DAWN OF THE
GOLDEN PROMISE

Also by B. J. Hoff
in Large Print:

The Captive Voice
Dark River Legacy
Heart of the Lonely Exile
Land of a Thousand Dreams
Masquerade
The Penny Whistle
Song of the Silent Harp
Sons of an Ancient Glory
Storm at Daybreak
The Tangled Web
Vow of Silence
Winds of Graystone Manor

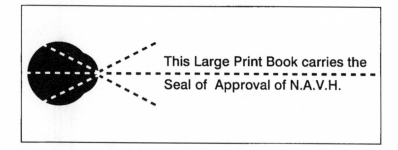

This Large Print Book carries the
Seal of Approval of N.A.V.H.

DAWN OF THE GOLDEN PROMISE

B. J. Hoff

Thorndike Press • Waterville, Maine

Published in 2002 by arrangement with Bethany House Publishers.

Thorndike Press Large Print Christian Fiction Series.

The tree indicium is a trademark of Thorndike Press.

The text of this Large Print edition is unabridged. Other aspects of the book may vary from the original edition.

Set in 16 pt. Plantin by Rick Gundberg.

Printed in the United States on permanent paper.

Library of Congress Cataloging-in-Publication Data

Hoff, B. J., 1940–
    Dawn of the golden promise / B. J. Hoff.
      p. cm.
    ISBN 0-7862-3578-0 (lg. print : hc : alk. paper)
    1. Irish Americans — Fiction. 2. Ireland — Fiction.
  3. Large type books. I. Title.
  PS3558.O34395 D38 2002
  813'.54—dc21   2001041555

In memory of Marty

At the author's request, a percentage of her royalties for *Dawn of the Golden Promise* are paid directly to World Relief Corporation, the international assistance arm of the National Association of Evangelicals (NAE). Founded in 1944, World Relief attempts to meet the physical and spiritual needs of people on every continent.

World Relief is a church-centered ministry of compassion, offering help and hope to victims of war and disaster, famine and poverty. In addition to their international projects, they assist with the resettlement needs of refugees in the United States. Information on World Relief can be obtained by writing to:

World Relief Corporation
P.O. Box WRC
Wheaton, IL 60189

Contents

PART TWO
THE PROMISE FULFILLED
HOPE FOR THE HELPLESS

PART THREE
THE PROMISE RENEWED
HOPE FOR THE FUTURE

Glossary

a gra	my love
alannah	my child
aroon	my dear, my love
bostoon	a worthless fellow
glunter	a stupid person
gorsoon	boy
gulpin	a clownish, uncouth person
macushla	my darling
ma girsha	my girl
mo chara	my friend
Seanchai	storyteller

The Heritage

This heritage to the race of kings,
Their children and their children's seed
Have wrought their prophecies in deed
Of terrible and splendid things.
JOSEPH PLUNKETT (1887–1916)

Killala, County Mayo, Ireland
December 1818

The winter's day was cold and grim, damp from last night's rain. Owen Kavanagh stood silently at the graveside of his two brothers: Owen's twin, Brian, seventeen, and Baby Dominic, scarcely a year. Both had been victims of the raging typhus epidemic claiming countless numbers throughout all Ireland.

Their wee Dominic had been a surprise to them all, born late, the last of six children. Of the six, Owen was the only one left.

In the village these days, voices hushed at the mention of Peg Kavanagh and the six sons she had birthed, only to bury them all, except for Owen. The deadly typhus had claimed Peg's three sons by her first husband, as well as two sired by her second man, Dan Kavanagh.

It would be up to Owen now to keep the birthright for the family and guard the *Harp of Caomhanach* — the Kavanagh Harp — for future generations. By rights the harp had belonged to Owen's twin, Brian, the eldest by no more than a minute. But with Brian gone, the harp now passed to Owen.

He knew what was said about him in the village, Owen did. That he was as unlikely an heir to the ancient harp as could be found anywhere in the family tree. The villagers knew, as he did, that the Kavanagh harp would not sing again for who could say how long a time. For in truth, Owen Kavanagh took after his father, Dan, who had not a note of music within him, not a note. Indeed, neither of the two had been able to manage the traditional lament over the graveside this day. Instead, they had sent for Tom O'Malley from Kilcummin to come and play.

Owen had known since he was but a lad that he was not suited for graceful things like music and books and conversation. Like his

12

da, he knew only the land, its strengths and its weaknesses, its defiance and its fickle ways. He was a long-legged, long-armed ploughboy who could figure simple sums and write the family names in the Holy Bible, and little more.

He was nothing like his twin, Brian, who had a voice that would charm the birds from the bushes and the bees from their hives. Brian, quick-witted and nimble-footed, who would dance at the crossing until daybreak, just as his uncle, Brian the Older, had been known to do before his hanging.

It would seem there had always been a branch of the bard and a branch of the farm boy in the Kavanagh tree, and there was no doubting which branch Owen had sprung from. But even though he could not pluck the strings and make the harp sing, he expected he was man enough to guard its legacy. And so he would.

One day, perhaps, he would have sons of his own, and when that time came, the eldest would inherit the ancient harp. Owen hoped he would have himself at least one boy from the same branch which had produced merry lads like his brother and his uncle. He thought it would be a fine thing indeed to have a son who could make the Kavanagh harp sing again in his own lifetime.

As he stood now between his parents, his father's hand upon his shoulder and Owen's arm about his mother to steady her in her grief, Owen shed his farewell tears for his two brothers. Even though it was another who strummed the harp and sang the lament which for generations had concluded the burial services of Kavanagh males, Owen reverently voiced each word in his heart:

> "My harp will sing across the land.
> across the past and years to be.
> No loss or grief nor death itself
> will still its faithful melody."

Owen felt his mother's thin body threaten to slump, and he tightened his grasp to support her. At the same time, his father increased the pressure of his hand on Owen's shoulder as the last strains of the Kavanagh lament rose and drifted out, across the graveyard:

> "To sing the presence of a God
> who conquers even exile's pain —
> Who heals the wandering pilgrim's
>   wound
> and leads him home in joy again."

Part One

THE PROMISE REMEMBERED

Hope in the Storm

The promise is for you and your children
and for all who are far off. . . .
ACTS 2:39

1

Dark Terror

For hope will expire
As the terror draws nigher,
And, with it, the Shame. . . .
JAMES CLARENCE MANGAN (1803–1849)

Near the coast of Portugal
Late June 1850

A little before midnight, Rook Mooney left his card game and went on deck. The starless night sky churned with low-hanging clouds, and although the wind was only beginning to blow up, Mooney knew the storm would be on them within the hour.

He hated sea storms at night, especially the ones that came up all of a sudden. The Atlantic was bad-tempered and unpredictable; she could turn vicious as a wounded witch without warning. Even the most seasoned sailor never took her for granted, and many a callow youth had been turned away from the sea for-ever by a particularly savage gale.

Had it not been for the brewing storm, Mooney would have been glad for the wind. Lisbon had been sultry, too warm for his liking. He was ready for Ireland's mild skies.

Hunched over the rail, he stared into the darkness. Although they were another night closer to Ireland, his mood was nearly as black as the sky. He had thought to see Dublin long before now, but instead he had spent three months in a filthy Tangier cell for breaking an innkeeper's skull.

The darkness deep within him rose up and began to spread. It was *her* fault. *The Innocent.* His hands tightened on the rail, his mouth twisting at the memory of her. All these months — more than a year now — and he still couldn't get her out of his mind. She was like a fire in his brain, boiling in him, torment-ing him, driving him half mad.

Nothing had gone right for him since that night at Gemma's Place. He spent his days with a drumming headache, his nights in a fog of whiskey and fever. His temper was a powder keg, ignited by the smallest spark. Even women were no good for him now. He could scarcely bear the sight of the used, worn-out strumpets who haunted the foreign ports. They all seemed dirty after her. Her, with her ivory skin and golden hair and fine clean scent.

Like some shadowy, infernal sea siren, she seemed to call to him. He was never free of her, could find no peace from her.

His grip on the rail increased. Soon, in only a few days now, they would reach Dublin. He would go back to Gemma's Place. This time he wouldn't go so easy on her. This time when he was finished with her, he would put an end to her witchery. He'd snuff out her life . . . and be free.

All at once rain drenched him. Waves churned up like rolling dunes, pitching the ship as if it were a flimsy child's toy. Angry and relentless, the gale whipped the deck. Salt from the sea mixed with the rain, burning Mooney's eyes and stinging his skin as the downpour slashed his face.

He swore into the raging night, anchoring himself to the rail. He felt no terror of the storm, only a feral kind of elation, as if the wildness of the wind had stirred a dark, waiting beast somewhere in the depths of his being.

Drogheda

The small cottage in the field seemed to sway in the wind. Frank Cassidy resisted the urge to duck his head against the thunder that shook the walls and the fierce lightning that streaked outside the window.

After months of following a maze of wrong turns, Cassidy could scarcely believe that he now sat across from the one person who might finally bring his search to an end. It had been a long, frustrating quest, and up until now a futile one. But tonight, in this small, barren cottage outside the old city where Black Cromwell had unleashed his obscene rage, his hopes were rising by the moment.

Friendship had motivated him to undertake the search for Finola Fitzgerald's past, but nothing more than the unwillingness to disappoint Morgan had kept him going. He owed his old friend a great deal — indeed, he would have done most anything the Fitzgerald had asked of him. But in recent months he had wondered more than once if this entire venture might not end in total defeat. Every road he had taken led only to failure. Every clue he had followed proved worthless.

Until now.

The possibility of finding his answers in Drogheda had first occurred to Cassidy months ago. A Dublin street musician's vague remark about an unsolved murder in the ancient city — a tragic mystery involving a young girl — had fired his interest and sent him on his way that same week.

According to the musician, a woman named Sally Kelly and her son Peter were likely to have information about the incident. Cassidy had wasted several days in Drogheda trying to locate the pair, only to discover that they had gone north some years past.

He started on to Cavan, eventually traveling as far west as Roscommon, but found no trace, not even a hint, of the Kellys. He started back to Drogheda, discouraged and uncertain about what to do next. To his astonishment, a casual conversation with a tinker on the road revealed that a youth named Peter Kelly had taken up a small tenant farm just outside the old city only weeks before.

Now, sitting across from the lad himself, Cassidy could barely contain his excitement. Even the brief, fragmented story he had managed to glean so far told him that this time he would not leave Drogheda empty-handed.

"If only you could have talked with me mum before she passed on," Peter Kelly was saying. "She more than likely could have told you all you want to know. There's so much I can't remember, don't you see."

Kelly was a strapping young man, with shirt sleeves rolled over muscled arms. His face was sunburned and freckled, his rusty hair crisp with tight curls.

21

"Still, I'd be grateful to hear what you do remember," Cassidy told him. "Anything at all."

Dipping one hand into the crock on the table, Kelly retrieved a small potato, still in its jacket, and began to peel it with his thumbnail. Motioning toward the crock, he indicated that Cassidy should help himself.

For a short time they sat in silence, perched on stools at the deal table eating their potatoes. The cottage was old, with but one room and a rough-hewn fireplace. Boxes pegged to the wall held crockery and plates. A straw mattress was draped with a frayed brown blanket. There were no other furnishings.

Peter Kelly had a friendly, honest face and intelligent eyes. "I don't mind telling you what I recall," he said, "but I fear it isn't much. 'Twas a good seven years ago, or more. I couldn't have been more than ten or eleven at the time, if that."

"And your mother was employed as cook?" prompted Cassidy.

The youth nodded. "Aye, she had been in service for Mr. Moran since I was but a wee wane. It was just the two of us. Me da had already passed on long before then."

"Tell me about Moran," Cassidy prompted. "Was he a wealthy man?"

Kelly took another bite of potato and

shrugged. "Not wealthy and not poor," he said. "He had an apothecary, but he also acted as a physician of sorts. His father before him left the business and the property. The land was fine, but not exceedingly large. There were some small crops and a few trees — and a lake."

"And Moran himself? What sort of a man was he?"

Again the lad shrugged. "I recall he was an elderly gentleman. All alone, except for the daughter. His wife died in childbirth, I believe. As best I remember, he treated Mum and me fine." He paused. "Mum said Mr. Moran doted on the daughter."

"You mentioned the day of the shooting," Cassidy urged. "I'd be grateful if you'd tell me about it."

Peter Kelly licked his fingers before reaching for another potato. "I recall it was a warm day. Spring or summer it must have been, for the trees were in leaf and the sun was bright. I was in the woods when I heard all the commotion. I wasn't supposed to go in the woods at all," he explained, glancing up, "for Mum was always fearful of the place. But I played there every chance I got, all the same."

Rubbing his big hands on his trouser legs, he went on. "But didn't I go flying out of there fast enough when I heard the screaming? Took off as if the devil himself was after me, I did."

Cassidy leaned forward, his muscles tensed. "What screaming would that have been?"

"Why, it sounded for all the world like a mountain cat in a trap! 'Twas too far away for me to see, but I could tell the ruckus was coming from near the lake, at the far end of the property. I took off running for the house."

He glanced at Cassidy, his expression slightly shamefaced. "I was but a lad," he muttered. "All I could think of was to get away from the terrible screaming without me mum finding out I'd been playing in the woods again. She was a stern woman."

"So you saw nothing at all?"

The boy shook his head, and Cassidy felt a shroud of familiar disappointment settle over him. Still, he wasn't about to give up. "And what happened then, lad?"

"Mum hauled me into the kitchen, then went for Mr. Moran. He told us to stay put while he went to investigate." He paused. "I saw a pistol in his hand, and I remember me mother was shaking something fierce. We heard the shots not long after Mr. Moran left the house with the gun."

Cassidy's interest piqued. He leaned forward. "Shots, did you say?"

Kelly nodded. "Mr. Moran was shot and killed that day." After a moment he added, "Everyone said it was the teacher who murdered him."

Curbing his impatience, Cassidy knotted his hands. "What teacher, Peter?"

Young Kelly scratched his head. "Why, I can't recall his name — it's been so long — but I do remember he was a Frenchman. Mr. Moran was determined his daughter would be educated, you see, and not in no hedge school, either. He hired the Frenchman as a tutor, and to coach her in the voice lessons. She was musical, you know."

Cassidy's mind raced. "This teacher — he lived with the family, did he?"

"He did. It seems to me he had a room upstairs in the house."

"But what reason would he have had to shoot James Moran?"

Peter Kelly met Cassidy's eyes across the table. "The story went that Mr. Moran must have been trying to save his daughter from the man's advances, but the Frenchman got the best of him. Mr. Moran was elderly, mind, and would have been no match for the teacher."

As Cassidy struggled to piece together what Kelly had told him, the youth went on. "I'm afraid I don't know much else, sir. Only that

Mr. Moran died from the shooting, and the daughter disappeared."

Cassidy looked at him. "Disappeared?"

"She was never seen after that day," said Kelly, crossing his arms over his chest. "Mum went looking for her after she found Mr. Moran dead, but there wasn't a trace of her, not a trace. Nothing but her tin whistle, which they found lying near the lake. No, they never found her nor the Frenchman." He drew in a long breath, adding, "Mum always said she didn't believe they tried any too hard, either."

Cassidy frowned. "Why would she think that?"

Peter Kelly twisted his mouth. "The police didn't care all that much, don't you see. The Morans weren't important enough for them to bother with, Mum said. They didn't know where to look, so they simply pretended to search."

Cassidy drummed his finger on the table. "Could the girl simply have run off with the Frenchman, do you think?"

The other shook his head forcefully. "No, sir, I'm certain it was nothing of the sort. Mum was convinced the Frenchman had done something terrible to the lass, and that was why Mr. Moran went after him. But Mr. Moran, he was that frail; a younger man would outmatch him easy enough, she said.

Mum was convinced until the day she died that the Frenchman murdered Mr. Moran and then ran off."

Cassidy rubbed his chin. "But that doesn't account for the girl," he said, thinking aloud. "What of her?"

"It pained me mum to think so, but she always believed the Frenchman took the lass with him."

"Abducted her, d'you mean?"

Peter nodded. "Aye, and perhaps murdered her as well." He seemed to reminisce for a moment. "Mum never liked that Frenchman, you see. Not a bit. He gave himself airs, she said, and had a devious eye."

Cassidy's every instinct proclaimed that at last he had found what he was searching for, but he had been thwarted too many times not to be cautious. Getting to his feet, he untied the pouch at his waist and withdrew the small portrait Morgan had sent him some months past.

He unfolded it, then handed it to Peter Kelly. "Would this be the girl?" he asked, his pulse pounding like the thunder outside. "Would the Moran lass resemble this portrait today, do you think?"

As Kelly studied the portrait, his eyes widened. "Why, 'tis her," he said, nodding slowly. "Sure, 'tis Miss Finola herself."

27

Cassidy stared at him. "Finola?" he said, his voice cracking. "That was her name — *Finola?*"

"It was indeed," the lad said. "And didn't it suit her well, at that? Tall and lovely, she was, and several years older than myself. Wee lad that I was, I thought her an enchanted creature. A princess . . . with golden hair."

A wave of exhilaration swept over Cassidy. He had all he could do not to shout. According to Morgan, the one thing Finola Fitzgerald had seemed to remember about her past was her given name.

"You're quite sure, lad?" he said, his voice none too steady. "It's been many a year since you last saw the lass, after all."

Kelly nodded, still studying the portrait. " 'Tis her. Sure, and she's a woman grown, but such a face is not easily forgotten, no matter the years."

"Now that is the truth," agreed Cassidy, smiling at the boy.

"Is she found then, sir, after all this time?" Kelly asked, returning the portrait to Cassidy.

Still smiling, Cassidy stared at the portrait. "Aye, lad," he said after a moment, his voice hoarse with excitement. "She is found. She is safe, and a married woman now."

"Ah . . . thanks be to God!" said Peter Kelly.

28

"Indeed," Cassidy echoed. "Thanks be to God."

Nelson Hall, Dublin

For the second time in a week, Finola's screams pierced the late night silence of the bedroom. Instantly awake, Morgan reached for her, then stopped. He had learned not to touch her until she was fully awake and had recognized him.

"Finola?" Leaning over her, he repeated her name softly. "Finola, 'tis Morgan. You're dreaming, *macushla*. You are safe. Safe with me."

Her body was rigid, her arms crossed in front of her face as if to ward off an attack. She thrashed, moaning and sobbing, her eyes still closed.

Outside, thunder rumbled in the distance and the lightning flared halfheartedly, then strengthened. As if sensing the approaching storm, Finola gave a startled cry.

Morgan continued to soothe her with his voice, speaking softly in the Irish. It was all he could do not to gather her in his arms. But when the nightmare had first begun, months ago, he had made the mistake of trying to rouse her from it. She had gone after him like a wild thing, pummeling him with her fists,

29

scraping his face with her nails as she fought him off.

Whatever went on in that dark, secret place of the dream must be an encounter of such dread, such horror, as to temporarily seize her sanity. The Finola trapped in that nightmare world was not in the least like the gentle, soft-voiced Finola he knew as his wife. In the throes of the dream she was a woman bound, terrorized by something too hideous to be endured.

No matter how he ached to rescue her, he could do nothing . . . nothing but wait.

In the netherworld of the dream, Finola stood in a dark and windswept cavern.

Seized by terror, she cupped her hands over her ears to shut out the howling of the wind.

The wind. She knew it was coming for her, could hear the angry, thunderous roar, feel the trembling of the ground beneath her feet as the storm raced toward her.

Faster now . . . a fury of a wind, gathering speed as it came, raging and swooping down upon her like a terrible bird of prey, gathering momentum as it hurled toward her . . . closing in, seizing her.

Black and fierce, it seemed alive as it dragged her closer . . . closer into its eye, as if trying to swallow her whole. As she struggled to break free, she heard in the farthest recesses of the darkness a strange, indefinable sound, a sound of sorrow, as if all the trees in the universe were sighing their grief.

She tried to run but was held captive by the force of the wind. It pounded her, squeezing the breath from her, dragging her into a darkness so dense it filled her eyes, her mouth, her lungs . . . oh, dear Jesus, it was crushing her . . . crushing her to nothing —

Finola sat straight up in bed, as if propelled by some raw force of terror. She gasped, as always, fighting for her breath.

Soaked in perspiration, Finola stared at Morgan, her gaze filled with horror.

Still he did not touch her. "You are safe, Finola *aroon*. 'Twas only a bad dream. You are here with me."

She put a hand to her throat and opened her mouth as if to speak, but made no sound. Finally . . . finally, she made a small whimper, like that of a frightened animal sprung free from a trap.

At last Morgan saw a glint of recognition. Finola moaned, then sagged into his waiting arms.

Stroking her hair, Morgan held her, crooning to her as he would a frightened child.

"There's nothing to harm you, my treasure. Nothing at all."

"Hold me . . . hold me . . ."

Tightening his arms about her still more, he began to rock her gently back and forth. "Shhh, now, *macushla* . . . everything is well. You are safe."

He felt her shudder against him, and he went on, lulling her with his voice, stroking her hair until at last he felt her grow still. "Was it the same as before?" he asked.

Her head nodded against his chest.

He knew it might be hours before she would be able to sleep again. So great was the dream's terror that she dreaded closing her eyes afterward. Sometimes she lay awake until dawn.

Her description of the nightmare never failed to chill Morgan. It had begun not long after their first physical union. Although he could scarcely bring himself to face the possibility, he could not help but wonder if their intimacy, though postponed, might not somehow be responsible.

At the outer fringes of his mind lurked a growing dread that by marrying her and taking her into his bed, he had somehow invoked the nightmare. He prayed it was not so, but if it continued, he would eventually have to admit his fear to Finola. They would have to speak of it.

But not yet. Not tonight. Tonight he would simply hold her until she no longer trembled, until she no longer clung to him as if he alone could banish the horror.

Unwilling to forsake the comforting warmth of Morgan's embrace, Finola lay, unmoving. Gradually she felt her own pulse slow to the steady rhythm of his heartbeat. "I'm sorry I woke you," she whispered.

He silenced her with a finger on her lips. "There is nothing to be sorry for. Hush, now, and let me hold you."

Something was coming. Something dark. Something cold and dark and . . . sinister. . . .

Thunder boomed like distant cannon, and Finola shivered. Wrapped safely in Morgan's arms, she struggled to resist the dark weight of foreboding that threatened to smother her.

It was always like this after the nightmare, as if the black wind in the dream still hovered oppressively near, waiting to overtake her after she was fully awake. Sometimes hours passed before she could completely banish the nightmare's terror.

Were it not for the safe wall of Morgan's presence to soothe and shield her, she thought she might go mad in the aftermath of the horror. But always he was there, his sturdy arms and quiet voice her stronghold of protection. Her haven.

"Better now, *macushla?*" he murmured against her hair.

Finola nodded, and he gently eased her back against the pillows, settling her snugly beside him, her head on his shoulder.

"Try to sleep," he said, brushing a kiss over the top of her head. "Nothing will hurt you this night. Nothing will ever hurt you again, I promise you."

Finola closed her eyes and forced herself to lie still. She knew Morgan would not allow himself to sleep until she did, so after a few moments she pretended to drift off; in a short while, she heard his breathing grow even and shallow.

After he fell asleep, she lay staring at the window, trying not to jump when lightning streaked and sliced the night. She hugged her arms to herself as the thunder groaned. In the shelter of Morgan's embrace, it was almost possible to believe that he was right, that nothing would hurt her ever again. She knew that with the first light of the morning, the nightmare would seem far distant, almost as if it had never happened.

But just as surely, she knew night would come again, and with the night would come the dream, with its dark wind and evil hidden somewhere deep within.

After a long time, Finola began to doze. But just as she sank toward the edge of unconsciousness, the wind shrieked. Like the sudden convulsion of a wren's wings, panic shook her and she jolted awake.

Feeling irrationally exposed and vulnerable, she listened to the storm play out its fury. Thunder hammered with such force that the great house seemed to shudder and groan, while the wind went on howling as if demanding entrance.

Again she closed her eyes, this time to pray.

2

Foreshadowings

I see in a vision the shadowy portal . . .
LADY WILDE (1824–1896)
"Speranza" — from *The Nation*, 1849

Annie Fitzgerald had held her tongue an excessively long time — certainly longer than was her custom — but on Saturday she decided that she had had enough.

Tierney Burke and the Gypsy seemed intent on ignoring her, but she would show them she could not be ignored. Not this morning.

She had learned from experience that the best way to get Tierney Burke's attention was to annoy him. To do that, all she needed to do was behave like the troublesome child he frequently accused her of being.

For close on half an hour now, while Jan Martova looked on, Annie had been watching Tierney shuffle an assortment of tools, all the while frowning and pretending to know exactly what he was doing — which, Annie suspected, was not the case at all. To her inquiries about the nature of his activities, she received only a muttered response to the effect that "as anyone should be able to tell," he was building a wagon.

"But *you* already have a wagon," she pointed out to the Gypsy.

Admittedly, Jan Martova was far more polite than his surly cohort. He at least acknowledged her presence with a smile before he replied. "We are building the wagon for Tierney, not for me."

Annie looked at him, then turned to Tierney. He had opened the storage chest at the back of the wagon and was rummaging through it. Fergus, the wolfhound, stood nearby, sniffing the chest's contents.

"And why would you be building a wagon for yourself?" Annie asked, directing her question to Tierney. "You're not a Romany."

Tierney Burke eyed the wolfhound at his side, then raised his head. Annie received a certain puckish pleasure from the impatient glare he turned on her.

"You and your hound are getting on my nerves. Don't you have chores to do inside the house?"

"I've already finished my chores, as it happens."

"Then why don't you run along and practice your sewing?"

He was deliberately goading her, of course; he delighted in it. He would provoke her until she either lost her temper and stamped off or else turned on him with a blistering tirade. Either way, he would pretend to find her amusing.

But not this time. The matter of a wagon for Tierney was peculiar enough that Annie's pride took second place to her curiosity. Although she called the wolfhound away from the wagon, she made no move to return to the house.

"Why would you be wanting a wagon?" she pressed, watching Tierney Burke put a drawknife to a piece of ash wood. "It isn't as if you need a wagon, after all. You're not a traveling person. And you already have two homes — one here at Nelson Hall and one in America."

He went on to split the wood, then reached for another piece. "You're making a nuisance of yourself, squirt," he said without looking at her.

Annie glared at him. It rankled her in the worst way when he called her *squirt*, and he knew it.

Because she could not voice the question at the back of her mind without being obvious, she merely continued to harangue him. "Planning a trip, are we?"

He shrugged. "I'm not planning anything as yet. I just want a wagon of my own." He glanced up. "Perhaps for a measure of privacy."

"But you *might* be planning a trip?"

"Did I say that, squirt?"

Annie studied him, looking intently at the handsome face, the rakish scar that made him look slightly dangerous. She felt an unexpected tightening in her throat. *Why else would he want a wagon for himself unless he was thinking of leaving Nelson Hall?*

Abruptly, before he could see her agitation, she turned away and started for the footbridge. Despite his incessant needling, Annie could not imagine Nelson Hall without Tierney Burke. She knew that at his advanced age of eighteen, he looked upon her as nothing more than an exasperating child. But without examining her feelings too closely, she also understood that she would rather suffer the worst of Tierney's condescension than be denied his presence altogether.

After all, at close on thirteen years, she was *not* the child he seemed to think her. He would have to notice that fact sooner or later, wouldn't he? Until then, she had resolved simply to ignore his constant teasing and his occasional impatience with her.

As they stepped off the footbridge, Fergus bounded toward the house. Annie made no attempt to call him back, but walked slowly, thinking.

Perhaps she should apply herself to behaving in a more mature manner. And to *looking* more grown-up, as well.

Although the idea didn't altogether appeal to her, it might have some merit. To begin with, she could ask Finola's help in dressing her hair more stylishly. But it was so infernally stubborn! Like a horse's tail, it was!

She frowned. Although she didn't much like getting all decked out in ribbons and laces, she supposed she could speak to the *Seanchai* about having new dresses made. Perhaps one of the more sophisticated French styles, something that would make her appear to have a bosom.

If only she were less of a stick! She had no curves as yet, none at all. And sometimes she despaired of ever growing taller. She still scarcely reached Finola's shoulder.

Finola insisted that Annie was going to be a "glory of a girl" someday. But Finola often said such things — almost certainly, Annie suspected, to make her feel better about herself.

What if she stayed just as she was now . . .

forever? What if, ten years hence, she still looked like a chicken-breasted twelve-year-old, with the same awful horsetail braids and the despised gap between her front teeth? Not to mention the same ungainly legs as a new foal.

After a moment, she gave an enormous sigh and stopped to watch Fergus dash across the field in pursuit of a hare. The small creature escaped into a stand of young oak trees, and the wolfhound, as if he hadn't been serious about the chase from the start, reversed his direction and trotted back toward Annie.

Again she sighed. Even the lumbering wolfhound, great lanky beast that he was, appeared more graceful than she.

Louisa stood at her bedroom window, watching young Annie and the faithful wolfhound as they sauntered toward the house. As always, the dog appeared extraordinarily pleased with himself. Perhaps the great beast was as simpleminded as she frequently accused him of being, for he did seem to wear a continual smile.

As for the girl, as always the braids were shaggy and askew, the hemline uneven, the gait that of a spindly legged colt. Louisa shook her head and smiled. She knew that it would not be long before a miracle of transformation would occur. The awkward foal would disappear, and the spirited thoroughbred would emerge. She had seen it time and time again, in countless classrooms over the years. Leggy girls with knobby elbows and too many teeth, girls who could not manage to enter a room without stumbling, would suddenly take on an unaccustomed grace, a new aura of loveliness. Freckles faded, hair tamed, angles became curves, and giggles turned into sighs.

From girl to woman: an amazing and wondrous thing entirely, yet as painful and frightening a process as it was splendid.

Already the first signs were apparent in the *Seanchai*'s precocious daughter. Studying looks in the mirror, impatient frowns with her appearance, experimental posturing. Covert glances across the table at the handsome — but surely treacherous — American boy. Temper tantrums and daydreaming. And, most telling of all, unaccountable spasms of weeping.

In young Annie's case, Louisa knew, the weeping went on behind closed doors, where she thought no one could hear. This one would not be caught unawares in a moment of weakness. Aine Fitzgerald would allow no one, except possibly Finola, a glimpse of her secret fears, her silent longings, her heart's whispered dreams.

Louisa expelled a long breath. Soon their girl would change, that much was certain. And if she were not sorely mistaken, the change would be momentous. More than once she had discussed with Finola their Aine's potential, and both agreed that she would one day be a beauty.

Blessedly, Annie seemed as yet to have no indication of the grand metamorphosis awaiting her. Indeed, the girl's conversation often contained veiled hints to the effect that she was certain she would never be anything other than the gangly yearling she was today.

Louisa smiled a little to herself. It was just as well that their Maker chose to keep such things well-hidden. The girl was difficult enough. Who could say what mischief she might wreak were she allowed a hint of what was ahead for her.

She lingered at the window for another moment, contemplating the Almighty's wisdom in concealing future events. She knew people who seemed eager to divine the days, as if knowing what lay ahead would give them some sort of power over it. For her part, she believed that wishing for the knowledge of one's fate was nothing less than madness itself.

Indeed, for many, she thought with a shudder, madness might well be the inevitable consequence of such knowledge.

★ ★ ★

In his bedchamber, Morgan Fitzgerald buttoned his shirt, then propped himself up in bed.

"You are displeased with the examination?" he said, watching the physician at the foot of the bed. The young doctor's chin was a fair barometer of his disposition on any given day. The lower the chin, the blacker the surgeon's mood. At the moment the chin sagged like the wattle of an aging turkey. Not a good sign.

The surgeon glanced up from closing his medical case. "Displeased? Oh — no, nothing of the sort. To the contrary, you seem remarkably fit. Your man Sandemon's regime has accomplished wonders."

"But?" Morgan pressed.

The doctor looked at him, delaying his answer. "I'm concerned," he finally said.

"About the shaking," Morgan said, knowing the answer.

Dr. Dunne came around the side of the bed to stand beside him. "There's that. But even without the tremors, I would urge you once again to seek the opinion of a specialist. I simply am not qualified in this area."

"Tell me what you think," Morgan said, as if he had not heard the surgeon's opinion before.

"And haven't I already done so?" The doctor sighed. "I wish I had more expertise. I can only repeat my concern that the paralysis could eventually expand — move upward."

Morgan cringed inwardly, trying to ignore the familiar swell of panic that rose in his throat at the physician's words.

"It would be to your benefit to seek the counsel of one far more qualified in this field than I. There is so much unknown in cases like yours."

In spite of the warmth of the room, Morgan shivered. "And what, exactly, do you think a specialist might do for me that you cannot?"

The physician met his eyes. Morgan did not miss the fleeting glint of sympathy in his gaze.

When Dunne replied, he was once more the consummate professional. "For one thing, he could give you a precise accounting of your condition and your options."

Morgan attempted a laugh. "I expect I can make that assessment on my own without benefit of a specialist."

"Prognosis isn't my only concern," the doctor said, looking directly at him. "What if there's a chance the bullet could be removed?"

Morgan glared at him. "I have been told by three purported experts that removal of the bullet is out of the question, unless I wish to risk ending up as a vegetable — or a corpse." He expelled a long breath. "You will understand, I trust, that I prefer my present condition to either alternative."

The doctor leaned toward him. "Of course I understand," he said, his gaze intent. "But advances have been made in surgery, even as recently as this past year. I have read papers from Paris, from Great Britain — and from the United States — that speak of exciting new procedures." He hesitated, as if undecided as to whether he should go on until Morgan nodded his assent.

"If there is even the slightest possibility that the paralysis might spread, surely you are bound to investigate all the possibilities."

Again Morgan felt chilled. He closed his eyes and attempted to suppress the rush that swept through him — fear mixed with a certain excitement.

He could not bring himself to face the idea that he might end up totally paralyzed. To live with useless legs was bad enough. But at least he still lived as a human being. He could still dress himself and feed himself and move about the house with some freedom. Even with his limited mobility, he could still be an active father to his children, a real husband to Finola. He could still call himself a *man*.

What if the paralysis should grow worse?

He thought death would be eminently preferable.

But if the bullet could be removed?

He opened his eyes. "So, then — what do you advise?"

Dr. Dunne's expression brightened. "There are two surgeons whose work would seem particularly promising. Do I have your permission to correspond with them in your behalf?"

Morgan moistened his lips, then nodded. "Where are these miracle workers? Surely not in Ireland."

"One is in London, actually. The other trained in Vienna, but his practice is in the States."

"I can't say I fancy the idea of an Englishman with a knife to my back," Morgan said dryly. "But I suppose it will do no harm to write to the both of them."

The doctor picked up his case and turned to go, but Morgan stopped him. "We will say nothing of this to my wife for now. You are aware of the difficulties she continues to experience."

Dr. Dunne nodded, waiting.

"The dreams and attacks of panic grow worse," Morgan went on, his concern for her renewed by each word. "I will do nothing to trouble her further. Whatever I decide will have to wait until she is stronger."

The surgeon's expression was skeptical. "I understand, naturally. Nevertheless, I would urge you not to delay. The longer you wait —" He broke off. "About your wife — as I've told you, I feel strongly that time will make all the difference for her condition. Time, and a normal, fulfilling life with you and the children."

After the doctor left the room, Morgan lay staring up at the ceiling, his arms locked behind his head. He tried not to think about paralysis or new surgeons or what might lie ahead for him. Instead, he turned his thoughts to Finola.

Time, Dr. Dunne had said. Time, and a normal, fulfilling life: that had been the physician's prescription for Finola's recovery.

But just how normal or fulfilling would life be for Finola if her husband were to end up paralyzed entirely?

Or dead?

If only she had someone besides himself to depend on. On the heels of the thought came the reminder that Finola very well *might* have someone else. Parents. Siblings. Other relatives. If only he knew where to find them.

He had hoped to hear from Cassidy long before now. At first, Frank had kept in touch fairly often, but of late his letters had grown further and further apart. There was no telling where he was these days. Apparently, he had learned nothing of any consequence, else he would have written.

Morgan's stomach churned at the prospect of what Cassidy's search might eventually disclose. There was no knowing, after all, what lay buried in Finola's past.

When she had first appeared at Nelson Hall, she had been mute and without the slightest memory of who she was or where she had come from. All she knew was her given name — and Morgan had occasionally wondered if even that bit of information was dependable. As time went on, very little in the way of remembrance had been granted her, and she seemed to have made peace with the missing pieces of her past. For her sake, Morgan had also tried to look ahead.

Yet, as much as he feared learning the truth about her background, if she had family somewhere who cared about her, who grieved for her absence, it could only be in Finola's best interests to locate them. Not only did she deserve to be reunited with the ones who loved her, but finding her family would also mean she wouldn't be left totally on her own if something should happen to him.

Morgan could not bear to think of her being alone, defenseless, with both Gabriel and Annie to look after. He could insure her financial security, of course — indeed, he had already seen to it. Most of his grandfather's considerable fortune would be at Finola's disposal in the event of his own death. But he wanted more than wealth. Her emotional turmoil still troubled him . . . she was still vulnerable in that regard. Her reluctance to appear in public, her sometimes irrational caution where the children were concerned, the ongoing nightmares — were these not indications that her wounds had yet to heal?

So in spite of his own misgivings as to what such a discovery might lead to, he continued to pray that Cassidy would somehow come upon the truth about Finola's past. At the same time, he could not help but implore the Almighty to allow nothing . . . not even the truth . . . to come between him and his beloved or bring still more grief to her already burdened spirit.

Just then she rapped lightly on his door and stepped inside. As always, the sight of her golden loveliness brought a breath-stealing wave of tenderness and love to his heart.

In spite of his somber thoughts of a moment ago, his smile for her required no effort. "Ah — and I thought the day was cloudy," he said, extending his hands to her. "But 'tis only that the sun has moved indoors."

She hesitated, and her inquisitive look turned to amusement. "Don't think to distract me by your blarney, sir," she said, crossing the room to catch his hands in hers. "I came to hear the surgeon's full report."

"He says I am an outrageous man."

She arched a brow. "How very perceptive our Dr. Dunne is."

"He also says I will continue to require a great deal of affection and attention from my beautiful wife. You may begin."

"You *are* an outrageous man."

Her bell-like laugh was delightful. Morgan never missed the slightest opportunity to coax the sound from her. He sometimes thought he could exist on nothing but the warmth of her smile and the music of her laughter.

3

House of Hope

The hope lives on, age after age . . .
GEORGE WILLIAM RUSSELL (AE)
(1867–1935)

Washington, D.C.

In the White House, which steamed with summer heat, President Zachary Taylor drew his last breath. It was an abrupt end to a brief term in office.

The President had fallen ill some days before, at the Independence Day cornerstone ceremony of the Washington Monument. He had served only a year and four months of his term.

His passing left a country enmeshed in a storm of bitter controversy over the issue of slavery. A country in turmoil because of the thousands of immigrants now swarming its shores — immigrants who filled the cities with strange speech, strange clothing, and even stranger customs. A country in conflict over the question of freedom, on which the young nation of America had allegedly been founded.

Freedom for *all*, the founding fathers had proclaimed.

Freedom for a *few*, the new, increasingly ugly voices of power demanded.

The concept of America as a refuge for those fleeing the tyranny and devastation of foreign nations suddenly seemed to be up for debate. To some, this aspect of America's image had always been dubious. To others, it was a sacred and unchallengeable ideal — to hold up the banner of hope to every refugee who stepped onto the shores of the United States.

In those cities whose ports now teemed with immigrants, a few courageous visionaries — themselves descended from immigrants — struggled to keep that banner of hope aloft.

New York City

It was a testament to the influence — and energy — of millionaire shipbuilder Lewis Farmington. Today, less than six months from the time the idea was first conceived and presented to him, Whittaker House would officially open its doors.

Already the city's newest children's home was licensed, at least partially renovated and furnished, and well on its way to being populated with its first young residents.

Farmington was also responsible for the dedication service, at which Pastor Jess Dalton officiated. The ceremony was held outdoors, on the wide front porch of the building. Despite the sweltering heat, an impressive number of philanthropists, clergy, and other notable dignitaries were in attendance.

When the speeches finally concluded and the benediction had been intoned, Evan Whittaker, the new establishment's superintendent, was presented with a sizable donation collected from various churches and private organizations throughout the city.

This, too, had been the doing of Lewis Farmington.

The new superintendent accepted the contribution with his customary British dignity and aplomb. Only the six small boys standing behind him — the first residents of the new children's home — detected the slight shaking of Whittaker's legs.

Those in the crowd who knew him best, however — including his frail but beaming wife — could not help but note the slender

Englishman's flush of embarrassment. But although he stuttered rather badly over his speech of acceptance, his final words came as a prayer, clear and unwavering:

"It is my deepest hope that God will make this place a house of refuge, where all His children, regardless of color or creed, may find safe shelter and nurture in His love."

Michael and Sara Burke were the first to shake Evan's hand after the ceremony, although Sara hung back for a moment before adding her good wishes to Michael's. For her, the proceedings had been fraught with emotion. In fact, the intensity of her response surprised her.

She had witnessed such incredible change in the lives of Evan and Nora Whittaker since that day on the Manhattan docks when they first arrived in New York — frightened, ailing immigrants who had left home and country for the promise of America. In scarcely more than three years, the two had endured illness and tragedy, broken dreams and grievous loss. Struggle and suffering had marked their experience of the United States in ways no one could have foreseen.

Yet, through it all Evan and Nora had believed in America's promise, had clung to that dream and to their God's faithfulness. And today, in spite of overwhelming obstacles and reverses, the promise had been fulfilled beyond their dreams.

Today Sara realized that the promise had not been for Evan and Nora alone, but for the children of New York City as well. Like a shining, golden gift, Whittaker House held forth the possibility of hope to those who had known little but despair in their young lives. Just as America offered the hope of survival and a better life to untold thousands of immigrants, this large, solid brick building extended the hope of survival and a better life to the unloved, forgotten children of New York.

Hope. Surely the word itself was one of the loveliest songs of the human heart.

Blinking back tears, she watched Michael put a hand to Evan's shoulder. "A grand day, Evan," he said, grinning broadly. "You and Sara's father have done a remarkable job."

Evan shook his head. "*Mr. Farmington* has d-done a remarkable job — he and the Lord. I'm still rather stunned b-by it all, I m-must confess."

"It's such a wonderful idea, Evan," Sara said, smiling at his characteristic self-effacement. "It must give you great joy to see your dream finally become reality."

He looked at her. "But it wasn't *m-my* dream, you know. Whittaker House was

God's idea, not m-mine. I would never have had the boldness to conceive of anything so m-marvelous."

Sara studied the lean-faced Englishman's honest features and knew he meant what he said. Yet she, like many others, had come to see a facet of Evan's character that apparently eluded him: a spirit that would always champion those in need, a nobility that, despite impossible odds or self-sacrifice, would somehow manage to persevere.

Perhaps this very trait made Evan Whittaker such an ideal instrument of God's grace. For truly, this humble man had become a source of blessing to many — not only his own family and circle of friends, but especially to those young souls who seemed to matter to no one else: the city's homeless, unwanted children.

"Well, whoever conceived it, it's an extraordinary idea," she said. "And you must know Father believes in this venture with all his heart, the way he's supported you in it."

"Even though he's still grinding his teeth over losing you from the shipyards," Michael put in. "He hasn't quite come to grips with it yet."

"Father says that's his own private sacrifice for the public good," Sara told Evan, smiling at the faint flush of pleasure that stole over his features. "He also says that Whittaker House will be filled to overflowing in no time, but he's hoping the idea will catch on throughout the city and lead to the opening of other shelters. Obviously, you can't begin to meet the demand that already exists."

Evan's eyes clouded. "I know. Why, we've taken in five children just this week — and that's in addition to B-Billy."

Sara nodded, glancing at little Billy Hogan, who stood at the bottom of the steps with another small boy. Both were eating cookies as they studied each other with measuring looks.

"The lad has bloomed under your care," Michael said. "It's good to see him looking like a normal little boy instead of a whipped pup."

"He's a wonderful b-boy," Evan said. "And I think he *is* happy with us. But he frets in the worst way over his younger b-brothers."

"I thought one of the immigrant societies was helping Billy's family," Sara said.

Evan nodded. "They are. And I think for the most part they're m-managing well. But Billy is concerned about what will happen if Sorley Dolan should be released from prison."

Sara shuddered. The memory of the merciless physical abuse Dolan had inflicted on the child was still all too fresh. Dolan, who had passed himself off as Billy's uncle — though he wasn't actually related to the boy at all — had almost killed little Billy with his violent beatings and forced starvation.

"I can't believe they would even *consider* letting that barbarian out of jail!" she said, turning to Michael. "Surely he'll be locked up for a long time."

Michael's expression darkened. "Don't count on it, Sara. It's a wonder he's been held as long as he has. With the jail cells packed as they are these days, there's many a sentence being cut short."

"Well, I should hope Sorley Dolan's won't be one of them," Sara said firmly.

Evan Whittaker's gaze went to the boys standing at the bottom of the steps. "Yes," he said quietly. "So d-do I."

Again Sara turned to her husband. "Michael, there must be something you can do to make sure Dolan isn't set free."

He looked at her, then shrugged. "A policeman has no influence in the courts, Sara. You know that. And the truth is, there's no room for even half the felons we haul in. Why, if we opened ten jails tomorrow, they'd be jammed to the walls in a day, every one of them. The situation is out of control."

Sara shook her head in disgust. "It seems to me the entire *city* is out of control."

"Most of the police force would agree," he admitted.

Sara saw his eyes suddenly go hard as his attention shifted to the other side of the street. "I expect we can thank the likes of blighters like her husband for much of the madness," he bit out, jerking his head in the direction of his gaze.

Frowning, Sara turned to look. On the opposite side of the street stood Alice Walsh, seemingly absorbed in a conversation with her children. Isabel Walsh, a rather thickset girl who looked dreadfully overdressed in a yellow ruffled frock, and Henry, a thin-faced boy with thick spectacles, stood on either side of their mother. Both seemed to be talking at once.

Evan, too, looked in Alice Walsh's direction. "I suppose," he said, "there is no disputing her husband's reputation. But as for M-Mrs. Walsh herself — I cannot say enough good things about her."

Michael nodded, but his tone was grudging. "Aye, Sara thinks well of the woman, too. She does seem a decent sort, but how do you account for her getting mixed up with an animal like Walsh?"

Sara heard the old, familiar animosity in his tone. It was always like this. The slightest mention of Patrick Walsh would ignite the spark of anger in his eyes and bring an edge of bitterness to his voice.

Sometimes she feared Michael had made the destruction of Patrick Walsh his life's work, to the exclusion of all else. She was convinced that he had even put aside his political ambitions, at least for the time being, because of his obsession with Walsh.

When she tried to talk to him about it, he only pretended to listen. He evaded her questions, and made light of her misgivings. Even though Walsh had been directly responsible for the brutal attack on Michael's son, Tierney — and the boy's forced exile to Ireland — Michael invariably denied Sara's suggestions that his fixation on Walsh might be excessive.

Yet Sara knew beyond the slightest doubt that Michael had set the entire force of his will to achieving one goal: to bring Patrick Walsh to justice. And he would not stop until he had accomplished his aim.

Despite the scorching temperature of the day, Sara shivered. She could not help but wonder whether Patrick Walsh was aware of Michael's enmity. And if he was, what ends might he go to in order to thwart him?

Alice Walsh was only half listening to Isabel's complaints about the heat and

Henry's criticism of the structural design of Whittaker House. Her thoughts kept darting back to the events of the day.

She was so pleased for Evan Whittaker and what this new venture was going to mean to the homeless children throughout the city. She longed to cross the street and congratulate him, but, seeing him in the company of Sara Burke and her husband, she decided against it.

Sara would be cordial, of course; she was unfailingly gracious, even friendly, when they met. But the captain . . .

Alice bit her lip, all too aware of what to expect from Captain Burke. The forced smile, the grudging concession to a polite greeting, followed by the fixed look that stopped just short of open disdain. It was always the same. She sensed that Captain Burke's reaction to her was kindled by his hostility toward Patrick, and his silent disapproval hurt.

She didn't understand the enmity between the policeman and her husband. Only lately had she begun to suspect that she might not want to understand. She felt a growing apprehension about the cause of the deep-seated animosity between the two men; indeed, she had found herself unwilling to probe too deeply, for fear of what she might discover.

Worse still, whenever she thought of the situation at all, she automatically blamed her husband, as if the fault were entirely his. There had been a time when it would have been virtually impossible for her to blame Patrick for *anything*. The fact that she did so now, and did it so readily, troubled her with a sense of guilt she could not easily dismiss.

In his hotel office nearby, Patrick Walsh glared once more at the letter in his hand, then crumpled it and tossed it into the ashtray on the corner of the desk. He struck a match, and in seconds the letter had burned to ashes.

The little fool! What in the world was she thinking of, writing him a threatening letter! As if threats from the likes of her would intimidate him.

He regretted his carelessness, certainly. There had been too many champagne dinners at her flat, too many late nights, entirely too little regard for the usual caution. He had been altogether too nonchalant, and it wouldn't happen again.

He should have known the little tramp would try to trap him. She wanted money, of course. That's what the line about "asking nothing for herself but a secure future for the baby" was all about. Clearly, she was going to try to take him for a bundle.

Well, she was in for a big disappointment.

She would get nothing from him — only enough to help with the doctor bills. Not a penny more.

He walked to the window and looked out on the sultry summer afternoon, thinking about the last time they had been together. Ruth had wept violently when he said good-bye. She always did, always begged him to stay longer. Sometimes he gave in, but not that night.

Even before then, he had been growing impatient with her transparent efforts to ensnare him, to coax some kind of a serious commitment from him. At first he had been merely amused by her feeble attempts at entrapment. Eventually, though, he had wearied of her whining and spent less and less time at her flat when he was in town.

Once he learned she was pregnant, he ended it. At least he thought he had.

She had never been important to him in the first place, merely an enjoyable diversion when he was in Chicago on business. The entire affair wouldn't have rated a second thought, had it not been for this latest ploy. She was actually threatening to come to New York!

Not that he really believed she would. She was far too timid; he couldn't imagine her finding the nerve to travel such a long distance alone. She had no self-assurance, no experience in getting along on her own. No, she wouldn't try anything so daring.

But what if she *did?* What if Alice should learn of the affair?

Worse, yet, what if Alice's *father* should find out?

In spite of the dim coolness of the office, Patrick's skin felt hot and moist. With his shirt sleeve, he wiped a band of perspiration from his forehead.

Jacob Braun would never forgive such a flagrant indiscretion on his son-in-law's part. He would see it as a mortal sin, a deliberate humiliation of his daughter — his adored, pampered, over-protected, *only* daughter.

Even though Alice's father had relinquished most of his involvement in the hotel business to his son-in-law long ago, Patrick knew that Jacob Braun could still hurt him. For one thing, Braun had a big mouth, and he wouldn't hesitate to shoot it off to anyone who would listen. He might not be able to wreak a great deal of financial damage on Patrick, but he was well-positioned enough to put serious strain on his political ambitions. He might even pull the plug on Alice's generous allowance . . . not to mention her inheritance.

Abruptly, Patrick turned back to the desk

and took up his pen. He would get a message off to Ruth Marriott yet today, a message she couldn't possibly misunderstand. He'd have one of his men deliver it. He would send money. A creditable amount of money. He hated giving her a dime, but perhaps that was the safest way, after all. Money would always buy silence.

Taut with anger and more apprehension than he cared to admit, he scrawled a hasty note, renewing his warning that he would accept no responsibility for the child. In language she could not possibly misinterpret, he let her know that he regarded what they had had together as no more than a casual affair.

The night she hit him with the news about the baby, he had insinuated he didn't necessarily believe he was the child's father. Now, in even stronger language, he reminded her of the same doubts, scratching his signature with almost vicious finality.

Opening the safe behind his desk, he withdrew a stack of bills. He counted out five hundred dollars, hesitated, then added five hundred more.

When Quinn O'Shea came looking for him later that afternoon, Evan was in the backyard, giving Teddy a horsey-back ride. The other boys were playing tag.

"Mr. Whittaker, could you please come to the front door, sir?"

Evan straightened, and Teddy increased his stranglehold about his neck. "Easy, son," he choked out. "N-not so tight."

He smiled at the young Irish girl. "What is it, Quinn?"

She hesitated. "There's a boy out front who insists on speaking with you, sir. Would you like me to take Teddy upstairs?"

Evan moved so she could free the toddler's grasp on him. "Why d-don't you just watch him and the other b-boys until I come back, if you don't mind."

On his way into the house, Evan reflected on their good fortune in finding Quinn O'Shea. She had been a godsend to them all. Not only was she an extraordinarily efficient housekeeper — the girl was a marvelous cook and household manager — but she was also quite good with the children. Best of all, she had somehow moved smoothly and unobtrusively into their family life, taking on more and more responsibilities, but in a quiet, unassuming manner that left Nora's dignity and sense of self-worth intact.

No longer did Nora look upon Quinn as an intrusion, Evan thought. Nor did she appear to be quite as frustrated by her own frailty these days. Again, he suspected that Quinn's tactful way of leaving the small, less wearying household tasks to Nora while she went about the more arduous jobs was at least partly responsible for Nora's acceptance.

Nora liked the girl, that much was obvious, and Quinn had taken to Nora with surprising warmth. Even though she maintained a certain aloofness with others, including Evan, the girl seemed to shed much of her reserve around Nora.

The front door was ajar, and Evan stepped into the open doorway. On the porch stood a small boy in a tattered shirt and raggedy short pants. A bundle tied to the end of a stick swung from one thin shoulder.

Evan cleared his throat, and the boy turned around, revealing caramel-colored skin stretched tightly over a small oval face. Two of the darkest eyes Evan had ever seen peered up at him. The boy looked as if he had not eaten a solid meal for weeks.

"You wanted to see m-me, young man?" Evan said.

The boy nodded. "Name's Oscar," he said without preamble. "Are you Mistah Whittaker?"

Evan guessed the slow drawl to be that of the deep South. The boy would appear to be a mulatto. He was a little fellow, no more than five or six years surely. And none too clean. "I am Mr. Whittaker, that's correct."

"You take little nigra boys here?"

Surprised, Evan hesitated. "Well, son . . ."

"I ain't *all* nigra, you understand," the child said. "My daddy was a white man."

"Yes . . . well, ah, where are your parents . . . Oscar?"

Evan noted the sharp, thin shoulders, the even sharper elbows. Not a spare pinch of flesh on him anywhere, poor lad.

"My mammy's dead," the boy replied matter-of-factly. "My daddy went away on a sailing ship. He didn't like us, I s'pose." He paused, then gestured to the bundle on the stick. "I brung my stuff."

Evan darted a look at the bundle.

"Can I stay?" the boy asked, his dark eyes fixed on Evan's.

Evan expelled a long breath. "D-don't you have anyone to take you in, son? Family? Friends?"

The boy shook his head. "Nope. I been living at the old Brewery building, down at the Five Points, since Mammy died. When I heard about your house for homeless boys, I decided to look you up."

Evan shuddered at the mention of the old Brewery. The place was a veritable pit of squalor and immorality. A den for thieves and drunkards, even murderers.

"If I allow you to stay here, you would have to work, Oscar."

The boy nodded. "Oh, I wasn't lookin' to stay for free, Mistah Whittaker. I'm six. I can work for my keep. I'll work hard."

Evan suppressed a smile. "Indeed, you will," he said gravely. "Our b-boys here work *very* hard. And we study, too. You would b-be responsible for certain chores, and for your studies. There is no thievery, no cursing, and no fighting at Whittaker House. And n-no gambling," he added, knowing the vice to be a favorite among the city's street children.

Oscar's chin fell just a fraction, but his reply was quick in coming. "That's okay, I s'pect." He paused. "But do you reckon I could have me some supper before I go to work, Mistah Whittaker? I'm awful hungry."

Evan stroked his beard for a moment. "Very well, Oscar. Come along with me," he said, motioning toward the big dining hall off to the right. "All our b-boys at Whittaker House take their meals together."

4

Young Dreams

I whispered, "I am too young."
And then, "I am old enough";
Wherefore I threw a penny
To find out if I might love.
W. B. YEATS (1865–1939)

The library was Quinn O'Shea's favorite part of Whittaker House. The friendly oak-paneled room had become a kind of retreat to her — even more than her own bedroom, which in itself was a cozy place with ruffled white curtains, a small fireplace, and a window seat.

During the first days of helping the family move into their quarters, there had been no time for exploring the rambling old house. Quinn had worked herself nearly to exhaustion each day. All the rooms, from the attic to basement, had to be thoroughly aired and cleaned; boxes unpacked; the pantry stocked

71

— all this in addition to looking after Mrs. Whittaker and wee Teddy.

The young girl, Johanna, helped whenever she was about, and the girl doted on Teddy. But she was often away at the Academy, an unusual school where they educated deaf children and taught them to speak.

Quinn thought it remarkable entirely that a child like Johanna could learn to use her voice — and without hearing a word she said. Nothing short of a miracle, and that was the truth.

But wasn't her own presence here at Whittaker House also something of a miracle? She truly enjoyed being with the Whittakers — they were fine people who treated her almost like family.

And the library — why, the library itself was a dream come true. To be given free access to such a treasure trove had at first seemed beyond belief. It had taken repeated assurances from Mr. Whittaker before Quinn finally felt at liberty to enter the room whenever she liked. Her first task had been to clean the premises thoroughly; while Daniel Kavanagh and Mr. Whittaker had sorted and organized, she had dusted and scrubbed, polished and painted, until the room actually seemed to take on a luster from her efforts.

Then, invited to choose any book on the

shelves for her own reading pleasure, she had fallen onto the entire collection with an almost ravenous hunger. From the moment she had first learned to read, Quinn had loved books: the heft of them, the fine smell of the leather, the sound of their pages rustling ever so quietly as she turned each one with reverent care.

Now as she stood in the middle of the room, she closed her eyes for a moment, savoring the experience of being utterly surrounded by books. More books, she was sure, than she could read in a lifetime.

The shelves were filled with a variety of volumes, many donated by Mr. Lewis Farmington from his private library, others collected from all over the state by ladies from various church societies. Mr. Whittaker said the library would be one of the most important features of the children's home; it was his intention that every child who took up shelter at Whittaker House eventually learn to read.

"There is a kind of freedom in these books," he had remarked to Quinn and Daniel during one of their organizing sessions. The three of them had spent the entire afternoon dusting books, then filling the shelves. As they worked, Mr. Whittaker had talked, explaining in his quiet, halting speech his personal conviction that the underprivileged children in their midst could eventually free themselves from poverty — by learning to read.

"For many, these books m-may represent their only opportunity for a better life."

He had smiled then, a fleeting, shy smile, as if embarrassed by his brief speech, but Quinn had taken his meaning right away. Somewhere in the rows and rows of books upon these shelves might well lie the key to *her* future. A *promising* future, not the squalid existence of just another starving Irish peasant. Something even beyond the respectable position in service she had found with the Whittakers, though sure, her present employment was far better than anything she had known before.

No, she was determined that her future would hold more. She would make a good life for herself, on her own efforts — a life that would include more than mere existence, more than a full stomach and an aching back at the end of the day. More than a sin-stained conscience. A life in which she would never again be forced to do anything for the sole purpose of survival.

She walked the length of each wall, passing her fingers lovingly over one book after another on the shelves. *I shall make my own future, my own place in the world,* she promised herself. *I shall build me a future of freedom and security . . . and respectability. No matter how long it takes or how hard I have to work, I will make a life for myself of real value. A life that matters.*

Her eyes drank in the storehouse of opportunity at her fingertips. Whittaker House . . . this room . . . was the beginning of that life. She could feel it.

But it was, she was quick to remind herself, *only* the beginning.

Unable to drag himself away, Daniel Kavanagh stood just outside the partially open door, watching Quinn O'Shea move along the library shelves. Something about the way she stroked the books, the warmth in her gaze, the faint movement of her lips, gave her actions all the intimacy of a caress.

This wasn't the first time he had covertly observed her as she paced the room or selected a book, her face rapt, her eyes shining. She came here almost every night, after the family had settled in their rooms upstairs and the boys in the dormitory were abed.

Daniel shared her love of the books, understood her pleasure in the library. But Quinn's passion for reading went far beyond his own experience. For him, it was a simple act of entertainment or a quest for knowledge. For her, the library seemed to hold a fascination bordering on obsession. Her entire countenance changed when she entered the room.

He saw it again now. Gone was the guarded watchfulness of her catlike eyes, the faintly cynical smile, the brisk resolve with which she went about her daily tasks. Years seemed to drop away, and with the years, the fortress of grim reserve and suspicion from which she rarely emerged.

Daniel enjoyed seeing her like this, yet at the same time he felt inexplicably threatened by the change in her. He was struck by the light of wonder in those strange, amber-flecked eyes, the unexpected softness of her features, the hint of vulnerability she revealed at no other time. Again he would realize that, instead of the flint-edged woman she seemed so intent on making herself out to be, Quinn O'Shea was in reality a mere slip of a girl — only months older than himself.

Did she suspect that he was mad for her?

The very possibility made his face heat with embarrassment. She obviously considered him no more than a green *gorsoon*, a foolish youth with the dust of barley still in his hair.

She treated him with the same detachment she might have afforded a slow-witted peddler. Although just to look at her made Daniel's heart leap into his mouth, she more often than not looked at *him* as if he did not exist at all.

At the best, she was tolerant of him — at the worst, impatient. She made it quite clear that he was little more than a clumsy interference when he hovered about. He was miserably aware that she suffered his presence only because he was a part of the family who employed her. She wasn't exactly rude to him, merely indifferent.

Daniel found her indifference humiliating. Yet he could not seem to stay away from her. Despite her obvious lack of interest, he was increasingly drawn to her, unreasonably attracted to her. At the same time, he occasionally felt something that bordered on resentment, almost as if his callow foolishness were somehow her fault.

He could only hope that Quinn O'Shea remained unaware of his feelings. As painful as her disregard for him might be, it would surely be preferable to her contempt.

Later that night, Evan lay quietly beside Nora in bed, reading.

Occasionally he would glance over at her to see if she was still awake. Each time she would meet his eyes and smile at him.

Finally he put his book down. "Is the lamp keeping you awake?"

She shook her head. She was propped up on a mountain of pillows to aid her breathing, and in the dim glow from the oil lamp, Evan could see the faint lines of fatigue about her eyes, the ashen hue of her skin.

"You ought to be sleeping." He reached to take her hand, and she turned to face him. "So, then — what do you m-make of our newest guest?" he asked her. "I saw you watching him at the table."

She smiled. "I expect your little Oscar could prove to be quite a handful." Her expression sobered. "Poor little tyke. He was nearly starved, did you notice?"

Evan nodded. The boy had eaten enough for three, wolfing down his dinner like a famished puppy. "I've n-no doubt you're right about his being a handful. B-but what else could I do? He had n-nowhere to go."

Still smiling, she squeezed his fingers. "Something tells me the walls of Whittaker House will be fit to burst in no time at all."

Evan sighed. "I wish I could take every one of them in. I would if it were somehow p-possible."

Nora put her free hand to his face. "Evan — you can't do it alone. Others will have to help."

"I only pray they will. There m-must be hundreds — perhaps thousands — of home-

78

less children out there, Nora. What's to become of them?" His thoughts went to the enormity of the task to which he had set himself . . . or rather, the task to which the *Lord* had set him. As always, he felt slightly overwhelmed by what he faced. And, as always, the reminder came that he wasn't alone in it.

"How many *will* we be able to take in, Evan?"

He thought about her question before answering. "Well . . . thanks to Aunt Winnie and Mr. Farmington — and other church sponsors, of course — we should be able to take care of at least twenty boys by the fall." He paused, doing some quick calculations in his head. "After Christmas, we'll hope for increased support. Perhaps then we can increase to twenty-five, or even more."

Nora was quiet for such a long time that Evan looked to see if she had fallen asleep. Instead, she tightened her grasp on his hand. "Evan — will we be able to help Daniel John go on to the university soon, do you think? I know he's saving all he can from his wages with Dr. Grafton, but he gives us most of it, I'm sure."

Evan tried not to show his uncertainty. "I expect we'll m-manage," he said. Wanting to reassure her, yet unwilling to deceive her, he went on in a tone that he hoped held more confidence than he felt. "We'll think of some-thing. If the Lord wants Daniel to be a doctor, He'll make a way."

"I'm worried about him, Evan," she said quietly.

He looked at her. "Why on earth would you be worried about Daniel?"

"Haven't you noticed how he acts around Quinn?"

Evan *had* noticed, of course, but he rather hoped Nora hadn't.

When he delayed his reply, she went on. "He's sweet on the girl, haven't you seen?"

"Oh, I d-don't know that that's quite the case, dear," he said evasively. "He m-might be somewhat infatuated with her, I suppose. Quinn is an attractive girl, after all. But I'm sure it's nothing . . . serious."

But he wasn't sure of any such thing; in-deed, he found Daniel's obvious attraction to their young housekeeper a matter of some concern. The girl had a hard edge to her, combined with a certain secretiveness that troubled Evan. He hadn't altogether forgot-ten Michael Burke's suspicion that Quinn might be running away from something. Or someone.

Yet despite his nagging uncertainty about Quinn O'Shea, there was no disputing the fact that in only months, the girl had made herself virtually indispensable to them. He hated to think what life would be like without her.

No matter how much they might need her, however, he understood Nora's concern. Daniel was sixteen years old, and in many ways far more mature than his years, yet he was still quite innocent. He would be especially vulnerable, Evan suspected, in matters of the heart.

Much as he himself had been at that age . . . and for a long time after.

"Has Daniel ever shown interest in girls b-before?" he asked abruptly.

"Only poor Katie, God rest her soul." Nora twisted to raise herself up on one elbow. "But that was only a childish affection. This is different, Evan."

She was right. The boy's awkward attempts to retain his composure in Quinn's presence, his quick blush of pleasure when she happened to notice him, the way his gaze followed her every movement across the room — all the signs pointed to a boy's first real passion of the heart.

Evan sighed. Because love had come late to him, he wasn't altogether able to identify with Daniel's youthful dilemma. But certainly he knew the anguish, the bewilderment, of those first painful steps toward love. His own had been agonizingly slow and brutally difficult.

Still, he was anxious to allay Nora's concern about the boy. The last thing she needed in her fragile condition was additional worry. Daniel was, after all, on the threshold of manhood, and he had always been a sensible boy. A good boy.

"We m-must realize, dear, that although Quinn is an attractive young woman, she's also exceedingly responsible. I can't think she would lead D-Daniel on."

He could see that she wasn't convinced.

"It's just that they're so different," Nora told him. "Quinn seems so much older than Daniel John, though there's not quite a year between them." She paused. "The girl seems so . . . hard, Evan. And Daniel John is such a gentle boy."

Evan said nothing, his mind drifting. He, too, had noticed the marked difference between their young housekeeper and Nora's amiable son. Though the two were close in years, they seemed ages apart in most other ways. Whereas Daniel was an idealist — thoughtful, noble-intentioned, and a bit of a dreamer — Evan suspected that Quinn O'Shea viewed life through the relentless eyes of a realist. His instincts told him that the girl had encountered too many of life's harsh realities to be otherwise.

To be sure, she had shown no undue interest in Daniel. Evan thought he might know the reason. "If you're aware of Daniel's attraction to the girl," he said, "then you m-must have noticed Sergeant Price's interest in her as well,"

Nora looked at him. "Sergeant Price?"

Evan nodded. "Surely you d-don't think he comes by as often as he does simply to check on B-Billy and the other boys?"

Nora sat up still more. Evan put out his hand to restrain her, but she shrugged it off.

"You think the sergeant is interested in Quinn?" Her entire expression brightened. "Truly, Evan?"

Evan smiled a little at the eagerness in her voice. "I shouldn't be at all surprised. He d-does seem to go out of his way to visit us, now doesn't he?"

Nora met his smile with one of her own. "Why, he does, now that you mention it," she said thoughtfully. "And wouldn't such a match make a great deal more sense? Though Quinn *is* a good many years younger than the sergeant."

"As you said, the girl seems years older than she actually is."

"And Sergeant Price is a fine looking man," Nora said, almost to herself. "And a bit of a charmer as well, according to Sara. No doubt

Quinn would find the sergeant much more interesting than a young boy like Daniel John."

Evan could hear her trying to convince herself — and doing an admirable job of it at that. "Well, then, you see . . . you've nothing to fret about. Nothing at all."

Nora still looked a bit uncertain. "I don't want to see Daniel John hurt, though. Even if I don't like his attraction to the girl, I'd hate to think she might actually scorn him."

Evan shook his head. Nora's reasoning — any woman's reasoning, for that matter, when it came to love — was a formidable challenge.

Finally Nora sank back against the pillows with a sigh. "You do like Quinn, don't you, Evan? I didn't mean to imply that she's anything but a decent girl, and her living right here in the house with us."

"I like Quinn very m-much," he said quickly. "And I'm sure she's a fine girl. But . . ."

When he hesitated, Nora frowned at him. "But what?" she prompted.

"Well, she does have a certain . . . reticence about her that sometimes puzzles me."

The truth was, he sometimes thought the girl was downright strange. He had to admit that he, too, would much rather see her take up with Sergeant Price than with Daniel. He doubted there was much of anything the good sergeant could not handle — including the mysterious Quinn O'Shea.

Releasing Nora's hand, Evan leaned to brush a light kiss over her forehead, then straightened. "We must simply pray that when the time comes, Daniel will find someone who will m-make him as happy as you've made me."

Her expression clouded. "Please, God, let her not be the *burden* I've been to you," she said, her voice low.

Dismayed, Evan hurried to reassure her. Bringing his face close to hers, he cupped her chin in his hand. "Oh, my beloved, never . . . *never* . . . say such a thing again! Why, m-most men go to their graves without ever knowing even a *taste* of the joy you've given me! I could never want anything m-more than your love, Nora. If you believe nothing else I've ever said to you, believe that."

She gave him a weak smile. "I don't deserve you, Evan Whittaker. I don't deserve you at all. But I thank God every day of my life for you, and that's the truth."

He touched a finger to her lips. "Then let us both thank Him for *this* day, beloved . . . and for every day He allows us to spend together. And then — you really m-must go to sleep."

Still clinging to Evan's hand, Nora fell asleep even before they finished praying together.

5

A Hardhearted Woman

Her hair was a waving bronze
and her eyes
Deep wells that might cover
a brooding soul;
And who, till he weighed it, could
ever surmise
That her heart was a cinder instead
of a coal?
JOHN BOYLE O'REILLY (1844–1890)

On Wednesday night Quinn settled herself at the kitchen table, book in hand. It was almost eight-thirty, and she was exhausted from yet another long day. All evening she had been looking forward to this time, when she could finally pamper herself by reading a book and indulging in her favorite snack of bread and cheese.

Tonight's book was one of the newer additions to the library: a volume of essays by the contemporary Irish poet and storyteller, Morgan Fitzgerald.

Although she was intrigued by the idea that Mrs. Whittaker had been a childhood friend of the legendary Fitzgerald — in fact, the Whittakers still maintained a friendship with him by way of correspondence — Quinn didn't idolize the rebel poet as many of her countrymen did. She didn't share Fitzgerald's devotion for the struggling, starving island of her birth, had never been able to see much of the ancient beauty and compelling secrets he attributed to it.

Certainly, she harbored no desire to return to the place. Not that she could return, even if she had a mind to — not, that is, unless she wanted to spend the rest of her life in gaol or end it with a noose about her neck.

There was no mercy in Ireland for an impoverished felon, man or woman. From the moment she boarded the ship to America, Quinn had determined to put all memory of her country behind her. Other than the aching reminders of her mother and her sister, Molly, she seldom allowed her thoughts to turn homeward . . . and never her heart.

Still, she was drawn by the power of Fitzgerald's writing. In Ireland, they said the Fitzgerald could make the angels weep or lure the faeries out of their hidey-holes with the music of his words. Despite her resistance to his nationalism, she found herself quickly caught up in the man's magic.

As eagerly as she savored the poet's rich imagery, so did she also relish the calm of the house this time of night. There was little enough peace and quiet at Whittaker House throughout the day; wee Teddy and a swarm of noisy little boys made the stillness of nighttime even more welcome.

Unfortunately, she usually nodded off to sleep soon after sitting down, too weary to really enjoy the time to herself. Tonight was no exception. She had put the book aside and was resting her head on top of her arms when a knock came at the back door.

She started awake, sitting bolt upright in the chair. She knew who it was even before she got up. Only one sturdy fist pounded with such uninhibited force at this time of night.

Yawning, she stumbled to the door, opening it with no real enthusiasm. "You're a bit late," she said dryly, taking in Sergeant Price's broad, good-natured features.

He looked at her. "Late?"

"Aye. 'Tis Wednesday. On Wednesday, you usually arrive by seven-thirty."

He grinned. "Ah. And can it be you were anxiously awaiting me, then?"

Quinn ignored the question, stepping aside

88

as he walked in without being invited. The fact was, Sergeant Denny Price had an open invitation from the Whittakers to drop by at any time. It wasn't her place to object, though at the moment she was tempted.

He stopped in the middle of the kitchen. "And how are you keeping, Quinn O'Shea?"

The man had been in the States long enough by half to rid himself of his thick Donegal speech. Instead, to Quinn's irritation, he seemed to cherish the brogue as if it were some sort of treasure.

"I'm very well, thank you." She deliberately made the effort to suppress her own Irish tongue. "And you, Sergeant?"

His grin was infectious, and in spite of her impatience with him, Quinn could not totally check an answering smile.

"Well, now, and wasn't I thinking that it's a splendid night for a stroll?" he said cheerfully. "Perhaps you'd join me?"

Although she would rather have remained in the quiet kitchen with her book, Quinn gave in. He was The Law, after all, and in especially good standing with her employers; they did seem to dote on the man. It might not do to slight him too frequently.

Besides, when he wasn't baiting her or flaunting his Irishness, the sergeant made surprisingly good company. He might be a bit rough, and he seemed altogether uninterested in bettering himself, but something about the thickset policeman made it difficult to actively dislike him.

For one thing, despite his being The Law and bold as a tinker, Quinn felt uncommonly at ease in his presence. He was almost always good-humored and seldom failed to make her laugh — a habit to which she wasn't ordinarily given. Quinn had not found very much in life all that amusing.

She hoped the man had no thought of anything more than a casual acquaintanceship. He had helped her out of a tight place on two occasions now, and for that, Quinn felt a certain amount of gratitude toward him. But that was all. Nothing more.

The last thing she wanted was a man's attention — especially a *policeman's* attention, and especially a policeman like Sergeant Price.

He was everything she did not admire in a man. He was gruff, uneducated, probably penniless — just another thick-necked, hard-headed Irishman. If the time ever came — and she couldn't conceive that it ever would — when she found herself able to tolerate a touch from a man, it most assuredly would not come from a rough Irish policeman. Instead, he would be sensitive, well-educated, ambitious, and considerate. A *gentleman*. In other words, a man who was everything Sergeant Price was *not*.

By the time they started back to the house, it was dark, and few people were about. Those who remained outside either sat talking on the front stoops of their houses or went about the evening business of pulling down blinds and locking up their stores.

Denny realized with some frustration that, as always, he and Quinn had exchanged no conversation of any real depth — only the usual superficial blather about the weather and the newest activities taking place at Whittaker House.

He had never had much trouble with the lasses — until this one. He had always had a pretty girl to take on a ferry boat ride or a picnic in the park, always a willing partner for the Saturday night socials at the hall.

Although Denny didn't exactly fancy himself a ladies' man, neither was he entirely unaware that he held a certain appeal for women — both young ones and not-so-young ones.

He had never thought much about this appeal one way or the other. He knew only that he enjoyed the company of women, and most seemed not to mind his. A lass did not have to be especially fair to attract Denny's interest, but he did like a girl with some spirit to her.

This Quinn O'Shea, now, she had more than her share of spirit. So far as her looks went, she was attractive enough, but not a beauty who would turn heads in a crowd — a bit too thin, a mere whippet of a lass, in truth. And those odd catlike eyes of hers could make a man downright uncomfortable. She had a way of peering at him as if he were a *gulpin* and nothing better.

But on those rare occasions when he managed to coax a genuine smile from her, Denny found himself delighted, and every time she laughed aloud, he felt an unaccountable rush of warmth rise up in his heart. He had sensed right from the beginning that Quinn O'Shea was not the sort who laughed easily or foolishly.

Sometimes he chastised himself for trailing after her so. She had a way of making him feel dull-witted and even clumsier than he actually was. No doubt she thought him a blockhead who could neither read nor write; but when he tried to think of a way to let her know he was no imbecile, he couldn't seem to get past that steely look of hers. And despite his strong discomfort in her presence, more often than not the very next evening would find him back on Elizabeth Street, heading for Whittaker House once again.

He simply could not seem to stay away from the girl. He was running out of excuses for calling so often, and he knew that soon he would have to confront her with his reasons for coming by — or else appear even more of a great fool than she already thought him.

But now here they were again, with her about to go inside, and as always they had discussed nothing of any consequence.

At the bottom of the steps, they stopped, and Denny found himself fumbling like a great *glunter* for something to say. "And how is Mrs. Whittaker getting on these days? I thought she was looking a bit brighter last week when I dropped by."

Quinn nodded. "She seems to be improving some. But she's still poorly. Too weak by far."

Denny nodded. "I'd hate to see anything happen to her. She's a fine lady."

She arched a eyebrow. "A lady, is it? I don't know as I've ever heard one of our own called a 'lady.'"

Denny studied her. "Well, now, it seems to me that being a lady has little to do with where you come from. Any fool can see that Mrs. Whittaker is indeed a lady."

"She is that," Quinn agreed. "But I doubt there are many who would acknowledge it, her being Irish."

Denny noted the tightness about her mouth and eyes, the edge to her voice. "You don't much take to being Irish, do you, lass?"

Her eyes went cold, but she merely shrugged off his question. " 'Tis what I am."

"Aye," he said softly. " 'Tis. And I for one do find it an acceptable thing to be."

"That's for you," she shot back. "There are some who might say there are better things."

Seeing the shutters draw down over her eyes, Denny moved to change tacks. He was reluctant to let her go after so brief an hour with her. "Have you heard from your little sister recently? 'Molly,' is it?"

Her face softened almost instantly. "Aye. She writes often. I taught her to read and write before I left, you see."

Denny smiled at her. "And did she ever receive the letters you had to write the second time — the ones you lost in the river at Tompkinsville?"

She nodded. "She says she has them all, and will keep them. She even used some of my own words from the letters when she wrote back. Molly was always a clever girl."

"You're still planning to bring her across, I expect."

Her chin went up. "I am. I will."

Denny liked watching her when she talked

of her young sister. It was the same as when he observed her with the wee orphan boys of Whittaker House: her features would brighten, and the wall of self-protection she seemed to live her life behind would slip, at least a little. At those moments, like now, she looked young and small and hopeful — almost happy.

She was good with those homeless little boys. They tagged along after her like shadows trailing the sun, and she seemed to have infinite patience with every wee one of them. There was no mistaking the look of affection in her eyes when she was bandaging a knee or wiping a nose.

Unwilling to part with her just yet, Denny kept up his attempts at conversation. "What of your mother, then? I expect she will be making the crossing with your little sister?"

As if snuffed out by a sudden gust of wind, the light in Quinn's eyes suddenly died. "No," was all she said, averting her gaze. "She wouldn't leave Athlone."

Denny frowned. "Not even for her daughters?"

"Not for this daughter anyhow." Abruptly, she turned away from him. "I must be going in now."

Impulsively, Denny caught her arm. "Stay a minute, won't you?"

She yanked her arm away as if a serpent had fallen upon it.

Taken aback — and sensing that she was about to bolt — Denny blurted out the first thing that came into his mind. "There's something I've been wanting to ask you, if I might."

Still shrinking back from him, she stared at Denny in a way that made him feel like a crude, clumsy bully-boy.

Was she really that revolted by him?

This was a new experience for Denny. Not that he hadn't been rejected once or twice by a woman, but so far as he could remember, none had ever looked at him with such disgust. For an instant he almost thought it might be fear in her eyes.

This unexpected response from her shook his confidence entirely. He groped for words. "The thing is . . . you may have been wondering about my coming by so uncommonly often. . . ."

Seeing no sign of encouragement from her, merely the same steady look, a look bordering on hostility, Denny faltered. His mouth dry, he deliberately avoided meeting her eyes as he hurried on. "In case you haven't realized, I . . . ah . . . I enjoy your company very much, lass."

Those few words out, he continued, but with even less confidence. "What I'm trying to say is that I'd like to see you on a more . . . regular basis." He paused. "I'd like to come calling, is what I mean."

Something flared in her eyes, then turned frigid. A hand went to the braid falling over one shoulder. "I don't keep company with men," she said.

She looked directly at him. Denny felt as if she were looking right *through* him.

He tried for a lighthearted tone. "I can't think why. Sure, you must have more than your share of lads coming about." A thought struck him. "If it's because of the years between us, I can understand —"

"The years having nothing to do with it," she interrupted.

Denny pulled in a long breath. A stab of disappointment shook him crown to toe. Obviously, she wanted nothing to do with him, whatever her reasons.

"Well, that's clear enough, then, isn't it? I'll just be on my way."

He swung around, anxious to escape before she could witness his humiliation.

Her voice stopped him. "Sergeant?"

Denny turned back reluctantly, waiting.

"It's . . . nothing to do with you, don't you see," she said in that same peculiar, dull tone of voice. She stared just past Denny's shoulder as she continued. "It's simply that I'm not

. . . in a position to keep company with anyone just now. I've no time for it, for one thing. But —" She stopped, biting at her lip as if uncertain how to go on. "I'd want you to feel free to come by whenever you wish, though. To see the Whittakers and the boys," she quickly added.

Denny nodded but said nothing. He was suddenly bent on getting away, putting as much distance as possible between himself and those somber, watchful eyes.

He berated himself all the way down the darkened street. Why had he even thought the girl would welcome his attentions? She hadn't given him the slightest hint of encouragement. Why, her treatment of him had never been anything but indifferent politeness.

What had he been thinking of, playing the fool, mooning about like a schoolboy, then working himself into a state when she gave him the mitten?

She was hardhearted, that one. It was just as well she had no interest in "keeping company with men." No man with a grain of self-respect would keep company with *her*, and that was the truth! Why, he was a sight better off without her. There was no misery like a hardhearted woman, his da had always said.

But try as he would, Denny could not entirely shake off the memory of the night when he had first seen her — a half-starved, wee stray of a thing, frightened and lost-looking. Even then, something about Quinn O'Shea had gone straight to his heart. And although it had been months before he saw her again, he never forgot her.

It was pity, no doubt. He had ever been the fool for the abandoned children of the city — even the stray animals. Didn't the other boyos on the force sometimes needle him about being soft for strays?

He felt sorry for the girl, that was all, and he had let his sympathy get out of hand.

But even as Denny turned the corner onto Hester Street, he knew that the feeling which had been growing inside him for Quinn O'Shea had little to do with pity. It was a different kind of feeling, unlike anything he had ever felt before . . . a feeling he couldn't begin to define, but not at all what he would feel for an orphaned child or a stray kitten.

Even though the wounded look in her eyes was much the same.

6

Of Age and Time

Believe me, if all those endearing
young charms,
Which I gaze on so fondly today,
Were to change by tomorrow, and fleet
in my arms,
Like fairy gifts fading away,
Thou wouldst still be ador'd, as this
moment thou art.
Let thy loveliness fade as it will,
And around the dear ruin each wish
of my heart
Would entwine itself verdantly still.
THOMAS MOORE (1779–1852)

On Sunday, Sara and Michael Burke at-
tended evening services at Jess Dalton's
small church on the edge of the Bowery.
They found themselves visiting the new
congregation more and more frequently, for
they had never stopped missing the big pas-

tor's presence at their own Fifth Avenue church. Although the pulpit had been quickly filled after Dalton's resignation, the new minister's influence seemed pitifully weak by comparison. Privately, Sara suspected that their distinguished new pastor, Dr. Stockley, was far more likely to bore the congregation to death than to offend or disturb them.

It was nearly dark when they started home in the buggy. With a sigh, she took Michael's hand. "Wasn't it good to hear a sermon with real substance?"

He grinned at her. "You mean a sermon with some real controversy, don't you?"

Sara shrugged. "I don't think Jess Dalton intends to be controversial. He simply attempts to preach the truth, and the truth often makes us uncomfortable. That's not the pastor's fault."

"Still, you're a bit hard on Dr. Stockley, now, aren't you?" Michael said, still smiling. "I've seen you biting your lip behind your white gloves. Your father would tell you — and not for the first time, I'm sure — that you'd best guard against a critical spirit."

"Really? Perhaps you didn't notice that Father himself nodded off more than once this morning."

"Understandable, after the first hour," Michael replied dryly.

Sara leaned her head back against the seat. "Anyway, it was good to see the Daltons; I miss them terribly. Did you see how little Amanda is growing? They've started the paperwork on her adoption, you know. But Father says there may be complications, with her parents having been immigrants."

"What isn't complicated where immigrants are concerned?" Michael muttered. "Nobody seems to know quite what to do about them."

"Well, I hope for Kerry's sake everything goes smoothly — and quickly. She's absolutely devoted to that little girl — they both are, of course. Amanda will have a wonderful home."

Michael nodded absently, and Sara could tell he was thinking of something else. Well, she had something more on *her* mind, too. She squeezed his hand. "I hope *we* have a child soon, Michael."

His surprise was obvious. "No doubt we will, sweetheart." He paused, searching her eyes. "Sure, you're not fretting about that already?"

Sara looked away. "We've been married over a year and a half, Michael. I *had* hoped that by now . . ."

She let her words drift off, incomplete.

After a moment, Sara felt his arm go around her. With his free hand, he turned her face toward his. "Ah, Sara," he said softly, shaking his head, "ever in a hurry. Even for a babe."

Sara tried to smile, but as always he saw past her pretense.

"We have time, sweetheart. Plenty of time."

"But you want children, too, Michael! You have Tierney, of course, but even before we were married, you admitted you wanted other children . . . our children."

He moved to take her by the shoulders. "I do, Sara *a gra*. As many as the good Lord sees fit to give us. But if either of us should be in a hurry, it ought to be me. I'm the one with silver in my hair, not you."

"It's different for a man," she said, brushing off his reference to the difference in their ages. "A woman has only so many childbearing years. If we want a large family, we need to get started."

"Right now?"

At the glint of amusement in his eye, Sara gave him a look.

His expression sobered. "Sara, I understand. I do, sweetheart," he insisted when Sara moved to protest. "And, yes, I want children with you. But do *you* understand that even if by some chance we *don't* have a child right away, it will make no difference to me?

None at all. You are enough family for me, Sara — you and Tierney. You will *always* be enough for me."

The tenderness in his eyes melted Sara's heart. "Oh, Michael! You're enough for me, too. I'm awful to want anything more than I already have, I know! It's just that seeing Kerry tonight with little Amanda . . . somehow it made me want a baby right *now!*"

He gave a soft laugh, then dipped his head to kiss her. "Well, then," he said, still holding her, "I suppose there's nothing for it but to get started on the nursery, for when you set your head to something, it's as good as done."

Later that night, Jess Dalton sat at his desk in the library, pretending to work on his most recent book, a collection of writings taken from former slaves who had escaped to the North. But he had accomplished little so far this evening. He was more intent on watching his wife entertain their son and little Amanda.

The door was open, and he could see directly across the hall into the parlor, where Kerry, Casey-Fitz, and the little girl they hoped to make their legal daughter were enjoying their evening story hour.

Amanda, not quite two, was perched on Kerry's lap, her curly blond head bobbing up and down as if she knew exactly what was coming next. Casey-Fitz was sprawled at his mother's feet. From the rapt look on the boy's face, Jess was certain that he was listening to one of Kerry's lively retellings of an Irish legend.

Tapping his pen, Jess studied the scene across the hall with a contented smile. It was difficult to realize that the fiery-haired little boy they had adopted a few years ago was now twelve. From all signs, Casey-Fitz would fulfill the promise of his childhood. He was fast maturing into an intelligent, sensitive lad who seemed destined to do something fine, something noble, with his life. He often spoke of becoming a physician, or perhaps a medical researcher.

Jess wondered again at how the boy, though adopted, resembled Kerry so closely in physical appearance. He no longer found the resemblance as surprising as he once had; the years had convinced him that the Lord must have handpicked Casey-Fitz especially for them — and particularly for Kerry.

Kerry. What a gift she was to him! He could still remember the first time he had seen her, when she stepped off the steamer at West Point: a feisty, achingly lovely, petite waif, with one copper curl escaping from the hood of her cloak and a look in her eye that plainly said she would rather be anywhere else than where she was.

She had come to him, reluctantly, as his ward, an arrangement accomplished by their fathers years before. When Kerry's father passed away she was still in her teens. Andrew Dalton — Jess's father, was also gone, leaving Jess to assume the responsibilities of Kerry's guardianship.

Already in his early thirties at the time, Jess was serving as chaplain at the U.S. Military Academy. For the most part, he had resigned himself to bachelorhood. But a lightning bolt struck him the day Kerry O'Neill stepped off the steamboat, and from that moment on his life was changed.

Smiling, he traced the memories as they unfolded through his mind: their courtship, after Kerry finally managed to convince him that the years between them didn't matter . . . their marriage in the academy chapel . . . their honeymoon in the Adirondacks. . . .

But his smile faded at the thought of their subsequent move to Washington, where Kerry had almost lost her life — along with that of their stillborn son — and where Jess himself had been shot by a fanatical politician with a virulent hatred for all abolitionists. The incident had left Kerry barren and bereft, and for a long time, Jess had questioned the

Lord's call on his life.

Yet out of the ashes of their anguish had come the unexpected, shining gift of an adopted son: Casey-Fitz. Then a small seven-year-old Irish orphan with ears too big for his face and eyes too old for his years, the boy had helped rescue Kerry from a fire. Eventually he also rescued her from the grief of her child-lessness.

And now . . . Amanda.

Jess looked at the tiny girl snuggled close to Kerry's heart. She was little more than a baby. He had brought her home after promising her dying mother that he would look after the child. His original intention had simply been to give Amanda a temporary place to live until her grandfather in England sent someone to claim her. But a few weeks after the death of the child's mother, word arrived that her grandfather had also passed on — without ever seeing Amanda.

By then, Jess and Kerry had taken the little girl to their hearts and could no longer imagine giving her up. Even Casey-Fitz quickly "adopted" Amanda as his little sister.

So Amanda had stayed, and now they were in the process of adopting her. Although Jess feared the process might not be without complications, he had been careful to hide his concern from Kerry. Ever since they had begun the legal proceedings, she could scarcely contain her excitement. She was like a child herself. She and Molly, the housekeeper who had been in Jess's family for years, had already made elaborate plans to redecorate the nursery. In the meantime, they spent hours each day sewing all sorts of dainty little-girl things, while Molly's husband, Mack, set his hand to building a rocking horse and a toy chest.

Resolved that Casey-Fitz should not feel left out of all the excitement going on around him, Kerry made a practice of telling him stories about his own adoption. "Why, it was even more of a rush with you," she would say, eyes sparkling. "We brought you home at practically a moment's notice! But Grandma Molly and Grandpa Mack had a fine new suit waiting for you when we arrived — and shiny black shoes as well! And weren't you proud of those new clothes! I suppose your father's told you that we didn't sleep for nights afterward — he says I talked his ear off with all my plans for you."

She had done exactly that, Jess remembered with a fond smile, and he had loved every minute of it. Nothing made him any happier than seeing Kerry happy. For that reason alone — aside from his own affection for Amanda — he would do whatever it took to make the child their own.

Later, in their bedroom, Jess sat down behind his wife at the vanity. Smiling at her reflection, he took the hairbrush from her hand and began to brush the copper curls he loved so well into a fiery cloud that fell halfway down her back.

She was unusually quiet for a time, and he knew her mind was racing. "What's going on in there?" he teased, dropping a light kiss on the crown of her head. "Planning Amanda's marriage? Or Casey's career? Which is it tonight?"

She wrinkled her nose at his reflection. "Actually, I was thinking about Sara."

Surprised, he slowed the brush strokes. "Sara? What about Sara?"

"She wants a baby, you know."

Jess lifted an eyebrow, then resumed brushing. "You have that for a fact, I suppose."

Kerry nodded. "She confided in me a few weeks ago. She feels somewhat . . . in a hurry, I think, because of her age. And Michael's."

Again he halted the brush. "Good heavens, Sara is little more than a girl herself! And Michael can't be all that old, surely."

She looked at him, all seriousness now: "No, Jess. Sara is older than I am — she's twenty-eight. And Michael is thirty-nine."

Jess considered her words, making an effort not to dwell on the fact that he had recently turned forty.

"Still, they're young," he said, half hoping she would agree with him.

She did, and he resumed brushing a little more cheerfully.

"Sara will make a wonderful mother, don't you think, Jess?"

He nodded. "Like you."

She smiled at him in the mirror. "We must pray for them. For a baby. I want everyone to be as happy as we are, don't you see?"

He smiled back, pulling the brush with great care through a particularly stubborn lock of hair. "Impossible," he said. "But I'm glad you and Sara are friends. At least you're not alone in being married to a patriarch."

She glared at him in the mirror. "Don't you *dare* start that nonsense again, Jess Dalton! You know it makes me angry. As if a few years makes the slightest bit of difference to you and me."

He grinned, amused at her scolding. "You truly don't mind, then, being married to a man in his dotage?"

One eyebrow arched. "You don't exactly behave like a man in his dotage, Mr. Dalton. Especially when we're alone."

Jess grinned. He laid the brush down on the

vanity so he could turn her around to face him. "Is that a fact, Mrs. Dalton?" he said, drawing her into his arms.

7

Uneasy Nights

Night grows uneasy near the dawn. . . .
W. B. YEATS (1865–1939)

Dublin
Late July

Dublin moved more slowly in the summer.

Her people strolled rather than rushed, talking and tending to their business in a more leisurely fashion. Visitors to the city took their time, viewing the Four Courts, the Custom House, and Dublin Castle with a slightly slower step than their cousins who came in the spring. Even the ragged children of the streets seemed to find less mischief in which to involve themselves. Some who traversed the Halfpenny Bridge said the River Liffey actually slowed its journey from the Wicklow Mountains to the Irish sea during summertime. It wasn't that the temperature rose to any

significant degree. Unlike the Irish themselves, the island's climate seldom climbed or
dipped to extremes. More likely it was the
sweetness of the season that accounted for the
less frenzied behavior, the more relaxed pace
of the entire city.

Summer was a winsome time. The breeze
coming down from the mountains was gentle,
almost intoxicating with fragrance; the hills
seemed to beckon the city people to come
away to a simpler life. At night, especially, the
wind was easy, the voices of the city were
carefree, the music sweet.

To the north of the city, however, at Nelson
Hall, movement on this fine summer's night
was brisk, even frantic. An event of great significance was approaching, and the household of Morgan Fitzgerald — the *Seanchai* —
was deep in preparation.

The family had agreed that some sort of
birthday celebration for Finola was long past
due. The problem had been how to schedule
such an event.

Because there was no way of knowing the
actual date of her birth, Finola had been
asked to choose a day to her liking. She in
turn requested that her husband select a date.
After some consideration, the *Seanchai* had
chosen August 1, explaining that this had

been his mother's birth date and he would be pleased if Finola would take it as her own.

And so, two nights before the birthday celebration, Sandemon and Sister Louisa were rushing to complete what was meant to be a very special gift for the occasion. A small linen press at the end of the hall had been converted to a prayer closet. Sandemon had done most of the pounding and scraping in one afternoon, while the *Seanchai*, who by this time had been let in on the secret, occupied Finola with a picnic by the stream.

After numerous late nights, and with considerable help from Sister Louisa and Annie, Sandemon had almost finished the task. Tonight they would complete the closet's furnishings.

"No doubt the *Seanchai* will present Mistress Finola with something fine and precious," Sandemon mused as he attached a carved wooden crucifix to a nail in the wall. "Jewelry, do you think?"

Sister Louisa gave a huff; worldly baubles, she clearly believed, were insignificant in comparison to spiritual riches. "Our gift will serve her better," she said, smoothing a soft white cloth over a table confiscated from one of the unused bedchambers in the east wing. "The girl needs privacy far more than pieces of glass."

Stepping back from the crucifix, Sandemon gave a satisfied nod. "You truly think she will be pleased?"

"And why wouldn't she be? The poor child doesn't know what it's like to have any time to herself. And it seems to me that it's beginning to tell on her. She's fretful and weepy of late — not herself at all."

Sandemon frowned. He eyed the candlestick Louisa placed at the end of the table, then leaned to move it slightly closer to the middle.

The black man lifted an eyebrow. "I have noticed that she is often sleepless," he said. "She roams the halls many a night, after everyone else is abed. Often, I have had to cease work in here, for fear of being discovered. I question whether the lack of privacy alone would cause such disquiet."

Louisa hadn't known about the sleeplessness, and it only added to her concern about the girl. "I didn't know," she admitted, setting the candlestick back in its original place. "Still, there is no denying that she is seldom alone. Young Annie follows her about like a shadow. And our Gabriel now toddles after her as if he would attach himself to her skirts. Then, of course, there is Lucy, who insists on hovering over the girl like a guardian angel." She paused. "Not to mention the *Seanchai*, who becomes positively wild-eyed if she's out of his sight for more than five minutes."

Placing a small missal and a copy of the Scriptures next to the candlestick, she stood appraising the tiny room. "There are many demands on a young wife and mother," she said distractedly. She bent to inspect the rag rug and prayer pillows, then straightened. "A few moments alone with the Lord each day will do her a world of good. Finola is devout, you know. She often steals away for a time of quiet in the chapel. But she is almost always followed by one of the children or the *Seanchai*. Even there, she seldom finds any real privacy."

The black man nodded. "Ah, well, here she can close the door to everyone — even lock it, if she wishes." He motioned to the small bolt he had installed. "Surely the household will respect her privacy to this extent. A person's time with God should be honored." Turning to Louisa, he crossed his arms over his chest and smiled. "Your idea was a fine one."

Louisa shrugged. "Ideas are easy enough to come by. It takes effort to give them life. You have worked hard," she conceded. "And everything looks splendid. Now," she added dryly, "if only our Annie can keep the secret just two days more."

Sandemon chuckled, turning for one last look at his handiwork. "She will," he said. "After the mayhem you've threatened, I can't think the child would dare whisper a word. Besides, she would not spoil the surprise. She dotes on the young mistress."

It occurred to Louisa that the entire household doted on Finola. With her shy smile, gentle ways, and unceasing kindness, the *Seanchai*'s young wife had endeared herself to the family — and to the entire staff of Nelson Hall, as well. Everyone, from the kitchen workers to the stable hands, wished only goodness and happiness for their lovely, soft-voiced mistress.

And that was as it should be, Louisa thought. When one so young and pure of heart had already endured such an incredible degree of pain, it seemed only right that she should now enjoy an abundance of blessing.

On the heels of this reflection came the unsettling reminder that life did not always balance its pain with an equal share of joy. Louisa firmly banished the thought but was unable to stop the slight shudder that accompanied it.

When she turned around, she saw that Sandemon had dropped to his knees. No doubt he was seeking the Lord's blessing on Finola's private haven. Without hesitating,

Louisa knelt to join his supplications with her own.

Rook Mooney stood hunched in the rain across the street from Gemma's Place. He had watched the upstairs' door every night for almost a week now, long enough to realize with growing fury that the Innocent no longer lived in the room at the top of the stairs.

She was gone. More than a year he had waited, the fire in his gut raging. Now he had come back for her, and she was gone. *Gone!*

With a rough hand, he brushed the rain from his face. Anger rose up in him like a scalded beast. For the past year he had lived for this time, when he would return to Dublin and put an end to the sickness she had bred in him.

He knew there was only one way to banish the fever from his brain, only one way to ever be free of her. In order to destroy her hold on him, he would have to destroy *her*.

But where to find her? There was a new woman in the room at the top of the stairs — an older woman, hard and unattractive. In five nights he had seen no sign of the golden-haired witch, no indication that she had ever existed, other than in his mind.

He spat into the street, then pushed away from the wall and began to walk. The rain came harder now, and he cursed as he stumbled into the night, his shoulders stooped against the driving downpour.

It wouldn't do to question the other whores. He didn't want to raise their curiosity.

Besides, he knew where he would find his answers well enough. Information could always be had on the docks, at least for a price. That was where he had heard about her in the first place.

His boots scraped, then slapped heavily through a puddle. He would find her. If not tonight, tomorrow. No matter how long it took, he would find her.

And this time when he was done with her, she would no longer haunt his sleep and poison his days. He would be free . . . because she would be dead.

Finola jerked awake, her heart hammering. She looked over at Morgan, relieved to see that he was still sleeping soundly.

Sometime in the night, the big arm that was usually wrapped securely about her had fallen away, and she suddenly felt cold. She tried to focus her eyes, reassured to see the candle beside the bed still flickering; she could not bear total darkness in a room.

Seeking Morgan's warmth, she moved

closer to the safe wall of his brawny shoulder. She took care not to rouse him, but lay quietly, trying to control the trembling of her body. Trying to think. Trying not to think.

She shuddered at the sound of the rain blowing against the house. Rain at night always seemed such a desolate sound, like the mournful drumbeat of a troubled heart.

Another strong blast of wind-driven rain hurled itself between the battlements outside and slammed against the window. Finola cringed, squeezing her eyes shut for a moment.

It wasn't the Dream that had awakened her this time, but the Feeling. A hideous, bleak sense of isolation, as if she were trapped in the vault of night itself. The darkness was dense and glacial, unyielding, bringing with it an overwhelming sense of betrayal that swept over her like a tidal wave of despair.

Again she had heard the faraway sound of music . . . strange, high-pitched — almost shrill — yet elusive, like the night wind sighing through the trees.

At the last she had felt the hands close about her throat . . . suffocating her . . . crushing the breath from her . . . stealing her life. . . .

And then, as always, she awakened with a start, panicked, terrified, filled with a sense of revulsion, as if she had been touched by something unclean.

The nausea came upon her in a wave, the sudden wash of sickness. Bracing herself, she resisted the urge to spring out of bed and escape the room. It would soon pass, as it always did.

Finally she was able to draw in one steadying breath, then another. Little by little the trembling subsided. Depleted, still dazed, she drew a fist against her mouth to choke down a sob of despair. Morgan stirred, and his hand moved to touch her hair, but he slept on.

She knew she would not sleep again this night. When the Dream or the Feeling woke her, it was impossible to return to the peace of sleep. She would lie awake in the dimly lighted bedroom, listening to the rambling old mansion creak and shudder around her. Or, if she grew too restless to stay abed, she would rise and walk the halls or go to the chapel and try to pray.

For now, though, she was reluctant to leave the comforting sound of Morgan's breathing, the safe haven of his bed.

What did it all mean, the evil dream and the poisonous feelings that continued to cause her so much anguish? Of all the night terrors she had endured since the attack, she thought these must surely be the most deadly. Not only did they rob her of hours of much-needed rest, but they spoiled her days as well, leaving her anxious and impatient. Of late, she had even begun to feel physically ill throughout the day.

She was failing her family, disappointing the entire household.

But what to do?

Sometimes she feared she had been stricken with some dreadful illness of the mind. Perhaps because of the dark chasm where no memory dwelt . . . perhaps because of the terrible thing that had been done to her.

Would it grow worse? Would she eventually lose her mind altogether?

Again she shuddered.

She looked at Morgan, studying his strong, beloved face in the candleglow. Then the tears came, spilling silently from her eyes.

He had suffered enough on her behalf, this good and noble man. She must give him no more pain, no more anguish of the soul. She would keep her silence; she would endure.

Carefully, she turned onto her side, away from him. She would not ever have him know that in the long hours of the night his wife lay weeping beside him.

8

A Casting of Shadows

*For back to the Past, though the
thought brings woe,
My memory ever glides. . . .*
JAMES CLARENCE MANGAN (1803–1849)

On the morning of Finola's birthday, Morgan was enduring a Latin recitation by one of the O'Higgins twins, at the same time keeping a watchful eye on the other scholars in the room.

He was impatient, not only with the boy standing across the desk from him, stumbling over his lesson, but even more with the subject itself. He detested the study — and the teaching — of Latin. It was too rigid, too precise a language for his taste. Although Sister Louisa had done her best on a number of occasions to point out its usefulness, Morgan's feelings had changed not at all since his own boyhood experience with the subject.

"Our young people would do far better to devote more time to their own language," he had argued with the nun. "The Irish is a sturdy, lively language. It has *spirit*. Latin is weak broth in comparison."

"*Latin* is the language of the *Church*," the nun returned pointedly. "A language of tradition and dignity. It also teaches one to think in a precise and orderly fashion, as well as providing —"

"— an understanding of all other grammatical relationships," Morgan finished for her. He knew her rebuttal by heart.

The woman could ever make him feel like an ignorant *bostoon!*

Glaring at Barry O'Higgins — or was this one Barnaby? — he offered no mercy as the boy ended yet another pathetic rendering of the daily assignment.

"Perhaps by now you have come to realize that one cannot conjugate *esse* in the passive voice, Mr. O'Higgins," he said, leveling a withering glare on the round, freckled face. "Would I be safe in assuming you did not bother to *read* the assignment before presenting it?"

Despite the flush that crept over his features, the lad's expression appeared entirely unrepentant. The quick downward glance didn't deceive Morgan for a moment. The

O'Higgins twins took nothing seriously until threatened with corporal punishment.

He sighed, wishing not for the first time that he had followed his earlier instincts and sent the both of them packing long ago. In truth, they owed their status as students to Sister Louisa, who insisted that even the O'Higgins twins could be both tamed and taught.

When the devil takes a holiday, Morgan thought, eyeing the difficult scholar. "Well, then, Barry —"

"— Barnaby, sir —"

"Very well, Barnaby — you may add to today's exercises the three sets in the appendix for chapter five, to be recited tomorrow."

"But you said no assignments today, sir!" the boy burst out. "It being the mistress's birthday and all."

Morgan lowered his eyeglasses on the bridge of his nose and stared at the boy. Finally he sighed. "So I did. Very well, then."

The boy beamed at him.

"But you will be prepared by Saturday morning," Morgan cautioned.

"Oh, I will, sir!"

"And you'd best set your mind on taking a more serious attitude toward your studies, else —"

A knock on the door interrupted him. Morgan motioned the boy back to his chair as Sandemon entered the room.

"Begging your pardon, sir, but there is a gentleman to see you."

Morgan frowned. It was only midmorning, early for a caller.

"A gentleman?"

"Mr. Cassidy, sir," replied the black man.

"*Cassidy?*" Morgan caught his breath, then tossed his grade book into the top drawer of the desk. "Show him into the library. I'll see him at once!"

As he propelled his chair into the library, Morgan fought down a wave of excitement and apprehension.

Something in the confident way Cassidy was standing — even though his smile appeared somewhat guarded — made Morgan's heart jump with anticipation.

They shook hands, and Morgan wheeled himself behind the desk. For a moment he studied the big white-haired man across from him. "So, Frank —" He motioned Cassidy to take a chair. "What news do you bring me?"

"I do have news at last," Cassidy said, lowering himself into the chair. "Though it's taken a terrible long time, I know."

Morgan swallowed against the tightness in

126

his throat. "Tell me," he said, his voice strained.

Cassidy knotted his big hands together on his knees as he leaned forward. Never one to dissemble, he started in right away. "It seems her name was Moran. The family was from Drogheda, but there would appear to be a distant blood-tie with Michael Moran."

Morgan gaped at him. "Zozimus?" Michael Moran, the blind street musician and legendary patriarch of the itinerant ballad singers, was better known by his nickname, *Zozimus*. So great was his fame that his reputation had spawned countless numbers of imitators.

Cassidy nodded. "Finola Moran is your wife's name, right enough."

Finola. So, then, her name really was Finola, *after all.*

Morgan fought to control the conflicting passions that warred within him. Hadn't he *wanted* to discover Finola's past and help her come through the darkness she battled? Yet now, selfish man that he was, all he could think of was the possibility that someone else, someone with a greater claim to her, might try to take her from him. He wanted what was best for Finola, of course, but . . . by all the saints, he couldn't face the possibility of losing her!

Trying to check the trembling of his hands,

Morgan clenched them on the desk in front of him. "And . . . did you find . . . the family?"

Cassidy shook his head. "There was only herself and the father. And the old man is dead." He paused. "Murdered, 'tis said, in a shooting incident. He was a widower, and the girl — Finola — his only child."

Relief poured over Morgan like a river, only to be replaced by a wave of guilt. Was he really so selfish that he could take comfort from Finola's loss?

"There is no one else, then?" he managed to ask, gripping his hands even tighter. "No one at all?"

Cassidy shook his head. "Only the two of them, the girl and the father — and him gone. James Moran owned an apothecary and raised some crops on a patch of land outside the city. A respected man, it would seem. 'Twas the son of his housekeeper from whom I finally heard the story — and a sad story it is."

Morgan squeezed his eyes shut.

There was no one out there waiting to take her away from him, no one else with a claim to her affection. Another stab of guilt, this time even sharper, pierced through him.

For so long he had dreaded the truth. . . .

Suddenly it struck him that Cassidy had mentioned a murder. "What's this about the father being murdered?" he managed to ask, opening his eyes. "Tell me everything you've learned."

In her bedroom, Annie sat at the small desk in the corner. She had completed her recitations with Sister Louisa and was now studying what she considered her most skillful piece of artwork to date.

She touched the tip of her sketching pencil to her lower lip, then gave a nod of satisfaction. At her side, Fergus uttered a soft bark, obviously intent on having a look for himself.

Annie glanced at the wolfhound. "Very well," she said, replacing the pencil in its box. "You may look at it. But you must be very careful not to drool. I'll not be giving Finola a portrait smudged by your great tongue."

She held up the sketch at a considerable distance from the wolfhound's huge head. He studied it, his expression sober. At last he gave a short bark.

"Don't be such a pup," Annie scolded. "Didn't I tell you the cat would be included in the portrait? 'Tis only right, her being Finola's special pet."

Fergus whimpered, but Annie ignored him as she resumed her study of the portrait. The sketch portrayed Finola, seated by the fire in the great room, with baby Gabriel on her lap and Small One, the cat, at her feet.

The sketch was quite good, if she did say so herself. Sister had promised to help her mat it later, which would make it even more presentable.

Annie did hope Finola would be pleased. From the beginning, she had determined to *make* her gift, wanting to give Finola something personal, something that would reflect a measure of effort and affection.

Propping one elbow on the desk, she rested her chin on her hand. "Finola doesn't seem altogether happy these days," she observed to Fergus, who cocked his head as if waiting for an explanation.

But Annie had no explanation. She only knew that there were times when Finola's lovely face grew sad and troubled, times when she seemed oblivious to conversation taking place all about her — even when the *Seanchai* was speaking.

Perhaps, Annie thought unhappily, Finola still fretted over a past she could not remember — where she had come from, who she had been, what she might have left behind. Wouldn't it be the natural thing, to puzzle over whether she had family somewhere, missing her, searching for her?

She put a hand to Fergus's head and began to stroke his ears. "I expect she *would* feel sad

130

sometimes," she said to the wolfhound. "It would be a terrible thing entirely not to know where you came from or who your people are. Even though my mum gave me up, at least I arrived with a *name*. But Finola doesn't even have that. She can't recall her mother or father, or sisters or brothers — no one."

Annie's heart wrenched. She wouldn't be so selfish as to hope that Finola had no other family outside Nelson Hall. Nor would she wish that Finola's memory of that family might never return. That would be a wicked thought altogether. But if such a family did indeed exist, would it be too cruel, she wondered, to hope that there was no younger sister?

By late afternoon, Morgan was so consumed by Cassidy's incredible tale that his head felt dangerously near to exploding. He had all he could do to keep from spoiling Finola's birthday celebration.

Now that at least some of the questions seemed to have been answered, he could not make up his mind what to do with the information. His first inclination had been to tell Finola the entire story at once. She had a right to know, after all, a right to have the missing pieces of her past finally set aright.

But what would it do to her?

131

Already her emotions were fragile. What if this new revelation proved to be more than she could bear? Was there a possibility it could damage the progress she had made, the healing she seemed to have gained since Gabriel's birth?

What if it turned out that she could not cope with the shock of such a disclosure? To learn that she had apparently been the victim of a savage assault not once, but *twice* — an assault that may well have cost her father his life — could such a horror really be borne without further devastation?

Just see what the truth had done to *him*. Even now, hours after listening to Cassidy's interpretation of the tale, he was still badly shaken, still half ill with the despair of knowing what Finola must have endured. He knew very well it would take a long, long time before he would be able to think on the entire story without a murderous rage or sick anguish. He could not fathom what this would mean to Finola, who had been the victim of the ugliness.

Besides, what possible good would be served by telling her? It was not as if there were a loving family out there, missing her. Evidently there was no one.

Did she really need to know? Might it not be the best thing — indeed, the loving thing

— simply to bury the past?

He shook his head as if to dispel the temptation. It would be unforgivable to let her go on anguishing over her identity when all the while he could provide her with the truth. Surely that would be the cruelest sort of deception, a virtual betrayal.

But how to tell her?

And when?

At the end of his wits he went at last in search of Sister Louisa. Perhaps the nun's unwavering good sense would help him to decide.

He found her upstairs in the sewing room with Annie and the wolfhound. Together they were matting the pencil portrait Annie had sketched for Finola's birthday gift.

"I would speak with Sister alone, Aine, if you don't mind," Morgan told her. "Perhaps you and Fergus could look in on Gabriel in the nursery."

The girl darted a curious glance from him to Sister, hesitating before leaving the room with the wolfhound at her feet.

Sister Louisa did not react as Morgan might have expected. After hearing the story, she sank down in the chair by the window, wringing her hands. She was, Morgan noted, frightfully pale.

"Oh, the poor lass," she said, her voice infinitely soft. She said it again, framing her face with trembling hands. "How could she survive such wickedness . . . such tragedy . . . more than once?"

Unnerved by the nun's rare display of agitation, Morgan wheeled his chair close to her. "Are you all right, Sister?"

She dropped her hands away from her face and looked at him. "Yes. Yes, of course." She said nothing more for a moment. When she finally did speak, her voice was still far from confident. "What will you do, *Seanchai?*"

Morgan shook his head. "I can't think *what* to do. I know I have no right to withhold the truth from her. She is tormented by the unknown secrets of her past, I think. But can she *bear* such ugliness, Sister?"

Sister Louisa frowned, then shook her head. "Finola is not strong. True, she has come a long way," she hastened to add. "There has been much healing. But . . ."

She did not need to finish. Morgan understood what was left unsaid. Finola was still wounded; she could, perhaps, still be broken.

"She still has nightmares." He spoke aloud, but more to himself than to the nun. "At night she dreams and cries out — sometimes she awakens in such terror, the demons of hell would seem to be hounding her!"

The nun looked at him, her expression sorrowful. "I know, *Seanchai*," she said softly. "Sandemon has heard."

Morgan felt sick. Sick and frightened and bewildered. "What shall I *do*, Sister? I don't know what to do!"

Again the nun remained silent for a time. Finally, she met his gaze. "This is what I think, *Seanchai*," she said, her tone once more strong, if quiet. "Today is our Finola's birthday. A day for celebration. We should allow nothing to cast a shadow on her joy. We must be very careful not to act in haste. Later, we will pray and see how God leads. But for today . . . tonight . . . let us celebrate Finola."

Rook Mooney trudged up the rain-slicked hillside to the place called Nelson Hall, silently congratulating himself on finding her so quickly.

It had taken scarcely any effort at all. A few pints with some of the wagging tongues on the docks, and within hours he had learned all he needed to know.

He had been outraged to hear that she was safely ensconced with the Big Lord on the hill. The *Seanchai*, they called him. A poet. And rich — rich as a king, they said.

A cripple! A cripple in a wheelchair!

A fresh surge of anger boiled through Mooney. He would have thought that he had spoiled her for any other man, especially gentry. Instead, the great fool had *married* her! Married her, and taken her to live among his own!

Women. They would stop at nothing to live the life of comfort — even bed with a cripple!

With the rain splattering his face, he stood staring at the immense ugly structure looming on the crest of the hill above him. Like an ancient castle, it was. Hulking and forbidding. What with its endless towers and battlements, the tall hedges and giant trees growing up all around it, it seemed to warn off any who would intrude.

Well, it would not stop *him*. He had come for her, and he would have her.

It took him the better part of an hour to cross the grounds. A bank sloped down toward a stream on the west side of the house, with woods rising tall and dense behind the property. Several buildings ringed the mansion — horse barns and storage sheds, a smith's stall, and a bakery.

His boots made a soft squashing sound in the mud around the stables as he moved quickly but stealthily toward the rear of the house.

By the time he finally settled on his hiding place — a large coach house with empty stables at the side — the heavens had opened, hurling torrents of rain down upon him in a fury. Lightning flashed, and the sky cracked with thunder as, cursing, Mooney ducked inside the coach house.

With one drenched sleeve, he caught the water pouring down his face. Wet all through and chilled, he traipsed the length of the building, carefully taking its measure.

It was just what he needed. The outside had a look of abandon. Inside, there were only two carriages — one a large and obviously well-maintained coach, the other smaller and dust-covered, as if it had not been used in some time.

The stables off to the right were deserted. Climbing up to the loft, he found nothing but hay and discarded harness. There was no sign that anyone had been in the upper reaches for a long time.

Mooney rooted about in the hay until he had himself a good view of the back of the house. Burrowing down for warmth, he lay watching the lighted windows.

She was in there, no doubt dressed in finery the cripple had bought for her, warm and safe and comfortable, while he hunkered in a hayloft, drenched and shivering.

It wasn't right. She didn't belong here, passing herself off as the grand lady, a respectable woman.

Didn't the great fool in the wheelchair know what had been done to her, that she was ruined? Didn't he realize he had married something despoiled, a simpleton with the body of a harlot?

But then, a cripple would have no pickings when it came to women, he supposed. The leavings of another man would be the best his kind could hope for.

Mooney ran a finger over the split at the corner of his mouth. No matter why the man endured her. He would soon have to find another baggage to warm his bed.

9

A Birthday at Nelson Hall

The radiance of Heaven illumines
her features,
Where the Snows and the Rose have erected
their throne;
It would seem that the sun had forgotten
all creatures
To shine on the Geraldine's Daughter alone!
EGAN O'RAHILLY (1670–1728)
Translation by James Clarence Mangan

Annie was pleased to see such happiness evident in Finola throughout the birthday festivities. The entire family was in attendance for the event. The scholars had also been invited, including, to her chagrin, the horrible O'Higgins twins.

Scrubbed and polished for the occasion, both Barry and Barnaby — *Beastly* and *Barbaric,* as she privately thought of them — were presently absorbed in stuffing their faces with

Mrs. Ryan's apple cake. Obviously, Annie thought with disgust, neither troublemaker had the slightest interest in the celebration apart from the food.

The unveiling of the prayer closet had been a great success, so much so that Finola could not stop talking of it during the meal. Indeed, she had been highly animated throughout the evening, praising Sandemon's ingenuity and the clever efforts of all involved, at the same time laughing into the *Seanchai*'s eyes each time their glances happened to meet.

Annie's own happiness was sharpened by Finola's obvious delight in the evening. When the *Seanchai* called upon Jan Martova to take up his fiddle, her anticipation heightened still more.

The Romany's music was a rare treat. Jan Martova seldom took his meals with the family. To Annie's indignation, both he and Tierney seemed to prefer fending for themselves outside, over an open fire, at least when weather permitted.

But tonight both of them had deigned to join the family. Annie watched the Gypsy as he went to stand in front of the vast stone fireplace at the end of the room. Eyes closed, he began to coax from the violin a slow, achingly sweet melody.

The room was hushed, as if in reverence,

until the end of the selection. But then the dark eyes snapped open and the fiddle came to life with a rousing Romany tune, followed by a country reel. Soon all the guests were clapping their hands to the music. Annie had all she could do to stay in her chair as the Gypsy fiddled his way through one lively, impassioned tune after another.

When the music ended, it was time for the birthday gifts to be presented. Now that the moment had actually arrived, Annie grew anxious, closely gauging Finola's response to each gift. She worried that perhaps she should have spent some of her weekly allotment on a more sophisticated present, rather than fashioning one entirely with her own efforts. What if Finola merely thought her too tightfisted to purchase a proper gift?

She squirmed on her chair, closely observing Finola's exclamations of pleasure as she opened each gift placed within her hands. The *Seanchai*'s gift, announced earlier, had been a surprise to everyone. Whereas they might have expected a piece of fine jewelry or an exotic scent, instead a generous donation had been made — at Finola's request and in her name — for the establishment of a new poor hospital near the docks.

To supplement that gift, however, the *Seanchai* now produced a newly published copy of his own poetry. The publication had been dedicated to Finola, who held the small book to her heart, eyes shining with love for her husband.

Annie sighed at the look that passed between them, and a feeling of restlessness stirred within her. She wondered if anyone would ever look at *her* in such a way. Her, with her scrawny legs and horsetail hair . . . would a man ever gaze at her as if the stars rose in her eyes, as if the world itself existed in her smile?

She sighed again, this time with real regret. She could not imagine how her thin face with its gap-toothed smile and hawkish nose could ever melt a manly heart. Perhaps she would eventually join a religious order, like Sister Louisa. She would live a holy life for the Lord and the Church.

Or perhaps she would become an actress and make the stage her One True Love.

But she decided it would be best not to let Sister in on *that* possibility. Nuns, no doubt, considered the stage little more than a paid arena for wickedness.

Morgan studied Jan Martova through narrowed eyes, unsettled by the way the boy was watching Annie. After a moment, he transferred his attention to the girl, who was obviously unaware of her admirer's scrutiny.

Admirer? The instinctive use of the word made his own appraisal of Annie turn yet more intense.

When had she changed so?

She was growing up, this adopted daughter of his.

Though the face was still a shade too thin, the black-marble eyes too large by far, there was a softness to her features he had not noticed before tonight. It was still a child's face, with a wide mouth and saucy nose, but someday soon, Morgan realized with a jolt, his Aine would be a startlingly beautiful young woman. Already the milk-white complexion had taken on a becoming flush, and the unruly mane of midnight hair seemed to be touched with bronze highlights; highlights which, he was quite certain, had not been there before.

She would not be a tall woman, like Finola, but no doubt what she lacked in height she would make up for in spirit.

Where had the time gone?

As if sensing his gaze on her, the girl turned and grinned at him. Morgan managed only the weakest of smiles in return. He was absurdly relieved to see that the gap between her two front teeth was still there.

Remembering what had set him off to begin

with, he returned his attention to Jan Martova. His jaw tightened. Had the object of the Romany's interest been anyone other than his thirteen-year-old daughter, he might have felt a touch of amusement at the furtive glances arcing in her direction. Young Martova had all the recognizable symptoms of hopeless adoration that Morgan recalled from his own youthful experiences with matters of the heart.

But *Annie?*

Unthinkable! She was a child still, for all the promise of approaching womanhood.

As for the Gypsy . . .

Morgan's mind touched on, then skittered past, the reminder of the youth's Romany blood. He refused to confront his feelings toward the Gypsies in general. If he were to be wholly honest, he would have to admit to at least some degree of prejudice.

Besides, there was more at issue here than a difference in blood or culture. Jan Martova must have passed his twentieth year by now. Despite Morgan's own tendency to think of him as a boy, the Gypsy was in fact a man, albeit a young one. Why, there were *years* between him and Annie!

Just as there were years between himself and Finola. . . .

He jerked as if he had taken a blow. He

144

glanced at Finola, reminding himself that the gap between their ages was different. Finola had not been a mere child when she came to him, but a woman.

Besides, *he* was not a Gypsy. . . .

Again the unpleasant hint of intolerance rose to the surface of his mind. Everyone knew that Gypsy men often took young girls in marriage, or at the least negotiated nuptial contracts with their parents. Even if these arranged marriages were delayed until the prospective brides were older — and Morgan wasn't so sure that was always the case — he found the prospect of a Romany ogling his daughter nothing less than outrageous.

Still young Martova *was* a believer, a Christian. And to his credit, he did seem devout, intent on living a decent life. Morgan had seen no sign of backsliding in the Gypsy.

Abruptly, he chastised himself for his own foolishness. *Whatever was he thinking?* Not only had he fallen into comparing the Gypsy and Annie with himself and Finola — had he taken to evaluating the youth's spiritual condition as well?

Preposterous!

He straightened in the wheelchair. Deliberately, he stared at the Gypsy youth until he caught his eye, then leveled his fiercest glare on him. The boy's dark skin flamed, as if

Morgan had found him out, and he quickly looked away.

Across the table, Annie roused herself to attention. She watched as Finola carefully placed the sky-blue shawl, knitted by Sister Louisa from the softest wool, alongside the small woven mat that Lucy had presented for the new prayer closet.

With a deep breath, she stood to hand Finola the portrait, wrapped in plain paper. She saw almost immediately that all her fretting had been for nothing.

After studying the sketch in silence for a moment, Finola turned to her with a brilliant smile and held out her arms. "Such a *wonderful* gift, Aine," she said, drawing Annie into a vigorous embrace. "I shall treasure it always!"

Pleased beyond words, Annie was content to watch as Finola opened Tierney Burke's gift — an imported silk fan. It occurred to her that he must have spent the better part of his stable wages on such a treasure. Perhaps this would show Sister Louisa, who had once deemed their American guest a "thoughtless, undisciplined *gorsoon,*" that Tierney did have generous instincts after all — when he thought to reveal them.

While Finola was still admiring the fan, Jan Martova approached her chair. "I, too, have a gift for you," he said quietly. As was his custom when in Finola's presence, he bowed his head in what appeared to be an instinctive gesture of respect.

Clearly surprised, Finola smiled at him as she accepted the gift. Still smiling, she drew back the folds of a brightly colored silk scarf to reveal a small penny whistle.

For a moment she simply sat staring at the tin whistle, almost as if she had never seen such a thing before. Suddenly she seemed to stiffen and go pale. Gasping for breath, she jumped to her feet and shook off the instrument as if a serpent had been tossed into her lap.

Then she screamed — a long, terrible wail that rent the room with anguish. Her eyes rolled back, and she went limp.

Annie leaped from her chair. At the same time the *Seanchai* flung out his arm in an attempt to hold Finola as she swayed. But it was Tierney Burke, still standing near Finola's chair, who caught her just before she crumpled to the floor.

10

The Storm Closes In

Woe to us, woe! the thunders have
spoken. . . .
Through the cleft thunder-cloud the
weird coursers are rushing —
Their hoofs will strike deep in the hearts they
are crushing. . . .
LADY WILDE (1824–1896)
"Speranza" — from *The Nation*, 1849

For a moment Morgan couldn't take in what
had happened. He froze as he saw Tierney
sweep Finola into his arms, not an instant
too late. His eyes darted to the tin whistle
flung onto the floor, the bright silk scarf discarded nearby.

Finally the sight of Finola, limp as a rag doll
in Tierney's arms, roused him, and he
whipped the wheelchair out from behind the
table. "Over there," he said. He motioned
Tierney to the rug in front of the hearth, and

followed him to the fireplace.

The moment the boy lowered Finola gently to the floor, both Sandemon and Sister Louisa knelt beside her. "A dead faint," Sister said, looking up at Morgan. "I'd best get the smelling salts."

Morgan blinked, his mind scrambling to understand what had happened. "Lay a fire, if you will," he said to Sandemon, without taking his eyes from Finola. "The room is cold."

"*Seanchai?*"

The soft entreaty from behind him made Morgan turn and stare. The Gypsy stood in the shadows near the sideboard. His dark eyes were troubled, his hands clenched. "Is it . . . something I did? She loves the music so, I thought only to give . . . I meant no harm . . ."

He let his words drift off, unfinished.

Morgan stared at him. For an instant, he felt his anger at the Gypsy boil up and threaten to explode. The feeling was irrational, he knew. Whatever had triggered Finola's bewildering behavior, obviously it had not been prompted by any malice on the part of Jan Martova. The Romany's confusion and misery were written all over his face.

"No blame is due you," he managed to concede. "Who can say what brought this on?"

Yet it was obvious that the penny whistle had in some way triggered the fainting spell. Morgan's mind raced. *What had Frank said? Something about a tin whistle being found by the lake, near the body of Finola's father. . . .*

Suddenly the rest of Cassidy's words came with dreadful clarity: *"The Kelly lad said she often walked along the lake, playing the penny whistle. Seems the music teacher — the Frenchman — gave it to her. . . ."*

Morgan felt a tremor of dread. The rain that had been falling throughout the evening now flung itself in wild torrents against the house. The wind was up, wailing and gusting through the dense fortress of trees all about the estate. Chilled, he crossed his arms over his chest and rubbed his shoulders as he studied Finola's still form.

He watched as Sister Louisa returned with the smelling salts and dropped down to administer them. Finola stirred slightly, moaning, then murmured something too soft to understand.

Morgan leaned forward. "What did she say?"

Sandemon had returned to kneel between Morgan and the prostrate Finola. Without turning, he shook his head. "A name, perhaps? I'm not sure."

Again Finola twisted in resistance to the

smelling salts. She whimpered as if in pain, her head thrashing from side to side.

Sister Louisa withdrew the stimulant, but Finola continued to writhe and utter soft sounds of protest.

Her moaning grew louder. *"Father! Oh, no, Father!"* She flailed her arms, crying out as if in agony. *"Garonne!"*

Garonne . . .

The word struck Morgan like a hammer blow. *A French name . . . the music teacher had been a Frenchman. . . .*

Suddenly, Finola gasped. Her eyes came open, and horror filled her gaze. The scream that ripped from her throat made Morgan draw back, startled.

"FATHER! NO. FATHER — NO!"

She looked to be in the throes of some sort of attack. Morgan stared at her, his muscles locked in anguish. He leaned forward, meaning to touch her, then drew his hand back.

Softly, he called her name, then again. "Finola . . . Finola, *macushla.* 'Tis all right. All is well. You are safe, Finola." Bracing one hand on the kneeling Sandemon's shoulders, he continued to lean toward Finola, calling her name quietly but firmly.

Slowly she turned her gaze on him, her features frozen in what appeared to be mortal terror. She began to tremble, slightly at first, then more violently. *"Garonne . . ."* she choked out.

"No, 'tis Morgan, *macushla*. Only Morgan . . ."

A glazed look of confusion washed over her features. Morgan waited, saying nothing. Finally, he saw the trembling subside a little. She struggled to sit up, and Sandemon hurried to help her. Immediately she reached for Morgan.

"Shh, now, *macushla*," he murmured, taking both her hands in his. He sensed that she was badly disoriented and would be distressed by all the attention turned upon her.

"Help us upstairs," he said to Sandemon, his voice low. "We would be alone."

With a nod, Sandemon lifted Finola gently into his arms and carried her from the room.

Behind them, Morgan stopped only long enough to press Annie's hand and look into the girl's frightened eyes.

"Seanchai? What is it? Is Finola all right?"

He squeezed her fingers. "She will be, *alannah*. She needs some quiet now, and rest, that's the thing. You will look in on Gabriel?"

Annie nodded, jumping at a loud crash of thunder. Again Morgan pressed her hand in his, sensing the fear she was trying to suppress. "Perhaps you should come up, too? No doubt the storm has made your little brother

152

and Lucy anxious. It might be well if you would stay with them until it passes."

As his gaze scanned the room, he noted that Tierney and Jan Martova were nowhere in sight.

That night, Morgan left Finola alone only long enough to speak with the doctor, who had come when summoned.

"You're sure she will be all right?"

"She should be perfectly fine after she has a rest," Dr. Dunne said. He hesitated. "You're quite certain it was the penny whistle that brought this on?"

Morgan nodded. Even in the dimly lighted hallway he could see the bafflement in the surgeon's eyes.

"I can't think it was anything else. Had you been here, you would understand. It was as if the thing had attacked her."

"And she has told you nothing since?"

Morgan hesitated, undecided as to how much he wanted to explain just yet, even to the physician. "Only one word . . . a name. Someone who . . . once caused her great distress, I think."

The doctor looked at him. "The man who attacked her?"

Morgan felt the old, bitter anger break over him. "There is reason to believe," he said tightly, looking away, "that she might have been assaulted . . . more than once. The first time . . . when she was quite young. Little more than a child."

The surgeon uttered a sound of dismay. "And you believe she has begun to remember?"

"I think it is a possibility, yes."

Their eyes met. For a moment neither spoke. "Will the laudanum help her to sleep?" Morgan finally asked.

"It will. And I've left more with Sister Louisa, should there be a need. She knows the dosage. I'm afraid there's really nothing else to do just now, except to keep a close watch. I will stop by again tomorrow to see how she's doing." He paused. "If you don't mind my saying so, Morgan . . ."

Morgan looked up. The doctor was eyeing him with the appraising look of a medical man.

"I don't like your color. You look quite exhausted."

Morgan waved off his concern. "I'm perfectly fine. Thank you for coming out on such a mean night, James. I appreciate it."

"I hope you've given some thought to the surgeon in America?" the physician ventured.

"This is hardly the time to be planning a crossing," Morgan snapped.

Immediately he regretted the sharpness of his tone. "I'm sorry, James. I didn't mean to be short. But it's *not* the time."

"Quite right." The doctor stepped back, although he continued to study Morgan a moment longer. "Send for me if you need me," he said gently, then turned to go.

After the doctor left, Morgan lay unmoving, holding Finola in his arms. At times she seemed to doze, fitfully. More often she sobbed or flailed her fists, as if warding off a blow. Once or twice she murmured something incomprehensible, then grew still.

He could almost feel the conflict raging inside her, as if she were fighting to remember. Or was she trying *not* to remember?

There was little he could do for her, other than to hold her close and attempt to comfort her as best he could. James had said it would be better if she remembered only a little at a time, but she seemed to be overwhelmed by an entire tide of memories.

Morgan felt the struggle draining her strength, both physically and emotionally. Yet now that the memories had finally come, he was reluctant to try to stem the flow. As he held her, he battled his own torrent of conflicting emotions.

Tonight he had finally caught a glimpse of

just how devastating the return of her memories could be. Even with his lack of medical expertise, he sensed it could be dangerous for her to remember too much too soon. How much should he — could he — tell her of what Cassidy had uncovered in Drogheda?

Morgan found himself gripped by the same dread, the same dark apprehension, as before. It was *fear*. Fear for Finola, and for himself.

Beyond what all this might mean to her emotional health, he could not deny a very real fear for its effect on their marriage, their love. Already there were times when he sensed her pulling away from him. He tried not to believe that his physical condition could be responsible for her occasional restraint, tried not to dwell on the reality that Finola was a beautiful young woman tied to an older man in a wheelchair. He tried not to wonder if her passion for him had begun to wane.

Perhaps it was, indeed, only the pain, the memories that had haunted and yet evaded her, that sometimes made her withdraw. Surely the violence inflicted upon her body and soul might cause some reluctance, if not actual aversion to intimacy, even with a man she loved.

And he did not doubt that Finola loved him.

But now . . . now he knew the hideous truth. Could he really bring himself to risk damaging what he held precious beyond all price . . . Finola's love? Could he tell her?

She stirred restlessly in his arms, and Morgan studied the exquisite face he had come to love more than life — a face now contorted with some silent anguish, some lonely struggle he found himself helpless to ease.

He drew her even closer, pressing her face against his shoulder, concealing the pain that threatened to obscure her loveliness. Outside, the rain continued to pelt the house, but the wind had diminished to a steady moan. Remembering many a night from his own troubled past when he had shivered beneath a cold rain on a lonely road, Morgan buried his face in the spun gold of Finola's hair and gave thanks for the shelter of her love . . . and the divine love that had brought them together.

Yet somehow he did not *feel* sheltered, not even with Finola's sweet warmth in his arms and a fire burning low across the room. Instead, he felt inexplicably chilled, his nerves drawn taut, his pulse too erratic by far.

"Garonne . . ."

Morgan started at the sound of the French name on her lips. He eased back to look at her. Her eyes were open, her expression stricken as she met his gaze.

157

"What is it, *macushla?*" he whispered, gently brushing a strand of hair away from her temple. "Who is this 'Garonne'?"

Her nails dug into his shoulders as she clung to him, but she made no reply.

The rainstorm had passed, leaving only a gentle dripping from the eaves and an occasional distant groan of thunder. But Morgan remained vigilant, his nerves on edge. He almost felt as if another storm were approaching, coming from a distant place . . . but coming quickly.

Sandemon stood staring out into the rainy night, becoming more unsettled with every hour that dragged on.

Not once this night had his mind grown still enough to sleep. There was no peace in his spirit, no quiet in his soul.

Part of his agitation, he knew, was due to the mysterious seizure of Mistress Finola. He had heard her broken sobs and moans of distress coming from the bedchamber, had heard as well the muffled efforts of the *Seanchai* to comfort her. So intense was his concern that it had been all he could do to leave them to themselves and not interfere.

Concern for the young mistress, however, was not the only burden on his spirit, nor was the rainstorm entirely to blame for his sleeplessness. Indeed, the rain had slackened, easing to a slow and steady pattering as the storm moved on.

But outside Nelson Hall something else — something dark and cold and threatening — rode the night wind. Something lurked in the darkness. Sandemon could feel it — palpable and foreboding.

Suddenly he shivered, then moved even closer to the window, straining to see outside. But the moon and stars were hidden, the night dense and black. Nothing moved in the darkness.

Turning, he looked around the room. The cold was pervasive, drawing in on him. Again he shivered. The need for warmth and light seized him, and he crossed the room to stoke the fire, then lit a second lamp.

It wasn't enough. Going to stand in front of the fire, Sandemon gripped his hands together, waiting for the heat to warm his bones . . . waiting for the Light to banish his sense of encroaching dread.

Finally, after a long time, he began to pray.

11

Long-Buried Secrets

But when the days of gold dreams had
perished,
And even Despair was powerless to destroy,
Then did I learn how existence could be
cherished,
Strengthened, and fed, without the aid of joy.
EMILY BRONTE (1818–1848)

Morgan's heart nearly broke as he lay holding Finola, watching her by the dim light of
the candle next to the bed. Her anguished
sobs came from deep within, as if her very
soul were rising up in torment.

How long could she go on like this? She was
obviously exhausted, and yet the weeping
continued, the deep, heartrending groans of a
spirit in the throes of a mighty battle.

He desperately wanted to comfort her, to
soothe and calm her, to still the inner storm
that buffeted her fragile body and racked her

mind. But he could do nothing.

All he could do was wait . . . stay beside her during this dark night of the soul and pray that somehow his presence would give her the strength to endure this torture.

Morgan had never felt so utterly helpless. He feared for Finola, and for himself. What would this revelation do to her . . . her mind . . . to her life . . . to *them?*

"Garonne . . ." As she called the Frenchman's name again, her entire frame shuddered in a convulsion that shook the great bed where they lay.

Morgan's arms tightened about her, and tears streamed down his face into his beard. "Finola, *aroon,*" he whispered fiercely. " 'Tis Morgan. I am here, *macushla . . .* I will not let you go."

"I will not let you go . . ."

The words pierced into Finola's soul like a hot knife. *Garonne!* Those were *his* words when she began to resist him.

"NO!" she screamed.

Still he came after her — this mentor turned monster. And suddenly, as she saw his obscene face looming above her, she remembered it all . . . everything. . . .

She remembered Henri Garonne, who had taken rooms with the Morans in the winter. He

161

had been employed to tutor her, not only in the classical subjects, but in the musical arts as well.

Finola could not have been more pleased. Garonne represented a curiosity, a departure from the dry, monotonous teaching of her previous tutor, the middle-aged Dr. Jennings, who had surprised everyone in Drogheda by marrying the Widow Browne and retiring to the country.

Garonne quickly became a familiar figure in the Moran household. Jocular and quick-witted, he entertained both Finola and her father with his stories of life in Paris. He praised her effusively for her accomplishments, especially in her musical pursuits. She was a wonder and a joy, he would say, patting her hand or squeezing her shoulder.

Finola blossomed under his tutorage, responding readily to his affectionate nature. Both she and her father trusted him completely, until that terrible day beside the lake . . .

Finola screamed and Morgan released her, his heart pounding. She gazed up at him with a wide, vacant expression, her eyes darting nervously about the room.

"It's all right, *macushla*," Morgan said gently.

Finola jerked her head around and cast a frightened glance at the bedroom door. Morgan's eyes followed hers, and with startling clarity, he understood. "The door is locked,"

162

he reassured her in a quiet voice. "No one can get to you, my Finola. You are safe."

At the word *safe,* Finola heaved a shuddering sigh and moved toward him again, burrowing her head against his shoulder. "I remember —" she began. Then the tears came once more, and she was unable to speak.

When at last her weeping had subsided, Morgan lifted her face to his and looked into her eyes. What he saw there shook him to the very core: raw terror, and a pain so deep he could not even imagine it. He could not bear to see her so hurt, so devastated. And yet instinctively he knew that they could not go *around* this mountain of pain and heartache. If they did, it would stand between them forever, would stand between Finola and the final healing of her soul and mind. They would have to go *through* this terrible darkness, and pray for light on the other side.

Morgan swallowed hard. He couldn't bear the thought of seeing her suffer still more, but he *must.*

"Can you talk about it?" he asked quietly.

Finola nodded — a stiff, childlike motion against his shoulder. She took a few gasping breaths and then began:

"Garonne was my tutor — a Frenchman. He was . . . I thought he was . . . a wonderful man. Encouraging, affectionate —" She gave an involuntary shudder. "I was young — only fourteen — and innocent in the ways of the world. If I had known, I could have —" An onrush of tears choked the words back.

Morgan pulled her close, and his own heart squeezed with her pain. "You were but a child, *macushla*. A child, do you hear? You could not have stopped him. He did a terrible thing to you, and it was not your fault." Finola looked up at him with a pleading, desperate expression. "It was not your fault," he repeated.

She sank back into his arms. "We were walking by the lake. We often studied outside when the weather was fine, and I loved being down by the water. I had taken along a tin whistle — a gift from Garonne." A shadow flitted across her face, and she winced slightly.

"I remember I was singing," she went on in a tight, strangled voice. "Sometimes, when I felt so, I would sing for hours. I was happy. Filled up with summer and music and young girl dreams. I felt light-headed and alive and utterly carefree. It was such a glorious feeling, it was almost painful. . . ."

Morgan nodded. It was a particularly apt description of youth. Her words brought to mind summer days of his own, days when he had literally ached with the sheer joy of the world all around him and the life yet to be lived.

But Finola's youth, at least a great part of it, had been stolen from her — ripped away by a man twice her age. . . .

"Garonne led me to a secluded place by a large oak on the bank of the lake," Finola continued. "I sat beside him next to the tree, and then —"

She broke off suddenly, and Morgan looked down at her. Her eyes were tightly shut, and her whole body tensed, shuddering, as if she were reliving the moment even as she spoke.

"He . . . he assaulted me!" she burst out. Tears streamed down her face, and her breath came in gasps, but she went on in a rush. "He pushed me down . . . I remember the tin whistle went flying out of my hand. He tore at my clothes, pressed himself on top of me . . . I was screaming. It was as if he had been transformed, mutated into someone else — or *something* else — entirely. Not the gentle tutor I had loved and trusted, but a madman, an animal."

Rage welled up in Morgan. How could anyone — *anyone* — do such a thing? How could any man take advantage of the trust of a young girl . . . a girl no older than his own Aine —

Annie! At the thought of his daughter, Morgan's fury crested. He would go mad if any man dared to assault his child as Finola had been assaulted. He would want to kill such a man — yes, he would — strangle him with his own bare hands, as he wanted now to strangle the Frenchman Garonne. . . .

"My father came running," Finola was saying. "Someone must have heard my screams. Suddenly Garonne stopped, and turned . . . and there was my father, pointing the gun at him." She put her hands to her face as if to shut out the sight. "Garonne — panicked, I think. He lunged for my father and knocked him down —"

Sobs choked back the rest of Finola's words. Her whole body shook as she remembered that terrible day. "I was on the ground," she went on at last. "My clothes . . . my clothes were ripped. I got up and ran toward Father, but Garonne shoved me away. I fell on the bank of the lake . . . nearly fell in the water. And then —"

She took a deep breath. "Garonne and Father wrestled for the gun, and then . . . Garonne *shot my father!* He just stood up, pointed the pistol at Father's head, and fired!

"I was screaming, crying . . . Garonne turned the gun on me, staring at me, and for a moment I thought he would shoot me, too.

166

Then he ran off, into the woods. I went to Father, but he wasn't breathing. . . ."

Finola looked up at Morgan. His face was hard, set like stone. Was he angry with her? Disappointed? Would he reject her outright, now that he knew the truth . . . now that *she* knew? Her heart sank, but she would finish . . . no matter what it cost.

"I think . . . I think I must have gone mad then," she whispered. "I ran into the woods . . . I remember screaming, over and over again. . . ."

She paused for a moment, gasping for breath. Outside, beyond the window, a faint rumble of thunder sounded in the distance, and Finola shivered.

"I don't remember anything else," she said. "I might have gone on running through the woods — I don't know how long I wandered. It could have been several days. The next thing I remember, I was in Dublin, at Gemma's Place. Lucy found me in the street and took me in. She and the other women at Gemma's looked after me."

She took a deep breath. "And then, after nearly four years at Gemma's, I found myself here . . . at Nelson Hall. . . ."

Finola kept her head lowered. She could not look at Morgan, could not bear to know what he was thinking, and yet she *had* to know. At last she raised her eyes slowly to his.

A look of infinite love filled his face. Tears tracked down his cheeks into his beard, and his eyes held an expression of pain and thankfulness.

"And for that, *macushla,* I will be forever grateful." His voice was husky with emotion, and he pulled her even closer. "You are a strong, courageous woman, Finola *aroon,*" he murmured, brushing a kiss over her hair. "And I am a blessed man entirely to have you for my wife."

Relief flooded through Finola as she saw Morgan smile at her through his tears.

"We have come to the truth at last," he whispered. "You now know the truth, and the truth will set you free."

Finola leaned against him and savored the warmth of his strong arms around her. At last, she was beginning to feel safe — safe, and free, and loved. And as she drifted to sleep in Morgan's embrace, she heard his voice, as from a great distance: "The worst is over, *macushla* . . . truly it is."

And her heart responded, *Please, God, let it be so. . . .*

12

Brady of Broadway

Like a spirit land of shadows
They in silence on me gaze,
And I feel my heart is beating
With the pulse of other days;
And I ask what great magician
Conjured forms like these afar?
Echo answers, 'tis the sunshine,
By its alchemist Daguerre.
CALEB LYON (1850, after a
visit to Brady's Portrait Gallery)

New York City

In the waiting room of Mathew Brady's gallery, Michael Burke sat on a straight-backed chair like a figure of doom. Not for the first time over the past hour, he silently railed at himself for his folly. It had been a weak moment indeed when he allowed his father-in-law and his wife to talk him into this daft idea.

169

Looking up, he glared at Sara, sitting across from him. She smiled sweetly in return, as if altogether unaware of his foul humor.

He could not help but notice that she was looking especially lovely today, decked out in the new blue suit which she'd had tailored for the portrait. For a moment he almost forgot to scowl. But only for a moment.

The waiting room of Brady's Gallery at Broadway and Fulton was an unpretentious place, not at all in keeping with the showy painting on the wall downstairs — a great, gaudy hand with one finger pointing to the stairway and the legend "THREE FLIGHTS UP."

Michael had expected something more on the order of Barnum's Museum across the street. But this plain and modest studio had little to distinguish it, other than the compelling portraits that lined the walls — and its owner's reputation.

Most of the portraits were of famous American citizens: politicians, inventors, showmen, and other notable personalities. As for Mathew Brady's reputation, it was equalled by none of the other daguerreotypists whose galleries lined Broadway.

Almost all photographers called themselves "artists," but Brady seemed to be one of the few who gave credence to the word. Brady's celebrated artistry brought the public scurrying to his door with more business than he could handle.

No doubt, Michael speculated sourly, the man's popularity accounted for his not being able to keep his appointments on time.

He looked up as one of Brady's assistants, a long-faced youth with rumpled linen and a slight tic, appeared in the doorway — for the third time — to announce rather timidly that "Mr. Brady will be ready for you soon, I'm sure."

"Would that be this afternoon or tomorrow, do you think?" Michael said evenly.

The boy twitched, then hurriedly retreated.

With a grunt of disgust, Michael again faced his wife. "I could have sworn your father said this would take only moments."

Sara's smile never wavered. "Try to be patient, darling. Mr. Brady is doing separate sittings of Father and Winnie, after all. And don't forget what a compliment it is, having Mathew Brady himself request an appointment."

"You know very well," Michael pointed out, "that the only reason we're here is because Brady wanted to photograph Mr. and Mrs. Lewis Farmington."

She merely shrugged, holding out one gloved hand to inspect it. "Mr. Brady requested that we sit for a portrait, too. He made his intentions very clear."

"The intentions were those of your wily father, I'm thinking."

After inspecting the other glove, Sara looked at him. "My father is not wily."

Michael quirked an eyebrow at her.

"Well . . ." Her mouth twitched. "I suppose he is a bit devious at times. Still, I think this is all very exciting. Pout if you must, but I intend to enjoy it. Besides, just imagine how splendid we will look to our grandchildren someday. You are wickedly handsome in your new suit, you know."

Michael relaxed a bit in spite of himself. "A lot of fuss for nothing, all the same."

At that moment Brady himself walked into the waiting room. "Captain. Mrs. Burke," he said. "I apologize for the delay. If you'd like to join Mr. and Mrs. Farmington now, we'll do the group portrait first. Then another of the two of you."

Following him into the other room, Michael was struck by Brady's youthful appearance. He might be one of the most famous photographers in the country, but even with a full beard he didn't look to be thirty as yet. He was a small man, his head barely reaching Michael's shoulder. His black broadcloth suit hung loosely on his slender frame, and a full head of curly dark hair diminished his stature even further. Even his thick-lensed spectacles seemed too large for the rest of him.

Mathew Brady was something of a mystery to New Yorkers. In spite of his phenomenal success and prosperity, he and his wife apparently lived a quiet, private life with virtually no involvement in New York's society.

There were any number of conflicting stories about the young photographer, some outrageously farfetched. Supposedly, his parents had been impoverished Irish immigrants, yet Brady claimed otherwise. He had been raised, he maintained, on a farm in eastern New York State, where his mother and father had been born.

Gossip also hinted that Brady could neither read nor write. Yet since entering the studio, Michael had seen the photographer scan his appointment register with his nearsighted gaze, then scrawl a message for one of his assistants to deliver.

Brady's failing eyesight, however, was obviously more than a rumor. The man seemed to have difficulty in making out his register entries, and he pressed his face almost to the page before writing. Apparently the problem had become so acute that he no longer operated his own cameras, relying instead on his assistants for the technical aspects of the business.

Still, there was no question that Brady was the real artist behind the gallery's success. Michael noted with interest the deft movements, the attention to detail, the quiet confidence that marked him as a master of his profession.

He also recognized something else about the renowned Brady of Broadway: the man clearly possessed the Irishman's traditional gift of storytelling. All through the sitting, the slight-figured photographer rattled off one anecdote after another, pausing between tales only long enough for a quick smile.

Brady took shots of both couples together, then of Michael and Sara, and finally individual portraits. When at last the click of the drop shutter proclaimed an end to the final sitting, Michael let out a relieved sigh.

"Excellent," Brady announced. "I personally guarantee portraits you will be pleased to pass down to future generations." The photographer looked at Michael, then broke into a boyish smile.

After the sitting, Sara waited with Winnie while the men exchanged small talk. Watching Michael, she was fairly certain he hadn't actually minded sitting for the daguerreotype as much as he'd previously let on. Both he and her father were laughing heartily as Mr. Brady led them through the door off the studio.

"I've only recently purchased a copy of your new book," her father was saying to the photographer. "I must say, I'm impressed with your portraiture, Brady. Fine work."

The book he referred to, Sara knew, was Brady's *Gallery of Illustrious Americans*. A massive work, the book was a collection of splendid portraits of eminent American citizens. It was said to weigh at least five pounds and sold for the exorbitant price of thirty dollars a copy.

"Well, Mr. Farmington, after today you can be sure that your own portrait will grace my next collection," Brady replied. Turning then to Michael, he peered at him closely through his thick eyeglasses. "You know, Captain, I've been entertaining the idea of doing a collection of our city officials, including the police force. But I must say the captains to whom I've broached the subject have been anything but enthusiastic."

Michael's dark eyes glinted with amusement. "I expect a number of the men might be as reluctant as I was to have their faces frozen for posterity. You might get further if you'd speak to Chief Matsell about the idea."

"Ah, I see. Thank you for the advice, Captain. Once I return from Europe, I'll do just that. I'm planning some rather extensive collections," Brady went on, stroking his beard. "Professional people. Stage stars. Public officials — the police force, the fire department. And political figures, of course. The mayor has already sat for me, as well as the governor. And some of our aldermen." He paused. "I've ah . . . heard tell that you might be considering a future in politics, Captain."

Michael merely smiled, not rising to the photographer's bait.

"If the rumor is true," Brady went on, "one of your future competitors is scheduled for a sitting next week. Perhaps you know Mr. Patrick Walsh?"

Michael reacted exactly as Sara would have expected. His features went rigid, his mouth tightening to a thin line below his moustache. He stood unmoving, both fists clenched at his side.

"Walsh?" he said, his voice as hard as his eyes.

Obviously unaware of the response he had provoked, Brady went on in a genial tone of voice. "Yes, in addition to his business connections, he's apparently planning a political career as well."

Sara watched Michael closely. His self-control was ordinarily impressive, but she had learned that when it came to Patrick Walsh, her husband could be highly unpredictable, even volatile.

"Politics, is it?" Michael's voice was edged with a mixture of disbelief and anger. "I wasn't aware that Walsh had any particular aspirations in that direction."

"Oh yes," Brady said, cheerfully rambling on. "He seems very enthusiastic about his prospects. Apparently he thinks his Tammany connections and business dealings will serve him well in the political arena."

"No doubt he's right," Michael said.

Although his expression never altered, Sara saw the flint in his eyes, heard the barely controlled contempt in his tone. Her mind raced for a way to end the exchange between the photographer and her husband before Michael's temper got in the way of his customary good manners. He could be a veritable bear when angered.

She drew a discreet sigh of relief when her father moved to intervene.

"If you're interested in politicians as subjects," he offered, "you might want to contact Simon Dabney." Sara's father spoke directly to the photographer, but his eyes were fixed on Michael. "Not only would Simon himself make a worthy subject for one of your collections, but he could bring you any number of other prospects as well. Do you know him?"

When Brady admitted that he had not had the pleasure, Sara's father offered to arrange an introduction. "For now, however, we probably should be on our way. Michael and I promised these lovely ladies dinner at the Astor House."

Sara didn't miss the firm grip her father applied to Michael's arm as he turned toward the door, then stopped. "You won't forget about the portraits of Sara's grandmother, will you, Brady?"

The photographer shook his head. "I'm looking forward to it. As soon as you advise me of a convenient time for Mrs. Platt, I'll make plans for a private sitting in her home."

Sara's father nodded, then gave Michael a little nudge. "Good. You'll hear from me soon."

Outside on the street, silence descended and hung over the four for a noticeably long time. Finally Winnie, ever sensitive to the moods of those close to her and always adept at breaking the tension, turned to Michael with a bright smile. "Why, Michael, don't you look positively thunderous! Was it really that bad, getting starched up and polished to have your portrait made?"

Michael blinked. "What? . . . Oh no. No,

perhaps not," he answered vaguely. "I expect I was thinking about something else."

For just an instant his eyes met Sara's; then he looked away.

That night, long after Sara had fallen asleep, Michael was still fully awake and restless. Finally he eased out of bed and, shrugging into his robe, crossed the room to the double doors that opened onto the balcony.

He stepped outside and stood looking into the night. Even for August, the air was warm and close. Not the slightest hint of a breeze stirred the enormous old oak trees surrounding the house. Yet the sky looked strangely heavy and low-hanging, as if it might open at any moment with a downpour.

As he stood gazing down on the stone walkway below, his thoughts were as dark as the night itself. He found himself wondering if he had made a foolish mistake, choosing to stay with the police force rather than taking up the political gauntlet previously held out by Simon Dabney.

If Mathew Brady had been right, if Walsh were actually to make a serious foray into politics, what could he hope to accomplish by staying on the force? The police were all but powerless when it came to crooked politicians.

Countless professional hoodlums already controlled much of the political world. Patrick Walsh would only add one more to their ranks. He had already attained considerable power, through his dishonest business practices and the intricate web of corruption he had woven throughout the city and the state.

Michael had been careful never to underestimate the influence of his old enemy. Patrick Walsh had, after all, almost gotten his clutches into Michael's son, Tierney. He exerted real power over the small-time crooks who populated his nefarious rackets across the state. Walsh pulled the strings of any number of local puppets at Tammany Hall as well. He could probably gather all the votes needed for any political office he set his sights on.

Politics would be a logical move for Walsh — a move that would only serve to make him more powerful, more dangerous, than he already was. Once he attained political position, there would be no stopping him. He would simply continue to rise, like a poisonous gas, beyond all possibility of containment.

Michael raked a hand over the back of his neck. His head throbbed from sleeplessness and tension. He could not bring himself to entertain the thought of Patrick Walsh completely beyond the reach of justice — unencumbered, free to wreak his depraved will in any manner he chose.

As things stood now, there was still the chance of trapping Walsh in his own unscrupulousness. But a lowly policeman — even a police *captain* — would have little hope of ensnaring a prominent politician, no matter what his offenses against society might happen to be. There was every likelihood that Walsh would manage to continue as he had in the past, keeping up the appearance of respectability while managing to stay one step ahead of the law.

Michael gripped the railing in front of him with both hands. He refused to accept the idea that a snake like Walsh could escape justice indefinitely. There had to be a way to stop him. There *had* to be.

Walsh would eventually make a mistake. He might be clever in his own way — cutthroat smart with all the scruples of a hyena. But at some point he would slip up.

Michael planned to be there when he fell.

13

Unwelcome Arrivals

I hardened my heart
For fear of my ruin. . . .
I hardened my heart,
And my love I quenched.
PADRAIC PEARSE (1879–1916)

Ruth Marriott arrived in New York on Saturday. It took her until Monday to gather the courage to confront Patrick Walsh.

She passed the weekend in a dingy hotel room in a district called the *Bowery*. According to the desk clerk, she was within walking distance of the hotel where Patrick kept his offices. But as she turned the corner of still another unfamiliar street, she worried that the clerk might have given her wrong directions.

By now she was beginning to wish she had followed her original instincts and spent some of her traveling funds on a hack. The August heat was oppressive, and her stomach felt more queasy with every step. If she didn't find Broadway soon, she would have to turn back.

But she *couldn't* turn back. She had come all this way to confront Patrick. The money he had sent would not last forever, and when it was gone, then what would she do?

As she walked, she gradually became aware that her surroundings were changing. Instead of taverns and freak shows, the buildings lining the street appeared to be small shops and decent, if not overly prosperous, businesses. Even the pedestrians around her looked to be more respectable, in marked contrast to the loud, dirty reprobates a few blocks back.

Perhaps she was headed in the right direction after all. Patrick's hotel would almost certainly be in a much finer neighborhood than where she was staying.

Unless he had lied about that, too.

Had he ever told her the truth about *anything?* From the beginning, he had deceived her with the worst lie of all: that he was an unmarried man. He had pretended to be a widower with adolescent children. Only when he learned about the baby had he told her the truth, that he did indeed have two children — and a wife who was very much alive — and thus could hardly be expected to take responsibility for her or her child.

Her child. As if he had had no part in the

unthinkable situation in which she now found herself.

Obviously, he assumed that sending a sum of cash by his contemptuous messenger would be enough to extricate himself from any further responsibility. The note had been matter-of-fact, with no hint of what they had once meant to each other. The money should "cover her medical bills and help her to get by until she could make arrangements for herself and the child."

He had even gone on to suggest that Ruth not have the baby at all. *There are women who take care of such things,* he had written in the same cold-blooded style. *You'd do well to consider that an option.*

The very thought made Ruth feel ill. How had it come to this, that the man who only months ago had claimed to adore her — who had promised to marry her as soon as his children were older — could now so casually suggest that she abort their child?

Patrick Walsh had taken her heart, her trust, her innocence, and left her with nothing but a crushing burden of shame — and a child he refused to acknowledge.

How could she have been so naive, so foolish? *So wicked . . .*

That's what Mother would call it, once she knew. *Wickedness.* She would turn her chilling, accusing look on Ruth and denounce her for the sinner she was. Then she would piously offer to pray for her and suggest a fitting penance for her transgressions.

Ruth was determined to keep her condition a secret from her mother for as long as possible. Her own shame and humiliation was bad enough. She didn't think she could endure the degradation her mother was certain to heap upon her.

Besides, Mother would demand that she give up the baby. Not for a moment would Amelia Marriott take the chance that her daughter's disgrace might become common knowledge to her ladies' society or her meddlesome neighbors.

She wouldn't do it! She wouldn't give her baby away! She regretted what she had done with Patrick . . . oh, how she regretted it! But she would not allow her child to suffer for her mistake. Somehow, she would take care of her baby. She would find a way.

Yet there was no one to whom she could turn for help. She had no friends, no family other than her mother.

When she made the decision to become Patrick's mistress, she had grown increasingly secretive. She had isolated herself until finally the only thing left to her had been her work and the clandestine life she shared with Patrick.

That life was gone and soon even her job would come to an end. It would be impossible to hide her condition much longer; the moment she told the administration the truth, the school would terminate her without notice. There was no place in an exclusive girls academy for a pregnant, unmarried teacher.

Somehow she had to convince Patrick to commit himself to provide for the baby's future. This resolve, combined with her growing desperation, had finally motivated her to come to New York and confront him. But now, as she turned the corner onto Broadway and saw the dark brick facade of the Braun Midtown Hotel looming just ahead, she felt an almost paralyzing wave of apprehension.

When she reached the hotel she stood in front of it for a long time, staring at the structure's solid imposing front, remembering all the times she had written to Patrick at this address.

"I spend far more time at the office than at home," he had told her. "I'll get your letters sooner if you send them to the hotel."

She had believed him. Now anger mingled with shame as she realized how quickly she had fallen prey to his lies, how easily she had allowed herself to be deceived.

With her eyes fixed on the sturdy double doors of the hotel's entrance, Ruth knotted her hands together at her waist. *He should pay.* He should pay for his treachery, for the unconscionable way he had manipulated and used her. It was only right that he pay.

Yet she knew she was no match for Patrick. If he remained unmoved by her plea for help, there was ultimately nothing she could do to persuade him. Nothing.

Except for the one thing she truly did not want to do. . . .

Swallowing down a hot swell of nausea, Ruth repeated Patrick's Staten Island address, information she had managed to get from one of the hotel messengers. At last, pulling in a long, shaky breath, she started toward the entrance of the hotel.

Jess Dalton looked up from his desk, smiling with pleasure at the sight of Nicholas Grafton in the doorway.

"Well — Nicholas! Kerry was just asking about you last night. Where have you been keeping yourself?"

The two men had become good friends over the past two years and had taken to dropping in on each other unannounced, when time allowed. Jess found even the briefest visit with the kind physician both pleasant and renewing.

As he got to his feet, his chair banged

against the wall behind him. The room that served as his office in the Bowery chapel was actually not much more than a closet. His considerable size made it seem even smaller than it was, but he had grown accustomed to the cramped quarters. Besides, he spent precious little time behind a desk these days.

"We've been missing you," he said, going around to shake hands. "Nothing wrong, I hope."

Before the doctor could reply, another man — this one a stranger — stepped into the room. Jess looked at him with interest. Only then did it occur to him that Nicholas's demeanor was uncommonly grave.

The stranger, like Nicholas Grafton, was not overly tall, but his stocky build made him appear a much larger man. Young, with fair hair and a pale complexion, he had the kind of piercing stare that hinted of boldness, even a certain arrogance.

As Jess waited for an introduction, he puzzled over the distress he sensed in Nicholas. His friend's expression seemed almost apologetic when he finally spoke.

"Jess," he finally said, his voice low, "this is Colin Winston." He paused. "Elizabeth Ward's brother."

Amanda's uncle . . .

Jess suddenly felt light-headed. His heart

plummeted, then raced. Stiffly, he extended his hand to the unsmiling Winston. But the younger man ignored the gesture, and after an awkward moment, Jess dropped his hand back to his side.

He could not have been more shocked. He had known that little Amanda supposedly had an uncle somewhere on the Continent, but after months of unsuccessful attempts to contact him, the attorneys in the States and in England had given the go-ahead to initiate adoption proceedings.

From the moment they took her into their home the previous winter, little Amanda had stolen both Jess's heart and Kerry's. Within days after the death of the child's mother, they began to discuss the possibility of adoption.

Nicholas Grafton had written numerous letters to Amanda's grandfather in England, but it seemed that Edward Winston's rejection of his daughter and her family was irrevocable. Every attempt to contact him was met by absolute silence.

As it happened, Lawrence Hancock, the attorney Jess had retained, eventually learned that Amanda's grandfather was dead. Moreover, the child's uncle — and her only living relative — had also been estranged from his elderly father for years. Colin Winston's whereabouts were unknown.

Until now.

"Jess?"

Nicholas Grafton's voice snapped Jess back to the present.

"You know that Mr. Winston is . . . Amanda's uncle."

"Yes," Jess said faintly, unable to venture more.

"He has come —" The doctor's voice faltered for an instant. "For Amanda. To take her . . . back to England with him."

Jess thought he would choke on the pain that knifed through him. "I see," was all he could manage. Abruptly he turned his back on both men.

His first thought was of Kerry — this would surely devastate her. Amanda had been like her own little girl from the first time she held her. Her delight in the child grew with every day that passed, and the bond between them was beautiful to behold.

His next thought was of himself, for he also adored the sunny little girl. He had come to call her his "curly-top," and he delighted in having a small daughter who seemed to consider him quite a prize. When she ran to him in the evening and stretched her arms up to be lifted onto his shoulder, no matter how difficult his day had been, he was suddenly renewed.

He could not imagine coming home to a house without Amanda.

Woodenly, he walked back to his desk and dropped into the chair. Lacing his fingers together, he sat staring at his hands for a long time. When he finally looked up, Nicholas was watching him with a look of undisguised sympathy, Colin Winston with an expression that appeared openly hostile.

"I plan to sail just as soon as I can make the arrangements," Winston said, his voice curt. "You'll prepare the child, I presume?"

Jess stared at the man. He suddenly felt very cold. Cold and weary and bereft, as if the sun had just gone down on his spirit.

Patrick Walsh drained still another cup of coffee. His nerves were already jangled, his mood vile, and he knew the coffee was a bad idea. But he was in no frame of mind to deny himself.

Hunched over his desk, he stared at the front page of the paper, which trumpeted yet another "achievement" on the part of the subcommission headed by Lewis Farmington. In particular, the article lauded Farmington's son-in-law, Captain Michael Burke, for his "vigilance and tenacity in bringing to justice those perpetrators of villainy against the innocent and unsuspecting."

The glowing article went on to explain that most recently Captain Burke had been instrumental in exposing the abuses of the Chatham Charity Women's Shelter. Its director, Ethelda Crane, was presently under investigation for misuse of both private and state funds — among other criminal charges. In the meantime, the shelter had been closed and its residents moved to other facilities.

Related to the same case was the opening of yet another investigation that involved a religious organization under the direction of one William Butterby — known by members of the sect as "Brother Will." A number of alleged offenses on the part of Butterby, including improper advances to female parishioners, had come under the scrutiny of the courts. Butterby was also suspected of some form of collusion with the aforementioned Ethelda Crane.

Patrick Walsh had no interest in the Chatham Women's Shelter, nor in the careless dolts who had managed to get themselves entangled by their own stupidity. But he was sick to death of reading about the accomplishments of the emigrant subcommission — and in particular the heroic exploits of *Captain Michael Burke.*

He should have followed his original instincts and had Burke finished off long before now. That thick-necked cop had been like a buzzard on his back for years. In the past few months the bad blood between them had finally reached a boiling point. Burke didn't even try to dissemble about his intentions: he was out to destroy Patrick Walsh by any means.

So far the bulldog policeman had managed to accomplish little more than to put a couple of Patrick's men in jail — where they had been summarily murdered before they could talk. But Burke had recently brought closure to two lucrative operations, including a highly profitable slave auction — and in the process stirred up speculation about the Walsh "enterprises." As a result, some of the Tammany bosses had begun to make disgruntled noises.

Patrick knew that real power — the kind of power he aspired to — lay not in financial control alone, but in political influence *coupled* with great wealth.

He was already a rich man; his prosperity continued to increase despite the paltry efforts of boorish policemen like Burke. But his larger ambition was to expand his rackets empire, while at the same time marshaling the even greater power to be found within the political arena.

Not for a moment did he intend to let an inconsequential police captain stop him.

He crumpled the front page, then tossed the rest of the newspaper to the floor. Something had to be done about Burke. It was nothing but foolishness to risk the man's further interference.

Patrick began to fantasize about what sort of torment he might inflict upon his nemesis before actually putting an end to him. On impulse he unlocked the middle drawer on the right side of his desk and sat staring at the pistol he carried back and forth between his home and the office every day.

After a moment he pushed the drawer shut and locked it. It would be foolhardy to deal with Burke himself, he acknowledged reluctantly. Far safer to leave the job to those he paid for risking their necks.

For a long time he sat tapping his fingers on the desk, thinking. Taking his pipe from its stand, he filled it, then lighted it. He wanted something special, something particularly nasty for Burke. He would send for Spicer Blaize. There was none better when it came to killing, and the man could be surprisingly inventive about his methods.

When a light knock sounded at his office door, Patrick frowned, annoyed. The door opened, and Glenn Stockton, his new assistant, stepped hesitantly inside.

"I'm sorry to bother you, Mr. Walsh, but there's ah . . . someone here to see you."

Patrick's frown deepened. "I thought I had no appointments scheduled till three."

The pinch-nosed Stockton nodded. "Yes . . . well, the thing is, she doesn't *have* an appointment. But she insists —"

"She?" Patrick looked past the narrow-shouldered Stockton but saw no one behind him.

"Yes, sir. A young lady." Stockton's pale eyes took on a sly glint. "A most *attractive* lady." His studying look was unusually bold, even conspiratorial.

Even more irritated, but curious as well, Patrick gestured curtly that Stockton should send the woman in.

With his pipe in his mouth, he leaned over to retrieve the newspaper from the floor. When he straightened, Ruth Marriott was standing across from his desk.

14

Bearers of Good and Bad Tidings

Let each person judge his own luck,
good or bad.
Irish Proverb

Quinn O'Shea made a halfhearted attempt to pick up some of the children's toys off the front porch of Whittaker House. The sun was scorching down like a furnace blast, and she had just decided to go back inside, where the high ceilings and draped windows offered at least some respite from the heat, when she saw Sergeant Denny Price round the corner of Elizabeth Street.

Quinn hesitated. The policeman called out, and at the sound of his Donegal brogue tripping over her name, she waited. The realization that she was actually glad to see the man set off an alarm in her.

Deliberately she chilled her greeting, offering only one curt word. "Sergeant."

He surprised her by not coming back with his usual impudent grin and cheerful salute. Curious, Quinn saw that he was wearing an uncommonly stern frown, and in one large hand clutched what appeared to be a book.

Taking the steps two at a time, he snapped out his only acknowledgment of her presence. "I need to see Mr. Whittaker right away. Is he in?"

His tone was abrupt, the words clipped. This, too, was a departure from the stream of Irish blarney she had come to expect from him.

"He is," she replied, studying him as he slowed his approach only slightly. "He's upstairs with the older boys, painting the hallway."

With a nod he marched by her and went inside. Quinn turned to watch, pushing back a faint stab of disappointment at his brusqueness. What was it to her, after all, if the man had other things on his mind today besides making a nuisance of himself? At least he wouldn't be trying to coax her out, for a change.

And didn't she have other fish to fry as well? Daniel Kavanagh was taking a rare afternoon for himself, coming home early to help the others with the painting. First, though, he had offered to help her with her grammar lesson.

Quinn had finally managed to swallow her pride and ask the Kavanagh lad to teach her how to speak correctly. She was a good reader, with a firm understanding of most of what she read. But when it came to conversation, her efforts were often awkward, if not altogether faulty.

Ever since coming to work for the Whittakers, she had been taken by the fine manners and proper ways of the family — especially Mr. Whittaker and Daniel. Mrs. Whittaker still carried a great deal of the old sod about her, most noticeable in her West of Ireland speech. But both Daniel and his stepfather were gentlemen, and their gentility was reflected in the way they used the language.

Part of Quinn's agenda on the way to becoming a lady — an *American* lady — was to learn to speak properly. But there was much she simply didn't understand about how to say things in an acceptable way. And Daniel Kavanagh seemed more than willing to teach her.

Mr. Whittaker would have been the ideal tutor, of course, for clearly he possessed a fine education. But the man's time was taken up from dawn to dark with his work; when he wasn't tending to the boyos or seeing to his own family, he would toil at the hulking piano in the dayroom, writing his music. Certainly he had no time left over for anything else.

Once in a while Quinn would sit in on the children's lessons, but for the most part their instruction was too basic to be of any real help to her.

Even before approaching Daniel Kavanagh with her request for help, she had known he wouldn't refuse. The lad could not quite manage to conceal his infatuation with her.

Now and again Quinn felt a nagging guilt that she might be taking advantage, but she did her best to ignore it. She had learned that opportunity was not a frequent visitor, and it was wise not to be too slow about opening the door when it arrived.

"I need to speak with you alone, Mr. Whittaker, if you please."

Evan noted the policeman's glance at Billy Hogan, who, along with three other boys, was in the midst of applying a generous coat of white paint to the hallway walls.

"Of course, Sergeant. B-boys, go right on with your p-painting. I'll be back directly."

Evan gestured toward the dormitory room across the hall. "We can talk in there."

As soon as Evan closed the door behind them, the sergeant came right to the point. "Sorley Dolan is out," he said, his voice hard.

"This morning. I thought you'd be wanting to know."

Evan stared at him, trying to comprehend. "You can't m-mean he's free? Not so soon!"

"Scarcely anyone serves their full time these days," the policeman said with a scowl. "The jails are jammed. There's not enough room for even half the felons we run in, and that's the truth."

Evan nodded. The city's overcrowded prison conditions had been the subject of frequent newspaper reports over the past year. Citizens were demanding reforms, while the politicians demanded bigger jails. The policemen, on the other hand, continued to urge the city to add more men to their number. It seemed that everyone had a solution, but meanwhile the problem continued to explode out of control.

"Most of the blighters are out the back door not long after we haul them through the front," the sergeant went on. "Even the lowest sort of riffraff are back out on the street in no time. There's simply no place for them. We need what cells we have for the murderers and madmen."

"But the m-madmen shouldn't be in ordinary jail cells at all," Evan couldn't resist pointing out. "They ought to be confined to hospitals or institutions, where they can get the kind of m-medical attention they need."

"Perhaps. But when the city can't find room for the hardened criminals, they're not likely to put themselves out for the lunatics."

The idea of murderers and madmen jolted Evan back to the purpose of the policeman's call. "Dolan has no legal rights so far as B-Billy is concerned, does he?"

The sergeant shook his head. "None whatever. But legal rights aren't going to be stopping a devil like Sorley Dolan. Especially if he's in his cups — which no doubt he will be by dark." He paused. "It might be well to keep an eye out for the lad just now, if you take my meaning."

Worry for Billy settled upon Evan like a blight. What if Dolan were to come after the boy? He was just irrational enough to blame Billy for his own savagery, when all the boy had done was to tell the truth.

The policeman seemed to read his thoughts. "I'll do what I can to keep track of Sorley, Mr. Whittaker. I'll be about, sure. And if you should happen to need help, just send one of the little lads running. Any of the men on the force will come."

Evan knew Sergeant Price meant to re-assure him, and he managed a weak smile. But the truth was, he didn't feel in the least re-assured.

"Ah — and I'm almost forgetting the other reason I came," said the sergeant, handing Evan the most recent selection he had borrowed from the library. "I didn't like this one as much as the Milton, I confess."

Evan regarded the sergeant with interest. The big policeman had been borrowing books from the library for weeks now. Evan still found it astonishing that Sergeant Price's interest seemed to lie almost entirely with poetry, especially classical poetry. His remarks upon returning each selection proved to be surprisingly incisive.

"What is it about Milton that fascinates you so, Sergeant — if you don't mind my asking?"

The policeman considered Evan's question only for a moment. "Why, in truth, Mr. Whittaker, I believe it's the man's earthiness."

Evan's interest was captured. "Earthiness? Milton?"

The sergeant nodded. "Aye. Though he was obviously a God-fearing man and eloquent entirely, he seems to have had a great deal of understanding about his own weaknesses. He's even a bit coarse at times, it seems to me. A man with his feet in the clay of humanity, so to speak, while his soul soars in the heavens. He can write about sin or sainthood, the loveliness of Eden or the darkness of the devil's domain itself. But no matter what he's saying, his words do make music, don't they?"

Evan stared at him. He thought he had never heard Milton described so succinctly as by this rough-hewn policeman with the enormous hands and gentle eyes.

"Please feel free to choose another book before you go, Sergeant, if you like," he said.

"Why, thank you, sir, but I'm in a bit of a rush today. Perhaps I'll stop by tomorrow, though, if you're sure you don't mind."

Evan shook his head. "You needn't feel you have to ask, Sergeant. You're always welcome."

As he watched the policeman descend the stairs, anxiety again swept over Evan. He opened his mouth to call Sergeant Price back, then changed his mind. The city's law officers already had far more than they could handle. They couldn't be expected to stand lookout for a drunken cad like Sorley Dolan.

Turning, he stood watching the boys at work at the other end of the hallway. He hated to spoil what was surely one of the few carefree moments in young Billy's life. Just now he appeared to be enjoying himself immensely, trading boyish jests and good-natured teasing with the others as they splashed paint on the walls. His wheat-colored hair was streaked with white paint, his thin face creased in a smile. The boy looked happy.

Billy *had* been happy of late, Evan thought, at least happier than he had been before coming to live with them. No longer did he wear that pinched look of worry; other than concern for his mother and two little half brothers, he seemed as free of life's troubles as a boy his age ought to be.

It was a shame to bring this newly found peace to an end. But since caution would seem to be their only real protection for now, he supposed there was nothing else to do but alert the boy.

Evan sighed and, with a heavy heart, started down the hall toward Billy and the others.

Downstairs, Denny Price would have stopped to talk with the cat-eyed Quinn O'Shea had the girl not been otherwise occupied.

He stood just inside the door, watching her and the Kavanagh lad — Daniel — on the porch out front. Denny's eyes narrowed as he took in the way the boy was gawking at Quinn. He looked about to swallow his tongue.

So that's how it was, was it? The lad was sweet on her.

Denny turned his attention to Quinn. Although there was no actual appearance of coquetry about the girl, she was smiling up at the long-legged *gorsoon* as if he were a man grown, and one to defer to at that.

Denny ground his teeth. Why, most times he was lucky to coax a civil word from the girl! Perhaps on a good day she might even give him a smile and take a stroll with him, but the whole time she looked as if she were ready to bolt and run.

Yet wasn't the little minx treating young Daniel like gentry? Sure, she could not have set her cap for a cow-eyed schoolboy! Why, he could not be much more than half Denny's age.

Young Daniel was a good enough sort, of course. He was known to be as decent and straight as they came. He was a smart boy, a fine boy — no denying it. All the same, he *was* still a boy.

And what of the girl? Denny studied her with the practiced, dispassionate eye of a policeman, suppressing his feelings for the moment. He couldn't be certain, of course, but he thought her smile might not be quite so strained, and those odd feline eyes of hers might not be quite so guarded, so suspicious, as they usually were.

But why? What was there about Daniel

Kavanagh that had apparently managed to sneak past her defenses?

The longer he watched them, the more Denny began to burn. Everything about the Kavanagh lad was quiet and refined: his looks, his voice, even his apparel. Irish or not, the boy had a kind of gentility about him that couldn't be denied. And his manner with the girl was nothing less than that of a knight with his lady. Respectful. Courtly. Gallant.

Jealousy crashed through Denny like a wild boar breaking through a forest. He could deny it all he wanted, but the truth was that he could see why Quinn might take a fancy to a boy like Daniel Kavanagh, young and callow though he was. He was a good-looking, sweet-talking, smooth-faced sort of boy — an educated lad. In comparison, Denny felt square and loud and brutish.

There was no mystery in how a fellow like that could attract a lass. More than likely, Daniel Kavanagh was just the kind of lad a girl like Quinn O'Shea would be drawn to.

Denny swallowed down his disappointment. He had felt all too keenly his own lack of appeal to her. When she wasn't being altogether obstinate, she looked at him as if he held all the interest of a tree stump.

He wasn't quite sure what accounted for her indifference. At times he thought she was just hostile to men in general. Other times he thought it was as simple as the fact that he was an Irishman. A big, uneducated, heavy-handed Irish cop.

Why couldn't he just stay away from her, then?

Disgruntled with himself, Denny made a fierce attempt to suppress his envy of the Kavanagh lad, at least for the moment. Sure, and a challenge was good for a man now and then. He wouldn't be much of a policeman if he turned tail in the face of combat, would he?

Finally he managed to plaster a big, confident smile on his face. Stepping out from the shadows, he walked onto the porch, where he wedged himself deliberately between the young knight and his lady.

In her opulent parlor on Staten Island, Alice Walsh sat on the piano stool smiling with considerable pleasure over the legal document propped up on the piano in front of her — and the letter beside it.

The legal paper was a contract issued by the New York publishing house of Firth, Pond & Co. Eventually, if everything went as it should, the contract would result in the publication of sheet music for a choral suite and two numbers for band instruments — all composed by Evan Whittaker.

Alice was as excited as if the contract had

been written on *her* behalf. Evan Whittaker had no knowledge of her efforts; only Harold Elliott, a member of the church choir and an employee of the publishing house, had been taken into her confidence.

For some time now, Alice had not only served as Evan Whittaker's accompanist, but had taken on the additional task of transcribing his choral and instrumental compositions. The diligent, mild-mannered Englishman already had more than enough to do. Composing at the keyboard had to be laborious for a man with only one arm; he certainly didn't need the added effort of copying his final arrangements.

A few months past, Alice had taken the liberty of showing some of Mr. Whittaker's arrangements to Harold Elliott for his opinion. To her delight, Harold had been enthusiastic enough to take the selections on to his superiors at Firth, Pond & Co. After a frustrating delay, during which Alice all but hounded poor Harold, the publishing house was at last offering a contract.

But almost as exciting as the contract itself was the letter beside it. Because Evan Whittaker was a new name to Firth, Pond, the publishers had approached one of their most popular composers, Stephen Foster, for an opinion on Mr. Whittaker's music. Foster had not only applauded the new music, but his enthusiasm had been such that he had written a personal letter of encouragement to the composer.

Like Alice, Evan Whittaker was a great fan of Stephen Foster's compositions. Now, not only was he being offered a contract by Foster's own publishing house, but he had received the composer's enthusiastic endorsement as well.

A publishing contract could mean a great deal to Evan Whittaker and his wife, Alice knew. Certainly the royalties, no matter how nominal, would be welcome. But somehow she sensed that this unexpected tribute from Stephen Foster might mean just as much, if not more, to the diffident Englishman as any monetary reward.

She could hardly wait to present him with the contract and letter — indeed, she had decided against waiting until the weekly Thursday rehearsal in Five Points. Instead, she would go to Whittaker House this very afternoon.

As her mother often said, bad news could always wait, but good news was never too early.

15

Feeble Breath of Hope

What good for me to call when hope
of help is gone?
EGAN O'RAHILLY (1670–1728)

For a moment Ruth felt a rush of satisfaction when she saw the stunned look on Patrick Walsh's face.

Obviously, he had not expected her to come to New York. Not for a minute would he have given her credit for that much courage. One of his pet names for her, after all, was his "pretty, timid sparrow." She presumed he meant it as an endearment, but the image had wounded her deeply.

Ruth had always been self-conscious to a fault. Patrick often praised her "good looks" and "fine figure," and Ruth was secretly pleased that he found her attractive, even though his compliments embarrassed her.

Where she perceived herself too tall and too thin, Patrick referred to her as "patrician." The heavy chestnut hair that was only stubborn and troublesome to her seemed to hold a certain attraction for him: he insisted her thick chignon gave her *style*.

And when she mentioned her self-consciousness, Patrick claimed to find her shyness charming. The one time she had openly objected to his teasing about her lack of confidence, he had quickly moved to reassure her. "I've always *disliked* overconfident, brazen women, my dear. I prefer you just the way you are."

Now, in the silent, tense moment that hung between them, an entire tide of memories surged through Ruth — memories followed by regret. Regret for lost love . . . lost years . . . lost innocence.

For an instant panic gripped her. Could she really go through with this, now that she was here? Could she actually confront and accuse this man whom she had loved so completely, so wholeheartedly?

So foolishly . . .

She struggled to recall the words of reason and appeal she had carefully rehearsed all the way from Chicago, but at this moment she could think of nothing but escape. Shrinking beneath his furious, incredulous glare, it was all she could do not to turn and bolt from the room.

He let go an oath and slammed his pipe into its stand. With his hands braced on the desk, he lunged to his feet, his eyes blazing. Then he spoke, and the thunderous rage of his words immobilized her. "What do you think you're doing, coming *here?* Have you lost your wits altogether?"

Ruth stood perfectly still, stunned by the venom lacing his tone. Taking in a deep, steadying breath, she struggled to keep her voice from trembling as she faced him. "I didn't want to come here, Patrick. I *had* to. I need help — remember?"

"As I recall, I've already sent you a generous sum of money," he shot back. The fire in his eyes suddenly banked to a cold stare, and his voice lowered to a threatening hiss. "You're wasting your time and mine if you're looking for more."

Her heart pounding, Ruth groped for some shred of her carefully scripted argument. "Patrick . . . I'm carrying your child!" Even to her ears, the tremulous tone sounded like the whining of a frightened schoolgirl. "You — you can't simply dismiss me. This is as much your problem as mine."

The stone mask remained unyielding. His words pierced her heart like shards of ice.

"You have a keen sense of drama, Ruth. But the fact that you find yourself in difficult straits doesn't mean you can foist your unwelcome little bundle onto me. Surely you don't expect me to believe I'm the only man you've been with?"

Ruth had to brace one hand on the back of a nearby chair to keep her legs from buckling. "You *are* the only man I've been with!" she choked out. "You know you are!"

His mouth twisted in an unpleasant smile. "Dear girl, I know nothing of the kind. To the contrary, as free and easy as you were with me, I find it difficult to believe you were ever as innocent as you'd like me to think."

His tone was impatient, and his expression held a distinct note of dismissal. Glancing down, he began to thumb idly through a stack of papers on his desk.

Hot tears welled up in Ruth's eyes, almost blinding her. Denial warred against reason as the truth began to penetrate. Still she fought against the reality of what was happening.

"How can you say that to me?" she burst out. "There was never anyone else but you. Never! Not before I met you — and certainly not after!"

He went on shuffling through the papers in front of him. "There's no need for you to defend yourself to me, Ruth. Your private life is none of my concern."

Without warning, resentment slammed into Ruth like a fist. "Perhaps you'd better *make* it your concern, Patrick!"

He looked up then, and the utter disdain in his eyes chilled Ruth's soul. A sickening dread washed over her. Threatening him had been a mistake.

"Get out." His voice was frigid, his words edged with the same ice that glazed his eyes. But his tone held an unmistakable note of warning that made Ruth take a step back. "Get out of my office, and get out of New York. Now, Ruth."

She was appalled that she could have deluded herself into believing that this cold, relentless man across the desk had ever cared for her. She didn't even know him. Only now did she realize that she had *never* known him.

Ruth tried to swallow, but anguish rose up in her, numbing her throat. Her mind registered the finality of his words even as she struggled to find some way of penetrating his indifference.

She stretched out a hand toward him. "Patrick . . . how can you do this . . . after everything we once meant to each other?"

He lifted his chin, and his pale, unblinking gaze raked over her, devastating her with contempt. "You stupid little baggage," he said in

214

an unbelievably casual tone of voice. "You never meant anything at all to me."

Ruth swayed, tightening her grasp on the wing of the chair to keep from pitching forward. "You . . . you are despicable!" She nearly strangled on her own words. "You won't get out of this so easily, Patrick!" she blurted out. "Perhaps your wife will be more interested in my predicament than you are!"

Before Ruth even knew what was happening, he was around the desk, his hand clutching her throat.

"Don't you dare threaten me, you little tramp!"

The face she had once thought so noble and handsome now held only menace — menace directed at her. The taut composure of his features had given way to a frenzied, contorted ugliness fired by rage.

"I'm warning you — stay away from my wife!"

Raw fury burned in his eyes. For the first time, Ruth was actually afraid of him. His fingers tightened around her neck, cutting off her breath. At that moment she believed he was entirely capable of killing her.

Gasping, she twisted, trying to shove him away.

"Patrick!" she choked out. "You're hurting me!"

His fingers eased their tension only slightly as he pushed his face into hers. The blazing hatred in his eyes seared her soul. "I haven't even begun to hurt you, you little fool! If you ever — *ever* — try to interfere in my life again, I'll teach you about *real* pain!"

Still gripping her throat, he let his furious gaze play over her face for another instant. "Now you're going to leave my office, Ruth. You're going to leave New York." His mouth twisted. "You're going to go back to Chicago and find some balding, dim-witted butcher to ply your questionable charms on. If you don't let any grass grow under your feet, you might even convince him that the brat in your belly belongs to *him*."

The cruelty of his words echoed in the silence. The physical pain he was inflicting on her throat was nothing compared to the self-disgust that impaled her.

He seized her shoulders and wrenched her around, then shoved her hard across the room and out the door.

Sobbing, her vision clouded with scalding tears, Ruth stumbled past the inquisitive stare of the narrow-faced man behind the reception desk.

The door to Patrick's office banged shut behind her.

In the tumult of her pain, the sound was

like the slamming of a coffin lid.

Ruth shuddered as somewhere deep inside her a dark abyss of despair slowly opened and drew her in.

The moment Colin Winston left the office, Nicholas Grafton turned back to Jess.

"You *are* going to fight him, aren't you?"

His head in his hands, Jess looked up at his friend. "Fight him?" he repeated thickly. "How? He's Amanda's uncle."

"But he's also a complete stranger to the child." Nicholas stopped. For a moment he stood fingering the chain of his pocket watch. "Jess . . . did you notice that he never once asked about Amanda? Never so much as inquired after her welfare? Doesn't that strike you as somewhat strange?"

Jess looked at him but said nothing.

"Something about that fellow," Nicholas went on, "doesn't register quite right with me. I'm not sure what it is, exactly — perhaps just the shock, and not wanting to see you lose Amanda — but I don't much like him."

Jess struggled to free himself from the fog enveloping his mind. It occurred to him that he had never heard the good-natured physician say anything derogatory about another human being. Nicholas Grafton usually had something good to say about most people, and if he didn't, he said nothing.

But he was right about Colin Winston's apparent indifference toward Amanda; it *was* peculiar. If Winston was really as concerned for her as he claimed to be, why hadn't he at least asked about the child, rather than simply demanding custody of her, as if she were nothing but a piece of property?

He looked up at Nicholas. The silver-haired physician had removed his eyeglasses and was rubbing the bridge of his nose as he regarded Jess. "If I were you," the doctor finally said, replacing his glasses, "I would talk with my attorney right away. There might be something Hancock can do to put Colin Winston off for a time — at least until you can find out more about the man, perhaps even have him investigated. You don't really mean to turn Amanda over to him without more information, do you?"

Jess shook his head as if to clear it. "We didn't expect anything like this. Not after so long a time. I'm not sure *what* to do."

He still could not believe what was happening. Only this morning at breakfast he and Kerry had been making plans with Casey-Fitz for him to take the larger guest room as his own so they could redecorate the smaller bedroom for Amanda. The three of them had discussed color choices and appropriate furnishings for the little girl's bedroom as seriously as if they had been deciding on a potential suitor for her.

But now . . . now there might never be a little girl's bedroom. . . .

"You love that child as if she were your own, Jess," Nicholas said quietly. "You told me so yourself."

"Yes," Jess answered, staring at his hands. "Yes, of course, I do. And Kerry —" He stopped, swallowing hard. Looking up, he met Nicholas's gaze. "Do you really think we'd still have a chance for adoption? Blood almost always wins out in matters like this. I can't think we have any real hope of keeping Amanda."

"There's always hope, Jess. Forgive me for sounding like a physician, but until the last breath is drawn there is always hope."

The doctor paused, giving Jess an intense look. "Do you know what they call you around town, by the way?"

"Call me?"

Nicholas nodded, smiling faintly. "Around the Bowery and Five Points, they call you the 'Fighting Parson.' "

Jess frowned. "What?"

"Oh, it's meant with respect," his friend assured him. "A number of the fellows down here like to boast that their preacher is 'a real

219

man — a fighting man,' when the circumstances call for it."

Jess groaned. "That's hardly a compliment to a man who considers himself a pacifist, Nicholas. Where did they get such an idea?"

"They mean well, Jess. You've won their respect — and that's no small accomplishment, I'd say. At any rate, they're not talking about fisticuffs. You're known as a man who's not afraid to fight for what's right — for what you believe in." He paused. "And I'd be the first to agree. That's why I know you won't simply give up Amanda without a fight. You'd be sending her off to another country with a man she's never laid eyes on — a man you know absolutely nothing about."

Jess looked at him for another moment, then got up. Going to the narrow-paned, clouded window, he stood, hands in his pockets, staring out onto the brick wall of the junk dealer's shed next door.

"I believe strongly in *family*, Nicholas. If Colin Winston is determined to take Amanda back to England, I'm not sure I have the right to try to prevent it. He's a blood relative — and the only family left to her."

There was silence for a moment. When the reply came, it was quiet but firm. "Blood doesn't make family, Jess. Love makes family. Love and commitment."

The words rang in Jess's ears, striking his heart like a bell. He turned around and met his friend's gaze. After a moment, he finally nodded. "You're right."

"Not always, but on occasion."

Still Jess hesitated. "Will you help us?"

Nicholas Grafton's eyes glinted. "In any way I can."

Outside, on the dusty street, Ruth Marriott stood with her shoulders hunched and her eyes lowered, trying to avoid the curious stares of passersby.

The heat was oppressive. The putrid smell of rotting garbage and horse droppings hung like a vile shroud over the street. Her stomach churned. She felt feverish and had to fight off wave after wave of dizzying nausea.

The sickening assault of Patrick's betrayal, combined with her physical condition, threatened to prostrate her in the middle of the street. She fought down a vicious swell of queasiness, at the same time groping for some semblance of reason.

She was on her own now. There was no longer any hope of help from Patrick. She had only herself . . . and the baby. No one else.

Below the surface of her anxiety rode an undercurrent of fear. She had never felt so isolated, so entirely alone, in her life.

She had no one to turn to, no one to count on. She would soon have no job, ultimately not even a place to live. And if her health continued to falter, she might not even be able to care for the baby without help.

At the fringes of her mind whispered what seemed to be her last remaining shred of hope. She had fought the idea from the beginning, disgusted with herself for even considering the possibility. It was the last thing she wanted to do.

But now it seemed the only thing she *could* do. She had to try . . . for the sake of her baby.

After a moment, she lifted her face and squared her shoulders. Bracing herself against the heat and the stench of decay, she finally mustered the nerve to ask a middle-aged man with a kindly countenance directions to the Staten Island Ferry.

16

Child of My Heart

Let me press thee closer still,
A gradh geal mo chroidhe;
To this scathed, bleeding heart,
Beloved as thou art,
for too soon, too soon we part,
A gradh geal mo chroidhe!
JOHN WALSH (1835–1881)

Jess Dalton didn't have to think twice before accepting Nicholas Grafton's offer to go home with him that afternoon.

He dreaded telling Kerry about Colin Winston, and when Nicholas offered to accompany him, he was immeasurably relieved. Until that moment he hadn't realized just how anxious he was about what this turn of events might do to Kerry.

She was the most precious thing in life to him, and he was about to break her heart.

As the buggy slowed and drew to a stop in

front of the house, he exchanged a long look with Nicholas. "I'd rather face almost anything than the pain this will cause her."

The physician nodded. "I know." He reached for his medical bag and stepped out of the buggy. "I'll take this along, just in case," he said, avoiding Jess's eyes.

This unexpected act of caution unnerved Jess even more.

They found Kerry at the kitchen table with Amanda. Kerry's hair was in disarray, and the pinafore apron over her dress appeared slightly rumpled. From the looks of things, the two had been having a late luncheon.

Kerry looked up in surprise as the men entered. "Why, Nicholas Grafton! And isn't it past time you were paying us a visit! But, Jess, whatever are you doing home at this time of day?"

She looked from one to the other. Jess saw the light of welcome in her eyes flicker and change to uncertainty. He went to kiss her, bracing himself for the ordeal ahead.

"Something's wrong. What is it?" Her voice suddenly sounded very young and small. She lifted a hand to her hair and began to tug at one stray ringlet.

By now Amanda was reaching for Jess, her face, smudged with potatoes, eager and bright. "Da!" she cried, thrusting her plump little arms toward him.

Kerry's hand went around the child's shoulder in a protective gesture. "Yes, love, it's Da." Her gaze searched Jess's face. "But you must finish your potatoes, like the good girl."

Even as she spoke, Kerry's eyes never left Jess's face. He saw her go pale and longed to deflect her questions, if only for a little while.

"Jess?"

He opened his mouth, but the words froze in his throat. Nicholas finally bridged the way to the bad news.

"I'm afraid we have something rather . . . difficult to tell you, Kerry." He stopped, then went on, his words coming more quickly than before. "But be assured that Jess and I are already taking steps to redeem the situation."

With that, he reached for Amanda, who went to him cheerfully. "Dokka Nick!" she cooed. She studied him for a moment, then giggled and pressed a chubby thumb over each lens of his eyeglasses.

Nicholas hoisted the child to his shoulder, smiling at her. "Why don't I take you to Molly, young lady? We're going to have to get rid of those potatoes around your nose before they take root."

He started for the door with the child in his arms, then turned. "I'll be right back."

When Jess finally forced himself to face his wife, her searching green eyes held an unmistakable glint of alarm. "It's about Amanda, isn't it?" she said.

Jess pulled up a chair beside her. "I'm afraid it is."

She went ashen.

"Kerry . . ."

"I shan't listen!" The words burst out unexpectedly, and she shook her head, refusing to look at him. "Whatever it is, I don't want to know!"

Jess stared at her in dismay, not quite knowing how to go on. "Kerry . . . love, I'm afraid you *must* know. Amanda's uncle . . . it seems that he's come for her. He's here, in New York, right now. He wants to take Amanda back to England with him."

Squeezing her eyes shut, Kerry continued to shake her head in denial. She looked like a child herself now, especially when a solitary tear escaped, slowly tracking down one side of her face.

Jess moved to gather her into his arms, holding her tightly against his chest, rocking her against him as he attempted to console her — and himself. At first she was rigid and unyielding, dazed, he suspected, with shock and grief. But finally he felt her go limp against him. Burying her face against his shoulder, she collapsed into a quiet, despairing weeping that rent his heart.

In that moment Jess vowed that, blood relative or not, Colin Winston would not have Amanda. He would do whatever he had to do, fight the man however he must, to keep their little curly-top with them . . . where she belonged. Unless God himself tore Amanda from their arms, they would not give her up.

Late that afternoon, Kerry took Amanda upstairs for a rest. She faltered at the landing at the top of the stairway, but both Jess and Nicholas were standing below, watching with concern, so she went on, taking slow but steady steps all the way down the hall.

Beside her, one small hand clutching Kerry's, Amanda trundled along, chortling happily. Somehow Kerry managed to murmur the appropriate replies to the little girl's cheerful prattle. But her heart felt like lead, and an anxiety bordering on hysteria hovered just at the edge of her emotions.

Rather than taking Amanda to her own room, Kerry led her to the master bedroom. Amanda seemed only slightly surprised at this departure in routine, scarcely pausing in her chatter as Kerry settled the two of them in the rocking chair by the window.

She kissed the small fingers tugging at her

own, her eyes taking in every dear, beloved feature of the little girl on her lap, as if to store the memories away, untouched and secure. Almost unaware of Amanda's squirming, Kerry saw only the tumbling blond curls and tiny nose, the darker brush strokes of eyelashes, the blue eyes that reflected none of Kerry's own fear, but only childish mischief and delight in the moment.

She knew she should pray. For a time she tried to summon prayerful words up through the chaos of fear and torment churning inside her. But the desperate plea of her heart remained unspoken, inexpressible.

They had made her listen to what they referred to as "the situation," speaking in hushed and uncertain tones. Jess explained it gently, carefully, as if he might have been reasoning with a babe. During the entire account, Kerry had bitten her lip with such force that she finally drew blood and had to swallow it down, along with the poisonous reality that again she was losing a child.

She had never seen her other baby, the poor little boy whose life had been snuffed out before he ever witnessed the light of day. She had never held him in her arms, spooned food into his mouth, sung lullabies to him at bedtime or whispered endearments as he slept. She had lost him before she ever knew him, and yet the anguish of his loss had left her grieving for months. Sometimes even now, in the long silent hours of the night, she would lie sleepless, wondering what he might have looked like had he lived.

But Amanda . . . oh, dear Lord, Amanda . . . I have rocked her to sleep, carried her up and down the stairs, bathed her, dried her tears, held her next to my heart . . . how can I bear to lose her, after all I have known of her?

Was there no end to the loss, to the pain of parting? Her mother had died not long after giving birth to Kerry. Her only brother, Liam, had wasted away on the crossing to America, and her da had died when she was just eighteen. Later, her babe, her pitiful wee babe, had been virtually torn from her womb. Then Arthur, the poor runaway black boy they had taken in and only begun to love, had died, victim of an inferno — and the racial hatred of the very city to which he had fled in search of freedom.

And now Amanda . . .

Oh, Lord . . . how much more? How much more loss?

She thought of Casey-Fitz, who had lost his own mother years before. Casey had found love and security with her and Jess. The lad doted on wee Amanda, had accepted her immediately as his little sister. He had been nearly devastated by Arthur's death; what would this do to him?

And Jess himself — how could he stand the loss of his little curly-top, the delight of his heart?

She looked down at the child on her lap. Amanda, curled into a ball, nestled her head snugly against Kerry's breast and gazed up at her with drowsy eyes. Somehow Kerry managed to smile through her tears, gently encircling the small body with her arms, gathering her as close as possible.

As the late afternoon shadows stole over the room, Kerry sat rocking the sleeping child. She held her with a mother's gentle arms, yet held her tightly, as if to guard against even the slightest threat to this darling one she loved so much.

A great sorrow settled over Kerry, a sense of the sun going down on the last light of her hope. Already she felt the cold gloom of emptiness.

17

The Sound of a World Ending

Gone, gone, forever gone
Are the hopes I cherished,
Changed like the sunny dawn
In sudden showers perished.
GERALD GRIFFIN (1803–1840)

Patrick Walsh paced the distance from his desk to the window several times before finally stopping to lean against the windowsill and stare down at the street. Outside, a curtain of gloom had begun to draw the city in, darkening the sky and the avenue with low-hanging shadows. Pedestrians hurried in and out of the stores and businesses, as if anxious to accomplish their errands and get home before the storm broke.

Abruptly he turned and went back to his desk, unlocking the middle drawer where he kept his gun. For a long time he stood staring down at the pistol, thinking.

He had made a mistake in giving Ruth the address of the hotel. He should have given her *nothing*. No address, no consideration — and no money. He should have dismissed her from his life the moment he tired of her, just as he had all the others.

She was none too stable, that much was evident. Otherwise she would never have come all the way from Chicago to threaten him.

But surely she wouldn't do anything so bold or so stupid as to go to his home and confront Alice. Ruth wasn't that foolish.

Even if she had the brass to make an attempt, she could never accomplish it. She had no way of knowing where he lived.

Unless she had made it her business to find out . . .

His eyes returned to the gun. After another moment, he grabbed the pistol and its shoulder holster and banged the drawer shut. Yanking his suit coat from the closet, he stormed out of his office.

"I'm leaving early," he barked at Stockton. "Tell Huston to get the boat and take me across."

In her upstairs bedroom, Alice Walsh gave a finishing pat to her hair, then smoothed the collar of her shirtwaist. She smiled in anticipation of her errand to Manhattan, already imagining Evan Whittaker's astonishment.

He would be stunned, his wife proud and pleased. Alice found enormous satisfaction in the knowledge that something good was coming the way of these two exceptional people. No one in New York labored more faithfully for their God than Evan Whittaker and his wife. They had made any number of sacrifices to help the less fortunate of the city. Even Mrs. Whittaker, though in chronic poor health, never flagged in her devotion to her husband or in her ministry to the city's abandoned children.

The hard-working immigrant couple seemed to thrive on pouring themselves out for others, at times to the detriment of their own health and livelihood. Perhaps soon, though, thanks to this unexpected publishing contract, their own financial burdens would be eased.

Not that they ever appeared burdened. Even with Mrs. Whittaker's health as fragile as it was, they seemed to enjoy life — and each other — to the fullest. In fact, Alice realized uncomfortably, there were times when she came close to envying them.

Her smile fled as a pang of regret stole over her. If Patrick had ever, even once, looked at *her* the way Evan Whittaker looked at his wife, she thought she might have lived on it forever.

But Patrick was not, had never been, a demonstrative man. He couldn't tolerate open displays of affection. Even in their most intimate moments, he was never what women in the popular novels would call *romantic*.

The truth was, Patrick often seemed cold and insensitive, even uncaring. Although Alice had never stopped wishing he might be more affectionate, for years she had managed to console herself with the reminder that her husband was a highly successful — and therefore extremely busy — man. He was occupied with more important matters than catering to her sentimental fancies. He might not be given to the time-consuming little acts of thoughtfulness that other men indulged in, but he was a good husband and father, all the same.

For the most part it had never been all that difficult to excuse his inattention. She simply reasoned that Patrick wasn't actually negligent — merely preoccupied.

At some juncture, however, that had changed. Over the past few months it had become increasingly difficult to defend him.

For a long time she had been aware of his lack of interest in her and the children. But recently she had begun to recognize his detachment for what is was: a lack of caring. The admission that Patrick was not as loving and devoted as she had believed him to be was difficult for Alice. Yet she could no longer deny that his only real affections seemed to lie in the areas of his own self-interest — primarily money and success, as well as an especially troubling need to dominate others. And the awareness had shaken her so badly that she could not bring herself to think about it further for weeks.

The turning point had come on Christmas Eve past. As was their yearly practice, the entire family, including Alice's parents, had come together after the late worship service to exchange their gifts. That night, as the children ripped into their presents, it occurred to Alice that Patrick was seeing the contents of each package for the first time. He had not shown the slightest inclination to offer suggestions, had taken no part in the selection or the wrapping of a single item.

Not that this was anything new. He routinely left all such matters to Alice. But for some reason the full extent of his indifference finally registered that night; suddenly her tolerance of Patrick's apathy seemed every bit as unacceptable as his neglect. And when her mother inadvertently let it slip that she, not Patrick, had selected his personal gifts for Alice, the disappointment, coupled with her own self-indictment, struck a wounding blow from which she had never quite recovered.

Since then there had been other occasions when Alice became aware of some character trait or flaw in Patrick as if for the first time. And yet she knew it was *not* the first time — merely the first time she had allowed herself to confront the truth.

And the truth was, her husband was an intrinsically selfish man, emotionally removed from her and his own children, even careless of his family's needs and feelings. From the beginning of their marriage she had made him something larger, something better, than his real self. She had never quite seen Patrick as the man he was — but only as the man she wanted him to be.

After the initial pain of that admission, his indifference had begun to take on a kind of cruelty in Alice's mind. She did not as yet know what to do with these discoveries about her husband. She knew only that for the first time in her marriage she was beginning to face reality. And for the sake of her children, she determined that she must not allow the bitter truth to destroy her.

But today was not the day for grim reality. It was a day for celebration — at least she hoped that's what it would be for the Whittakers. And being the messenger of such good tidings gave her a genuine pleasure that helped ease the sting of her personal pain.

She forced a smile at her reflection in the mirror, scanning her appearance one last time before collecting her gloves and handbag.

Just as she reached the bedroom door, Nancy, the housemaid, knocked and announced, "Beg pardon, Mrs. Walsh, but there's a caller."

Alice opened the door. Nancy — shorter than Alice and considerably plumper — stood outside. The girl's round face was flushed and fixed in an expression of disapproval.

Ordinarily Alice would have been pleased by the prospect of unexpected company. Callers were rare, except for peddlers and the occasional business acquaintance of Patrick's.

But to receive a caller now would mean missing the ferry.

"I wasn't expecting anyone today," she said uncertainly, peering past Nancy's shoulder into the hall.

"And didn't I tell her that you would be going out any moment now?" The youthful maid emphasized her annoyance by crossing her arms firmly over her starched apron front. "But the woman insisted on seeing you anyway."

Alice frowned. "Then it's someone I know?"

Nancy shrugged and arched her eyebrows. "I'd not think it likely." Nancy gave a sniff of disdain. "Didn't she decline to give her name? And her not even having a *card!*" The maid's casual behavior and exaggerated Irish brogue irritated Patrick in the worst way, but Alice found the girl mildly amusing.

"Well, I think you'd best ask her to come back tomorrow," Alice said, impatient to be on her way. "I'll be happy to receive her then."

Grumbling, the maid turned and stepped out into the hall. Alice followed her but stopped just outside the door, where the vast winding stairway, which ascended three entire floors, broke off at a landing.

Alice crossed to the banister. There was a clear view to the entrance hall below, and a young woman was standing at the foot of the staircase, looking up. Obviously she had taken it upon herself to enter without being invited.

"Why, what cheek!" Nancy exclaimed. "I'll be getting rid of her this moment, just see if I don't!"

Something in the forlorn expression of the young woman below held Alice captive. She stood staring down at her, and as she met the dark gaze lifted in her direction, she felt a sudden presentiment of dread.

She put a hand to Nancy's arm. "No," she said, her voice none too steady, "show her upstairs, to the sitting room."

Ruth Marriott had never envisioned Patrick's wife looking even remotely like the woman who stood across the room, studying her with a guarded but not unfriendly expression.

She wasn't sure how she *had* imagined Alice Walsh, once she learned of her existence. But it was certainly nothing like this short, plump woman in the plainly tailored rose-hued suit. She would have expected a much taller woman, elegantly dressed, with a lofty demeanor and suspicious eyes.

She would never have conceived the pleasant, surprisingly sweet face, the air of vulnerability, the uncertain smile. This woman, who stood regarding Ruth with far more kindness than she deserved, appeared warm and unassuming — and much younger than Ruth knew she must be.

For a moment Ruth stood frozen under the directness of the other's searching eyes.

"We haven't met before, have we?" Alice Walsh asked, her gaze growing more intent. "I'm afraid I didn't even get your name."

"I . . . it's Ruth. Ruth Marriott."

Ruth watched for some hint of response to

her name, but of course there was none. "We . . . no, we haven't met," she continued. "I came —"

Her throat suddenly felt burned and swollen. She stood, mute, unable to go on.

Something flickered in Alice Walsh's clear blue gaze, and guilt assailed Ruth as she realized the enormity of what she was about to inflict upon this woman.

"Mrs. Walsh . . . I didn't want to come here. . . ."

Alice Walsh remained perfectly still, her expression cautious and perhaps slightly less charitable.

Ruth felt faintly nauseous. "I'm sorry," she choked out. "I'm . . . very tired. If I could sit down for a moment . . ."

A fleeting look of apprehension crossed the other woman's features. But she was very much the lady, responding at once to Ruth's appeal.

She gestured to a plum-colored upholstered chair. "Would you like some water?"

The thought of putting anything into her stomach, even water, made Ruth almost buckle with revulsion. She shook her head, stumbled to the chair, and collapsed.

For a few moments Ruth could do nothing more than sit staring at her hands, tightly knotted in her lap. Even when the nausea began to subside, she remained silent, miserable in the growing awareness of what she had done to herself . . . and to the woman across the room.

Finally Alice Walsh broke the silence. "You are obviously distressed about something, Miss Marriott. May I ask why you've come?"

Slowly Ruth dragged her eyes away from her hands to meet Alice Walsh's troubled frown. "I came . . . to you . . . because I didn't know what to do, where else to go. Patrick . . . your husband . . . warned me not to come, but I didn't feel I had a choice."

Alice Walsh's gaze never wavered, though Ruth could tell that she was badly shaken. "I'm afraid I don't understand. How is it that you happen to know my husband?"

Ruth was suddenly overcome with the conviction that the woman standing in the middle of the room was a fine and decent person, no doubt altogether ignorant of her husband's betrayal. Alice Walsh had probably never hurt anyone in her life or given anyone reason to hurt her.

This was a woman, Ruth sensed, who lived a good life in a safe, secure world where people did not betray or wound one another. And now, through no fault of her own, a total stranger was about to bring that world crashing down around her. Alice Walsh's life would never be the same again.

Ruth opened her mouth to speak, but nothing came. Dragging in a long, tremulous breath, she finally forced the words up from her throat. "Mrs. Walsh . . . I'm sorry. But I have to tell you that . . . I'm carrying your husband's child."

18

The Worst Deceit of All

A man lives alone with his mistakes.
A woman shares them.
Irish Proverb

The rain began, not gradually or gently, as hinted by the storm's slow building throughout the afternoon, but all at once, a sudden downpour bursting from the sky. A crash of thunder shook the house, rattling the windows. Lightning streaked, illuminating the sitting room for an instant with a sweeping flash of silver.

Alice stared at Ruth Marriott. In the eerie incandescence filling the room, the younger woman appeared to be trapped in a blaze of phosphor. Her gray suit took on a faint green hue, and her dark eyes smoldered like hot coals against the iridescent gleam of her skin, giving her an almost spectral appearance.

This is not real, Alice told herself. *It's not*

happening. The light faded, and once again shadows draped the room, broken only by an occasional arc of lightning at the window.

Finally Alice managed to speak, although her voice sounded thin and tremulous, like that of an old woman who has been threatened or vilified. "I think it best that you leave, Miss Marriott. Right away."

Slowly, the dark eyes never leaving Alice's face, the young woman rose to her feet. Alice did not miss the effort the movement seemed to require. In a moment of alarm, she feared that Ruth Marriott was about to drop into a dead faint.

But the younger woman stood facing her. "Mrs. Walsh —"

Alice had no intention of hearing anything further from this deluded stranger. "I can't imagine what all this is about, but you've done a very unwise thing in coming here like this, saying such a thing to me about my husband!"

She knew she was rambling, could feel herself losing control. *So foolish, getting worked up over what was obviously either a horrible mistake or some sort of cruel scheme . . .*

"Please, Mrs. Walsh, I think you should hear what I have to say. I know this is painful for you —"

"Painful?" Alice repeated incredulously.

"Hardly painful, I can assure you! It's absurd! Now, I really must insist that you leave my home." Alice had meant to sound firm and in control. Instead, a faint note of hysteria seemed to have crept into her voice, and she cringed.

Unbelievably, Ruth Marriott stood her ground, watching Alice with an expression that seemed to hold both regret and resolve.

"I'm telling you the truth, Mrs. Walsh," she insisted quietly. "Your husband . . . Patrick —" She stopped, dropping her gaze to the floor. "We've been having an affair for months. I'm going to have a baby, and Patrick is the father."

"You are *lying!*" Suddenly angry, Alice felt an irrational desire to strike the pale young woman standing so still, so solemnly, across from her. "My husband would never be unfaithful to me!"

Ruth Marriott looked at her with a strangely pitying expression. "But he *has* been unfaithful, Mrs. Walsh, though I can certainly understand why you find it difficult to believe. Patrick . . . is a most convincing liar. He lied to *me* right from the beginning. He told me that . . . his wife was dead."

Stunned, Alice reeled as if from a blow. *"How dare you?"* she choked out. *"You're* the liar! I want you out of my house this instant!"

Again the young woman regarded her with that unaccountable look of regret, as if she found Alice a pathetic figure, one to be treated with great pity.

For the first time since this strange young woman had leveled her outrageous charge against Patrick, Alice found herself doubting her husband's fidelity. A sickness rose up inside her, and an acrid taste filled her mouth.

"I could tell you things about your husband, Mrs. Walsh . . . intimate things . . . that only you would know. Please don't make me do that." Ruth Marriott spoke more quietly now, a flush spreading over her face. "For both our sakes, please don't."

Dazed as she was, Alice heard the threat and hesitated. Her mind raced. Even if Patrick had, during a lapse of judgment, trifled with the girl, it didn't necessarily mean that he had fathered her child. Obviously, she was bent on extortion.

"Why did you come here?" Alice demanded. "What do you want?"

"I want your husband to take responsibility for his behavior." The woman answered firmly, her words almost muffled by a peal of thunder. "I'm going to need help — financial help — in raising my child. *Patrick's* child. He tried to buy me off with a thousand dollars, but he's not going to get rid of me so easily. I stand to lose my job, my apartment — everything — any day now, and I'm going to need help caring for the baby."

Alice stared at her. "Patrick . . . has given you money?" she said thickly, dread twisting inside her. "You've actually confronted him with this?"

Ruth Marriott's face contorted into a mask of bitterness. "Oh, yes," she said acidly. "I confronted him. Patrick's solution is for me to either have an abortion — or marry a 'fat, balding butcher'! He refuses to take any responsibility whatsoever for the baby. I warned him that I would come to you, but he didn't believe me. He threw me out of his office."

Alice stood utterly still. A crawling sensation of cold traveled down her shoulders and along her spine. Rain drummed against the window so hard that the glass seemed likely to shatter, while lightning flared and crackled. Alice trembled as if caught in the throes of a fever. She steeled herself against the weakness, clenching her fists until pain shot all the way up her forearms.

"I don't know what you thought you could possibly gain by coming here with your lies," she said as firmly as she could manage, "but you should have spared us both. I must tell you that if you don't leave, I will have to see that you are forcibly removed."

"You know I'm telling the truth."

Again Alice would have denied the woman's accusations, but something in the quiet, even voice and unwavering gaze made her hesitate.

"Mrs. Walsh, I didn't want to do this. I didn't want to come here. You must believe that if I had known Patrick was lying, if I had known he wasn't really a widower, I would never have become involved with him." She stopped, pressing a hand to her abdomen in a thoroughly maternal gesture. "I'm not a bad woman, Mrs. Walsh. At least, I never was before I met Patrick. But he promised to *marry* me. As soon as the children were older, he said, we would be married. Please, try to understand how it happened."

Something in the appeal of those desperate words, some plea in the wounded dark eyes, pierced Alice's heart. She knew then, with an awful, wrenching certainty, that Ruth Marriott was telling the truth.

She turned her back on the younger woman and crossed the room, sinking down onto the sofa near the fireplace.

Incredibly, Alice felt no sense of outrage. Somehow she knew that the woman across from her was not the first with whom Patrick had betrayed their marriage vows, not the first to become involved in an illicit affair with him

. . . and probably not the first to be so carelessly discarded when he tired of her.

Strange, that she could summon no real anger for the way he had lied to her, humilated her. For the first time she realized that she had been *lying to herself* all along, had indeed been deceiving *herself* for years.

"Perhaps," she said, barely able to force the words out, "you should tell me . . . everything."

All the way across to the island, Patrick Walsh's insides churned in rhythm with the storm-driven waves. His head pounded with the thunder, and every furious heave of the boat brought an answering slam from his heart.

Hunched inside the rough, makeshift cabin, he watched the lightning swoop down and skate over the water. He shouldn't have started across in such a storm; even the ferry wasn't running. But he wasn't willing to risk the chance that Ruth might be foolhardy enough to go to his wife.

Not that Alice would believe her, he reassured himself. Not Alice. Not in a lifetime. She trusted him implicitly, always had. Of course, he had been discreet with his affairs over the years, never taking up with local women but instead favoring those assignations convenient to his out-of-town "business trips." He suspected that for the most part his caution had been unnecessary; Alice, he was sure, would never have thought to question his fidelity.

Alice didn't think much about anything at all, so far as he could tell. Certainly she would pay no heed to someone like Ruth Marriott. No, his wife would never be susceptible to a strange woman making wild-eyed accusations.

But it was better to be sure. He had worked too hard, had had too much incredible luck, to risk losing even the smallest part of what he had attained over the years.

One little doxy couldn't do him all that much damage, of course. The worst that might come from her foolishness would be that Jacob Braun, Alice's father, could turn on him and take back control of one of the hotels and some of the real estate. If it came to that, he had more than enough on the books in legitimate businesses to cover himself, not to mention the taverns and tenements in Five Points.

But it wasn't money that worried him. Money had never been his primary aim, but the means to attain the power that *was* his ultimate objective. He already had more money than he could ever spend in a lifetime, certainly enough to ensure future political position and its accompanying power — with the proper backing and brokerage, of course. Over the past few months he had pulled all the strings, taken all the steps that would be required to play the game of politics from a winning position.

But if old man Braun lost his temper and went against him, even managed to turn Alice against him — unlikely as that seemed — there could be a messy scandal. His political aspirations would end up dust.

Everyone knew that most of the politicians in the state — at least the successful ones — were as rotten as bad meat. No one paid much heed to their crooked schemes, so long as they came through with what their constituents demanded. But just let one of them get caught being unfaithful to his wife, and all of a sudden everyone had a conscience. A man who cheated on his wife — and got found out — made some of the big bosses squirm. And a *divorced* man was dead in the water. There were too many Irish Catholics and straitlaced Protestants to appease. The voters wouldn't make their mark for a man who had openly shamed his wife, and the politicos knew it. They would dump a known philanderer without blinking.

Clinging to the rail to keep from sliding

against the wall, Patrick reminded himself that Alice would never turn on him, much less seek a divorce. She was totally devoted to him.

Still, it was best not to take chances. He'd feel better once he got home. That way, if Ruth *did* happen to show up, he'd be there to toss her out before she could get to Alice.

Silently he cursed the little fool for complicating things. Thunder crashed, and the boat gave a violent lurch. He tightened his grip on the rail, for a moment imagining the iron bar under his hands to be Ruth Marriott's throat.

19

Confrontation

Day of the damned, descend,
And bring man's deceit to an end.
Day of dread, now reveal
What darkness would strive to conceal.
Anonymous

Utterly drenched from the storm and ridden by a growing anxiety, Patrick Walsh flung the heavy front door open so hard it banged against the wall. Inside, he shook himself like a dog to shed some of the water.

When the housemaid came rushing to see about the noise, he shouted at her. "I could do with a towel! You should have had one ready!"

The maid — Nancy — gaped, wringing her hands at her waist. Her fearful expression only irritated him more. "I'm sorry, sir," she stammered, "we weren't expecting you so early! The children aren't even home from school yet, and they're usually in long before you arrive."

He ignored her blather, ordered her to fetch a towel, then stopped her before she could obey. "Where's my wife?" he snapped, shaking the water from his hair and clothes with no regard for the polished floor under his feet.

The maid turned back, blinking furiously as if she couldn't quite take in his question. "Why . . . Mrs. Walsh is upstairs in the sitting room, sir. She has a caller."

Patrick straightened, staring at her. "A caller?" His stomach knotted. "Who?" Shrugging out of his suit coat, he removed the pistol from the shoulder holster and pocketed it in his trousers.

The woman squinted at the gun for an instant, then pulled her moon face into the exaggerated scowl of disapproval that never failed to annoy him.

"The lady — the caller — didn't give her name, sir. Invited herself in as if she was royalty, with no calling card at all. But Mrs. Walsh, she said to show her up anyway. They've been up there, in the sitting room, for well over an hour now," she added, darting a glance upstairs.

Then, as if she'd forgotten, she brought a hand to her mouth. "Oh, your towel, sir! I'll be getting it right away!"

"Never mind." Patrick stood for a moment looking up at the second floor landing. "Go to your quarters," he said shortly.

"But, sir, you'll catch your death —"

"And stay there until you're sent for!"

He waited until the maid had disappeared down the hall that led to her room behind the kitchen. Then he started up the stairs two at a time.

Alice heard the front door bang open, followed by voices — Patrick's voice scolding Nancy, and the maid's shrill return.

With dread settling over her, she got to her feet. "He's come home early."

Ruth Marriott also stood, her expression fearful. "He'll be furious! I must leave at once."

Alice shook her head. "No, it's time he faced . . . the two of us. Together."

"But he *threatened* me. He — I thought he was going to strangle me right there in his office!"

Alice had listened to the younger woman's detailed account of her plight for the better part of an hour. She had sat silently, her pulse pounding, her heart breaking, as she heard what she recognized to be a truthful rendering of her husband's betrayal. As the narrative progressed, she had moved past disbelief and anger, even beyond humiliation, to an unexpected, unexplainable kind of sympathy for the other woman's dilemma.

But at the moment she felt only impatience. "Patrick may be an . . . adulterer," she said, her tone sharp, "but he would never put a hand to a woman. I insist that you stay. There can be no thought of assistance to you until he admits the truth. To both of us."

Alice was surprised by her own calm. Had she ever once envisioned the agonizing scene of this afternoon, she might have expected that she would collapse with shock and grief, at the least give in to hysterical weeping. Instead, she felt only a gaping emptiness within, as if her very self had been stripped away, leaving nothing but a dry husk, devoid of all feeling, all emotion.

She didn't even feel anything when she looked up to find Patrick in the doorway. He stood there unmoving, his eyes darting from Ruth Marriott to Alice. "I can't believe you opened the door to this woman! Surely you realize that she's utterly mad!"

He was dripping wet, his hair slicked to his head, his face beaded with water. His shirt and trousers looked to be soaked.

Ordinarily, Alice would have run to him and begun to fuss. Now she merely stood watching him as he turned a murderous look on Ruth Marriott.

"What exactly is going on here?" he demanded. As always his tone was authoritative, imperious. But it seemed to Alice that his manner lacked some of its usual confidence.

"You haven't listened to her preposterous stories, I hope," he said, turning back to Alice. "I told you, the woman is deranged."

Alice met his gaze straight on. Her throat felt as if it were lined with gravel, her mouth dry as dust. But she surprised herself by answering him in a quiet, even tone. "How I wish that were the case, Patrick. But Miss Marriott doesn't strike me as deranged. Not in the least."

His jaw tightened. "You can disregard whatever she's told you. She's quite mad, and I can't believe you didn't see as much right away."

"Please don't do this," Alice said. She felt heavy, her arms and legs weighted and cumbersome. "Don't try to lie. You're only making it harder on all of us. There's already been entirely too much lying."

Incredibly, his look was one of reproach. "You can't be serious! For the love of heaven, Alice, this woman is a lunatic! You'd listen to the ravings of a madwoman rather than believe your own husband?"

Alice looked at him. A dark, bitter sorrow rose up in her as she recognized what a consummate actor Patrick had always been. Even now, when he had been found out, when he stood in the very presence of the two women he had betrayed — even now, he was frighteningly convincing. She could almost believe his indignation, his outrage, could almost accept his protests of innocence.

Almost . . .

Before she could weaken, she deliberately allowed fragments of Ruth Marriott's accusations to surface. The woman obviously knew Patrick well. Intimately.

Disgust renewed itself, and for a moment she turned away from both of them. Ruth Marriott had spoken of things meant to be private, hidden between husband and wife, secrets never intended to be shared outside the sanctity of marriage. Alice shuddered, forcing down a wave of nausea.

She turned around to find Patrick glaring at Ruth Marriott with an expression of undisguised malice, his features contorted to an ugly mask. The other woman apparently failed to recognize the intensity of his anger, for she seemed bent on pressing him to some sort of agreement.

"At least your wife understands my predicament," she was saying. "You might just as well stop trying to deny it, Patrick! She knows, and she's willing to help me."

Alice saw the last of his control shatter, inverting to a dark, pulsing rage. He raised a hand as if to strike Ruth Marriott, who shrank away from him with a look of pure horror.

"You little slut!" he roared, looming over her. "I warned you! I told you not to come here!"

Ruth stumbled back from him, but he caught her wrists and held her with one hand while grasping her throat with the other.

Alice rushed at him. *"Patrick! No!"*

He seemed deaf to her scream, gave no sign that he even knew she was in the room. At last he released Ruth's throat, gripped her by the shoulders, and shoved her to the open doorway.

The woman's terror was unmistakable, yet she seemed determined to stand her ground. "You can't do this! Your wife believes me. She knows I'm telling the truth!"

Patrick shot a look at Alice over his shoulder as if to say he would deal with her later. She cringed at the fury burning out of his eyes.

He swung back to Ruth Marriott. "You've gone too far, you little fool! I warned you!"

Alice watched in disbelief as he began shaking Ruth like a worthless doll. She tried to wrest free of him, but he yanked her around, forcing her out the door and into the hall.

Alice ran after them. At the landing, Patrick was pushing Ruth Marriott backward toward the staircase. With one hand locked about her throat he held her captive, while with the other hand he leveled a gun at her head.

The terrified woman was trying to free herself, flailing her arms, pounding him with her fists as she gasped for breath. But Patrick seemed possessed. Livid in his fury, he bent over her, and Alice suddenly realized what he intended.

She clutched the banister and screamed at him, *"Dear Lord — Patrick, no! You can't!"*

If he heard her choked cry, he ignored it.

Ruth Marriott's eyes, filled with horror, locked on Patrick's. Her skin had faded to a deathly gray, and all at once her body seemed to fold. Her knees buckled, and she went limp.

Alice forgot her own fear, her trembling legs, her heart which threatened to explode at any instant. Pushing away from the banister, she charged at Patrick.

But she was too late. Even as she reached him, he shoved Ruth Marriott hard. The woman tumbled backward, crashing down one step after another until she hit the bottom and lay like a broken doll, sprawled and silent.

Crying out, Alice started down the steps after her. But Patrick caught her arm in a vise-like grip, yanking her back and holding her fast with his left hand.

Then with his right hand, he raised the pistol and aimed it at the woman at the bottom of the steps.

"Oh, dear God no, Patrick! *No!*"

"Shut up! Stay out of this!"

His grip on her arm tightened. "I intend to make sure she can't cause any more trouble!"

"You can't do this! I won't let you!"

Alice seized his right arm, clinging to him, trying to force him to lower the gun.

Patrick turned on her, his face distorted. His eyes were savage, the eyes of a wild animal out of control. Alice knew in a white-hot instant of clarity that something had been unleashed in him, something that had always been there, lurking just below the surface. Something cruel and corrupt . . . and utterly evil.

Suddenly she saw the truth — he would murder her if she persisted. She mattered little more to him than Ruth Marriott — if indeed she had ever mattered at all.

The realization hit her like a blow, and she faltered. As if in slow motion, Alice's senses took in everything at once . . . the still form of Ruth Marriott, surely dead, at the bottom of the stairway . . . the maid, Nancy, appearing in the hallway below, shrieking hysterically . . . Patrick pushing at her, trying to throw her off him . . . her own weakness, the awful sickness welling up in her. . . .

Pure instinct made her grapple for the gun. She pulled at his arm with all her strength and felt cold steel under her fingers. Patrick roared in fury and gave one last violent shove. The gun exploded.

He uttered a hoarse cry of surprise, and the pistol clattered to the floor.

Patrick looked at her, his eyes wide with shock. *"Alice?"* he gasped.

Then he doubled over, sinking to his knees, clutching his chest. With a shudder, he collapsed.

Alice stared at him. Somewhere she heard someone screaming, and as darkness closed around her, she realized the tortured cries were her own.

Part Two

THE PROMISE FULFILLED

Hope for the Helpless

Be sure of this: The wicked will not go
unpunished,
but those who are righteous will go free.
PROVERBS 11:21

20

Dark Corner
of the Mind

Why do those eyes lie open in sleep,
What's hid in the black of his mind?
F. R. HIGGINS (1896–1941)

Dublin, Ireland
August

Rook Mooney turned over, still wide awake, though it was long after midnight. The mattress on the sagging bed was nothing but straw, thin and ridged.

Like sleeping on a washboard.

The bed went with the rest of the room — a cramped, dingy pesthole with one window and a broken-down washstand as the only furnishing besides the bed. The place was little more than a pantry, hot and filthy, but it was all he could afford; he had left most of his money in the gambling pits in Lisbon.

Sprawled on his back, he stared up at the

ceiling, its mottled layers revealed by the faint wedge of moonlight filtering through the grime-encrusted window. After a moment he raised himself up on one elbow to swill from the bottle of whiskey he had brought to bed with him.

This would be his last night in this hellhole, and good riddance. Tomorrow he would go back to the big house on the hill.

Nelson Hall, it was called. As if a house merited a name. As if it was gentry like those who lived inside.

Curse them all! They'd not be so uppity when he was done.

He had stayed two days up there the first time, holed up like a rat. It hadn't stopped raining the whole time. Finally, hungry and cold, he had given it over and come back to the city.

But he had seen her. Seen her at the window upstairs, peering out. Looking straight at the coach house, as if she knew he was there, waiting for her.

Maybe she *did* know. Maybe she felt his closeness, smelled his rage. Knew he was coming after her.

He hoped so. He wanted her afraid. Scared out of her wits. Just like before.

He remembered how she had tried to scream, the choking sound that had come out instead.

He scowled and took another swig of whiskey. Just the sight of him had scared her plenty.

Well, she'd be scared this time too. More than before, and not just because of his face. One look at the knife would set her off good. He'd teach her.

He'd have to be careful of that big black, though.

The cripple in the wheelchair would be no problem. No more trouble than a flea on a dog. But that black devil was something else. Maybe he ought to get rid of him first thing.

And those Gypsy dogs on the other side of the stream. They could be trouble, too.

He caught the sweat on his face with his sleeve and took another drink. What kind of people were they anyhow, letting those filthy Gypsies squat on their land?

Even his Aunt Fee wouldn't have taken up with a Gypsy. The old witch had hauled just about everything else into her bed, but never a Gypsy.

He twisted his face at the memory of his aunt, one finger going to the split lip she had given him. If the old hag hadn't gone after him with a knife, he would have had himself a decent job. The women wouldn't get wild-eyed at the sight of him. He wouldn't have to pay to get them to be nice to him, or else beat it out of them. . . .

His mind went back to his plans. The black, that was the one he'd have to be careful of. Him and the dog.

Cussed wolfhound. Devil's own, that's what they were. More wolf than dog, and that was the truth. And this was a big one. The biggest he'd ever seen.

He glanced at the half-empty bottle in his hand, then tipped it again. No use saving it. He had another to take with him.

He ought to get some sleep. Needed to be fit tomorrow.

But he couldn't stop thinking about her. It had been almost two weeks since he had hidden in the coach house the first time, since he'd seen her at the window. Long enough to stoke his rage and his need.

Soon. It oughtn't to take long, but this time he was going prepared to stay as long as need be. He had spent the last of his coins on some bread and cheese — and a spare bottle.

He had everything he needed to wait it out.

Until he got what he came for.

He reached underneath the bed, drew out the knife, and ran his thumb along the sharp steel of the blade. This time, she wouldn't get off so easy.

21

In the Vale of Love

*Your love creates for me
a haven, a holy place,
where we abide.*
MORGAN FITZGERALD (1850)

Glendalough, Ireland

Morgan Fitzgerald no longer remembered when the idea of a brief retreat for himself and Finola had first occurred to him. He only knew he would always be grateful for these past three days.

Basking in utter contentment, he sat in his wheelchair in a clearing near the round tower, watching a Wicklow sunset. Finola, lounging on the grass beside him, leaned against the chair.

He felt inordinately pleased to have been the one to introduce her to the Vale of Glendalough — the Valley of Two Lakes. The isolated mountain setting, so rich in natural beauty and ancient history, had long been special to him. One of the loveliest spots in Ireland, Glendalough was a place where the past, with all its romance and legend, seemed to reign untouched, unmarred by the Island's troubles and tragedy. Even the famine's devastation could almost be forgotten amid the serenity and beauty of this secluded valley.

He had always found a kind of healing here, as though the site itself held restorative powers. Perhaps the ruins of the Seven Churches, those antiquities scattered throughout the valley, were responsible for giving the area a sense of time forgotten. Possibly the mystique of the place centered about Saint Kevin, the sixth-century Celtic mystic who had lived a hermit existence here. Certainly, those legends played a part in the mood of reverence and sanctuary that seemed to engulf the entire locale.

Or perhaps it was simply the valley's remoteness, its solitude, which Morgan found renewing. Whatever it was, there was nowhere he would rather be at this moment — and no one he would rather share it with than Finola.

If she had ever been here before, she had no memory of it. And because it was all new for her, Morgan almost felt as if he were seeing it for the first time as well, through her eyes.

He sighed a great sigh, and felt her hand tighten on his.

"Are you tiring, Morgan?"

He turned to look at her. With her hair tied back in a blue ribbon and a faint blush of color on her face from their hours in the sun, she looked wonderfully young and healthy.

And happy?

"I have never felt better in my life, *macushla,* and that is the truth."

She smiled and again pressed his hand. "This was a fine idea you had for us. I will always be glad we came."

"Truly? I had hoped it would be special for you."

"Oh, it has been, Morgan. I can't tell you how special! Why, if I weren't eager to get back to our Gabriel and Aine, it would make me sad to think of leaving."

He nodded, sharing her feelings. Despite missing the children, this trip had been a kind of gift. As brief as it had been, it was in fact their wedding journey at last — their first time to go away by themselves.

Sad to say, he had never had the opportunity to court his wife, never played the suitor, never wooed her. He had been her friend and her husband, her companion, and her lover.

But he had never been Romeo to his Juliet, never really pursued her or romanced her.

Circumstances had forced them to forgo the traditional courtship. Because they had moved — leaped, actually — from friendship to marriage, Finola had missed much that other young women took for granted.

Even now, as husband and wife, they found precious little time to be alone. They lived in a large household, and a busy one. Because of his own physical limitations, Morgan needed to have Sandemon nearby most of the time. As for Finola, wee Gabriel shadowed her everywhere. Precious few were the moments she had alone, except for those times when the wee one slept or when she managed to slip away to her prayer closet.

Even Annie tagged after her relentlessly, for Finola seemed to have become to the lass a combination of mother, older sister, and best friend.

Predictably, Finola insisted that she did not mind. "Aine is the sister of my heart, don't you see, Morgan?" she would say. "I delight in her."

In addition to the immediate family, there were also the scholars drifting in and out of the halls of the academic wing. And Sister Louisa, of course; the incredible nun seemed to be everywhere at once, virtually materializing without warning.

Morgan did not mind for himself. He savored the feeling of family after so many years of the solitary life. To be head of his own household, to be the husband of Finola, to spend his days in the warmth of her love, to fall asleep with her safe in his arms — what more could he ask?

But he did hope to make up for at least a part of what *she* had missed, especially now that he knew the tragedy of her girlhood. He was determined to give her some of the beauty and carefree moments — and, yes, the romance — she had not known.

So he had persuaded her to come away with him, just the two of them. Alone. He had pushed aside his insecurities about traveling without Sandemon, leaving him in charge of Nelson Hall and its inhabitants. Strict orders were given to Annie and to everyone else — including Tierney Burke and his Gypsy cohort — that whoever displeased Sandemon would be in serious trouble when Morgan returned.

With only a coach and a driver, they had set off for a small, remote inn in the valley of Glendalough. For three glorious days, they had soaked up sunshine and mountain breezes, visited the antiquities of the area, talked, laughed, and even dreamed a little.

It was the best time of their marriage, and especially significant now, in these days when the memories of Finola's past seemed to be virtually bursting upon them in a great, final rush of clarity.

Now that most of it was out in the open, now that he had seen the strength with which she had confronted the terrors lurking at the edge of her consciousness, he had finally come to believe that she would be all right. She would not only endure: she would overcome.

There had been a number of bad times since that first night when the memories had begun to emerge, times when he could do nothing but hold her and allow her to weep, shuddering against him like an inconsolable child. Later, there had been anger — a fierce, heated anger. Acting on instinct, he had encouraged her to give it rein, had even allowed her to see his own anger, his outrage.

There had also been times of silence. At these moments he could sense she was remembering something more, experiencing it again in her thoughts, in her feelings, and sometimes, later, in her dreams.

But in the midst of it all, he remained hopeful. For at last she had opened her heart to him — her heart and her very soul — drawing him in, letting him share her terror, her pain, her anger, even her nightmares.

He had suffered with her, and in the suffering they had become closer than they had ever been before.

Except in the marriage bed . . .

He had not attempted to make love to her since the night of her birthday, the night Jan Martova had given her the simple tin whistle that had triggered the return of her memories. He sensed that she was resistant to, perhaps even incapable of physical intimacy just yet.

Not for anything would he risk a setback in her healing process. Somehow he managed to conceal his disappointment and hurt when she flinched at his embrace or merely endured his chaste good-night kisses.

Time, he again reminded himself. Only time would help to restore her passion, only time would free her from the tyranny, the terrors of her past, and allow her to be at ease in his arms again. Until then, he would treasure the emotional intimacy they enjoyed, if not the physical.

"Morgan? What are you thinking about?"

Her soft voice and the tug on his hand brought him back to his surroundings. With his knuckles, he lightly traced the smooth line of her cheek. "I am thinking," he said, smiling at her, "how very proud I am of you."

She tilted her head up still more to study him. "*Proud* of me? Why would you say such a thing?"

Gazing at her for a moment, he felt his heart swell with love. "For many reasons, *macushla*. But especially because you are so brave. Brave enough to face your fears and strong enough to overcome them. You have survived more horror than most of us can even imagine, yet you have not let that horror defeat you or embitter you. You are a beautiful, strong-hearted woman, and, yes, I am quite proud of you."

Her eyes filled. "I am not brave, Morgan, though you are kind to say so. The truth is, if I have been able to 'face my fears,' as you believe, it is only because we have faced them together. You are my strength," she said softly, looking away. "You and our Lord . . . you are my strength."

After a moment she turned back to him, her expression grave. "I think there is something you have not shared with *me*, however, and I cannot help but wonder why."

Now his smile turned questioning. "What are you talking about? I keep nothing from you, *macushla*."

Her eyes searched his. "Then tell me about the doctor in America," she said softly.

Anger at James Dunne blazed up in him.

"You weren't supposed to know about that yet —"

The words fell between them, ringing with significance. Hadn't he only seconds ago claimed to keep nothing from her?

For a moment Morgan couldn't think what to say. Obviously, she expected an explanation, and she had every right to one.

"It was wrong of James to tell you," he said shortly.

She studied him. "I think it was wrong of *you* not to tell me, but we will not argue that now. It was an innocent blunder on his part; he meant only to encourage me.

"He was telling me how pleased he was with my progress in recovering from the amnesia," she went on to explain. "In the course of the conversation, he let it slip that perhaps now he could convince you to see the American surgeon."

Slightly mollified, but still chagrined to think he had added yet another burden to that which she already bore, Morgan said nothing for a moment.

She moved, just enough to face him more easily, then reached to enfold his hand between both of hers. "Dr. Dunne felt wretched that he had broken your confidence, Morgan, truly he did. I didn't press him for more, because he clearly thought you should tell me yourself." She paused. "I've been waiting for you to do so ever since."

The last crescent of the sun was slipping down behind the mountain. Soon the sky's gold and crimson ribbons would darken. Already the air had turned cooler. Morgan lifted his free hand to stroke her hair, then her cheek. Her eyes were almost violet in the sunset, her features expectant — and noticeably apprehensive.

He knew he could no longer put off telling her, but dear heaven, how he wished he could. They needed more time. Time to ensure her own healing, time for him to consider the decision that daily weighed on him like a monolith.

But if James Dunne were right, time was the very thing he could not count on. It might indeed be slipping away from him even now, like the sun sliding down behind the mountain in the west.

The chill that suddenly gripped him had little to do with the night air. He looked at Finola. When he bent to brush a kiss over the top of her head, she surprised him by lifting her face to meet his lips.

The intensity of the kiss left him shaken. She framed his face with her hands, her gaze never wavering. "Let's go inside," she said quietly. "I want . . . to be close with you.

We can watch the sun go down from our room."

Then she kissed him again, gently. "Later you can tell me about the doctor in America. We will face your fears together, Morgan, you and I."

22

Preparations for the Journey

What that fate may be hereafter
Is to us a thing unknown. . . .
"A Southern" from Samuel B. Oldham
collection (1848)

By the day after their return from Glenda-lough, Morgan had begun to cast an occasional longing thought back to the peace and quiet they had left behind. Almost from the moment of their arrival, they had been besieged by family and staff with three days of tales to tell, grievances to air, and problems to solve.

Annie was put out because Tierney Burke and Jan Martova would be leaving tomorrow morning on a journey across Ireland, just the two of them. Wee Gabriel had turned into a veritable firestorm of energy and chatter, scurrying after Finola if she so much as crossed from one corner of the room to the other. On the adult level, Sandemon had found one of the root cellars flooded and suspected mice in the west wing, while Sister Louisa seemed to have been counting the hours until she could advise Morgan of the heathen O'Higgins twins' latest mischief — something to do with beetle husks in the cook's flour barrel.

By late afternoon, Morgan's head was swimming, and he wheeled himself outside in search of some peace and quiet. He had scarcely reached the west lawn when Annie, tight-lipped and fiery-eyed, came charging up like a young war-horse and planted herself in front of him, arms locked across her chest.

So much for peace and quiet.

"They think themselves such *men!*"

Morgan sighed. It was a perfect summer's day, resplendent with sunshine and vibrant with the lush, late-blooming flowers and greenery of the season. He wanted nothing more than to sit quietly and bask in the lazy peace of the afternoon.

Instead, he squeezed out a smile, bracing himself for the expected stream of complaints. "You refer to Tierney Burke and Jan Martova, no doubt?"

"Indeed. One would think the fate of all Ireland were hinged upon the door of a Gypsy wagon!"

Now Morgan found himself wanting to smile in earnest, but he suppressed the urge when her frown darkened. " 'Tis only natural they would be excited about the journey," he said reasonably. "Surely you can understand."

"I am that tired of hearing about their *tour of Ireland!* They can speak of nothing else."

She stopped, as if expecting a response from him. When there was none, she went on. "The entire household grows weary of their endless blather. I for one will be glad when they are finally on their way tomorrow!"

Morgan recognized her frustration for what it was. Only this morning Finola had alluded to the girl's resentment. " 'Tis disappointment, don't you see? Aine had hoped we would all take such a journey, as we discussed. Because we can't, she thinks the boys should have waited."

Morgan understood the girl's disappointment. He had felt no small measure of regret himself, although he chose not to voice it. He had looked forward to taking the family on an excursion across the country — in truth, he had wanted to be the one to acquaint Michael's son with Ireland. But circumstances had intervened to make it impractical, if not impossible.

Gabriel's arrival, for one thing. Still, the

tyke was old enough now, and given his genial disposition, he would present no real problem on a journey. But there had also been Finola to consider; she had not been strong to begin with, and the boy's birth and her emotional struggles had weakened her still more.

More to the point was the possibility of another, even more extensive journey: the anticipated voyage to the United States. Annie knew nothing of the trip, of course — nor did anyone else except Sandemon. Morgan and Finola had only just come to the decision themselves, on their last day at Glendalough. But once the lass knew, he felt certain her disappointment would be appeased.

For now, however, he supposed the best he could do was to allow her to vent her frustration.

To his surprise, however, his daughter's stormy expression turned contemplative. "Sometimes, *Seanchai,* I wish I had been born a boy."

Never knowing what to expect from this mercurial child, Morgan remained silent, regarding her with a certain caution, still poised for another volley of resentment.

Instead, she gave a somewhat dramatic sigh and shook her head. "I expect that I shall never have an adventure of my own."

With that she turned and started up the

pathway toward the house. The thin shoulders seemed to slump as he watched. Even the dark braids appeared to hang more heavily than usual, rather than swinging from side to side as they usually did when she flounced off.

He called after her, but she went on, and Morgan decided to let her go. He could not fathom these flashes of mood the girl exhibited, and when he spoke of it to Finola or Sister, he received nothing more than a look that said of course he did not understand — how could he?

The *Seanchai* did not understand, Annie knew. He cared about her feelings, of course. But he did not understand.

How could he, he being a man?

Upstairs in her bedroom she stood peering out the window, watching the two boys hoist yet more boxes into the back of the wagon. Under her breath, she repeated the same statement she had made to the *Seanchai* only moments before. At times she *did* wish she had been born a boy!

Only boys, it seemed, could have *true adventures,* while girls, on the other hand, were left to keep the fire and tend to the babes. Boys could simply go off on a trek across the entire countryside, had they a mind to do so, but girls must dress like uncomfortable ninnies and sit at home, pricking their fingers with the endless darning or boring themselves witless as they learned to *manage the home.*

It wasn't a bit fair. Tomorrow Tierney Burke and Jan Martova would rise before dawn, turn their selfish backs on Nelson Hall, and depart upon their journey.

They might have waited until the *Seanchai* and the other family members could be included in their expedition. But no. They would go *now,* or be bound.

And didn't they presume to justify their behavior with pointless statements such as, "We must set out before the weather turns," or, "We shall *all* go later, of course, when the *Seanchai* can get away. This is just a short jaunt to have a look at the island."

Annie was quite sure neither cared a stitch about whether the *Seanchai* and the rest of them ever managed such a journey. They were selfish boys entirely, taking on airs, pretending to be worldly men of consequence.

She would ignore them from now on.

Perhaps she wouldn't even say goodbye when they departed in the morning. Certainly she would not stoop to tagging along this evening, although they had invited her. They would be taking the *Seanchai* and Sandemon for a brief turn in the wagon before dinner —

"to give it a try before setting out in the morning."

Well, she guessed she had made it clear enough that she wasn't at all interested in having a ride in their bumpy old wagon. Besides, Tierney Burke had spoiled the gesture by making it clear that it had been Jan Martova's idea, not his, for her to come along.

Jan was nice enough, Annie had to admit, and she would miss him. For a Gypsy, he was extraordinarily well-mannered: quiet-spoken, always polite and sensitive to others. He treated her with the utmost respect — not as if she were a mindless child. His dark eyes held nothing but kindness and a sort of awkward uncertainty she found rather sweet, though why he should feel awkward she could not fathom.

Tierney Burke, on the other hand, when he condescended to pay her any attention at all, either teased her unmercifully or else relegated her to the role of a bothersome child. It seemed to Annie that *he* was the childish one, with his boorish teasing and thoughtless remarks.

Annie sighed, aware that she was feeling unduly irritable. The truth was that she would miss *both* of them, annoying as they often were. Things would not be the same without them. Although to some extent they kept themselves removed from the rest of the household, the days would not seem complete when they were gone.

She carefully kept such feelings to herself, as well as the notion that of the two, she would miss Tierney Burke most. Why that should be, she could not say. She only knew that she would prefer his exasperating joke-playing and taunts to his absence . . . and she found the knowledge unsettling.

She turned away from the window, unwilling to watch them any longer. More restless now than ever, she considered going in search of company, then remembered there was no one to seek out.

Gabriel and Finola were napping. She thought of Sister Louisa, but the nun and Lucy Hoy had set out for the city earlier in the afternoon, intending to visit the homeless on the docks. More than likely they wouldn't be back much before dusk, since they'd insisted on walking.

Sister seemed to have some sort of fixation about matters such as walking and eating healthy food: *keeping fit,* she called it. It was Annie's observation that nuns tended to be somewhat obsessed about matters such as healthiness and holiness.

Even Fergus the wolfhound was unavailable. He had whined like a pup to accompany

Sister and Lucy, and they had given in and allowed him to go along.

There was Small One, but Finola's cat wasn't at all friendly. She was a lazy creature, wanting to do nothing more taxing than sleep in the sun or groom her coat with halfhearted licks.

With a long sigh, Annie plopped down in the middle of the bed. She might just as well have a rest. Perhaps later she would go and visit the stables.

At least the horses seemed to enjoy her company.

Not long after Annie went into the house, Morgan followed. He could do with something to eat. Tea had been early, and now he regretted it; they would not dine until later tonight, after the wagon ride with the lads.

In the kitchen, Mrs. Ryan, busy with the preliminaries for the evening meal, made it clear that his foraging expedition was unwelcome. Morgan ignored her glare just long enough to spoon a ladle of savory broth over a wedge of bread, immediately wheeling himself into the pantry to enjoy it in private.

A few minutes later he left for the library, where he sat at his desk for a long time, considering the two letters that lay open in front of him.

James Dunne had persisted in making inquiries of American surgeons. His queries had resulted in correspondence from two physicians, one in Philadelphia, the other in New York.

Morgan had read both letters numerous times before the trip to Glendalough, but it was the response from the New York surgeon, Jakob Gunther, that interested him most — though it was anything but encouraging. According to James Dunne, this Dr. Gunther had trained under some of the finest physicians in Vienna before emigrating to the United States. Apparently he was doing a great deal of "experimental" surgery with some success.

It was the *experimental* aspects of the man's work that concerned Morgan. He was not inclined to present himself as a laboratory rat for some eccentric surgeon's experiments. And Gunther sounded more than a little eccentric, not to mention insufferably arrogant.

Yet there was something in the barely legible scrawl — a kind of confidence that seemed to burn from the words themselves — that drew him in spite of his reservations.

With a long breath, he put on his eyeglasses and began to read the last part of the letter again. . . .

. . . As I wrote to your Dr. Dunne, I could not speculate on the possibilities of a surgical procedure for you without a thorough examination. Even then, should I be willing to discuss surgery, you must understand that my methods are quite new, considered highly experimental, and not without significant risk. While I am admittedly a surgeon non pareil, *I can make you no guarantees, no promises.*

Morgan smiled grimly. With such persuasion, he scarcely could restrain his eagerness to proceed.

Gunther *did* condescend to grant him an examination, after which he would render a decision about the advisability of surgery.

. . . I must tell you that, based on Dr. Dunne's information, I believe time to be your enemy. There may already be extensive nerve damage, and if the bullet should reposition itself, paralysis might also extend to your upper extremities. That you submit to an evaluation as soon as possible is imperative, but you should hold no unrealistic expectations.

Leaning forward, Morgan passed his hand over the letter several times to smooth it, while resting his head in his other hand to ease the dull ache that had only now begun. He had not shown the letter to Finola, unwilling to inflict the full impact of Gunther's discouraging tone upon her. But neither had he tried to minimize the risk.

Ever since he had first made her aware of the correspondence, she had insisted that the decision should be his. Yet, despite the unmistakable glint of fear in her eyes when they discussed the subject, he had known from the beginning she thought he ought to at least explore the possibilities.

He would not — could not — make such a decision alone. The consequences were too important to both of them. But she had steadfastly refused to try to influence him in any manner, insisting only that she would support him in whatever he chose to do.

"It is between you and our Lord, Morgan," she had told him repeatedly. "I will understand, whatever you decide. But one thing — if you go to America, I shall go with you."

There had been a note of resolve in her voice, a surprising firmness when she ignored his every attempt to dissuade her. "No, you will not do this alone. We shall go together, as a family. You and I . . . and the children. We shall take Gabriel and Aine with us. You should have your family with you at such a time."

The truth was, of course, that he desperately *wanted* her with him. And so, after much discussion and agonizing and prayer, the decision had finally been made. He would at least subject himself to an examination by Jakob Gunther. He would go to America, and Finola would have her way — she would go with him, as would Annie and Gabriel.

Such a journey for all of them would mean a great deal of planning and organization before he could leave with an easy mind. His absence from the estate and the school for so long a time — not to mention arrangements for passage and lodging once they arrived in the States — would require much preparation. He had already taken the first steps — writing to Gunther, and then penning a request to Michael for help in locating lodging for an indefinite time.

In addition, he intended to have the edited manuscript for Father Joseph's diary completed and in hand when he arrived in America. Even if nothing else were accomplished by this journey, he was determined to arrange publication of the priest's record of the famine. This might be his best, perhaps his only, opportunity to get the truth about Ireland's tragedy across the sea.

He felt a sudden urgency to discuss it all with Finola, and he hurriedly wheeled himself out of the library. The house was uncommonly quiet as he started down the hall. Annie would be in her room, brooding, no doubt, and apparently Sister Louisa and Lucy Hoy had not yet returned from the city. As for Sandemon, he had gone across the stream earlier to help the lads with a final check of provisions for the journey.

He went on down the hall, fairly certain he knew where he would find Finola. At this time of day one of her favorite places was the sunroom that opened onto the west garden.

He stopped just inside the door. His wife and wee Gabriel were curled up together on the divan, asleep. Struck by the sight, he sat watching them, smiling at the picture they made. Finola lay with both arms wrapped securely about the tyke. The sun fell like a blessing over both golden heads, and Morgan could almost feel the warm silk of their hair between his fingers. Resisting the urge to approach and touch them, he instead left the room, closing the door quietly behind him.

There would be time enough later to talk. In fact, he thought that tonight at dinner might be an auspicious time to announce the journey. Perhaps the anticipation of such an event would dispel Annie's gloom. The lass had been mourning her lack of adventure. A crossing to America should go far in restoring her enthusiasm for life.

How he wished it might do the same for him. He was, certainly, eager to see Nora and Michael again, and equally enthusiastic about the possibility of getting Joseph's journal published. But the prospect of the American journey engendered any number of conflicting emotions in him. And at the moment, apprehension outweighed them all.

23

Dark Forces

Like shadows in the corners of the night,
elusive, deceptive,
whispering threats we cannot hear
of things the spirit cannot bear,
are dark forces who battle secretly
with the light.
MORGAN FITZGERALD (1850)

Annie jolted awake, startled by the awareness of someone or something on the bed with her, prodding her arm.

Her eyes snapped open to see a small, rosy-cheeked face pressed almost nose to nose with her.

"Gabriel?" Still groggy, she took a moment more to gain her wits. "What are you doing in here? I thought you were downstairs —"

She sat bolt upright, pulling him onto her lap. "Where is Finola?" she asked him. "Where is your mama?"

His smile only brightened as he twisted to look over his shoulder. "Down!"

He chuckled as if he had made a grand announcement.

Annie clasped both his chubby hands in hers. "Downstairs? Your mama is still asleep downstairs?"

He grinned at her. "Down!"

"Gabriel," she demanded, "did you climb the steps alone?"

He beamed, and Annie knew he had done exactly that. A rush of fear swept through her at the thought of her baby brother on the steep main stairway by himself.

She pulled him close to her, as much to reassure herself as to keep him from tumbling off the bed.

"You are such a monkey," she scolded, with no real exasperation. "You know you're not supposed to be on the stairs without someone watching after you."

He was a climber, their Gabriel. Ever since he had begun to walk, he'd been able to reach all sorts of places a babe was not meant to go. He could haul himself up onto any of the adults' beds, could reach the biscuit tin in the pantry — had even been caught trying to climb the bookshelves in the *Seanchai*'s library!

"Aye, you are a monkey," she said again,

still hugging him against her.

He squirmed, then reached up to pull at her braid. "Play," he demanded. "An-ye play."

Annie considered the invitation. "Let's go and see the horses," she suggested. "Perhaps the *Seanchai* and Sand-Man will return while we're outside."

He regarded her with a sober stare. "Orsies?"

"Horses," she corrected, smiling at him. He was ever so bright for such a wee boy. He had walked long before he was a year old, and he knew a number of words already.

He gave her hair another tug. Annie felt pleased and proud to be one of her little brother's favorites. The *Seanchai* and Finola often remarked about Gabriel's affection for his "An-ye."

Giving him another squeeze, she set him to the floor to wait while she put on her shoes.

"We must be careful not to wake your mama," she told him, taking his hand and starting for the door. "We'll go down the kitchen stairs."

Feeling more cheerful than she had most of the day, she led him quietly along the hall, to the back stairway.

"Down," said Gabriel, trundling along beside her.

"Aye, down," Annie agreed. "But this time you will hold on to my hand."

Rook Mooney could scarcely contain his excitement.

When he saw the cripple go off in the wagon with the black man and the two Gypsies, he knew the time he'd been waiting for had finally come.

With the four of them gone, it should be easy. The wolfhound was also off somewhere, had set out with the nun and another woman earlier in the afternoon. There would never be a better time than tonight.

He scrambled to his knees and looked out the window of the loft. His eyes swept the surroundings from the small abandoned barn stable to his left, across the path leading to the west side of the Big House.

Then, crouching, he went to the window on his right, where he could look out and see the field across the stream.

They were gone right enough. Only one wagon remained. The black mare usually tethered nearby was nowhere in sight. There was not a sign of anyone about.

He looked up at the sky. The sun would be going down soon. But not soon enough to suit him. He would have to wait until it was completely dark to make his move.

Halfway down the ladder he looked over his shoulder and froze. From the sliding wooden windows above the great door, he saw the dark-haired girl, the lanky one with the braids, coming down the path from the back of the house. She had a tyke in hand, a boy with golden hair.

Mooney thought for a moment that the two were coming to the coach house, but instead they passed on by. He could hear them going round the side of the building, the little one babbling to the girl.

He took the last few rungs of the ladder quickly, hurrying to the back of the building. Cracking the door, he watched them cross the field to the stone stables and go inside.

He hadn't known there was a wee wane. He was little more than a babe. Did he belong to her, to the Innocent? Sure, with that cap of fair hair, he just might.

As he had before, he wondered about the girl with the braids. Not that he fancied the likes of her. He wanted a real woman, not a scrawny schoolgirl. Of course, if he happened to manage the time for both, why not?

After a moment he went back to the ladder, climbing just high enough that he could look out the windows above the door. Bracing himself halfway up, he studied the back of the Big House, particularly the second story amid the battlements. His eyes locked on the tall window — her bedchamber, he'd warrant.

Was she up there now? Waiting for him?

Heat blazed up in him, heat fueled more by fury than by need. Did she sense his presence, his rage? Was she cowering in the corner, filled with dread at what was to come?

He willed her to appear at the window, and when she didn't, he tried to picture her face, the fear that would overcome her when she saw him again. He imagined her trying to scream in that peculiar whisper of a voice, as she had before.

His mouth went dry, and he licked the jagged split at the corner of his lip. It had to be tonight. There might never be a chance like this again . . .

Finola awakened slowly. At first she couldn't think where she was. When she finally focused her eyes on the glass wall of the sunroom, she realized the day's light was almost gone.

She had slept much longer than she intended. Now she felt like a sluggard, slow and heavy.

Suddenly she remembered Gabriel. He was nowhere in sight.

She leaped to her feet, stumbling in her haste. "Gabriel?"

He loved to hide, her wee son. He delighted in tucking himself in a remote corner — and there were endless such places in Nelson Hall — until someone came to find him. Then he would chortle and stretch out his arms to be picked up.

"Gabriel, where are you? Come to Mama at once."

Quickly, she checked behind the divan, then the chair.

No Gabriel. Not a sign of him.

How could she have been so irresponsible as to fall asleep and leave him to himself? Her pulse raced as she went to the door that opened onto the garden and stepped out. "Gabriel — you must not hide from Mama! You are being very naughty."

No answer.

Panic began to crowd in on her — unreasonable fear, she told herself. The babe was either hiding or playing somewhere close-by, that was all. She would find him burrowed behind one of the shrubs, laughing at her.

While he was standing there on the ladder, plotting his alternatives, Mooney caught a glimpse of movement off to the right of the house. He squinted, straining to see.

For a moment he thought someone was moving about in the garden, and he caught his breath, waiting. But all was still, and after a time he turned his attention back to the house.

Where was she?

Impatience jabbed at him, and he decided he had wasted enough time. He could not stay out here forever. He would do whatever he must to end the waiting.

And he would do it tonight.

Finola's hasty search of the garden proved futile. Her heart sped out of control as she hurried back inside, trying to think where to look next.

Aine . . .

Of course! The girl must have come and taken her little brother off to play.

Or had he awakened and gone to look for *her?*

The idea of her tiny son wandering off on his own brought a stab of real terror to her heart. It was such a big house . . . the grounds so vast . . . there were so many things dangerous to a baby like Gabriel, so many ways he could harm himself. . . .

She ran down the hall to the stairway and, gathering her skirts, took the steps two at a time, calling their names as she went.

By the time she reached Aine's room, she was out of breath. But when she found the girl's bedchamber empty, she raced on down the hall to the nursery. Surely she would find them there.

The nursery was silent.

She stood in the middle of the room, staring. *She had to find her son!*

She must stay calm.

She would go for Morgan . . . he would know what to do. . . .

Then she remembered. Both Morgan and Sandemon had planned to go for a ride in the new wagon before dinner. More than likely they were already gone.

Turning, she retraced her steps, calling Morgan's name as she hurried downstairs. Without waiting for an answer, she ran to the front door, flung it open, and tore across the lawn.

Tierney's wagon was gone.

For a moment she hesitated. Bewildered, frightened, she could not think what to do.

Standing there in the deepening shadows of evening, with no sound but the soft keening of the wind through the trees and the slow running of the stream, Finola was suddenly overcome by a feeling of dread. A terrible weight of apprehension came bearing down upon her with relentless force.

She whipped around, staring at the house. The ancient structure, with its endless wings and battlements, its densely shadowed windows, seemed to take on a chillingly ominous appearance, like that of an unfriendly stranger.

Finola shuddered, then deliberately shook off the flash of foreboding. Pulling in a deep, steadying breath, she steeled herself to think rationally, without panic. Gabriel was perfectly safe. Why wouldn't he be, after all? He could not have wandered far. Those little legs, still wobbly, would not take him any distance. He must still be within the confines of his own home and family.

She strongly hoped he was with Aine . . . *please, Lord, let it be* . . . so the thing to do was consider where they would have gone, the two of them.

If not the nursery or the garden or Aine's bedchamber, where, then?

The stables . . . Aine's favorite place . . .

Of course! How could she have forgotten the stables?

Still breathless, clinging to the fragile threads of her self-control, she forced herself to walk rather than run up the gentle swell of lawn that rose toward the house. But instead of going inside, she went around, through the garden to the back.

For a moment she stopped, staring straight ahead at the wide stone stables set well behind the property, at the rear of the coach house. It would soon be dark. Already the grounds were draped in dense shadows, obscure and strangely threatening beneath the lowering clouds and hovering old trees that lined the property.

When Finola realized she was trembling, she felt an instant of disgust with herself, that after all she had been through she could still be frightened so easily. Then, chiding herself for her foolishness, she stepped out onto the path that led toward the stables.

He saw her the moment she came round the side of the house.

At the sight of her he jerked so sharply he almost pitched off the ladder.

Leaning forward, he held his breath.

She was walking toward him, a pale specter, the evening wind ruffling the golden hair and the flowing dress, as the last light slowly drained from the day.

Watching her, Mooney felt his breath choke off. He suddenly recalled to mind with aching clarity the clean scent of her, the silken feel of her skin under his hands, the throbbing of her pulse at the base of her throat.

His hand tightened on the ladder. His heart began to bang violently against his chest as he watched her approach, then pass on by.

She was on her way to the stables. No doubt in search of the girl and the boy.

His blood churned through him like a fury, surging to great waves of almost blinding force.

He dropped from the ladder and tore across the coach house to the back door, stopping just long enough to watch her enter the stables.

With his eyes still locked on the double doors, he bent to pull his knife from his boot.

He could not have planned it so well. It would be just like before. She would be helpless to stop him.

Then he would rid himself of her for once and for all. She would plague him no more.

He would make the younger one watch; then he'd have her as well. He would kill them both.

A surprise for the cripple.

His gut churned with excitement as he gave the door a push and stepped outside.

24

In the Gloaming

In haunted glens the meadow-sweet
Flings to the night wind
Her mystic mournful perfume;
The sad spearmint by holy wells
Breathes melancholy balm.
JOHN TODHUNTER (1839–1916)

Not for anything would Louisa have admitted that she wished they had taken the carriage to the city.

It was nearly dark, the road seemed uncommonly rough, and her feet cried out for relief. But they were over halfway home by now. Too late for complaining.

Her aching feet and troublesome back put her in agony, but she would not let on to Lucy Hoy what she had only begun to admit to herself: she was no longer young. Only months ago the walk to and from the city had seemed as nothing. She had reveled in the

fresh air of the countryside and the accelerated pace of her blood.

Louisa had always maintained that her frequent constitutional kept her feeling fit and
rather younger than her age, which was an
indisputable fifty-one years. At the moment,
however, she did not feel all that fit — and she
most certainly felt her age. She reminded herself that she had stood in a classroom almost
the entire morning, after which she had gone
on to polish the furniture in her bedchamber.
That careless upstairs maid seemed to have
no use for polish; she would rather get by with
a languid swipe of the feather duster.

She ought to have given the wolfhound a
bath as well, she thought, watching him trot
along beside her. He was looking downright
scruffy, though she and young Aine had
soaped him end to end only a week past.

As if sensing her intentions, the beast
glanced at her out of the corner of his eye — a
disconcertingly human-like eye, Louisa had
always thought — and immediately veered off
to traipse a ways ahead.

"I don't know about you, Sister," said Lucy
Hoy with undisguised weariness, "but I'm
wishing we had taken the carriage. Me poor
feet feel as if the squirrels had been gnawing at
them. Couldn't we rest for a bit?"

"We will soon be home," Louisa said, resisting the other's suggestion to rest, much as she would have liked to. Instead, she lifted her chin and made a deliberate effort to pick up her pace, ignoring the protest sent up by her lower back.

"If you would walk with me more often, you'd not find the effort so taxing." The sanctimonious tone in her own voice revolted her. She was even beginning to *sound* old. A sour old nun, that's what she sounded like.

Lucy Hoy gave her a dubious look but said nothing.

Louisa would have judged the other woman to be years younger than she, but a good deal rounder and of a more phlegmatic disposition. Lucy's idea of physical exercise, no doubt, was half an hour in a rocking chair.

But she was a faithful soul, an excellent nurse for their Gabriel, and the sort who did not grumble about tasks that others might find demeaning. She had accompanied Louisa today simply because she worried over "Sister being on the road alone," and Louisa was glad of her concern.

Reflecting on her companion's good heart, Louisa now softened and let down her own defenses. Slowing her stride, she said, "In truth, Lucy, *my* feet are hurting, too, as is my back. I'd rather not stop, though, or everyone will be fretting about us."

With a sigh of relief, Lucy slowed her steps to match Louisa's, and for a time they walked along in comfortable silence. After a few moments, Louisa offered a rare glimpse into her private thoughts. "You know, Lucy, I am beginning to feel my age, and I must confess that I don't like the idea all that much."

"Oh, Sister, you're not a bit old!" Lucy protested. "Not you! Why, you could outrun the wolfhound, if you'd a mind to, I'll warrant."

"Humph! You have obviously not seen him go flying after the poor hares in the meadow. He fancies himself still a pup, that one."

The great shaggy beast trotted on, a spirited wave of the tail the only indication that he was not deaf entirely to these personal remarks. Louisa suspected that at least in the years of a dog's life, even the wolfhound was much younger than she.

But then, these days it did seem as if everyone was.

Morgan was surprised and touched by the makeshift ramp the two lads had provided for their wheelchair-bound passenger, as well as the way they insisted on securing him to the wheelchair with a belt — "in case of sudden stops." But he was equally impressed with the wagon's workmanship. The boys had worked hard, and their attention to detail was evident throughout.

Although Tierney had opted for slightly less garish colors than those of a typical Gypsy wagon, overall the finished product could easily have passed for a Romany *vardo*. The inside was comfort itself, with gaily printed cushions and rugs, a small table with two chairs, and new pallets with heavy ticking. An array of copper and tin utensils hung on hooks from the ceiling, giving the interior an unexpected homelike atmosphere.

Tierney gave full credit for the superior craftsmanship to Jan Martova, but Morgan knew the lad had learned a great deal from his Gypsy friend and had worked every bit as diligently. The American scamp might have his faults, but indolence was not one of them.

It was a little after eight when they started back to Nelson Hall. Jan Martova and Sandemon shared the driving, leaving Morgan and Tierney to ride together inside the wagon. Morgan had welcomed the arrangement, wanting to talk with the boy alone about the prospects of a crossing to America.

He was surprised and a bit disappointed to learn that the lad had no intention of accompanying the family to the States. Tierney insisted that his troubles with the New York crime lord, Patrick Walsh, made his return well nigh impossible.

As he talked, the lad absently fingered the scar that ran from his left eye down the side of his cheek — a visible reminder of Walsh's intentions to silence him. No doubt Patrick Walsh and his henchmen were a threat to the boy, Morgan conceded. But he thought he detected something else in the lad's excuses, some underlying indifference that was as surprising as it was puzzling.

"But surely you miss your family," he said, not yet willing to drop the subject.

With his eyes averted, the boy merely shrugged. "There's only Da."

"And his wife — Sara," Morgan pointed out. "You said she was good to you. And our lad, Daniel John."

Still not looking at Morgan, Tierney nodded. "Sara's a good enough sort, I suppose. But I'd not pretend to be fond of her. I scarcely know her. As for Daniel, he's hardly ever about. He stays busy working for the doctor."

"Your father would be expecting you to accompany us, don't you think? It's more than a year now since you left home. Once he knows we're coming, his hopes will be set on seeing you."

Finally the boy turned his gaze to Morgan. "It's as I told you: I can't go back. Not now.

I'm eager for this trip with Jan. But even if I were willing to give it up, I couldn't go back to the States. Walsh would have his hatchet men on me in a shake. I'd be a goner before I ever stepped off the docks."

"You don't think there's a possibility all that has been settled by now?"

Tierney shook his head. "Da would have written. He'll get the word to me as soon as it's safe to go back."

Morgan had to agree. He was sure Michael would waste no time letting his son know that he could come home.

He studied the boy for a moment. "Do you ever miss the States at all?"

Tierney glanced out the window, delaying his answer. "I miss home sometimes, sure. Da, my friends. But I don't miss the crowds and the noise and the stink, I can tell you. Not a bit."

He turned to look at Morgan. "I'm living my dream, don't you see? How many people can say as much? This is what I've wanted ever since I was just a tyke. To come here, to Ireland. Even if I could go back," he added, "I wouldn't just now. Not yet."

Morgan made no reply, but merely nodded. The truth was, he did understand. He understood all too well.

Ireland was not the boy's dream. It was his

obsession, and had been for years, doubtless. Tierney's imagination had made the island his mistress, if a remote one. And now that he was here at last, he was determined to claim her as his own, to fuse his soul with hers.

From bitter experience Morgan knew the fascination, the passion, the terrible yearnings that in time could lead a man to madness, even ruin, with such a mistress as Eire. He knew what it was to love this small, suffering island to the very brink of despair, even to the point of his own destruction.

And he knew . . . ah, how well he knew . . . that there was nothing he or anyone else could say or do to change the boy's mind, to break the spell. Tierney would follow his own road, just as Morgan himself had. And those who cared about him would be able to do nothing — nothing but pray that somewhere along that road he would find salvation instead of destruction.

They were quiet for a long time, Morgan so caught up in his own thoughts that the boy's next words were almost jarring.

"Morgan — sir —"

Morgan blinked, looking at him, half expecting a request for additional funds for the coming journey. The lad had asked for nothing other than his stable wages since his arrival at Nelson Hall. As matters would have it, Morgan had already planned to make a contribution to the venture, even if no request was forthcoming.

"Since we'll be leaving first thing in the morning," Tierney said, "and with you now considering a journey of your own, there's something I'd like you to know. I just want to say . . ."

He hesitated, and Morgan gave an encouraging nod, now even more curious as to the boy's intention.

"I want you to know how much I appreciate everything you've done for me."

The unexpected words spilled out all in a rush. Morgan could sense the lad's awkwardness as he went on. "You've been swell to me, right from the beginning, even though I haven't always deserved it. I just wanted you to know . . . I *am* grateful."

His voice fell away at the end, and he seemed to be looking everywhere but at Morgan.

"You are more than welcome, I'm sure," Morgan replied, suppressing a smile. The boy was entirely right: he had *not* always deserved fair treatment, the young rogue.

"I wish you well, lad," he told him, meaning it. "I hope you find whatever it is you're looking for."

Tierney met his eyes. "I'm not at all sure I

know what I'm looking for," he said frankly. "But I think I'll recognize it when I find it."

"Let us hope so," Morgan said, his voice low. He felt strangely unsettled by how much the haunted look in the boy's eyes reminded him of his own yearning soul in times past.

"Do you know what I wish for you, lad?" he asked, surprised by his own question, yet thoroughly convicted by the emotion that prompted it.

Tierney looked at him.

"More than everything, Tierney, son of Michael, I wish you the grace to live at peace with God . . . and with yourself. That will be my constant prayer for you throughout your journey."

After an awkward silence between them, Morgan turned to his own thoughts. He felt unaccountably anxious to get back to the house, to Finola and the children. Ever since the American journey had become a real possibility, he had found himself even more intent than usual on spending every possible moment with his family, often growing impatient with those distractions that would take him away from them. He seemed to covet each precious hour that might be spent together.

Perhaps, he admitted somewhat grimly, because he knew those hours might soon be all too few.

★ ★ ★

Sandemon stared out into the gathering darkness, unsettled by a feeling too vague to identify. For several moments now it had come and gone, a distant tide drifting in and out upon the shore of his emotions.

Twice he had almost taken hold of Jan Martova's arm and urged him to increase the pace of the black mare pulling the wagon. Both times he had checked himself from doing so. The elusive darkness rose and fell within him; perhaps he was simply reacting to the twilight shadows closing in on them.

They were driving through a particularly remote area leading off from the city, a lonely road over which few coaches traveled these days. The only sounds were the sawing of crickets and the click and scrape of the wagon wheels over the rugged road.

He was so caught up in his attempt to distinguish his feelings that the comment from the Gypsy boy at his side almost startled him.

It took him a moment to focus. "Forgive me," he said. "I must have been wool gathering."

"I said I am going to miss you. I will miss our talks and your good teaching."

Sandemon smiled a little. "And I will miss the companionship. But I think this is a good thing you are doing. An adventure such as this can be a learning experience like no other. Still, you will both be missed, you can be sure."

Jan Martova looked straight ahead. "Much will have changed by the time we return, I expect."

Sandemon nodded, still smiling. "I shall be older, for one thing."

The Gypsy looked at him. "Impossible. I think the mighty Sandemon will never age. But others will. The *Seanchaí*'s little Golden Boy, for one. Just think what a difference even a few months will make in that one."

"Indeed." Sandemon studied him. "And in the *Seanchaí*'s daughter as well, eh?"

The youth blinked but kept his gaze fixed on the road.

"Today she stands upon the bridge between childhood and womanhood," Sandemon went on. "By the time you return, no doubt she will have crossed over."

Jan Martova turned his head only slightly, enough to meet Sandemon's eyes. "Is there no hiding anything from you?"

It occurred to Sandemon that only a blind man would have failed to see the youth's infatuation, but he said nothing.

The Gypsy youth, however, seemed to want to pursue the subject further. "So, then . . . you know I have feelings for the *Seanchaí*'s daughter?"

Again Sandemon nodded. "I suspected as much, yes. But she is far too young for such feelings, you know."

Jan Martova looked back to the road. "Not in the world of the Romany."

"But she does not live in the world of the Romany, my young friend," Sandemon said gently. "Nor, for that matter, do you."

The other sighed. "I know. I suppose, under the circumstances, you feel it's best that I'm going away. With her being so young, and my being a Gypsy . . ." He let his words drift away, incomplete.

Sandemon looked around. It was taking more and more effort on his part to concentrate on the conversation, yet he recognized the seriousness of the young man's dilemma.

"You must understand," he said, trying to focus his attention on Jan Martova, "that in the *Seanchai*'s estimation, his daughter is still very much a child. Frankly, I expect he will continue to see her as such for quite some time yet."

"And I, of course, am still very much a Gypsy in his eyes," said Jan Martova heavily. "Even though I have been cast out from my tribe. To a doting father, however, I suppose even a *renegade* Gypsy is still a Gypsy."

He looked over at Sandemon. "Surely you, at least, can trust me? My interest may seem inappropriate to a *Gorgio*, but I can assure you I bear the *Seanchai*'s daughter nothing but the purest of affection and respect. And I do understand that, at least for now, my feelings can be nothing but those of a friend or brother. Besides," he said, looking back at the road, "she cannot see me, hidden as I am by the shadow of Tierney Burke."

Sandemon gave no indication of agreement, but he wasn't surprised at the boy's remark. The Romany youth was far too intelligent, too discerning, not to have noticed the girl's fancy for his American friend.

"As you said, the passing of time brings many changes," he offered mildly. "Our part is to use the time wisely and accept what God gives."

Without warning, the darkness inside him swelled, while the darkness around them seemed to turn sullen and threatening. Shadows cast from the low-hanging branches of roadside trees loomed larger, taking on menacing, grotesque shapes as they swayed in the night wind.

Sandemon shuddered. The nagging uneasiness that had distracted him most of the evening now surged to a rising tide of foreboding.

Badly shaken, he turned to grip Jan Martova's arm. "We must hurry," he urged, offering no explanation. Indeed, he *had* no explanation, other than the wave of panic coursing through him.

"Something is wrong," he said, more to himself than to the Gypsy youth. "Something is . . . very wrong. We must get back at once."

Jan Martova whipped around to look at him, his eyes questioning. Rising to a crouch, he snapped the reins, clicking his tongue to urge the mare on.

25

Night Terrors

And the dark lava-fires of madness
Once more sweep through my brain.
JAMES CLARENCE MANGAN (1803–1849)

Entering the stables, Finola lighted a lantern from the shelf near the door. She stood for a moment, looking about, her heart still racing with apprehension. Where could they be, Aine and her Gabriel?

The air in the building was warm and close, pungent with the smell of hay and harness and horseflesh. In the stalls, the horses were quiet. Other than an occasional soft neigh or stirring, Finola heard nothing but the sound of her own thundering pulse.

She held her breath as she started down the far left side of the stables, hay whispering beneath her feet with each step. She would check Pilgrim's stall first. The big red stallion, Morgan's own, was a keen attraction for both

Aine and Gabriel. They almost always rushed to his stall first when they visited the stables.

She had taken only a few steps when she heard a high squeal of laughter.

Gabriel!

Almost immediately came the sound of Aine's robust laugh in response.

Finola stopped where she was, squeezing her eyes shut and putting a hand to her throat. Overwhelmed with relief, she let the fear drain out of her for a moment. When she opened her eyes, she again headed toward Pilgrim's stall in the back of the stables.

The closer to home they came, the lower the clouds seemed to hang. It was becoming difficult now to see their way. Only the wolfhound seemed fully comfortable with the night, so the two women followed his lead.

Louisa was still cross with herself for not thinking to bring along a lantern. Of course, they hadn't intended to stay so long on the docks; they never did. But invariably they found so many poor souls languishing there — more every day, it seemed. With each trip it grew more difficult to leave. It wrenched one's soul to pass them by without at least an assurance of the Lord's love and a brief prayer for their deliverance.

Dublin was, had always been, a city with a

great heart, Louisa thought proudly. Her people seemed naturally inclined toward giving, even sacrificial giving. But these days the city could not possibly take care of her own needy, much less all those who came from the lengths of the countryside in search of work or shelter or, as a last resort, the means of immigration.

She suspected the reason she felt so weary, so depleted, had more to do with the misery and despair she had absorbed earlier in the day than any real physical fatigue. The hopelessness of the poor wretches on Dublin's docks was enough to devastate even the most stouthearted. Certainly, she thought, giving a long, heavy sigh, the experience never failed to weary her to the point of exhaustion.

She hadn't realized that she had slowed her stride almost to a complete halt until Lucy Hoy, beside her, roused her with a question. "Are you all right, Sister?" The other woman pressed her face close to Louisa's, peering at her in the darkness.

"I will be perfectly fine," Louisa said firmly, "once we reach Nelson Hall and I can draw a nice foot bath. I fully intend to indulge my poor feet the rest of the evening, provided there is no unforeseen calamity awaiting us."

Lucy gave her a strange look. "Why would you say such a thing, Sister?"

Louisa frowned. The woman looked inexplicably frightened. Moreover, she was quite sure she saw Lucy shiver before drawing the sign of the cross over herself.

"Ach, Lucy, wasn't I but making a joke?" She had almost forgotten that poor Lucy was given to great leaps of imagination and could be superstitious to a fault.

With a nod, Louisa resumed her usual brisk pace. The wolfhound, who had been waiting for them with exaggerated patience, again took up his role as guide, leading the way without actually distancing himself from the two women.

"Haven't we had conversation about these vapors of yours?" Louisa chided as they walked. "Such hysteria is not at all consistent with a life of faith, you know."

Head down, Lucy trudged along. "I do know, Sister, and I'm sorry. But something came over me, was all, when you said what you did about a calamity." She was quiet for a moment. "I'll try harder, I will, Sister."

"You must do exactly that," Louisa replied. But despite her assurance to the other, she was momentarily distracted by her own faint sense of disquiet, doubtless a reaction to Lucy Hoy's foolishness.

In the stables, Finola saw Gabriel first. He

peeked around the corner of the end stall, covering his mouth, then laughing into his hand as if he had carried off a grand feat.

Aine, holding on to his hand, was also smiling. Finola lifted the lantern for a better look at the two.

"He woke me up," the girl said quickly. "I was napping, and all at once, there he was, on top of the bed with me. I thought we would pay Pilgrim a visit and let you sleep."

Finola stood looking at the two of them, too relieved to offer more than a perfunctory scolding. "You must not go off like this again without telling someone."

Aine seemed instantly contrite. "I'm sorry, Finola. I didn't think."

Suddenly struck by another thought, Finola drew in a sharp breath. "You found Gabriel upstairs, in your bedroom?"

At the girl's nod, Finola hung the lantern on a wall peg, then stooped to confront her small son. "You climbed the big stairway by yourself, Gabriel? *Did* you?"

The boy's happy smile wavered. He glanced up at Aine with a look of uncertainty, lifting a thumb to his mouth before turning back to his mother.

"Oh, Gabriel! What am I to do with you?"

The thought of her tiny son groping up the enormous main stairway made Finola shudder. "If you should fall, you could be badly hurt, don't you see? You must never do that again!"

The child blinked, and Finola saw that his baby pleasure in his grand accomplishment had dimmed. With one hand, he rubbed his eyes, now clouded with tears.

Instinctively, Finola reached for him, but he hung back, his tear-filled gaze avoiding hers.

His wounded expression was like a knife to Finola's heart. "Ah, now, 'tis over," she murmured quietly. "You are my fine, good boy. Come, give Mama a kiss."

His gaze landed on Finola for only an instant, then deflected beyond her.

Thinking him still uncertain, she again opened her arms to him. But instead of running to her as he ordinarily would have, he hesitated, his eyes widening, his small mouth rounding to a wondering circle.

Bewildered, Finola bent lower to coax him, but a strangled gasp from Aine diverted her attention. The girl had gone chalk white. Something about that pale, taut countenance made the blood drain from Finola's face as well.

Her mouth went dry as she looked from one to the other. Outside, leaves whispered in the wind, breaking the silence of the night. A rope of fear twisted through her.

Aine's dark eyes swung from Finola to something behind her. Finola straightened, the crawling sensation along her spine spreading across her back like a cold tide rushing over the shore.

She seemed unable to look away from Aine's eyes, now wide with unconcealed terror. Her heart felt as if it had leaped into her throat, each violent throb almost strangling her.

Only a supreme act of will finally enabled her to turn around.

When she did, she found herself trapped in her own worst nightmare.

The wagon shot forward without warning, clattering wildly into the night as if a legion of demons were hard upon them.

Inside, Tierney saw Morgan grasp both arms of the wheelchair and rear back with a sharp grunt of surprise. Seated on the floor across from him, Tierney pitched sideways, flinging out a hand against the wall to brace himself.

"Something must have spooked the mare," he said, clambering to his feet. "I'll go and see."

Hanging on to the brass rail that ran along the side of the wagon, he made his way to the double doors behind the driving bench. When he stepped onto the connecting platform, the dim glow from the front lanterns revealed Jan Martova at a crouch, leaning forward over the mare. Sandemon, his face taut and set straight ahead, gripped the bench with both hands.

Planting one foot between the two, Tierney watched Jan Martova. "What's going on?"

It was fully dark now, the moon completely concealed by dense clouds. The wind was up, whipping the tree limbs that hung over each side of the road as the wagon raced through the night.

Jan Martova glanced back at Tierney, then at Sandemon, who merely shook his head.

"Sandemon . . . feels anxious," Jan replied, his attention again on the road. "He thinks something might be wrong at the Big House."

Tierney looked from Jan to Sandemon, who still remained rigidly silent. He typically placed little if any stock in the "feelings" and premonitions of others. But he had lived around the West Indies black man too long not to take him seriously.

He thought Sandemon was downright strange sometimes. More often than not the black man could sense what a person was thinking the way other people sensed a change in the weather. There was also his way with animals, especially horses. Jan Martova said even the Gypsies didn't understand horses as Sandemon did.

If Sandemon thought "something might be wrong," it probably was.

He shivered. "What do I tell Morgan?" he asked, looking from Jan to the black man.

It was Sandemon who answered. "Tell the *Seanchai* we knew he would be anxious to return, with night coming on."

The black man remained silent for a moment. When he finally spoke again, there was a raw edge to his voice Tierney had not heard before. "After we arrive, stay with him," he said, still not taking his eyes from the road. "Be sure he is not left alone."

He glanced back over his shoulder, his eyes meeting Tierney's for only an instant. But something in that dark, inscrutable gaze made the skin at the back of Tierney's neck prickle.

After a moment he turned and went back inside the wagon.

All reason deserted Finola.

The nightmare was real.

This was her darkest dream, in the flesh, standing close enough that she could see the madness in his eyes.

It was him . . . the monster from the black chamber of her night terrors.

An irrational, numbing sense of dread over-took her, sharpening her senses. In the dim lantern light of the stables, every line, every shape, now became clearly defined, high-lighted by the pulsing glow of terror.

He stepped toward her, stopping only an arm's length away.

In the flickering glow from the lantern, his face was shadowed, eerily pale, hideously familiar.

The same wolfish, predatory face . . . same torn, misshapen mouth. But the eyes . . . the eyes were different, more frightening than before, filled with rage as well as lust, burning with madness.

Behind her she heard Gabriel begin to whimper. But shock had frozen Finola in place. She could not turn, could not look at her son or at Aine, could only stand and let her own fear wash over her like an icy water-fall.

His mouth cracked to an ugly smile. "Well, now, I see you remember me. I had hoped you wouldn't forget."

She would never forget . . . how could she hope to forget?

His voice hit her with a flood of sick re-membrance. Unnatural, chilling, a grating rasp of a voice that spewed words from that mutilated mouth like bullets from a gun.

Behind her, Aine was silent, but Gabriel

331

continued to cry, harder now, huge choking sobs of childish despair.

The monster pressed closer, waved something in his hand.

A knife . . . oh, Lord, have mercy, he has a knife . . .

She heard Aine gasp. Gabriel stopped sobbing, letting out a high, steady whine that seemed to go on and on.

"Shut him up! *Now!*"

He was close enough that Finola could smell his unwashed body. Again a mind-shattering memory swooped over her. Like before, he reeked of sweat and cheap whiskey.

And something else.

Hatred . . .

A blistering, savage hatred emanated from him, a force so intense, so bestial, it made him seem less than human.

He came at her. Two steps, and now his foul breath heated her skin, making her turn away in disgust.

He caught her arm, holding her fast with a bruising grip.

Finola closed her eyes, trying to deny the monster holding her captive, trying to convince herself it was all a nightmare, that she would awaken any instant to find him gone.

But when she opened her eyes he was still there.

26

Echoes of a Nightmare

To our misfortune, a thing
Will sometimes prove
As deadly as it seems
In the darkest of our dreams.
Anonymous

This was no nightmare. It was hideously real. He was here.

She was trapped. Just like before.

No . . . not like before. This time at least, she had a voice!

Somehow she forced a scream up from her throat, past the terror choking off her windpipe. *"Aine — run! Take Gabriel and run!"*

In one blinding movement the man caught her right arm, yanking it behind her with such force Finola thought it would surely break. "You can talk!" he grated into her ear. The idea seemed to enrage him even further, as if she had betrayed him somehow, harbored forbidden secrets.

She screamed again, but he seemed not to hear. He dragged her over to Aine and Gabriel, who stood wide-eyed, clearly terror-stricken, as he whipped the knife over their heads.

"Either of you move so much as a hair, I'll rip your hearts out!" He snapped the knife back to wave it in front of Finola. "And hers as well!"

Finola stumbled as a storm of ugly memories exploded in her mind, whipping through her with the driving force of a hurricane.

How could it be happening again? Merciful Lord, are you really going to let it happen again?

One rough hand yanked her to her feet, while the other stabbed the air with the knife, over her head, in the direction of the children.

"Now you stay put, the both of you! Not a move. Not a sound."

His eyes blazed as he turned his attention back to Finola. "And you — if you don't want the both of them butchered as you watch, you'll keep still, mind! Not a word, understand? Not a word!" His reddened, watery eyes went over her, searing her skin, making her feel dirty, diseased.

Finola could feel his rage, the dangerous lunacy that burned from him like smoke from a fire.

"How long?" he snarled. "How long have you been able to talk? What was it with you before? An act? A game?"

Finola turned her face away, almost overcome by the stench of his breath, the raw malignance in his eyes.

He caught a handful of her hair, jerking it so hard that pain shot through her like a furnace blast. When she shrieked in agony, he pulled her hair again, pressing his face even closer. "You'll look at me when I'm talking to you, witch!"

Finola groaned. The tears she'd been trying so desperately to suppress finally spilled over.

"Stop your blubbering! Didn't I tell you to keep quiet?"

He released her hair and locked his hand around both her wrists, pinning her arms behind as he bent her backward. To keep from crying out, Finola bit her tongue with such force she drew blood.

He brought the knife blade flush against her throat. "Don't worry, lassie. I got no intention of using this unless you force me to." He cracked a predatory smile. "At least not until I've taken my pleasure."

Finola's blood turned to ice at his words. She had to steel herself, keep herself from flying apart. She knew if she started screaming, she would never stop.

Abruptly he wrenched her upright. "Who does the brat belong to?" he demanded, jabbing the knife toward Gabriel.

Finola's heart stopped. For one insane moment she considered telling him the truth. Would it make a difference if he knew?

Seeing her look of dismay, he sneered. "So he *is* yours, then? I figured as much, with that yellow hair."

Appalled at the thought that had crossed her mind, she immediately quelled it. She would *never* allow this monster to know that Gabriel was of his flesh! Never! In her heart, he wasn't. Her son was not the offspring of some monstrous sin, but a living testament to God's grace — a precious gift of joy. Gabriel was *Morgan's* son . . . and God's.

His ugly laugh jarred her back to her reality. "He's not the cripple's, sure?" he goaded. "It takes a whole man to sire a son."

Morgan. She could not bear even the mention of his name on this madman's tongue.

Her legs shook violently beneath her. Her heart was racing out of control, hammering against her chest so furiously she felt she might die where she stood. She knew she was dangerously close to fainting.

She despised herself for her fear, her weakness. Only her resolve to protect Gabriel and Aine kept her from surrendering to the darkness closing in on her. She dared not leave them to fend for themselves with this monster.

If only someone would come! She had lost track of time, but surely someone would be returning before long.

Please . . . oh, please, sweet Savior, bring someone soon. . . .

In the same instant, she almost recanted the silent prayer of her heart. What might this animal do to Morgan, to anyone who happened to step into his path?

To her horror, she realized that Gabriel had begun to cry again, louder than before. His childish fear might soon give way to genuine hysteria. Racked with hard, heaving sobs, he sounded shrill, terrified, as if he might strangle on his own tears at any moment.

Finola could hear Aine's shallow breathing and saw both horror and anger in her stare. She feared the girl might try something desperate that would only make things worse for all of them. Their eyes met, and Finola gave a small shake of her head. *Please, Aine,* she begged silently, *do nothing foolish, or we may all die. . . .*

Almost from the instant she had set eyes on him, Annie had known the identity of the man with the knife.

This was the beast who had attacked Finola, had very nearly murdered her.

Just for a fraction of a second it occurred to her that he was also Gabriel's father. She glanced down at the wee wane clinging to her hand, and immediately denied the thought. The *Seanchai* was Gabriel's father, himself alone! This monster could not possibly be sire to anything but evil!

Poor Gabriel was crying ever so hard now, tears streaming down his cheeks like rivers, his breath coming in loud, strangling gasps. She squeezed his hand, then put a trembling finger to her own lips to try to silence him. When he merely stared up at her and went on sobbing, she bent to gather him up in her arms.

She turned to watch the man with Finola. He was big, not so big as Sandemon or the *Seanchai*, but a hulk of a man all the same. And he was scary looking entirely, with his crazed eyes and misshapen mouth.

The thought of the *Seanchai* and Sandemon made her heart leap. Surely they would be arriving at any moment now, the two of them, with Tierney Burke and Jan Martova!

Sister and Lucy Hoy ought to be coming back soon as well. But they would be of little help against the beast with the knife.

She had to do something *now*. The man

with the knife was obviously a lunatic. There was no telling what he might do unless he were stopped.

She wanted desperately to fly at him, claw his face, strike him with murderous blows. She wanted to hurt him in the worst way, make him pay for what he had done to Finola.

But he had turned Finola about to face them, and she was signaling Annie with her eyes to do nothing rash.

A riot of conflicting emotions raged through Annie. It seemed to her that if she and Finola rushed him at the same time, they could bring him down. It would be the two of them — and they were not weaklings, after all — against him alone.

But there was the knife . . . and Gabriel.

Again her gaze met Finola's. The message was the same: *do nothing. At least for now.*

So she would wait, if reluctantly. She would watch him and wait for her chance. Perhaps she could find a weapon of some sort, or figure a way to outwit him.

Sister said his sort of man had a terrible anger inside, a need to punish others, to assert power by inflicting pain and degradation. That was why they often picked on women to hurt. They considered them weaker, less likely to fight back.

Perhaps for now she must let him think just

that. She would pretend to be weak, give him no sign she meant to fight. But she *would* fight, given even half a chance, one timely moment. She would . . .

A muffled sob against her neck and a renewed fit of wailing brought her back to the dread reality of their situation. She whispered a reassurance to wee Gabriel, who had turned in her arms and was looking at his mother with a pitiful expression that nearly broke Annie's heart.

I won't let him hurt you, Little Brother, she promised silently. *I will die before I let him hurt you.*

Behind the children, in the back of the stables, Morgan's stallion, Pilgrim, snorted, then whinnied and began to bump at the door of his stall. Gradually, Finola heard the other horses throughout the building join in, squealing and snorting, pounding at the ground with their hooves and thrashing against the stalls, setting up a terrible din in the stables.

Pilgrim reared in the stall and let go a furious protest. The noise seemed to set the man off like a torch to tinder. For a moment he appeared to forget Finola, releasing her hands as he whirled about to bellow in rage at the horses.

In the split second as he released her, Finola sprang away, bolting toward Aine and Gabriel, intent on making a run for the back door of the stables. Aine saw, and pivoted toward her, pressing Gabriel tightly against her shoulder.

But the man was too quick. He was upon Finola in an instant, grabbing her and yanking her against him.

He was a big man, much heavier than Finola, but she was nearly as tall. Trying not to think about the knife, she twisted, kicking behind her, catching him on his shin bones.

The blows stopped him, at least long enough for her to pull free.

"WITCH!" He began to chant the word at the top of his lungs, like some sort of macabre incantation. He came at her again, both hands raised above his head, one balled to a fist, the other gripping the knife. *"Witch, witch, witch!"*

He was on her again, one thick arm wedged under her throat, dragging her backward with such force her feet left the ground.

Finola saw Aine move to help. *"No, Aine!"* she screamed at her. *"Stay back!"*

Still carrying Gabriel, the girl backed off. But after a moment she set her brother to his feet, then stood poised, as if waiting for an opportunity to strike.

The heavy arm around Finola's neck unexpectedly dropped away, then circled her waist so tightly she lost her breath. With his other hand he brought the knife around to her throat.

Facing Aine and Gabriel, Finola could not escape the horror in their eyes. Her son was clinging to Aine's hand, but seeing his mother entrapped, he now strained to press forward, to run to Finola.

"No, Gabriel!"

Immediately she realized that the fear in her voice had communicated to the child. He stopped, then began to cry — terrible, heart-wrenching wails that pierced Finola's heart and threatened to sever her last remaining cord of sanity.

She knew her life, and probably the lives of both children, depended on her not losing control. Somehow she managed to lower her voice, to inject a note of calm into her tone. For the sake of her son and Aine, she swallowed her own terror, strangling on a knot of panic even as she tried to soothe him.

"Gabriel . . . my precious, stay with Aine," she choked out. "Mama is all right. All is well." Her eyes went to Aine's, silently pleading for her to restrain him.

But as she watched, Aine's stricken face turned hard. White-lipped, rage blazing in her eyes, she looked at Finola as if searching for a sign, a signal of some sort.

Terrified, Finola raised a hand as if to hold her back. "Aine . . . no," she warned, her voice low and unsteady. "You must not."

Slowly the girl's thin shoulders sagged, then slumped in defeat. But her dark eyes still burned with helpless rage as she stood, unmoving, holding her brother's hand.

Finola swayed on her feet, then squeezed her eyes shut. She could not bear Aine's look of utter desolation or the bewildered terror in her son's small face.

27

Dread and Despair

The bravest heart
No more is brave.
From an article in
Illustrated London News, 1848
Author Unknown

Sandemon was more familiar with the road
than Jan Martova; he knew about the wicked
turn just ahead. But for the past several minutes he had deliberately shut out his surroundings in an effort to pray.

Only moments before, the dread that had
been growing within him all evening had risen
to the surface in one chilling instant of awareness, driving him to seek the Presence. His
own spirit was far too agitated, his concentration too fragmented, to gain any measure of
peace for himself. But he had at last identified
the urging of the Spirit to seek divine protection — and intervention — for those he loved.

Because of his inattention, they were almost into the sharp bend before he realized it. He shouted a warning as they approached, but it was too late.

The road was spongy from the recent rains, rutted from neglect and covered with debris. Although Jan Martova instantly tried to pull back on the mare, they were already too deep into the turn to recover.

The horse and the front wheels made it around, but when Sandemon felt the back wheels begin to skid, he knew what was about to happen. He whipped around, fumbling at the door that opened into the wagon.

"Brace yourselves!" It was all he had time to cry out before the wagon went into a sickening skid.

He thought they would surely capsize, but at the last instant the wagon careened, shuddered, then lurched to a dead stop.

Tierney had already felt the wagon begin to skid out of control. The instant he heard Sandemon's warning, he dived for the wheelchair.

Throwing himself between the chair and the brass railing at the side of the wagon, he barely managed to break the impact of Morgan's crash against the wall.

There was silence for a moment, then the

sound of raised voices outside, coupled with the nervous whinnying of the mare.

He pried himself free, watching Morgan. "Are you hurt?"

Morgan seemed stunned, but otherwise all right. He waved off Tierney's concern. "No damage, thanks to you. Go and see what's wrong."

Outside, Tierney found Jan Martova and Sandemon bending over the wagon's right front wheel, which looked to be firmly lodged in the roadside ditch.

"What happened?"

Jan Martova glanced back over his shoulder. "I took a bend in the road too quickly. But we're fine, I think. The axle held, and the wheel looks secure."

Tierney eyed the listing wagon. "Can we put her back up?"

Jan nodded. "Nothing seems broken."

Straightening, Sandemon looked around for a moment, then turned his gaze in the direction of the house, which was still not in view.

"We must hurry," he said, his voice strained.

Both Tierney and Jan Martova looked at him, then at each other.

Sandemon reached out to clasp Jan Martova's shoulder. "I have seen you with the wolfhound, running in the meadow. You are as fleet of foot as the red deer. Run now," he urged, his eyes burning in their intensity. "Run to the house, as fast as you can. Tierney Burke and I are strong enough to raise the wagon without you. But neither of us can run as you do. Go now!"

Jan Martova's black eyes searched Sandemon's face for another moment. Then he murmured a sound of assent and turned toward the road.

Sandemon stopped him with a restraining hand. "Your knife — do you have it with you?"

Jan Martova looked at him, then drew his right leg up slightly to tap his boot.

Sandemon nodded. "Go now! We will follow as soon as we can."

Driven by desperation, Finola searched and found deep within herself a semblance of self-control, a thread of sanity that still held. Forcing her voice above the cacophony in the stables — the horses' frantic pounding and whinnying, Gabriel's relentless weeping — she swallowed down her own fear and loathing in an attempt to reason with the man who held the knife to her throat.

"Please . . . please, don't do this," she ventured, cringing at the trembling she could hear in her voice. "You'll be caught, don't you see? My husband and his man will be back any moment . . . and there are others . . . you can't possibly hope to get away with this!"

To her dismay, he laughed at her. Whipping her around to face him, he held her with one arm about her waist. He pressed close to her, unbearably close, bringing the knife so near she could smell the metal of the blade.

"Your husband the cripple will stop me, is that it? And what will he do, run me down with his wheelchair?" Again he laughed, an ugly explosion that split the torn mouth even more.

Behind her, Gabriel wailed louder.

"SHUT UP, I TOLD YOU! JUST SHUT UP!"

In his rage, he suddenly threw Finola off, giving her a hard shove toward Aine and Gabriel. "You quiet him down! I mean it, or so help me, I'll cut his throat before I even start on you!"

Finola's shoulder slammed into the wall. Stunned, she sank down beside her weeping child, reaching for him and drawing him up against her heart as she tried to comfort him.

The warmth of Gabriel's small body gave Finola a strength she wouldn't have believed possible. She began to stroke his hair and croon to him in the Irish, pressing his face against her body. In no time her bodice was wet with his tears, though his muffled cries grew slightly less frenzied.

The man came to stand over them, legs spread, knife held blade up. He watched them for another moment.

Abruptly, he turned his attention to Aine. Without warning he grabbed her and hauled her up by one arm. She screamed, and he swore at her, raising the knife in warning.

Dismayed, Finola saw Aine's self-control snap.

The girl twisted and bucked like a wild mare, kicking frantically at the man's legs, shrieking and flailing her arms as she tried to fight him off. *"Leave me alone!"*

"You little alley cat! You're not worth the trouble! I'll be done with you *now!*"

With the knife clutched in one hand, he seized Aine's throat with the other, shaking her as if she were nothing more than an empty sack of feed.

Finola stumbled to her feet, still holding Gabriel in her arms, pressing his face against her shoulder so he could not see what was happening.

Her mind froze. She felt weak, dazed, as if none of this were real. The stables seemed to recede from her view, dissolving into a mist. The sounds of the anxious horses faded, and even her son's heart-wrenching sobs waned. Shadows rose, darkening everything about her, until the only thing that seemed real was the madman and his victim.

It was almost as if she had stepped back through the years and stood watching herself. She had been scarcely older than Aine the first time a man had attacked her, still little more than a girl when the second assault came — from the monster who now held Aine captive.

Suddenly, reality came rushing back, with all its ugliness and clamor and mind-crushing terror. In front of her, Aine was pummeling her attacker with her fists in an attempt to free herself.

The man thrust the girl back and slapped her hard across the face. She screamed in pain. The assailant began to taunt her with the knife, pulling it back, then thrusting it closer.

Somewhere inside Finola, something snapped. The fear that only a moment before had been close to paralyzing her now vanished. In its place rose an anger she had never known, a rage so fierce, so intense, that the very force of it threatened to whip her into a frenzy.

Her ears drummed with the beat of her wildly racing pulse. She felt lightheaded, weightless, yet at the same time sensed a power welling up in her that had not been there before.

Her eyes swept her surroundings for a weapon and locked on a piece of harness with brass fittings carelessly looped over Pilgrim's stall.

She set Gabriel to the ground against the wall with his back toward Aine and her lunatic assailant. Immediately the boy looked around and reached for her, renewing his wailing.

Everything inside Finola longed to scoop him up and try to flee the stables with him, but she could no more leave Aine to face this horror alone than she could have abandoned her son. Resisting his pitiful cries, she told him firmly in the Irish that he must stay where he was, that he must not move from this spot, no matter what. The child cowered into the corner, still crying.

Yanking the piece of harness off the door of the stall, Finola rushed the madman from behind. She went after her nemesis like a fury, using the harness as a whip, flogging him across the back with as much force as she could muster, which was considerable. She screamed as she drove into him, turning years of suppressed rage and pain into a battle cry. Like one of the ancient warrior-queens, she brandished her weapon against her old enemy.

The victim had become the attacker.

The house was now in sight, but they were still far enough way that Louisa was again tempted to sit down beside the road to have a rest. Only the thought that she could soon remove her shoes and soak her feet in a nice warm bucket of water kept her going without complaint.

Beside her, Lucy was huffing as if they'd been walking the entire day without respite.

The wolfhound had pulled ahead a bit, though ever so often he would slow his gait and come back, prancing and circling them as if to urge them on. *"Can't you go any faster?"* he seemed to be saying.

He was clearly agitated, unusually fidgety. During the past few minutes Louisa had accelerated her own pace — not to humor the wolfhound, though his anxiety *did* unnerve her, but more because her own apprehension had continued to heighten. Her growing uneasiness was out of proportion, given the fact that it seemed to have no basis, but that did nothing to alleviate the dread. Now *she* was falling prey to Lucy Hoy's infamous superstitions.

She glanced over at Lucy, and saw that the

woman had her face set straight ahead, toward Nelson Hall, and was taking the road at as fast a stride as her short legs would allow. If Lucy sensed Louisa's look, she didn't return it.

"We will be home soon," Louisa said somewhat breathlessly.

Lucy gave a nod. With her eyes still set on the house, she began to walk even faster. "I think we must hurry, Sister," she said. "See, even the wolfhound knows that we must hurry."

Louisa looked at her, then at Fergus, who indeed had pulled ahead and was taking the road at a much faster gait. Abruptly, he stopped and turned, the uncannily intelligent eyes watching them. He barked once, then again, with an air of impatience and frustration.

After studying them for another second or two, Fergus seemed to make a decision. He barked once more, turned, and broke into a furious run toward the house.

Louisa had never panicked easily, indeed seldom panicked at all. But she panicked now. Seized by an icy shudder, she ignored her sore, burning feet, gathered her skirts, and began to run. Out of the corner of her eye, she saw Lucy falter for only an instant before following her lead.

28

Battle to the Death

What brings death to one
Brings life to another.
Irish Proverb

Taken completely off guard by the unexpected attack, the man tossed Aine from him
and spun around to face Finola. The knife
fell when he pushed Aine away.

Finola's eyes went to the blade, but her
courage faltered when she saw his expression. A look of utter amazement exploded
into a spasm of murderous rage. He crouched,
hunching his shoulders and thrusting his
head forward like a mad bull about to
charge.

Finola gave him no time. She swung the
harness as hard as she could at his head.

He threw up his hands to protect his face,
lost his balance, and went down on one knee.
It took him a moment to recover, and in that

time Finola rushed him again with the harness.

The brass buckle at the end of the leather smacked his cheekbone, cracking the skin. Blood spurted, adding a crimson trail to his skin's furious red flush.

He shrieked with pain. Down on both knees now, he roared an oath at her. He scrambled to his feet, covering his wounded cheek with one hand.

Finola saw his furtive gaze sweep the ground nearby. He was looking for the knife.

She slanted a look at Aine. Conscious but obviously dazed, the girl lay on her side, knees drawn up to her chin like a babe, rubbing her throat with one hand.

The blade lay within an arm's length of her.

"AINE — THE KNIFE!" Finola screamed. "GET THE KNIFE!"

The girl stared at her with a disoriented look, her eyes dull and blank.

Finola shouted again, and this time the warning seemed to register. But it was too late. Even as Aine uncoiled herself and scooted sideways to retrieve the knife, the man lunged for it and grabbed it up.

He turned back toward Finola, his face contorted, his eyes flaming.

Within a fraction of a second, her mind

clicked through three decisions: she would not, could not, run and leave the children. She would kill the madman if she could, rather than endure for the second time his hideous abuse. But if she failed, she would not resign herself to death and make it easy for him; she would fight him to the end.

He came at her then, his face cut and bleeding, his lips pulled back over his teeth, his eyes blazing. He was sweating, panting, cursing with every breath. He was no longer even partially sane, but had degenerated to something savage, a primal beast driven entirely by blind, mindless rage.

He had recovered from her attack and was fast and surefooted again, with the quick, instinctive movements of a wild animal in deadly combat. Finola had lost all the advantage of surprise, and she was tiring. Her throat burned, and her chest hammered with pain from exertion and terror.

But something had also been released in her, some instinct so ancient, so fundamental, that it fueled and energized her, equipping her for the conflict. At this moment in time, she was no longer a victim, but simply a woman, a woman fighting with every part of her being, with her very life, to save her loved ones.

At this moment, her own life had value to

her only as it provided a kind of weapon — a weapon to ensure the protection . . . the *deliverance* . . . of her son and stepdaughter.

And so as the beast came for her, crazed and more dangerous than ever in his rage, she risked it all — her strength, her sanity, her flesh, her life — in one last desperate attempt to stop him. Something deep in her spirit cried out a great, impassioned plea to God and all his angels, and sent it roaring up inside her to explode into a deafening battle cry as she rushed headlong against her enemy.

Through glazed eyes and a cloud of pain, Annie saw Finola raise the piece of harness high above her head, leaving herself open and vulnerable to the knife.

Finola gave a terrible scream, and the harness slashed down with a singing blow over the madman's head just as he charged her.

Annie rubbed her aching throat as she watched, breathless.

The man roared in agony but didn't go down.

Wheezing, gasping, Finola attempted to evade the thrust of the knife by hurling herself to the floor and rolling off to the side, then scrambling on her knees into the open track between the stalls, only a short distance from the back of the stable. She pushed herself to her feet, glanced behind her, then looked toward the stable door.

Stunned, Annie thought for an instant that Finola was about to desert them, was going to run out the stable door, leaving her and Gabriel behind.

But as she gradually regained her senses, she grew angry with herself for even thinking such a thing. Finola would never abandon them, never!

As Annie watched, Finola turned to face the madman. Her clear blue gaze, usually so gentle, now blazed with fury. Her long hair was tossed and tangled, hanging in wild disarray about her face. She stood as if daring the man to advance: legs planted wide, teeth bared, the piece of harness still looped about her wrist.

A fire burned out from her, and she looked for all the world like one of the wild warrior women of the ancient legends.

Annie felt a surge of wonder and pride as she witnessed Finola's courage. But her elation was short-lived. With a piece of harness as her only weapon, even a warrior queen would have little hope of defeating such a formidable enemy.

She tried to haul herself up off the stable floor to help, but was struck by such a sickening wave of dizziness she reeled and fell back.

Weak beyond belief, she could do nothing but lie in the dust and pray.

Trembling, Finola saw that her attack had only fueled the madman's rage. Snarling, growling like the mindless beast he had become, he lunged at her, flung himself on her. He threw her to the ground and fell onto her back, pressing her face down into the hay-strewn floor. At any moment, the vicious knife blade would slice into her flesh. But she would not give up.

As she struggled against the weight of the madman on her back, Finola's mind flashed to the family she loved. She thought of Gabriel, her tiny son . . . and Aine, the step-daughter she had come to cherish as if she were flesh of her flesh. She thought of Morgan, and her heart wrenched with a great sorrow. She prayed that somehow God would deliver her loved ones, that they would not fall victims to this monstrous savagery.

Darkness was fast bearing down on her. Still she struggled, trying to throw him off, covering her head to ward off the attacker's blows.

When the howling and snarling rose to a clamoring din, a roar so thunderous the stable walls seemed to pound and shake, she felt the instant of her death had surely come. If this were the end, she would go down fighting.

The last image before her eyes would be her son, and the last word on her lips would be the name of her Savior. She lifted her head out of the dust. . . .

Suddenly, through the veil of her tears and the blur of her pain, she saw a brindled gray thunderhead explode through the open hay doors at the back of the stable and come flying toward her.

For one chilling moment she thought the murderer at her back had been, after all, Satan incarnate, and that he had called up his fiendish minions to finish her off. She saw the bared fangs, the snarling mouth, the eyes, savage and blazing with fury, barreling down upon her, and knew an instant of utter, mindless panic.

And then she saw that it was no hellish demon roaring toward her, but instead their own Fergus, the wolfhound.

The madman was still upon her, but his blows had abruptly ceased.

Instinctively, she began to scream the blessed wolfhound's name, over and over again, like a litany.

"FERGUS . . . FERGUS . . . FERGUS!"

She felt the man-beast roll off her back, his savage growls cut dead. There was a final bleat of terror, then a howling, inhuman scream of agony.

Wrenching around, Finola watched in stunned disbelief as the massive wolfhound, great chest heaving, buried his snarling, tearing jaws in the madman's throat. He gave one violent shake, and in an instant the stables were silent.

Less than an hour later, the wolfhound had been ordered away from his kill. He lay panting near the back door, removed from, but keenly mindful of, the shrouded body nearby. The great beast's eyes were solemn but alert as he kept watch.

Only Sandemon and Sister Louisa remained in the stables. Tierney Burke and Jan Martova had been sent to fetch the law and a death cart. Lucy Hoy had taken the *Seanchai*'s daughter and small son to the house, where they would receive the care they needed.

After recovering from the shock, the *Seanchai* had insisted on taking the mistress Finola to the house. Although she had obviously suffered a cruel battering and appeared to be nearly prostrate with exhaustion, she remained adamant in her insistence that she did not need medical attention; only with great reluctance and to ease her husband's concern did she finally agree to summon the surgeon.

★ ★ ★

Sandemon held a lantern aloft as he stood looking down over the covered body at his feet. Across from him, Sister Louisa clutched her hands at her waist.

Her wimple was askew, her habit rumpled and dusty. Her voice, when she spoke, sounded uncommonly thin and tremulous to her ears. "Is it sinful, do you think, to feel nothing but relief at the death of a man like this? I should feel despair at the loss of his soul, but I find myself consumed with relief instead."

Sandemon considered her words in silence, his eyes still downcast. "Even an evil man," he finally said, his voice quiet, "is not without choices. A man chooses the way he will walk, whether the way of life, or the way of death. This man chose death."

Sister Louisa shuddered. "I cannot help but think there has been a terrible . . . *justice* done this night."

Sandemon nodded, saying nothing. But knowing the taciturn man as she did, Louisa was fairly certain he had already had the same thought.

"He would have silenced our Finola for all time," she said, not without anger.

"Instead, it is *he* who has been silenced," Sandemon completed her thought. "We do not always see justice done this side of heaven," he went on, his expression thoughtful. "Much tragedy and horror seem to go unpunished, and we question why. Yet God has promised that evil will not go unavenged forever, and we know He is true to His Word."

Slowly, he raised his eyes to hers. "Tonight, in this place, I think justice has been done: delivered, it would seem, by a wolfhound."

Inexplicably, Louisa felt that something was still unfinished, undone. Words remained unsaid, questions unanswered. But there *were* no answers, no final words at such a time. Why, then, did she feel so unsettled, so . . . dissatisfied?

"I will not pretend to be sorry, you know," she said to Sandemon. "I don't believe for a moment that our Finola would have lived had *he* not died."

Again the black man inclined his head in agreement. "I have no real sorrow for him either, I confess. Only for our Lord, whose heart must grieve that one of His creation, intended for love and a life of faith, should choose wickedness and destruction instead. And yet . . ."

Louisa looked at him sharply, ready to rebuff any attempt on his part to wax philosophical or inject a note of compassion into the situation. She was depleted entirely, incapable of rational thought, and she was not feeling the least bit charitable.

The black man lowered his eyes to the lifeless form on the ground between them. In the flickering light of the lantern Louisa saw that the night's ordeal had also taken its toll on Sandemon. The strong features, the regal bearing, showed telltale signs of strain and fatigue.

"One cannot help but wonder," he said, "what sort of torment or evil, what nightmares of his own, he might have endured that had a part in making him . . . what he was."

Louisa stared at him, resisting the unbidden, unwelcome emotion she sensed pressing in on her. But despite her restraint, another feeling now threatened her grim satisfaction that justice had been served. It was something more than understanding, yet less than genuine mercy, and she would fling it away . . . if only she could.

"As you said," she pointed out, thinking to extinguish the unwanted stirring of emotion by ignoring it, "even a wicked man has choices. This man clearly made the wrong ones."

Sandemon lowered the lantern slightly. "But are not some of us blessed with loving people in our lives to *help* us make our choices? People who teach us how to choose what is good, what is best?" He stopped. His eyes took on a distant expression, as if he had retreated to another time or another place.

"Others," he went on, his voice lower still, "are not so fortunate, I fear. They spend their lives unwanted and unloved, stumbling along life's pathways, often ending up on the road that leads to destruction — because there is no one who cares enough to show them a better way."

He gave Louisa a long, searching look. "I have told you of my own life, and its turning point. I can only believe that, had it not been for the patient, unconditional love of that godly man — my friend, Father Ben — in all likelihood I, too, would have taken the road to eternal damnation. It seems to me that with enough love and guidance, the lives of those we count as *lost* might take drastically different turns.

"Above all else," he went on, his voice stronger and more confident now, "we must remember that our God can turn to good even that which is meant for evil. Think of our Gabriel, the golden child of sun and light who now brightens the rooms of Nelson Hall. He was born out of the violence of this doomed man, yet created as a wondrous gift, a miracle. When I think of him, I stand in awe of our

God and His working in our lives."

Louisa shivered, and not from the night air. She looked from Sandemon, who, even in the shadows, seemed to radiate a nobility of spirit, a steady goodness and strength of soul . . . then to the shrouded corpse between them.

Shaken, she felt herself seized by a totally unexpected impulse to weep — in sorrow, for the senseless waste of a life, and at the same time in relief, for the lives that had been saved.

Her legs ached as she dropped to her knees in the dust. She had never been one for praying for the dead, though of course the Church sanctioned it. The time to intercede, it seemed to her, was when the living still had breath and their wits about them, when prayer could still make a difference.

The best she could do, she decided, staring with dry eyes at the blanketed body in front of her, was to offer a prayer of thanksgiving for the beautiful, precious lives that had been spared — and a prayer of supplication that she would not take her own life for granted. For she was one of the fortunate ones Sandemon had spoken of, whose family had nurtured and protected her, loved her and guided her into choosing the Light rather than the darkness.

For the immeasurable gift of people who loved her, she would be eternally grateful . . . even more so, she was sure, after this night.

She also found herself moved to pray that their Lord might raise up more of the faithful to love and protect, to teach and guide. Many young, unfortunate souls were alone this night throughout the world, frightened and in desperate need of someone to care . . . someone who would care enough to make a difference. She prayed that these little ones might not end up wasted and doomed, like the unknown, lifeless body beneath the shroud.

She opened her eyes for an instant and saw that Sandemon, too, was on his knees before the Throne.

29

Secret Pursuits

I had a thought for no one's but your ears . . .
W. B. YEATS (1865–1939)

New York City
Late August

Billy Hogan stopped in front of the Old Brewery building, looking at his surroundings. His stomach knotted as he stood amid the filth and squalor of Paradise Square. Leprous tenements, garbage-littered streets, raggedy children sifting through the barrels in search of food, their eyes as hungry as their bellies.

A flood of memories, all of them unhappy, came rushing at him. Tears stung his eyes, and for a moment he wished with all his heart he hadn't come.

It made it worse that he was here against Mister Evan's wishes. He wasn't supposed to come anywhere near the Five Points, although he hadn't actually *promised* he would not.

Mister Evan had said it would be "wiser" if he weren't to visit his mother and brothers just now, what with Sorley being out of jail.

Billy no longer called him *Uncle Sorley*. They had never been blood anyway, and now that Mister Evan had helped him to understand that he hadn't done anything to deserve the beatings and mistreatment Sorley had inflicted upon him, the word *Uncle* would have stuck in his throat.

Still, he couldn't stay away from his family forever, though he wasn't at all sure it would matter to his mother if he did. The last time he had stopped by, she seemed too worn out and downhearted to even take notice of him.

It was different with Liam and Patrick, his little brothers. They were half brothers, in fact, what with them and Billy having different fathers — but he never thought of them that way. Those two always looked forward to his visits, and they let him know it. No doubt part of their excitement had to do with the treats he usually took along; Miss Nora always saw to it that he had some cookies or other sweets to share when he went for a visit. Doubtless, it was the only time the wee wanes tasted anything besides potatoes or stirabout.

Billy hadn't been to see them since Sorley got out of jail, close on a month ago. Mister Evan was worried about his getting hurt again, Billy knew. He had been uncommonly stern when he told him to "stay close-by" Whittaker House for a spell.

But he missed his brothers something fierce, and even if Mum didn't care whether he was there or gone, he still missed *her*. Besides, the boys wouldn't understand such a long absence.

He worried for the little ones, which was another reason he could stay away no longer. Even though they were Sorley's own natural-born sons, Billy wasn't convinced they were entirely safe from his meanness.

He knew Mister Evan would have come with him, had he insisted. But if Billy allowed it and something went wrong — if Sorley should be at the flat and in his cups, for instance — Mister Evan could get hurt. He wasn't all that strong, and what with his only having the one arm, he would have no chance at all against Sorley's brutish strength.

Evan Whittaker was the best man Billy had ever known, aside from his da, who had died before they ever left Ireland. In secret, he sometimes pretended Mister Evan and Miss Nora were his real parents. Perhaps it was wicked to play at such thoughts when his own mother was still alive, but *wouldn't* it be a fine thing to have a dad and a mum who loved him proper, who seemed to want his company more often than not?

In any event, he would not be able to bear it if something bad were to happen to Mister Evan. And what would the other orphan boys at Whittaker House do without him?

He had had a hard time getting away from Finbar. The motley colored, cross-eyed kitten who had once disrupted Mister Evan's choir rehearsal was now a sleek and powerful mouser — still cross-eyed, but of great service to Whittaker House. Finbar was now Billy's cat — following him everywhere, sleeping on his bed, sitting on his lap and purring loudly during lessons.

Finbar had wanted to go with him today. Billy had had to distract him with a stolen bit of fish from the kitchen so that he could slip out the front door. It being a Thursday, there were no late afternoon classes, and he had seen to most of his chores before leaving. All that was left were his after-supper jobs, and he intended to be back well in time for those. So he had sneaked away early in the afternoon, not telling a soul what he was about.

He smiled at the memory of the wee kitten, tucked inside his jacket, howling off-key his very first rehearsal with Mister Evan's choir.

Only then did it strike him like a blow — *choir rehearsal!* He had completely forgotten. Thursday afternoons were reserved for the boys to practice their music. That was the very reason classes were dismissed early.

He groaned, disgusted with his carelessness. Not only was he missing one of his favorite activities of the week, but by not showing up at the practice, he was ensuring the fact that Mister Evan would know he was gone.

It couldn't be helped now, but he fretted all the same. He should have planned more carefully. His only consolation was the thought of his little brothers, how their eyes would light up when they saw him after so long a time.

With his small sack of treats clutched tightly in his left hand, he started off toward Mulberry Street, trying not to think about Mister Whittaker.

At Whittaker House, Quinn O'Shea descended the main stairway at a dash. For two Thursdays past now, an envelope had come for her, slipped under the door in the early afternoon, when no one was about. Her first thought when she awoke this morning was to wonder whether another envelope would arrive today.

She saw it at once, on the floor just past the

threshold. After a quick glance around to make sure she was alone, she grabbed it up and hurried upstairs to the privacy of her room.

With a quickening pulse she inspected the long, slender envelope on which her name had been written in a broad but neat hand: *Miss Quinn O'Shea, Whittaker House.*

Quinn's fingers trembled slightly as she opened the envelope and scanned the lines. The first poem she had received had rhymed; the second had not — instead, had sounded more like a letter, the words respectfully impersonal, yet complimentary, with an allusion to admiring someone from a distance, caring for someone in secret.

Today's poem, written in the same precise hand, was gentle, even lyrical. With a strong yet subtle rhyme, it was as if the poet wished to say much in few words, and say it without offending:

> "I cannot pass you by
> with a careless eye,
> Although I try,
> But like a candle's light
> at dead of night
> you draw me nigh. . . ."

There were only a few more lines, each

carefully worded with the spare, rhythmic flow Quinn had come to recognize. She read them over again, unwillingly stirred, yet disquieted.

Daniel Kavanagh had penned the poems, of course. It could not be anyone else.

She had been aware of the boy's infatuation for months. He had hardly kept it a secret, after all. He was young and patently innocent, unlikely to have had much skill at dissembling, and seemingly not the least bit cunning. In truth, Quinn was almost surprised the boy had mustered the courage to go *this* far with his attentions.

It bothered her that she invariably thought of Daniel Kavanagh as a *boy*, when in actuality he wasn't even a full year younger than she. She supposed it was his innocence that made him seem ever so green, at least when it came to girls. He was clever enough about everything else, that much was certain.

He had done wonders, for example, in helping her to improve her grammar during their weekly hour of instruction. In the little extra time they could manage, he had even worked in a smattering of other subjects, including the basics of home nursing, learned from his experience with Dr. Grafton.

He was ever to be found with his nose in a book, Daniel was. If not a medical book lent to him by the doctor, then a history or geography book from the house library.

Apparently, he favored poetry as well.

Despite their time together, he had lost almost none of his shyness around Quinn. He still stumbled over his tongue more often than not, still turned crimson when he entered a room and found her there.

Obviously the poems represented his attempts to express himself and still protect his anonymity.

Quinn drew a long sigh. The boy was sweet, really. Sweet and smart and altogether decent. A prince of a young man, and a handsome one at that — one to turn heads, she supposed, with that curly ink-black hair and stunning blue eyes. Why didn't he realize he could have had his pick of girls, that he needn't be settling for one he *couldn't* have?

More the pity. Even if she were to find some feeling for the lad, she could never let him suspect as much. A young man like Daniel Kavanagh deserved a fine girl — a girl as decent and innocent as himself. A girl who would make him proud.

Quinn bit her lip. She would never be one to make a man proud. She was used and spent and ruined, all by one who had been the scum of the earth. Had it not been for the knife, she might still be enslaved to him today.

Sometimes she felt like an old woman already, not a girl of seventeen years.

Seventeen . . . and already a fugitive and a fallen woman. Certainly not a girl for the likes of Daniel Kavanagh, and so she must be careful not to encourage him in his foolishness. The last thing he needed was an entanglement with someone like her. He deserved better, much better. Why, even a rough, bold Irishman like the mulish Sergeant Price would think twice before taking up with someone like Quinn O'Shea, did he but know her for what she was.

The thought of the burly policeman brought a grim smile to her face. Sure, there was nothing subtle about *that* one. Sergeant Denny Price would never be the man for keeping his intentions to himself, now that was the truth.

But even the hardheaded policeman would not be so eager to hang on her sleeve if he knew what lay in the darkness of her past. Not likely.

She sat there for a long time, staring at the paper in her hand without really seeing the words. Finally, the sound of music from downstairs brought her back to her surroundings. Voices — boys' voices — coming from the cavernous dayroom on the first floor reminded her that Mister Whittaker would be rehearsing the singers by now. The younger boys not a part of the group would need attention, and since Johanna was still at school, Mrs. Whittaker would be requiring help with wee Teddy so she could have her afternoon rest.

She got up, stretching her arms up over her head full length. No more time for lolling about like a great lump of a girl, letting her wits run to mush. Quickly, even a little fiercely, she folded the paper back inside the envelope, then crossed the room to tuck it away with the others.

What she must do from now on, though carefully, so as not to hurt the lad's feelings, was to discourage Daniel Kavanagh from his regard. Perhaps she should start by avoiding him as much as possible.

The grammar lessons should probably cease, though she was reluctant to bring them to an end before she had learned all she could. Still, she wasn't all that comfortable with Daniel as it was, and lately she had found herself more awkward than ever.

Odd, that she would be so ill at ease with one as attentive and so obviously enamored of her as Daniel Kavanagh, yet she could feel almost comfortable — at least some of the time — with the exasperating Sergeant Price. For someone who had never known anything but oppression and intimidation from the law, it seemed peculiar entirely that she could be more herself, even occasionally enjoy herself, in the company of a policeman.

True, he could set her teeth to grinding when he acted the buffoon or flashed that wide-mouthed, smug grin at the most inappropriate times. But as insufferably thickheaded as she sometimes found him, Quinn would give the man this much: he could make her laugh. At the least likely times, on the most unexpected occasions, the big sergeant could make her laugh, even at herself.

At those times she could almost forget that he was a policeman.

But not for long.

Within ten minutes after the start of rehearsal, Evan Whittaker considered the possibility of canceling *all* rehearsals until Alice Walsh returned.

If she returned . . . please, God.

He had seen her only twice since her husband's death. The burial service had been private, with no calling hours beforehand, but he had gone to Staten Island anyway, just to express his concern for the family.

He had found Mrs. Walsh terribly shaken, but seemingly glad to see him. There had been a heavy sorrow about her, of course, but with more composure than he would have expected. But then, Alice Walsh had always impressed him as being a strong, resourceful woman. Depending on the outcome of next month's hearing, Evan had hopes she would eventually move past this ordeal and make a life for herself and her children. He fervently hoped that life would include her returning to help him with the singers and the band.

The entire sordid situation had to be unbelievably difficult for her. It was a hideous story, blown out of all proportion because of the potential for scandal. Supposedly, Walsh's mistress, who had been carrying the man's child, had confronted both Patrick Walsh and poor Alice that dreadful day, with disastrous consequences. Walsh had cold-bloodedly murdered his paramour by shoving her down the stairway. Evidently Walsh had meant to put a bullet into her, just to make absolutely certain she was dead. Alice had tried to stop him, and he had been shot in a struggle for the gun.

Apparently Sara Farmington Burke was the only person to whom Alice Walsh had confided the ugly facts of the situation. According to Sara, it was nothing less than remarkable that Alice Walsh had not suffered a total nervous collapse from the ordeal.

For his part, Evan was convinced that Mrs.

Walsh would bear up, if only for the sake of her children. Still, to learn that her husband had been unfaithful — and to learn the ugly truth from the other woman herself — would surely be enough to devastate even the strongest will. And to have to live with the fact that she had shot him, albeit accidentally — well, it would be no easy road for her to follow.

Yet a few days after her husband's burial service, Alice Walsh had surprised him and Nora by appearing at Whittaker House, bearing a sheaf of papers and even managing a faint smile as she gave them the exciting news: Firth, Pond was offering a publishing contract to Evan for some of his instrumental and choral arrangements.

It was almost inconceivable that, in the midst of her own personal anguish, she would make the effort to travel from Staten Island on an errand of goodwill for others. Evan had virtually been struck dumb by her selfless generosity.

Even now, weeks later, he still found his astonishing good fortune, which had come about almost entirely through Alice Walsh's efforts, nearly impossible to believe, especially coming as it had on the heels of her own personal tragedy. He would be unceasingly grateful for her encouragement. He wished there were some way to repay her, but she had asked for nothing in return but his and Nora's prayers on behalf of her and the children.

Certainly he was becoming more and more aware of just how much Mrs. Walsh contributed to the boys' choir as he tried to muddle along without her each week. Being a one-armed director, he conceded grimly, was difficult enough in itself. But attempting to be a one-armed director *and* a one-handed pianist was simply impossible.

For the moment, however, he would have to make do. The boys were clearly waiting for his lead. With a sigh, he scanned the familiar faces, his intention being to choose one of the older lads to help beat time, leaving Evan free to pick out parts on the piano.

Only then did he realize that Billy Hogan was missing.

"Where is Billy?" he asked. His eyes scanned the group, an assortment of ages and skin colors. One or two shrugs and a number of blank expressions were his only reply.

While waiting for Oscar, the group's newest and youngest member, to go and fetch Billy, Evan rehearsed the others in a quick review of some of their favorite songs. A few of the older boys had left the singing group altogether, opting for the military-style band Evan had recently formed some months back — again with the help of Alice Walsh. Others had chosen to be active in both groups.

Although most of the members still lived in the Five Points district, Evan had recently moved rehearsals to the house here on Elizabeth Street, an easy walk from the notorious slum. This enabled him to keep a close eye on the smaller boys now living at Whittaker House, and at the same time be available to Nora. Besides, he was convinced it did the boys good to get out of that ghastly pit, even if for only an hour or so a week.

When Oscar didn't return right away, Evan grew impatient and inexplicably disturbed. He had been worried about Billy Hogan for some weeks now, fearful that, against all practical advice, the boy would take it upon himself to go and see his family. Although Evan had made the strongest sort of appeal that Billy avoid the Five Points — thereby staying out of the abusive Sorley Dolan's reach — he had stopped short of forbidding him to go. In reality, he had no right to forbid the boy anything, since he was not his legal guardian.

That prompted another thought, one which occurred frequently these days, but which he had so far kept to himself. He wasn't sure how to broach the subject with Nora — or with Billy, for that matter. But he sometimes considered trying to gain legal custody of the boy

. . . if Billy were willing, that is — and if Nora approved.

From what he could tell, the child's mother was virtually indifferent to him. There had been no attempt to contact Billy, no communication of any sort, in weeks. Even with Dolan hanging about the premises, the woman could surely manage to get in touch with her son, if only to warn him to stay away. But there hadn't been a word from her, and Evan had sensed the boy's bewilderment and hurt.

His heart ached for Billy Hogan. He had come to care a great deal for the little fellow with the straw-colored hair and fine-boned features and angelic voice. He wouldn't mind at all calling Billy his own. But he hadn't the slightest idea how *Billy* might feel about the possibility.

The appearance of Oscar roused him out of his thoughts.

"Can't find Billy nowhere 'tall, Mistah Evan. Miss Quinn says she ain't seen him either. And the cat, Finbar — seems like he's disappeared, too."

Evan stared at the small mulatto boy for a moment, then turned back to the others. "Has *anyone* seen Billy? Billy Hogan?"

Again there was no reply. A growing sense of uneasiness swept over Evan. He was almost certain he knew what Billy was up to.

The boy seemed to relish every rehearsal, usually showing up early and hanging back after the hour was over. Billy simply would not miss for no reason.

Evan made the reluctant decision to go on with rehearsal. If Billy did not return before the end of the hour, he would leave at once for the Five Points.

He might not be legally responsible for Billy Hogan, but certainly his heart held him accountable all the same.

30

Travesty of Justice

For Man's grim Justice goes its way,
And will not swerve aside;
It slays the weak, it slays the strong,
It has a deadly stride. . . .
OSCAR WILDE (1854–1900)

When Michael Burke stopped by Jess Dalton's office in the Bowery early that same Thursday afternoon, he found the big curly headed preacher considerably more cheerful than when they had last met.

The pastor's handshake was vigorous, his smile quick. "Michael! Good to see you. You've come with the clothing collection your enterprising wife promised, I expect. Come in, come in!"

Michael sank down in the chair Dalton indicated, while the pastor went to sit behind the desk.

"I promised Sara to ask after your wife and

family first thing," Michael said.

Jess Dalton's smile remained cheerful. "Kerry is doing well enough, considering the circumstances. Casey-Fitz is a great help to her. And we've had some good news about Amanda, as a matter of fact. The court has granted an extension of our petition; Winston can't take Amanda *anywhere* for another month."

Michael leaned forward. "That's wonderful, Pastor. You must be greatly relieved."

A muscle tightened at the corner of Dalton's eye, and his smile faded. "We're grateful, of course. At least this will give our attorney more time to investigate Winston's background and prepare a stronger case in our behalf. But as long as there's even the slightest chance that we might lose Amanda —" He stopped, looking down at his clenched hands on the desk. "Well, it's difficult."

"You'll have the girl before all is done," Michael said. "I can't believe any judge with half a heart would send the child off with a virtual stranger. Why, she's little more than a babe."

A worried expression settled over Dalton's features. "I pray you're right. But the fact is that Winston isn't exactly a stranger to Amanda any longer. The court has allowed him to see her each week — only for an hour, but that's probably long enough for him to ingratiate himself with her. She's a very trusting little girl."

He shook his head, then glanced up. "Ah, Michael, I have a veritable war going on inside me these days. At times I think that if I truly want what's best for Amanda, and if Winston is prepared to make a good life for her, perhaps I shouldn't fight him. But then I see the anguish in Kerry's eyes or feel the knife twist in my own heart, and I can't seem to get beyond the terror that we might actually lose her — or my rage at Colin Winston for being the cause of it all."

Michael nodded but said nothing. He knew about rage well enough these days.

Since the death of Patrick Walsh, he had harbored a silent but steady fury. He knew the resentment simmering in him was wrong. He called himself a Christian, had tried to live as one most of his life. But a real Christian possessed the grace of forgiveness, didn't he? A real Christian left the business of judgment up to God. Yet despite a fundamental belief that God was fair and would eventually bring His perfect justice to pass, he could not seem to rid himself of the growing bitterness in his heart. He felt disillusioned, cheated — and angry.

There had been a time when he had vowed

to bring down Patrick Walsh, to make him pay for all the evil he had wrought, the lives he had ruined — including that of Michael's own son, Tierney. Instead, Walsh had ultimately been destroyed by his own weakness of the flesh. Confronted by his mistress, the woman he had wronged, he was slain, if accidentally, by the hand of his wife . . . the woman he had betrayed.

Somehow it seemed grossly unfair. There should be the very devil to pay for a man like that, a man without scruples, without conscience.

Walsh had been thoroughly corrupt, a pirate who had pillaged uncounted numbers of the city's immigrant population. From his merciless dock runners, preying on those just off the ships, the shameful tenements from which even the rats tried to escape, the taverns and gambling dens and brothels, he had unleashed almost every form of depravity and corruption upon the city. He had even tried to corrupt Michael's own son, and failing that, had tried to have Tierney killed.

Michael could not help but believe there should be a merciless retribution for one who had caused so much misery, so much tragedy, in the lives of thousands. There ought to be *justice*.

And for longer than he could remember, he

had intended to be an agent of that justice.

But now Walsh was gone, killed in an instant, no doubt surrendering his life with little suffering and no remorse. The vermin had gotten off entirely too easily.

Michael's stomach wrenched. He and Sara had argued about his "irrational obsession," as she called it, again this morning. She was being affected by his helpless rage at Walsh's death, but still he couldn't seem to help himself. Or maybe he didn't *want* to.

His mouth filled with the vile taste of his own bitterness. He looked up to find Jess Dalton studying him with a curious expression.

"Why do I think you're angry, too, my friend?" The pastor's voice was gentle. "What burdens you so?"

Michael blinked, regarding the kind features of the big man across the desk. For a moment he was tempted to unburden himself and seek Dalton's counsel. Preacher or not, he obviously understood anger. Jess Dalton wasn't one to condemn another man for his feelings.

But what was the point? Walsh was dead. There was no changing fate, no going back. And words, no matter how wise or well-intentioned, would not extinguish the coals of bitterness that still smoked in his own heart.

He gave a tight smile and shrugged. "No

burden, Pastor. Just some things I need to work out. But tell me about this Winston character. Last time we talked, you were making plans to have him investigated."

The big preacher's unsettling blue gaze searched Michael's for another moment, then cleared. "Yes. Hancock — Lawrence Hancock, our attorney — is doing just that. He has a man in England working on it, and another here. So far we've learned little more than we already knew. Winston was estranged from his father — Amanda's grandfather — and had been for some time. Before Amanda's mother died, she told Nicholas Grafton that her brother drank and gambled heavily. Apparently, he was altogether irresponsible. Their father ordered him out of the house more than once because of his profligate ways."

Dalton stopped, again frowning. "But that's not necessarily going to keep the court from awarding him custody of Amanda."

"So you *are* suing for custody, then?"

"Oh yes. We had the preliminary adoption papers under way when Winston showed up, but now we've had to go back and institute an actual suit for temporary custody."

Michael frowned. "It seems obvious to me, Pastor, that almost any judge would find you and your wife far more acceptable guardians for the child. Especially since she's already been in your home for several months."

Jess Dalton shook his head. "But Colin Winston is her *uncle*. That makes all the difference. Or at least it may, unless we can find evidence — significant evidence — to absolutely prove he would be an unfit guardian. We need something rather drastic, I'm afraid."

"That might not be as difficult as you think," Michael offered, getting to his feet. "It's been my experience that a man who spends his life at the bottle and the gaming tables often leaves a wide and dirty trail behind him. I don't know that there's much I can do to help, but I'll nose about to see what I can turn up. For now, though, I'd best be off. Where would you like the clothing boxes, by the way?"

Dalton stood, coming around to again shake Michael's hand. "In the hall will be fine. Tell Sara we're grateful, as always. And you know we'd appreciate any help you can give us with Amanda." He paused, his friendly, bearded face close enough that Michael could see the question in his eyes. "And, Michael — if I can ever help *you,* you've only to ask."

Once more the preacher's compelling gaze seemed to probe Michael's soul.

An uncomfortable idea altogether, he realized, given his soul's present condition.

Colin Winston scanned the marquee of the dime museum with distaste. The display left little doubt as to what waited inside.

The place was no museum at all, of course, but a freak show. In this dreadful slum called the *Bowery,* such places seemed to abound. Apparently Americans were fascinated by the grotesque.

Still, it ought to be just the place to find the sort of ruffian he was looking for. Not necessarily among the freaks themselves, although that was a possibility. He thought it more likely that one of the disgusting creatures inside might point him to the sort of thug required for the business at hand. If not, he would try the rough-looking blighters milling about on the corner.

He paid his admission to a scowling barker with a drooping moustache and a flashing diamond ring on every finger, then passed by the mean-looking dwarf manning the door. Winston met the loathsome creature's scowl with a sneer of his own and went inside.

He paid scant attention to the human monstrosities on stage, registering only the vaguest awareness of a bearded lady and a revolting youth without legs billed as the *Turtle Boy.* He turned his gaze to a decidedly ugly specimen being introduced as the *Strong Man.* An enormous thick neck joined a head like that of an iron bull to a body that looked as invincible as an oak tree. Beside the Strong Man, at the end of the row, stood a tall, thin albino, almost spectral in appearance, and beside him, a man with two empty sleeves and a horribly scarred face.

Winston shuddered and hurried on, exiting the exhibition hall through a side door he thought might lead backstage. A wizened old man on a stool near the door stopped him, gruffly asking his business.

"Actually I'm looking for a particular chap," Winston said pleasantly. "Perhaps you could help, or at least might direct me to someone who could."

The other simply stared at him, obviously unsoftened by Winston's forced cordiality.

"Large fellow," Winston chattered on, attempting to describe the sort of criminal type he hoped to find. "Bit of a rogue. Somewhat unsavory, I'm afraid. Anyone come to mind?"

The old man eyed him with contempt. "No more than a couple of hundred or so is all."

Still sour-faced, the grizzled custodian raked Winston with a knowing look. " 'Tis the Stump you want to be talkin' to. If he's of a mind to talk, that is. He knows most of the ugly mugs about the Bowery, I'd wager. He's the one who can put you in touch."

"The Stump?"

"He's on stage right now. The one what has no arms."

Winston swallowed. His reluctance to confront one of the freaks in residence warred with his anxiousness to finish the nasty job still ahead.

After a moment his impatience won out. "Is there somewhere I can wait for him?" he asked the scowling custodian.

"Two doors down on the right." The old man stabbed a finger in the direction of a dark, narrow hallway.

Winston's gaze went to the shadowed corridor behind the irascible custodian. A shiver trailed down his spine. He imagined all manner of ghastly abominations lurking in the corners, could almost smell the vile odors that surely permeated such a place.

He steeled himself, looking straight ahead as he started down the dim, scaling hallway. He fumed as he went at his deceased father — and at Dalton, the hulking dolt of a clergyman who had forced him to such a pass.

His original plan had been simply to collect the girl and take her back to England. Once there, he would rely on his old chum, Charley Seagrave, a jaded solicitor with even less scruples than Winston's own, to arrange a legal guardianship and see to the details of the will. His niece could be dealt with later, after he'd had time to plan more thoroughly.

But Dalton had gotten hostile and moved to delay things. Now the entire matter couldn't be resolved for at least another month.

Just enough time for Dalton to launch an investigation, an investigation that *could* lead to Winston's losing the girl altogether. Even out here among the savages, the courts might not look kindly on a *profligate,* to use his dear departed father's favorite indictment of his only son. Especially a profligate whose gambling debts exceeded half the value of the family estate, and whose thirst for whiskey was practically legendary in London.

So as distasteful and inconvenient as it was, he had effected a swift change of plans. He would have the girl abducted and gotten rid of *before* she was placed in his custody. That would keep him clear of the law. As soon as the deed was discovered and his unfortunate niece out of the way, he would be on *his* way back to England, to his inheritance and a new life — a much more comfortable life.

At the door the old man had indicated, Winston stopped, sniffing the stale air in the corridor. He leaned against the wall — gingerly, with only one shoulder, for the plaster was filthy — and stood brooding over his lot as he waited for the one called Stump.

None of this was his fault, really. All credit went to his intractable, puritanical father, who had taken it upon himself to punish his wayward children for their rebellion.

No doubt his father would view it all as divine justice, since he had always thought himself to be in league with the Divine. A duly appointed administrator of righteous retribution.

Heaven's Hangman.

First, poor Elizabeth had been banished and disinherited for marrying her boorish Irish stable hand. Then, after a change of heart, the old man restored Elizabeth and her little brat to his will, this time leaving his son's — Colin's — inheritance in question. Only in the event of Elizabeth's death would Winston gain control of a part of the vast estate — and only with his niece out of the picture could he count on ever being as sinfully rich as he intended to be one day.

It could not come too soon. Footsteps sounded in the corridor, and Winston pushed away from the wall. With a fixed smile, he smoothed his collar, forcing down the sour taste of revulsion as the creature called Stump slowly came into view.

31

Abandoned

Only the ashes that smoulder not,
Their blaze was long ago,
And the empty space for kettle and pot
Where once they stood in a row.
Anonymous (1847)

By the time he dismissed the boys from rehearsal, Evan was nearly ill with worry. He knew his panic was irrational; small boys occasionally got it into their heads to forgo a responsibility, or even a privilege, for that matter. It wasn't all that inconceivable that Billy had simply gone off on his own for the afternoon.

No doubt he was foolish to fret so. More than likely the boy had taken up with one of his chums and forgotten the time. Or perhaps Quinn had sent him off on an errand without mentioning it to anyone.

She had not. When Evan approached her in

the hallway as the boys filed out, she gave him a puzzled look. "Why, no, sir. I haven't seen Billy at all this afternoon."

"You're quite sure?"

"I am, sir. Is something wrong, Mr. Whittaker?"

"I certainly hope not," Evan said, distracted. "It's not like B-Billy to m-miss rehearsal. Not like him at all. I wonder if I shouldn't —" He stopped, looked at the girl. "Quinn, would you m-mind very much going for Sergeant Price while I speak with Mrs. Whittaker? I'm going to b-be leaving for a time, and I want her to know. If you can't find the sergeant, ask after him, would you? One of the officers is usually close-by."

"Aye, sir — I mean, yes, sir, I'll be glad to." She paused. "Billy Hogan is not in trouble, I hope?"

Evan looked at her. He knew their young housekeeper was partial to Billy. He had seen her with the boy on frequent occasions, had noted her obvious affection for him. Of course, Quinn was quite good with all the boys, but she did seem to have a particular fondness for Billy Hogan. Perhaps the solemn-faced little fellow helped to ease her loneliness for her younger sister back in Ireland.

"Mrs. Whittaker and I told you about B-Billy's family — the mother's neglect, his . . .

stepfather's abuse?"

Quinn nodded, her eyes darkening. "And the brute is out of jail already, so I hear."

"Yes, and that's why I'm concerned. I'm afraid B-Billy may have gone to see his family and encountered Dolan. There's n-no telling what the man might do, especially if he's drunk. And he almost always is."

Before Evan had even finished his explanation, the girl turned to go. She yanked off her apron, giving it a toss as she started for the door.

"I'll find the sergeant," she said, glancing back over her shoulder. "Don't you worry, Mr. Whittaker. We'll find Billy Hogan, we will."

As he watched her hurry out the door, Evan fervently hoped she was right.

Billy Hogan took the darkened stairway up to the flat as slowly and as quietly as he could. When he reached the door, he put his ear to it a moment, listening.

There was nothing but total silence on the other side. He tried the knob and, finding the door unlocked, edged it open with caution.

Although he saw nothing, heard nothing, he half expected Sorley to come flying at him, drunk and in a rage. But when he stepped the rest of the way into the room, he was greeted by an eerie quiet, a strange hollowness, in which the beat of his heart seemed to echo like a drum.

He knew an instant of relief that Sorley was not on the premises, quickly followed by a prickling of concern when no one else appeared.

"Mum?"

He flinched at the sound of his voice in the stillness, lowering his tone even more to call the names of his brothers. "Patrick? Liam? 'Tis Billy, your brother. If you're hiding, come out now."

Nothing stirred except the growing wave of uneasiness rising in him.

Billy stood unmoving, looking about. For the first time he saw that the room was virtually empty.

His pulse hammered faster as his mind took in the barrenness of the room. The dilapidated table and all four chairs were gone. The grease-covered cookstove still squatted in the corner, but without his mother's teapot. There was no sign of crockery or kettles, not even a tin cup.

"Mum?" he said again, choking down a lump in his throat that had not been there a moment before.

His legs felt wooden as he started toward the doorway to the bedroom. The curtain separating the bedroom from the kitchen was still hanging, and he pulled it aside with a trembling hand, holding his breath as he stepped inside.

The bedroom was dark and shadowed without a window, but Billy could clearly see that it was as vacant as the kitchen. The sagging iron bed his mum and Sorley had shared was gone, as were the pallets the boys had slept on. No dirty clothes littered the floor, no blankets lay tossed in the corners.

There was no sign that anyone had ever lived here.

Billy stood staring into the emptiness for a long time before whispering into the silence. "Mum?"

His eye caught a glimpse of color in the corner where he and his brothers had once slept, and he crossed the room, bent over and picked up a small blue sock in need of darning.

As he stood there a bitter cold wind seemed to blow through the flat, chilling him to the bone, leaving him numb and dazed.

They were gone. Without so much as a word of goodbye, with not even a letter to explain, they were gone.

For an instant he considered running downstairs to see if perhaps they had left word as to their whereabouts with Mr. Hudgins.

But almost as quickly as the idea appeared, he knew it to be futile.

Mr. Hudgins would know nothing. Nothing at all.

They had simply packed up and left him to his own keeping. His mother, his brothers — all of them.

He was abandoned. Alone.

Sorley's doing, he supposed. But perhaps not entirely. His mum could have sent word, at least. If she cared for him at all, she could have sent word.

Slowly, he sank down to the floor, his back against the wall, his knees propped up to his chin. In the ominous silence of the empty room, his ears heard but his mind did not register the quiet, padded tapping of soft footsteps coming up the stairs. With the small sock clutched tightly in his fist, Billy squeezed his eyes shut against the tears he refused to shed.

Quinn had surprised herself by insisting on accompanying the sergeant and Mr. Whittaker to the Five Points. Sergeant Price, as she might have expected, argued against her going, reminding her that the slum was a vile and treacherous place entirely, filled with desperate men and vicious women.

He started his harangue the moment she

fetched him from his perch in front of Diley's Bakery, and the man didn't let up until they collected Mr. Whittaker.

Clearly, though, Mr. Whittaker did not mind her coming. Indeed, he almost seemed glad that she had offered, saying she'd be a comfort to Billy once they found him.

The afternoon shadows deepened with the early gloom of lowering clouds as the three of them took the distance to Mulberry Street almost at a run. The closer they came to Billy's former home, the less they spoke among themselves . . . as if each harbored a silent fear of what waited ahead.

Sergeant Price led the way up the dark steps to the second floor, easily taking two at a time, his nightstick in hand.

Upstairs, they found the door to the flat ajar. Quinn saw the sergeant withdraw his gun before tucking his nightstick under his arm. With his free hand, he pushed the door open.

"Nell?" he called out, his voice lower that usual. "Nell, 'tis Sergeant Price, come to see about you and the lads. We'll be coming in now."

The moment they stepped across the threshold Quinn was struck by a strong sensation of emptiness. The room was bare, except for a cookstove and frayed curtains at the window. She had the feeling that even a whisper would echo indefinitely in the desolate silence.

Mr. Whittaker broke the quiet, his voice taut and thin. "Why . . . it looks as if n-nobody is here, as if . . . they've m-moved . . ." He let his words fall away as the sergeant went to pull the curtain to the adjoining room.

The policeman stood in the doorway for a moment. Then Quinn saw the broad back stiffen, the hand with the gun drop slowly to his side.

His voice sounded peculiar when he spoke, as if he were strangling on his words. "Mr. Whittaker," he said quietly. "In here."

Quinn rushed to Sergeant Price's side and peered past him. There, in the grim, shabby bedroom, Billy Hogan sat against the wall, staring into the gathering darkness. Beside him, like a faithful sentry, lay Finbar the cat, his crossed eyes wide and watchful, his sleek body curled against Billy's legs.

Quinn hung back for a moment. The two men moved past her into the bedroom. By the time she stepped through the doorway, Mr. Whittaker was on his knees on the floor beside Billy. The sergeant, too, dropped down beside the boy.

Billy Hogan looked from one man to the other, his eyes enormous and smudged with sadness, red-rimmed but dry. Quinn recognized the look for what it was: the slightly dazed, disbelieving stare of one who has been abandoned, rejected by the very people in his life who were supposed to care.

Oh, she knew the look, right enough. And well did she know the feeling.

"They're gone, Mister Whittaker," said Billy Hogan in a terrible, hollow voice. "My mum, my brothers . . . they're gone. Gone without a word. I'm alone."

Mr. Whittaker — the kindest man Quinn had ever known — shook his head. He reached to clasp the boy's shoulder, almost losing his balance in the effort. Sergeant Price quickly steadied him with one large hand.

Quinn's throat felt tight and swollen as Sergeant Price gently lifted the cat and placed the purring, warm bundle into the boy's lap.

"No, Billy," said Mr. Whittaker, his voice infinitely gentle. "You are *not* alone. You have another family. You have m-me, and Mrs. Whittaker — and Miss Quinn. And don't forget Teddy and all the other b-boys at Whittaker House." Mr. Whittaker removed his hand from Billy's shoulder and stroked the cat, whose purring grew louder. "And Finbar. He obviously loves you very m-much." He paused and swallowed hard. "We all love you."

As he spoke his hand moved to Billy's hair, and Quinn could sense the soothing effect his touch and his words were beginning to work on the sorrowful-eyed little boy.

"It seems to m-me, Billy, that you have quite a large family indeed, wouldn't you say?"

The boy hugged Finbar to his chest, and his eyes rose to meet Evan Whittaker's. Finally he nodded, slowly.

"And, Billy — I promise you, son," Mr. Whittaker went on, "that we will never leave you. Perhaps your mother and brothers will return one day soon, b-but even if they don't, you will always have us. You have m-my word on it, Billy. And I do not break my word."

The boy studied Evan Whittaker's face for another moment. Then, his expression solemn, he lifted his chin slightly and said, "Thank you, Mister Whittaker. I'll be very good, I promise. I'll try to make you proud."

Quinn saw Sergeant Price's eyes mist and knew an instant of surprise. She wouldn't have believed the big hardheaded policeman capable of a tender thought.

Her own eyes clouded over as she watched the sergeant pick the boy up in his sturdy arms and hoist him, still holding the cat, onto his back.

"Why don't we just be giving you and

Finbar a lift home, Billy?" he said cheerfully. "Hang on, now, and we'll be back at Whittaker House in a shake."

As Quinn watched, the boy smiled wanly. Then, cradling the cat in one arm, he locked his other arm about the sergeant's neck and hitched both legs about the man's middle. An unfamiliar feeling caught her sharply off guard. Her heart seemed to vault to her throat as an enormous wave of tenderness swept over her. She felt herself drawn to the policeman's strength, yet moved beyond measure that this big, powerful bear of a man could be so easily gentled by a small boy's need.

Shaken, Quinn reminded herself that strength could just as quickly transform to cruelty, a most formidable weapon when turned upon the unsuspecting.

With a deliberate act of will, she suppressed the temporary softening of her heart. If and when she ever allowed herself a woman's affection for a man, he would need to be as gentle, as kind and tenderhearted, as the poet behind her weekly letters: Daniel Kavanagh.

That man could not *be* Daniel Kavanagh, of course. But at the very least, he would have to be a great deal like him.

She avoided the sergeant's eyes as she reached to squeeze Billy's shoulder and reassure him. The boy gave her a smile, and

Quinn smiled back, then quickly turned away before the policeman could catch her eye.

She set her face straight ahead, her eyes averted, as they started for Whittaker House. Deliberately, she avoided looking at Billy and the policeman during the long walk home.

32

Justice or Mercy?

Is God unjust? Not at all!
For he says to Moses,
"I will have mercy
on whom I have mercy,
and I will have compassion
on whom I have compassion."
ROMANS 9:14–15

After not finding Michael at the station later that afternoon, Denny Price decided to go by the Burke residence.

In truth the rambling old mansion on Thirty-fourth Street was the home of Mrs. Burke's grandmother, but Mike and his wife had moved in with the elderly Mrs. Platt right after their marriage.

As a rule, Denny would have felt out of place entirely in such grand surroundings, but Mike was his friend, not just his captain — and Mrs. Burke treated everyone the same, beggar or king. She was just as quick as Mike to make a body feel right at home, and it pleased him no end that she seemed to approve wholeheartedly of his and Mike's friendship.

As he crossed the street and started toward the house, Denny was aware that today he *needed* a friend. It had been a black day for the most part, capped by the incident with the poor little Hogan lad. Sure, it would do him good just to sit with Mike for a time and compare stories about each other's day.

As he closed the iron gate behind him and started up the walk, it began to rain, a light but steady drizzle, the kind likely to go on for hours. The thought of Billy Hogan pressed in on him again. The cowl of gloom that had set in when they found the boy alone in the deserted flat was still upon him, darker now than ever.

Denny had been a policeman since he was little more than a lad, yet he could still be astounded by the treachery of human beings. Were it not for decent Christian folks such as Evan Whittaker and his kind, only the dear Lord knew what would become of the city's innocent. Many were lost as it was, but the Whittakers and others like them had managed to rescue a few, God bless them.

He had lost count by now of just how many

ragged boys filled the beds at Whittaker House, but he had no doubt but what all of them were treated as fine as if they were the Whittakers' own. *Family*, that's what they called themselves at Whittaker House. *God's* family.

There had been a time, when he was but a stripling with all the carefree notions of youth, that Denny had given little thought to the importance of family, his own or others. Back then his mind had been almost entirely occupied with becoming a man, becoming an American, and becoming a policeman . . . in that order.

But these days, now that he had accomplished some of his earlier goals, he found himself thinking more often about family. Not only about a family of his own, although that was a part of it, but about the importance of families everywhere. That's what America was, after all — a country of families, working the land, building the cities, raising their children. Children who would one day grow up and have families of their own.

He had begun to realize how empty two rooms could be when occupied alone. The truth was, he was tired of his solitary life. He had had his years of squiring the lasses, a different one on his arm every week, and it was grand, when he was younger. But he no longer wanted those idle days.

He knew in his heart the time had come for him to be a husband, a father. The time had come to find someone with whom to share his life.

Ah, but there was the rub. He *had* found her, had found just the girl.

Who would have thought it, though, that he would tumble for a razor-tongued slip of a lass who had trouble written all over her face? A lass who thought him as dumb as a tree stump.

There were countless fine-looking girls about the city who would be quick to give a man the attention and affection he craved. Fairer girls by far than the uppity Miss Quinn O'Shea, and with civil tongues in their heads as well.

And the lot of them might just as well not even exist, for all he noticed or cared. . . .

As he walked up to the front door of the house, Denny wondered if Mike had ever considered his good fortune in having found, not one, but two women willing to give their hearts to him. Mike's first wife had died years ago, when their son Tierney was still a little boy. But apparently they had shared a good life together, albeit a brief one. And now he had his Sara. Sure, there was no mistaking the feelings between the two.

Denny drew a deep sigh, then shook the rain off his shoulders and knocked on the door. Perhaps a bit of their glow would rub off on him, at least enough to take the chill from the rain when he started back to his empty flat.

He found Mike in the library, grim-visaged and sitting alone by a cold fireplace.

Although he smiled when Denny entered, his expression sobered almost at once.

"Sara will be sorry to have missed you," he said after they exchanged pleasantries.

Denny took the chair Mike offered across from his own and started right in to tell him about Billy Hogan and the events of the day.

"Poor little fellow," Mike said, shaking his head. "We can be thankful he has Whittaker and the other boys. He'll make out all right with them, I expect."

With a nod, Denny inquired after Mike's wife.

"I doubt she'll be down," Mike replied somewhat glumly. "She's . . . indisposed just now."

"She's not ill, I hope?"

Mike seemed to hesitate. "In truth," he said, his eyes darting away from Denny, "I expect she's avoiding me. We had a bit of a, ah, row this morning, you see."

He attempted a smile, but it faltered. "That's the reason I came home early this afternoon, in hopes of making things up with her." He paused, his lower lip dropping even more. "It would seem, however, that she isn't quite ready to talk with me yet."

Denny blinked, trying not to show his surprise. Why, he wouldn't have thought it of Mike and his Sara, could not conceive of them at odds with each other.

"Sara thinks I'm making big out of little over the Walsh incident," Mike volunteered. "She says I'm like a dog with a bone, that I don't know when to give it over."

Denny said nothing, sensing the wisdom of silence.

"She also seems to think I would rather have shot the scoundrel myself."

Denny's eyes widened, but still he ventured no remark.

With a sigh, Mike looked away. "I expect she may be right."

"Oh, I hardly think that's the case, Mike. Not you."

The other locked his hands together over his chest, meeting Denny's gaze straight on. "As it happens, Sara knows me too well. The truth is, Denny, and it shames me to admit it, that I find myself wishing exactly that. Or at least that Walsh had suffered before he died."

He paused. "I did not realize I had such a brutal streak in me, but there it is. I can hardly blame Sara for being put off by it."

Startled, but quick to take his friend's part, Denny leaned forward. "No doubt 'tis difficult for others to understand a copper's life, Mike. Our hearts tend to get hard over the years, no matter how we may try to protect them."

As if he hadn't heard, Mike went on. "It was all too easy, the way he went. A snake like Walsh shouldn't have met his end so easily."

He dropped his hands to the arms of the chair with another sigh. "Sara gets very impatient with this side of me, you see. She insists it's not for me to question the judgment meted out to a man. And she's right, of course. I can't argue otherwise."

"For what it's worth," Denny said, "I've felt the same about Walsh. It does seem the rogue got off too easy entirely."

Mike lifted both eyebrows, this time managing a grimace of a smile. "Ah, well, Denny — the women would like us to be the good fellows they think they married. When we don't measure up, I expect it's disappointing."

Silence fell between them for a time. More than once Denny was tempted to voice his own disappointments, but it was clear that

Mike's thoughts were already troubled. It didn't seem right to burden him further.

Just when the stillness was beginning to feel awkward, Mike leaned forward, studying Denny with an interest that hadn't been there before. "If you don't mind my saying so, Denny, you don't seem quite yourself today. Is there something more on your mind, I wonder?"

Denny looked at him, deliberating how much, if anything, he might say. Mike was his friend, his only close friend if truth were told, but he was also his captain. He wouldn't want Mike to think one of his sergeants had turned into a weak sister.

But in spite of his caution, he suddenly found himself letting go, pouring out in one explosive rush of disjointed words his feelings, his frustrations, and his fears in regard to Quinn O'Shea. He confessed the urge that sometimes came upon him to shake the girl for her obstinacy, an urge which could just as easily change to a desire to embrace her with great tenderness. He admitted to the hurt he felt when she avoided him or shied away as if he were a wild beast — like a spear to his heart, that feeling. He told Mike how it incensed him when she took on airs and tried to play the grand lady, making him feel like a great bumbling eejit. He even confessed to the terrible fierce jealousy that overcame him when he chanced to see her acting a bit too chummy with the Kavanagh lad.

Mike listened, as he always did when one of his men spoke his mind or his heart, saying not a word the entire time, but rather suffering Denny's rambling tirade. He had a way, Mike did, of patiently hearing a man out, as if his problem was the most momentous event of the hour, worthy of a captain's undivided attention.

Only when Denny finally slumped back in the monster of a chair, spent and weak as an old woman, did Mike lean forward and smile at him — a kind, brotherly sort of smile that let Denny know at once that he had not lost his friend's respect or strained his patience.

"Denny, my boy," Mike said kindly, "it is clear that you are finally in love."

"Surely not," Denny protested, at the same time acknowledging his own suspicions. He sat up straight, knotting his hands on his knees. "I am altogether miserable, Mike."

Mike nodded, a look of great wisdom upon him. "Aye. It is as I said. Poor lad, you are finally in love."

In his room at the end of the corridor, Bhima the Turtle Boy listened with growing anger as the Stump unraveled his narrative

417

about the stranger and his gruesome offer.

All manner of sick jokes were routinely bantered about at the expense of Bhima, who had no legs, when he was seen in the company of Fritz Cochran — the Stump — who had no arms. Despite the cruel humor their companionship incurred, the two had become good friends over the years.

Bhima scooted the cart that bore his legless torso a little closer to his friend. "What did you tell him?"

"I told him it would take a bit of time, but I thought I knew just the sort of roughneck who might be willing to handle the job for him."

Bhima's eyes widened, and Fritz rushed to explain. "I thought it best to let him believe he'd found his man. Otherwise he might go looking elsewhere, don't you see?"

Bhima did see, and he was thankful for his friend's quick wits. "How are you to contact him again? And when?"

"He's to stop by later tonight. I told him I'd set up a meeting by then." He paused. "So — what do we do?"

Bhima's mind raced. "We have to tell Pastor Dalton right away, of course."

"He's over to the mission now, or at least he was. I'll go and fetch him."

"Wait. We need to send for Captain Burke as well. I'd not want to risk making a mistake

418

and somehow jeopardize the little girl. The captain will know what to do."

Fritz nodded. "I'll get Pauley to go for the captain, while I fetch the preacher."

"Be careful," Bhima cautioned as Fritz turned to go. "Whatever we do, we mustn't let word of this slip to anyone else. There's a great deal at stake here. And it's our chance to help Pastor Dalton."

"That's true. The Lord knows that good man has given up enough to help us. The least we can do is return his kindness."

As soon as Denny Price was out the door, Michael went upstairs to the bedroom. He fully expected to find Sara napping. Instead, she was sitting in the rocking chair, looking out the window.

It was unlike her to be idle. On those rare occasions when she sat quietly in the afternoons, it was usually with a book or some mending.

Guilt stabbed at Michael. Apparently his behavior had distressed her more than he would have thought.

She looked at him when he entered the room, but immediately turned back to the window.

After closing the door, he went to stand behind her, his hand on either post of the rocking chair.

He cleared his throat. "Denny Price was here," he said. "He asked after you."

She nodded but made no reply.

Michael hesitated for a moment, his insides aching at her coolness. "Denny is in love, it would seem," he ventured lightly, hoping to thaw her icy composure.

She slowed the rocking motion of the chair but made no move to look at him. "Denny Price? In love with whom?"

Encouraged, Michael came around to stand in front of her. "You'll not believe it. 'Tis Quinn O'Shea. He has fallen for Quinn O'Shea."

She stopped rocking altogether now, and he could almost hear her busy mind wheeling with possibilities. "Quinn O'Shea and Denny Price?" She hesitated, then started rocking again. "I'm not at all surprised."

Michael stared at her. "Well, I am! The girl doesn't strike me as the sort to turn the head of a charmer like Denny Price."

She shrugged. "I'd say they would be a good match. Quinn is enterprising, intelligent, and high-spirited."

"She's spirited, right enough," Michael muttered.

Sara gave him a sharp look. "And Denny Price is enterprising, intelligent — and *hard-headed*. It should be an ideal relationship."

"There is no 'relationship,'" Michael pointed out. "Denny says the girl wants nothing to do with him."

She lifted one eyebrow. "I find that hard to believe. From what I've been told, women practically fall at Denny's feet."

"Nothing quite so dramatic as that, but he does seem to have a way with the ladies."

She appeared to be warming to the conversation. Determined to put their tiff of the morning behind them, Michael hurried on. "Denny insists that the girl avoids him. Even when they're together, he says she's as guarded as a cornered wildcat."

Sara seemed to consider his words. "I suppose it might be the difference in their ages. Quinn's awfully young."

That stopped Michael for a moment, long enough for him to do some quick calculations. "There's not all that much more difference in *their* ages than there is in *ours,*" he said. His tone sounded defensive, but he couldn't entirely keep his hurt feelings under wraps.

She looked at him, her expression unreadable. "I suppose that's true."

He ground his teeth. She was still riled, all right.

"Sara . . . can we talk about this morning?"

She looked away. "I can't think why. There

doesn't seem to be any reaching you on the subject, Michael."

"The subject of Patrick Walsh, you mean."

She nodded.

"Why can't you understand how I feel?"

She turned her gaze back to him, and he was surprised to see concern in her eyes rather than exasperation. "Oh, Michael — I *do* understand how you feel! That's what upsets me so. None of this is like you."

"*What* isn't like me?" he countered stiffly.

She studied him for a moment. "To be so . . . coldhearted! I understand your bitterness about Patrick Walsh, but —"

"So I'm bitter, am I?"

"Yes, you *are!* You're bitter and resentful and angry. Perhaps you don't realize it, but when you talk about Walsh and how — how 'easy' he got off, I hear this terrible anger in you. Why can't you just accept what happened to the man and go on?"

He looked at her for a moment, then began to pace the room. "Sara — I'm a policeman. Try to understand, if you will, why I feel the way I do about Patrick Walsh. I deal with the lowest sort of human being almost every day of my life. Some are little more than mindless beasts. They steal from the poor, they swindle the honest, they lie and they murder and they rape — they destroy *lives,* Sara. And more often than not, they get away clean with it all."

He stopped by the window again but did not face her. Instead, he turned to look out into the rain-veiled afternoon.

"I know it must seem to you that by now I should have learned how to shake it off — the cruelty, the madness, the injustice of it all. That I ought to be able to just — put it behind me." He turned back to her. "Most of the time I can do just that. Otherwise, I expect I would have gone mad long before now."

He raked his hands down both sides of his face and expelled a long breath. "The thing is, Sara," he said, struggling to articulate his feelings, "once in a great while, a cop comes up against a true monster. There are real monsters out there, Sara, believe me. Monsters who spend their entire lives preying on the innocent, taking — always taking — whatever they can from the unsuspecting or the helpless. They destroy the lives of almost everyone they touch. Sometimes they even destroy the lives of those who love them."

Suddenly bone-weary, he sank down on the window seat. The rain had brought a dull ache to his knees, and he rubbed them as he went on. "Patrick Walsh was just such a monster. That sort has no conscience. No heart. I recognized him for what he was the first time I met him. I *knew*, Sara. I just knew."

He looked up. The indifferent glare had disappeared from her eyes, and she was leaning toward him, understanding softening her face. *Her dear face . . .*

"I can't explain what Walsh provoked in me," he went on. "Contempt. Disgust. Anger, most of all. It enraged me that he had become so successful and powerful — and obscenely wealthy — at the expense of those less fortunate. That he simply didn't care what he did, how many lives he ruined. Even ours, in a way. If it hadn't been for him, Tierney wouldn't be in exile in Ireland. Tierney will forever bear the scars of Patrick Walsh's evil ambition.

"I simply couldn't stop him. Every time I thought I had him on the ropes, he slipped away. Every attempt I made to bring him down failed. For so long I lived with such a terrible feeling of *helplessness* inside me because of the man, don't you see? And then, all of a sudden —" He pulled in a shuddering breath, spreading his hands palms up. "All of a sudden, he was gone. In an instant. Just like that, he was gone."

He looked at her, almost pleading for her understanding.

"Ah, Sara — I felt so incredibly *cheated!* I felt as if justice itself had been violated. It was almost as if Walsh's death was just one more escape — one more time he had managed to evade the punishment he deserved! He was a monster, and I wanted him to pay, and when he didn't —" He stopped, shaking his head, for there were no more words.

"Oh, Michael . . . Michael . . ."

She drew him into her arms, and he had all he could do not to blubber like a babe. For so long he had carried the weight of his emotions alone. Any longer and he thought he might have died with the burden.

He took the rocking chair now, pulling her onto his lap, into his arms. She pressed his head against her heart, soothing him as she might have a hurting child.

"Do you understand now, Sara?" His voice was muffled against her warmth. "Do you?"

"Oh, Michael, yes! Yes, I do! You don't have to defend yourself to me. This morning . . . this morning, I was foolish. I was only trying to help you — and instead I ended up accusing you. I'm so sorry."

He put a finger to her lips to hush her. "Don't you dare be sorry, *ma girsha*. Don't you dare. I've been a bear to live with, I know, and you have every right to call me to account. I'm the one who's sorry, and I will try to change my ways, I promise you."

They remained as they were for a long time, locked closely together, rocking slowly forward and back, comforting each other.

At last she eased back just enough to search his face. "Michael? Would it surprise you to know I've had some of the same feelings you have, about Patrick Walsh?"

He frowned at her in disbelief.

"Truly, Michael, I have. I even talked with Jess Dalton about them. I was angry, too, Michael, like you."

"You never told me. Why wouldn't you tell me, Sara?"

"I'm not sure. I knew you were hurting even more, and I suppose I was afraid my anger might only make things worse for you. I wanted to give you the time . . . and the freedom . . . to work through your feelings in your own way."

He pulled her head down and brushed his lips over her forehead.

"Do you want to know what Jess Dalton told me, Michael?"

He smiled to himself. "Of course, sweetheart." She would tell him in any event.

"Well . . . you know how he is. He seems to understand how you feel, even if he doesn't agree. After I'd bared my soul, he leaned back in that dilapidated old chair of his — I'm always afraid it's going to collapse beneath him — and smiled at me. Then he said something very strange, or at least I thought it strange at the time. He said that if we really understood what we were asking for when we demanded justice, we wouldn't be so quick to ask."

Michael went on stroking her hair, waiting for her to explain.

"When I asked him what he meant, he got the most peculiar look in his eyes. 'Sara,' he said, 'two thousand years ago, if God had given us justice instead of a cross, where do you think we'd all be today?' "

Michael stopped rocking, although he continued to hold her even more tightly. He could almost hear Jess Dalton's deep, gentle voice as Sara went on.

"He talked about the fact that while we all *deserve* God's justice, He gave us mercy instead. For which we can be eternally thankful, of course," she added quietly.

Michael swallowed, his mind scrambling to grasp the significance of her words — Jess Dalton's words.

"And then he said something else, Michael, something that really made me think. Of course, Jess Dalton has a way of doing that, doesn't he? Saying things that make you think, even when you would really rather not. He said, 'As to punishment for Patrick Walsh, I won't presume to speculate on what awaits a man like that on the other side. But I do believe with all my heart that the loss of heaven is the most grievous punishment of all. To lose all hope of eternity with our Lord is surely a most terrible, terrible judgment. And I daily thank my Savior that He has granted me His mercy, rather than the justice I deserve.' "

Michael wrapped his arms around her and again tried not to weep. The words she had spoken seemed to linger, echoing throughout the room, in his mind, in his soul. And in that moment, in the stillness of their bedroom with his wife's love draped all about him like a curtain shutting out the world, he felt something stir deep inside him, felt the beginnings of a healing and a peace that he knew could only have come from the Father of Mercy.

Anxious to be home out of the rain, Denny Price had run most of the distance from Mike's house when he met up with Pauley Runyan — the "Strong Man" from Brewster's dime museum in the Bowery.

This was not the sort of neighborhood where a boy from a dime museum might ordinarily be found. Indeed, Denny thought he probably wouldn't have recognized Pauley at all, had the lad not stopped him in his tracks.

Pauley was wearing the sort of open-throated shirt and dark work trousers common to any of the factory workers throughout the city, rather than the abbreviated stage costume that showed off his enormous size and muscles. He looked, Denny decided as he studied him, surprisingly ordinary.

"Well, Pauley, what are you doing up here — and in such a hurry at that?"

The lad was puffing as if he, too, had run most of the way. "Sergeant," he said after catching his breath, "I've been sent to fetch Captain Burke. I went to the station first, and Officer Ryan said the captain would be at home."

"He is. I've only just left him. Something wrong, Pauley?"

The youth took off his wet cap and ran a hand through his hair, a riot of dark brown curls. "Bhima said to ask the captain to come to the museum at once! Said it concerns the little girl taken in by the preacher."

Denny's interest quickened. "Pastor Dalton's little lass, do you mean?"

"That's the one, sir. Stump went to fetch the preacher from the mission while I was sent for Captain Burke." He caught a breath, then went on. "Bhima said I should ask the captain to come as quickly as possible."

Denny considered the boy's explanation for only an instant. "You know the captain's house, do you?"

Pauley shook his head. "No, sir, but I'll find it. On West Thirty-fourth," Bhima said.

Denny nodded, thinking. "I'll fetch the captain. You go on back to the museum. If there's trouble, Bhima may need you."

The boy hesitated only a moment. "All right, sir. But will you tell the captain, Bhima says it's urgent?"

"I will. Go on now."

Denny stood watching Pauley's muscular back for another second or two, then turned and took off at a run in the opposite direction.

33

A Well-Intentioned Deception

For who can say by what strange way
Christ brings His will to light. . . .
OSCAR WILDE (1854–1900)

The steadily increasing rain brought an early darkness to the day. In Bhima's small room at the back of the dime museum, the oil lamp gave just enough light to reveal the men huddled close to one another in the shadows.

Their faces were intense, troubled, lined with varying degrees of anger and speculation. As the discussion among them grew more heated, their expressions grew even more strained.

"Surely we would have evidence enough," said Jess Dalton, his usually genial voice now edged with worry, "without resorting to such measures."

Captain Burke shook his head. "I fear not,

Pastor." He darted a glance to the sergeant.

Sergeant Price, his red hair still slicked to his head, his shirt wet and clinging, looked from the captain to the preacher, giving a nod to indicate his agreement.

"It seems so extreme," Jess Dalton persisted. "And dangerous."

Bhima looked at him. "I say this with all respect, Pastor, but the real danger is to your little girl unless we act immediately."

For a fleeting moment Bhima saw a look of utter panic fill the pastor's eyes — the expression of a drowning man going down for the last time and finding not so much as a scrap of driftwood to cling to. "But do we have to bring her *here?*" he asked. "Couldn't we . . . isn't there some way . . . ?"

Captain Burke turned a look of understanding on the anxious preacher. "We'll do whatever it takes to keep her safe, Pastor," he said quietly. "We'll try to bluff him, but if Winston calls our hand, we may have to produce the lass. Still, we'll protect her with our lives, if it comes to that."

The big preacher frowned and ran a hand through his dark curly hair. "All right. We'll do whatever you say, Michael." His voice was resigned. "But it still doesn't make sense to me. Why can't you just arrest Winston on the strength of his proposition? Surely he's incriminated himself simply by approaching Fritz with such a scheme."

The captain's gaze traveled from the pastor to Fritz, then came to rest on Bhima for a second or two. Bhima sensed the policeman's dilemma and moved to rescue him. "I expect what Captain Burke is trying to avoid saying, Pastor, is that no court would be likely to accept the word of people such as us. You might say we have no real, ah, *credibility*, with the law. It would be the word of a man of English gentry against . . . us."

Captain Burke shot him a look that was both embarrassed and grateful. Jess Dalton studied Bhima for a moment, a look of understanding dawning in his eyes.

"If you will allow my opinion, Pastor," Bhima said quietly, "I believe Captain Burke's way is best."

"He's right, Pastor," Sergeant Price put in, turning toward the captain at his side. "The court can hardly ignore firsthand evidence from two city policemen. And it's for me to do the job."

A good man, the sergeant, thought Bhima. Decent and sturdy, a man who respected all the right things, such as truth and justice and the law. In that regard, he bore a close similarity to Captain Burke, who now stood glaring at the man beside him.

"It is *not* for you," declared the captain. "You will stay here with the pastor and back me up when I return."

"No, Mike — er, Captain. Begging your pardon, but you don't have the looks for such a nasty business, don't you see?"

The captain's eyes narrowed, but before he could make a rebuttal the sergeant hurried on. "Ah, Mike, no offense, but you're just a shade too civilized-looking for such a job." With a good-natured grin, he crossed his arms over his chest. "This kind of ugly business calls for a mean mug like my own, don't you see? Why, there's little effort it will take for me to play the outlaw, and that's the truth!"

Bhima found the sergeant's appraisal of himself altogether too harsh, but his observation about the captain's "civilized" appearance was incisive. He doubted that Captain Burke had it in him to make a very convincing hoodlum.

The friendship between the two policemen was evident as they stood searching each other's eyes, just as the conflict taking place inside the captain was unmistakable. "No doubt you'll make a more believable felon than I," he said dryly. "But I still outrank you, Sergeant, and you will remember that."

Sergeant Price, still grinning, merely shrugged.

The captain regarded him for another moment, then gave a gesture of concession with his hand. "All right, then. You'll do the job."

He turned to Fritz Cochran. "When Winston returns for your answer, set the deed for later tonight. Tell him it's absolutely no deal unless he hands the money over himself when the lass is — delivered." He paused. "You have to demand this very thing, mind: he must bring the money tonight, and bring it *here*. No later than ten o'clock. No exceptions."

Fritz nodded. "Ten o'clock," he said solemnly.

"Pastor —" The captain turned to Pastor Dalton. "Will your wife cooperate? We'll need her agreement to pull this off."

The preacher didn't answer right away. When he finally spoke, his voice was none too confident. "I'll have to convince her. Kerry has been terribly distraught about Amanda. But once she realizes . . . yes, I think she'll consent."

When the captain turned back to Sergeant Price, his face was as hard as Bhima had ever seen it. "You do realize, do you not, Denny," he said, his voice low and tight, "that a blighter capable of ordering the abduction and murder of his own niece will not give a second thought to killing a cop?"

The sergeant was no longer smiling. "You need not fret yourself, Mike — Captain. I can handle a white-livered Englishman with no great fuss."

The captain's expression remained dour, but the deal had been made. From this point on, Bhima knew, there was nothing he and the others could do except to wait . . . and pray.

Later that night, Kerry Dalton waited inside the darkened kitchen on Thirty-fourth Street, her arms trembling as she cradled her sleeping little girl. Molly Mackenzie, the Daltons' tall, pragmatic housekeeper, stood beside Kerry, arms folded across her sturdy chest, dark eyes watchful. Every now and then she would try to convince Kerry to let her hold Amanda. But Kerry could not bear to let her child out of her arms until the last moment, the last second.

When the knock came at the back door, Kerry, still holding Amanda, opened it herself. She was completely unprepared for what she saw.

A grimy, hard-looking hooligan of a man stood before her — his face blackened with soot, a day-old growth of beard stubbling his chin, a worn cap pulled down menacingly over his eyes.

Kerry's heart leaped into her throat, and her pulse began to pound. Instinctively she shrank back. Her terror must have been obvious, for the intruder instantly whipped off the cap and smiled gently at her.

" 'Tis me, Mrs. Dalton," he said softly, stepping into the kitchen. "Denny Price."

Kerry let out a tense breath and tried to force a smile. "Sergeant Price . . . well. Jess told me you could play the role, but I didn't expect . . ."

"Didn't expect me to look quite so convincing, now?" He grinned in earnest.

Kerry looked him up and down. He did look the felon, and that was the truth. Then her gaze fell on a tattered, lumpy carpetbag gripped in his left hand. A large bag, large enough to hold a small . . .

She gasped and drew Amanda closer. "No!"

Sergeant Price's eyes followed her gaze to the bag. "It's a bluff," he said hurriedly. "Didn't the pastor tell you?"

"You — you mean," she stammered, "you're going to try to convince Winston that my daughter's body —" She choked on the word.

The sergeant nodded almost apologetically.

"I won't let her go!" Kerry said fiercely.

"You don't need her. You've got . . . *that*." She shuddered, fighting to maintain some semblance of composure.

"Winston is determined to see the bod . . . the lass," Sergeant Price answered grimly. "We hope he won't insist on looking inside. But if he does, we'll have to be able to produce the girl. To get the evidence we need, you see."

Sergeant Price regarded her steadily. "My life upon it, Mrs. Dalton," he said firmly. "I'll not let the lass be harmed." He set down the carpetbag and held out his arms for Amanda.

The sleeping child's warmth could not begin to penetrate the cold tide of dread that swept through Kerry as she dragged her gaze from Sergeant Price's soot-streaked face to his waiting arms.

She took a jerky step backward, stopping when Molly steadied her with a restraining hand.

"Trust me," he murmured. His eyes, still compassionate, held Kerry's.

Finally, her throat closing, her heart breaking, she transferred the warm, infinitely precious bundle from her arms to his.

When Winston had not shown up at the dime museum by ten past ten, Michael's stomach was so sour as to make him ill. As he stood, gun in hand, listening through the paper-thin wall separating this room from Bhima's, perspiration ringed his neck and trailed down his back, leaving him clammy and uncomfortable.

If they had launched this bizarre exploit for nothing, he thought he would never be able to look Jess Dalton in the eye again. To put the kindly preacher and his wife through such an ordeal only to have it fail —

It couldn't fail. Please, God, don't let it fail.

In the next room, Bhima's room, only Fritz Cochran — the Stump — waited for Winston's arrival. Here, behind Michael on the small cot that served Pauley Runyan as a bed, Jess Dalton kept his vigil with his daughter, who had finally fallen back to sleep in her daddy's arms. With them, Bhima and Pauley — the museum's Strong Man — waited in tense silence.

Michael knew the torment the pastor must be going through. He could only hope the man would be able to stay put until this was over.

While he waited, he worried that something had gone wrong, something had happened to spoil their scheme. But what? What *could* go wrong, at least until Winston himself showed up?

The light knock at the door of the next room was hesitant, uncertain, but Michael heard it at once.

Behind him, the others stirred. He lifted a hand to warn them to silence.

The walls were so thin that they muffled the voices scarcely at all. His heart leaped to his throat when he heard the clipped tones of the unmistakable British accent, followed by an oath. . . .

"Abominable slum! It's hard to say which is worse, the dogs running loose in the streets or those squalid little beggars trying to bleed money from a man!"

Fritz Cochran said nothing as the Englishman charged through the door, brushing rain from the shoulders of his jacket. "I took a hack, but the driver could scarcely get past all the filthy little savages in the street! What a hellhole!"

He stopped in the middle of the room, looking around. "Where is he?"

"He'll be here," Fritz said, carefully concealing his own emotions. "Any minute, now, I'm sure."

Winston continued to shake the rain from his hair and clothing. "I cannot *wait* to get out of this loathsome pit! It's hard to believe people actually live in such squalor."

Fritz watched him, saying nothing.

Winston, finally still, frowned at Fritz. "You're quite sure you can depend on this thug you hired? You said he was a bad sort altogether."

Fritz nodded. "He'll show. You can count on him."

Winston snorted. "I rather doubt *that*."

"He'll do the job. That's all that matters to you, isn't it?" He paused. "You do have the money? Mine as well as his?"

Winston eyed him for a second or two. "I have the money. But it stays right here" — he patted his breast pocket — "until I see the proof."

Fritz had all he could do not to kick the man. It was true he had no arms, but life in the Bowery had taught him clever use of his feet.

"You actually intend to view the child's body?" he said, wondering at a man who could stoop so low.

Winston lifted an eyebrow. "For the amount I'm paying you and your roughneck friend, I'll see what I've bought. But if he doesn't show up before long, you can say goodbye to your own profit. If he reneges on the job, neither of you sees the money, remember?"

"He'll show," Fritz said again, praying it would be soon.

When the rap on the door finally came, Fritz jumped, watching nervously as the man stepped inside.

Sergeant Price certainly *looked* the part of the felon, with his dirty, rumpled clothes and soot-streaked face. He carried a lumpy, tattered carpetbag in one hand. Fritz held his breath and waited.

The Englishman's gaze raked the newcomer.

"Well?" he snapped.

"Not so loud," the abductor warned, his tone harsh. "You're the Brit?"

"I'll ask the questions, if you don't mind! Have you done the job I'm paying you for?"

Price regarded his interrogator. With his cap pulled low and a fierce glare in his eyes, he gave off a strong aura of menace. "You haven't paid me for nothin' yet," he answered sullenly. His eyes flickered to the large carpetbag he held in his hand.

Winston's face flamed, and his eyes narrowed. "Let me see," he breathed.

"Not until I have my money," Price returned. His grip tightened on the handle of the bag.

"Let me see the evidence, you fool —

now!" The Englishman grabbed the heavy carpetbag, heaved it onto the narrow cot, and jerked it open. With his back to both men, he froze. For a moment complete silence descended over the tiny room.

Fritz's blood ran cold. Sergeant Price had better be convincing — very convincing — or they were both dead men.

At last, as if in a daze, Winston lifted a sack of sand out of the carpetbag and held it in his palm as if measuring the weight. He wheeled around and shook it in Price's face.

"What is the meaning of this?" he screamed. "Where is the girl?"

For a moment Winston looked as if he might lunge at the abductor. But Price held his ground, and the Englishman seemed to be considering his opponent's superior size and bulk. Price held him off with a steely glare.

"The girl is just where I left her. And there she will stay until I see some cash."

"Do you mean she's still *alive?*" Winston rasped the words out with a look of raw fury.

Price straightened to his full height and fixed a withering stare on Winston. "I'm not fool enough to commit murder on the promise of an *Englishman.*" He spat out the last word. "The lass is alive — and she will stay alive until I see your good intentions, your *honor.*"

"That wasn't the arrangement."

Price stared him down. "The *arrangement,*" he grated out in the same rough voice, "was abduction and murder. Half the job is done, mister. Now, unless you want to do the other half yourself, I'll see my money."

"You —"

Price took a step toward Winston. The Englishman stumbled backward.

"Have you got the money or not, mister?"

"I have it! I told him —" He jabbed a finger toward Fritz. "I said when the job was finished!"

Price's eyes flashed. "And I said I'll finish the job after I'm paid. And that's the *last* time I will say it, Brit. You pay me now — me and Stump — or I gather up the little lassie and take her home."

Fritz's heart stopped as he watched the two face off. Only when the Englishman slowly reached inside his breast pocket did he let out a ragged breath.

"Very well," Winston muttered. "Here's your money. And his!" He scowled, then tossed a small money bag to Fritz, a larger one to Sergeant Price. "Now do what you've been paid to do!"

The Sergeant's eyes glinted. "Aye, that I will, your honor. That I will."

At that instant the room exploded. Michael

444

crashed through the door, gun leveled on Colin Winston as Denny Price reached behind his back to pull his own pistol from his belt.

With one sharp motion, Denny jerked the gun in Winston's face and gave a nasty grin of satisfaction. "I am doing what I've been paid to do, Mr. Winston. I am placing you under arrest for conspiring to kidnap and commit murder. If you'll be so kind as to cuff the gentleman, Captain?"

Michael felt an almost dizzying sense of gratification as he watched the incredulity in Winston's eyes change to understanding, then fury.

The Englishman turned on Fritz Cochran. *"Why, you filthy, treacherous freak —"*

For just an instant Michael entertained a brief but gratifying mental image of beating Colin Winston senseless. Instead, he jerked the raving Englishman around and put the cuffs on him. Denny Price, he noted, seemed to be enjoying himself immensely as he let go an entire stream of descriptive epithets at the crimson-faced Winston. Denny was not a lad given to profanity, but he still managed to express in unmistakable terms his contempt for a man who would order the murder of his own niece.

For the first time in a very long time, Michael felt good about being a policeman.

Less than half an hour later, having received the awaited message, the officer who had been posted at the Daltons' house throughout the evening delivered Kerry Dalton to the dime museum.

Sergeant Price was waiting at the back door and flung it open the moment he saw her.

Kerry rushed inside, her heart hammering. She stopped short when she saw the big policeman. For a moment she stood searching his eyes, her legs shaking beneath her.

The sergeant smiled — a wide, beaming, thoroughly Irish smile that made his eyes dance. He dipped his head in a small bow to her. "You have come to collect your wee lass, I expect, Mrs. Dalton. It will be my personal pleasure to take you to her."

Relief poured over Kerry, threatening to leave her faint. When the sergeant offered her his arm, she quickly accepted it, releasing him only when she stepped inside Bhima's room.

Her gaze took in the entire room in one sweep, coming to rest on the group huddled in the corner. "Jess!" she cried. He turned, his face lighting up at the sight of her. He broke free of the others and strode rapidly across the room.

"Kerry — it's all right! Winston is in custody. Michael Burke and another officer have already left with him."

Kerry didn't care about Winston. She could not think of anything at this moment but her little girl.

"Jess — where *is* she? Where's Amanda?"

Jess wrapped an arm about her shoulder and pulled her to his side. But before he could answer, Kerry heard the high, delighted laughter that always made her think of a bubbling fountain.

She turned from Jess, putting a hand to her mouth as she watched the group across the room part. Out of their midst, whirring toward Kerry and Jess, came Bhima, the sweet, gentle-natured boy who had no legs, on the small cart that served as his means of transport. Seated on the cart in front of him was Amanda, laughing excitedly, obviously having the time of her life.

She spied Kerry immediately and threw both arms in the air. "Mumma!"

Bhima brought them to a stop directly in front of Kerry. "What a perfectly delightful daughter you have, Mrs. Dalton," he said. "Although after tonight, you may have to buy her a wagon. I'm afraid we've indulged her no end."

The tears ran freely down Kerry's face as she lifted her baby girl into her arms. "How

447

can I ever thank you . . . all of you?" she choked out.

Her eyes went to Sergeant Price, now leaning against the opposite wall of the room, a tired but contented smile creasing his soot-smudged face. "And especially you, Sergeant. I can never thank you enough! You risked your own life for Amanda."

"Ah, now, Mrs. Dalton," the sergeant said, pushing away from the wall and thrusting his hands into his pockets. "There was never really any danger at all, don't you see? Giving a black-hearted Englishman like Winston his just desserts is no more trouble than bringing a cowardly dog to heel, and that's the truth."

He grinned at her. "Though I'll admit," he added, "it might be a bit more satisfying."

Part Three

THE PROMISE RENEWED

Hope for the Future

There I will give back her vineyards,
and will make the Valley of Troubles
a Door of Hope.
HOSEA 2:15

34

Nation of Exiles, Land of Liberty

The nation has a smell all its own,
a scent that drifts out upon the water
to fill the air and the senses
of those countless numbers
standing at the ship's rail
with longing eyes and yearning hearts. . . .
It is the very breath of freedom,
borne on the wind of hope.
MORGAN FITZGERALD (1850)

Late September

Before leaving for the harbor, Sara made one last-minute inspection of the east wing, which had been aired and partly redecorated for the Fitzgeralds. Her grandmother followed her every step of the way, commenting or criticizing, as the condition warranted.

"I do wish there had been time to have more of the furniture replaced." Her grandmother leaned on her cane as together they appraised the second largest bedroom in the wing. "We really haven't changed anything since you and your brother used to spend weekends with us, when your grandfather was still alive. Most of the pieces are terribly dated."

"Oh, Grandy, the furniture is just fine. The little Fitzgerald boy is scarcely more than a baby, after all. I doubt that he'll care whether the furniture is old or new."

Her grandmother didn't look convinced. "Still, the girl will be sharing the room with her little brother. And she's old enough to be sensitive to her surroundings."

"That's why we moved the brass bed and Mother's desk in here. And the dolls." Sara smiled fondly at the rag and china dolls propped randomly around the room. She had selected them from her own girlhood collection, and the sight of them brought back a stream of memories, all of them pleasant. "Annie Fitzgerald is going to love this room. I'm sure of it." She frowned. "I only wish Tierney were coming, too. Michael is so disappointed."

Her grandmother pursed her lips. "I know, dear. But boys that age are bound to strike out on their own — adventure, that sort of thing. I'm sure Michael understands." Grandy paused, still considering. "Well, at least the Fitzgeralds can have a nice, large sitting room off the bedchamber. And the blue room turned out just splendidly for their servant. What's his name again? Sandemon. Yes, we've put him right next door to the Fitzgeralds."

Sara nodded. "That's just fine, Grandy. But try to remember that Sandemon isn't a servant. I believe Morgan refers to him as 'his man.' They're quite close, almost like family, according to Michael."

"Well, he sounds like a veritable wonder. I find myself almost as eager to meet the amazing Sandemon as Morgan Fitzgerald himself. At any rate, my first consideration is to make sure things are comfortable and cheerful for all of them, so they'll feel at home."

"I'm sure they will," Sara said, crossing the room to remove a stray pin in one of the draperies. "I'm more concerned that we've anticipated Morgan's needs. It must be difficult enough being confined to a wheelchair when you're in your own home and can adapt things accordingly. I'm sure there's no telling all the problems he must encounter when he travels. Michael helped me, and we tried to plan as carefully as possible, but I still worry that we might have forgotten something."

It had been Michael's idea to install a ramp leading off the side entrance, and he himself had made some additions to the plumbing to compensate for his friend's disability. In deference to Morgan's size, they had even invested in a new, much larger bed for the guest room that he and his wife would share.

They seemed to have accomplished a great deal in only a few weeks, but Sara continued to fuss about details, anxious that nothing of any consequence be overlooked. "Michael says Morgan wouldn't want us to go to any trouble on their account, but we're both too excited about their visit to think of the preparations as 'trouble.' "

Sara held on to her grandmother's arm as they walked out of the room into the hallway. "Grandy, I want to thank you again for inviting them to stay here. It will be so good for Michael. He's been so happy ever since we found out they're coming."

Her grandmother stopped for a moment to adjust her cane. "I'm really quite excited about this visit, you know. It's an honor to entertain someone of Morgan Fitzgerald's caliber. The man is quite a dignitary, even if Michael does howl every time I say so."

Her grandmother went on talking as they started down the hall. "As I told you and Michael, dear, I plan to enjoy their company immensely. Your grandfather and I used to have guests regularly, and I rather miss all the bustle and excitement. Besides," she added, her eyes lighting with amusement, "I'm looking forward to some dinner conversation that includes something more than the exploits of cops and robbers. For now, though, if we don't want the poor man and his family stranded in the harbor, you'd best collect Michael and your father from the parlor and be on your way. I'm sure both of them are pacing the floor by now."

Nora peered into the mirror of her vanity, trying to be objective about her appearance as she considered, somewhat reluctantly, how she might look to Morgan after so long a time.

Older, that much was certain. Most of the hair at her temples had gone to silver, and there were faint lines at her mouth and the corners of her eyes that had not been there before.

Although she and Morgan were nearly the same age — thirty-six — Nora knew she looked older than her years. And what about Morgan? No doubt both of them had changed a great deal since their last parting.

It would be difficult, seeing him in the wheelchair. Even though she had eventually grown used to the idea, she still worried over how she would respond when faced with the reality.

How many changes they had been through since their childhood days in the village . . . Morgan, Michael, and herself.

Tragic changes, some of them. Even as a young man, Michael had lost a wife. And Morgan, in the prime of his manhood, had been crippled by an unknown assailant. He had been left almost entirely alone after the death of his brother Thomas, then his niece Katie and nephew Tom — both of whom had died after reaching America.

As for herself, Nora had known her own tragedies, her own losses. Her first husband, Owen, their wee daughter, Ellie, and soon after, Tahg, their eldest son. Her health had almost been destroyed by the famine and scarlet fever, her heart weakened, her strength depleted.

But for all the tragedy in their lives, they had not been left without joy. There had been gifts of love for each of them: new mates, children, and a very special and enduring friendship.

She wondered anxiously what it would be like for them today, when they were finally reunited after so long a time. Would they be strangers, unnatural and ill at ease with each other? Or would the tie that had somehow bound them throughout the years, even an ocean apart, prove to be as strong as she had long believed?

Evan walked in, rousing her from her thoughts as he came to stand behind her at the vanity. With a smile, he clasped her shoulder. "You look lovely," he told her, leaning to kiss her cheek. "As always. But, Nora, are you quite sure you feel strong enough to go this m-morning?"

She nodded. "What does it take to convince you? 'Tis just as I've been telling you, Evan — I feel stronger and more fit than I have for an age; I have felt so for days now. You mustn't take on."

"B-but you'll be careful not to overdo."

"I'll be very careful, I promise you. But I want to be there today, with you and Michael. You do understand, don't you?"

He straightened, his hand still clinging to her shoulder. "Of course, I understand." He studied her for a minute, as if he wanted to say something more but didn't quite know how.

"Evan?"

He shook his head. When he avoided her gaze in the mirror, Nora turned to face him. "Something is troubling you, Evan. What is it?"

Slowly he turned back to her. "I . . . feel ashamed to tell you," he said quietly. "Perhaps I'm b-being altogether foolish, but as m-much as I'm looking forward to seeing Fitzgerald again — I can't help feeling somewhat . . . anxious."

Nora frowned, unable to read his expression. "Anxious? Why would you feel anxious about Morgan? He admires you entirely."

Again he looked away. "You — the two of you — once cared very d-deeply for each other. You loved each other. . . ."

Nora stared at him in dismay, understanding finally dawning upon her. "Oh, Evan . . . surely you do not mean . . . you cannot think . . ."

She reached for his hand. "Oh, Evan . . . Evan! How can it be, that you are unsure of my love, after all this time? Can you really doubt me, after everything we've been to each other?"

He looked thoroughly miserable. Nora was grieved that he could feel anything less than total confidence in her love, yet she thought she understood. But before she could move to reassure him, he turned away from her.

"I'm sorry," he said, his voice almost inaudible. "I would never question your faithfulness, Nora. Never. I suppose . . . it's m-myself I doubt. A m-man like Fitzgerald, after all — such a great man — even in a wheelchair, he surely overshadows m-most men. And you *did* love him. And he, you."

With his back still turned to her, he touched his empty sleeve — an unthinking gesture, Nora suspected, but not an entirely meaningless one.

Slowly, she got to her feet and put a hand to his shoulder. "Evan . . . look at me," she said quietly but firmly.

When he finally turned back to her, she stepped closer, gripping his hand with both of hers. Her eyes went over his face . . . that good, strong, kind face, with its polished spectacles and precisely trimmed beard and scrubbed cheeks.

Oh, how she did love this man!

It brought such pain to know he thought himself wanting in her eyes because of stature or a missing arm or his halting speech . . . or any of the other traits he seemed to view as weaknesses. In truth, those things only endeared him to her that much more. It even made her angry somehow, to realize how lightly he held himself in his own estimation.

"Evan — you foolish, foolish man!" she burst out, unable to stop the tears that spilled over with her words.

He blinked, looking altogether stunned. "Why, Nora, what did I —"

"*You* are my love, Evan Whittaker! You are my husband, my best friend — and my love!

Don't you understand? Yes, Morgan *was* the love of my girlhood. He was my hero-lad, the love of my youth. But, Evan, you — *you* are the love of my *life!*"

She stepped back from him, bringing her hands to her face. "There is something I would tell you, Evan," she said, dropping her voice to little more than a whisper. "It shames me to admit such a thing, a thing better left a secret, but I will tell you in spite of my shame . . . because you deserve to know the truth."

With a deep shudder, she dropped her hands away to face him directly. "Not only do I love you more than I ever loved Morgan Fitzgerald, but in truth I love you more than I loved Owen — Owen Kavanagh, my husband . . . and Daniel's father. Do you hear me, Evan? Do you understand what I am saying to you? I . . . love . . . you . . . *more!* I have never loved *any* man as I love you, Evan Whittaker. And you must never dare to question my love again, after my telling you such a thing. Never!"

His features had gone slack, his skin chalk-white. With a stricken look, he reached to draw her to him. But Nora resisted, searching his eyes for something she could not quite define.

"Oh, Nora . . . dearest . . . can you forgive me? I'm so sorry! I *have* been foolish, and now

look what it's cost you." He stopped. "Nora
— thank you! Thank you for telling me something so . . . private. You can't imagine how
m-much it means to me, hearing those words
from you."

Nora saw what she was looking for, the
quiet assurance that had not been there before. She took a step toward him, then
stopped. "You must promise you will never
again doubt my love for you, Evan."

He extended his hand to her. His eyes behind the spectacles were bright, glistening
with some new light of confidence. "I promise, Nora. I do."

Nora felt spent, but strangely relieved to
have finally spoken such a stark truth about
her feelings. Warmed by the assurance her
confession seemed to have inspired in Evan,
she moved into his embrace.

For a moment they stood, saying nothing,
her head resting lightly against his shoulder.
"Nora?" Evan finally said. "Though I've
promised never again to question how m-
much you love me, I wonder . . . do you suppose you m-might just remind me every now
and then?"

Nora smiled to herself, then lifted her face
for his kiss.

Morgan and his entire entourage had been

on deck for well over an hour, awaiting their first sight of the American shoreline.

All about them the water was polluted with debris, refuse thrown overboard from emigrant ships entering New York Harbor. Apparently this was a common practice.

Terrible things bobbed up and down with the current, forcing one to look away. Morgan could not help but cringe at the sight. He was accustomed to the clean waters of Ireland, had not imagined that his first look at the States would include the carelessly dumped garbage of her newest arrivals.

At least the ship on which they had crossed had strict regulations about such negligence. All round, the *Destiny* was a wondrous improvement over what he had been told about other vessels, especially the British emigrant ships on which bodies were herded together in steerage like cattle, doomed to pass the entire voyage in squalor and filth and disease.

The *Destiny* was a new vessel, reputedly the fastest of the Farmington line, and clean, with spacious quarters for all. Morgan had not been able to descend into steerage, but Sandemon had gone as his emissary and found the emigrant bunks more than adequate.

It would seem that Michael's father-in-law was a man of conscience. In the beginning,

Morgan had found it difficult to accept Farmington's offer of free cabin passage on his newest packet. He had always assumed that if he ever made the crossing to America, he would make it as most of his people had before him: in the dank, mean quarters of steerage, suffering the same desperate conditions.

But back then he had not known that he would make the voyage as a crippled man in a wheelchair, with a wife and two children. After reluctantly accepting Lewis Farmington's largesse, he had been gratified to learn that the man kept a decent ship, with fair conditions for all, even the exiles. It would have seemed obscene to travel in comfort while other poor wretches suffered in misery below.

It was an auspicious morning for their arrival, clear with a brilliant autumn sun overhead, and brisk without being chill. They began to see other vessels at a distance, heard murmuring all round that they were close now, approaching land.

They were all eager, none more so than Annie, who was fairly dancing with anticipation. Gabriel, held securely in Sandemon's sturdy arms, was growing restless, but Morgan insisted the boy remain on deck. Although Gabriel was likely too young to recall this early glimpse of the States, the memory would still be his own, tucked away in that deepest part of the mind that time and change could not alter.

Beside Morgan, on his left, stood Finola, her hand clasping his shoulder. Her usual serenity seemed to have vanished as her anticipation grew.

He lifted his hand to cover hers. "So, *macushla*, are you eager?"

"I am," she said, sounding slightly breathless. "I have dreamed of seeing America, but never thought it would come to pass." She paused. "But you, Morgan — you must find the waiting unbearable. In no time now you will be reunited with your friends and your little niece."

"Not so little by now, I'll warrant." Mentally, he calculated Johanna's years. "Johanna and our Aine are close on the same age, thirteen years."

"Shall we be friends, do you think, *Seanchai?*" Annie spoke up. "Your niece, Johanna, and I?"

His daughter's voice sounded somewhat anxious, and Morgan realized anew what a momentous event this was for her. "I can't think anything else, *alannah*," he said. "But you recall that Johanna cannot hear? You must remember to face her when you speak so that she can read the words on your lips."

"But she *does* speak?"

"By God's grace, she does, though there's no telling how well. It has been only a short time since she discovered she had a voice."

"No doubt she will be wild to see you again, Morgan," Finola said.

"I only hope she will remember me."

He spoke more to himself than to the others standing nearby, but Sandemon had heard him. "Blood remembers," the black man said quietly. "It has not been so long ago, after all, that you parted."

"Aye, but a few years can make a large difference to the young. And she has never seen me in the chair."

"I doubt that your niece will even take note of the wheelchair," Annie said brightly, as if she already knew Johanna and held a good opinion of her. "She will be far too happy to see you again to bother about anything else."

Morgan nodded, determined not to surrender to the veiled melancholy that had been nipping at the heels of his spirit most of the morning. He had resolved upon sailing that he would not allow thoughts of the pending surgery — if indeed there were to *be* a surgery — to cloud the enjoyment and high spirits of his family during the crossing.

Soon now, this very day, he would be reunited with friends and family. Michael.

Nora. Johanna and Daniel John. The delightful Whittaker.

Moreover, steps had already been taken by Michael's father-in-law and a clergyman-friend of the family to bring Joseph Mahon's famine diary to the attention of an American publisher. There seemed to be real hope for the diary's publication — reason enough in itself for this voyage, to Morgan's way of thinking. If he accomplished nothing else than getting the truth about England's perfidy and unconscionable indifference past the British press, the journey would be well-served.

Throughout the coming days he would be in the company of loved ones as he explored this vigorous, important new nation about which he had read volumes. Perhaps he would also meet people of consequence who might make a difference for Ireland.

So, while it was true that a dark unknown — perhaps even a dread unknown — awaited him further on in this adventure, he would not dwell on it today. Today he would discover America.

"LAND!" someone down the deck shouted. Someone else took up the call, and the words rolled across the ship like thunder claps. "AMERICA! BY THE GRACE OF GOD! AMERICA AT LAST!"

Morgan felt a thrill ripple through him. He

gripped Finola's hand more tightly as his gaze swept their surroundings. He had not expected to see so many hills, all splashed with vivid autumn hues. The waters were placid, though dotted with countless other vessels. Clippers and longboats. Smaller craft, some flying medical flags, zigzagged in and out among the larger ships. A few emigrant vessels bravely displayed tattered banners of green and gold, along with laundry hung on the rigging: Ireland's tattered frieze and frayed red petticoats, mostly.

From Michael's description Morgan knew they were passing through the Narrows, the channel running between Staten Island and Brooklyn. The docks had come into view, teeming with people and activity.

The entire spectacle was bright and busy, a scene of energy and color and excitement.

Breathtaking!

The steerage passengers had come above decks, and everywhere people embraced and wept and called out to one another. Some fell to their knees and gave thanks, while others stood in mute amazement.

Morgan felt Finola's hand in his tighten still more. Behind him, he heard Sandemon's deep-chested "Ah!" and turned to see his comrade lift wee Gabriel high on the wide expanse of his shoulders.

"Do you see, Gabriel?" Morgan shouted above the din all around them. "We have come to America! Remember this day, lad, for one day you can claim knowledge of a country known above all others. This nation of exiles is called the Golden Shore, the Land of Liberty."

With his face still set on the docks just ahead, he murmured to himself: "Aye, she is all that and more, this gracious land. To the millions, she has become a door to hope, a promise, a gift of God. And may she always be so."

35

Welcome to New York

There are those in this city who would
brighten, to me,
the darkest winter-day that
ever glimmered . . .
and before whose presence even
Home grew dim. . . .
CHARLES DICKENS (1812–1870)
From *American Notes*

Thanks to the forethought and influence of Lewis Farmington, the Fitzgerald party was passed through the usual debarkation procedures with extreme ease and all possible speed.

As soon as Sandemon wheeled him down the gangplank, Morgan began to search the crowds for a familiar face. Nora, of course, he would recognize, no doubt Johanna and Daniel John as well. But he knew it was unlikely that he would be able to locate Michael in a horde such as this, not after twenty years.

Finola and Annie, eyes wide, had come to a stop beside him. Gabriel stood between the two, his arms stretched upward, a hand securely anchored in each one of theirs.

The docks were so dense with milling crowds that it was virtually impossible to move more than a few feet in any direction. Although Morgan had heard any number of tales about the bedlam that greeted passengers leaving the ships in New York, nothing could have prepared him for the reality.

The cacophony of shouting and weeping battled with the sound of running feet tearing off down the wharves and the sailors' boisterous exchange ringing back and forth from adjoining ships. Morgan's ear singled out at least six foreign tongues, as well as all manner of accents and brogues, the most common by far being Irish.

In only moments he saw the runners Michael had described in his letters: hard-looking men with knives between their teeth or an occasional musket in hand, literally shoving people aside in their haste to board the ships or hawk their services to disembarking passengers. Most of the bounders were Irish themselves, knaves who preyed on unsuspecting emigrants from their own country. Greedy and brutal, they would stop at nothing, would even seize an entire family's belongings as a means of forcing them into their "protection," then promptly lead them off the docks to an abysmal boardinghouse or tenement run by other pirates like themselves.

One such scoundrel came snaking his way through the crowd at that very moment, jostling the wheelchair, stopping only long enough to level an oath at Morgan. Sandemon reached one large hand to the blackguard's shoulder to stop him, but Morgan gestured to let him go.

"Have a care," he muttered to his friend. "According to Michael, a black man does not dare to lay a hand on a white for any reason, not even here in New York."

Sandemon looked at him, and Morgan wondered if they weren't both thinking the same thing: that even in this land of liberty, freedom had its limits.

Carefully, he tucked his harp next to him in the chair — he had not been willing to trust it with the rest of the baggage — then stretched his neck in an effort to scan the dense throngs of people lining the docks. It was almost impossible to see anything, and after being caught in the same place for more than ten minutes, they made their way a little farther down the docks.

By now Gabriel was growing agitated from

the noise and confusion. No doubt the tyke was hungry as well. In any event, he began to set up a fuss of his own. Finola lifted him into her arms and tried to quiet him, but he went on squirming.

Morgan knew it wouldn't take long before Finola also would react to the clamor and chaos. Uncomfortable in crowds, she could quickly become unnerved by excessive noise and disturbance.

He supposed it had been sheer presumption on his part, expecting that someone would be here to greet them. Their arrival had been delayed past the initial date, after all. The storms they encountered early on had slowed their speed considerably. Nonetheless, he could not curb an edge of disappointment. It would have been a cheering sight to find some welcoming smiles amid the crowd.

That not being the case, he decided the sensible thing to do was to hire a conveyance to take them to Michael's house. He turned to say as much to Sandemon. At the same instant his attention was diverted by a commotion off to his left. A broad-shouldered fellow with dark hair and a moustache came whipping down the docks, parting the crowds to make his own lane, leading what looked to be a small procession behind him. He scowled as he came, threading himself and his party past one startled bevy of onlookers after another, waving his hand like a warning.

As he drew closer, Morgan could see that the fellow held what appeared to be some sort of badge, star-shaped, of copper tint. This must be one of the New York City "coppers," one of Michael Burke's number. A strapping fellow, he appeared altogether hard and sturdy — not brutish at all, in fact, rather dashing, but with an edge of flint about him that clearly said he was not a man to be trifled with.

Morgan's glance strayed to the others in the fellow's wake. With his vantage point obscured by the crowds, he could make out very little: two women, a girl with gleaming red hair, followed by a distinguished-looking man, obviously a gentleman, a younger lad, and a thin-faced fellow with spectacles and a beard.

He craned his neck to follow the progress of the approaching train. Only when his gaze lighted on one of the two women did his senses quicken. There was something about the diminutive stature and uncertain tilt of the head. . . .

Morgan tensed, glancing to the others. The bearded man had an empty sleeve, neatly pinned to his jacket, and he carried a babe against his other shoulder. His eyes went to the tall youth with the head of raven curls, then back to the women, one of whom walked with a slight limp. Finally he turned his gaze to the fellow blazing the way for the others — the snapping dark eyes, the roguish good looks, the air of authority.

He gripped the arms of the chair until his knuckles cracked. They were almost upon him now. Morgan held his breath.

They stopped, and Morgan snapped his head up, his eyes sweeping the lot of them. At the same time, out of the corner of his eye, he saw the small woman step out from the others. At her side was the tall youth with the long, handsome face and curly hair.

No . . . it could not be . . . she was too thin, had too much silver in her hair . . . the boy was too tall, too mature, a man grown.

He stared at them both, and recognition hit him like a hammer blow.

Nora squeezed her eyes shut for an instant, grasping Daniel John's hand before stepping out to approach Morgan. She must not, would not, allow him to see the pain that had seized her when she caught her first glimpse of his once vigorous body now confined to the wheelchair.

Other than the legs that would no longer support him, he seemed to have changed

474

scarcely at all. The great, noble head, the flaming copper hair and darker beard, the soul-piercing green eyes, the aura of strength and power — all the attributes about the man that gave him the bearing of an ancient chieftain, a Celtic prince, seemed to have endured, unchanged.

Yet he sat immobile, a stricken giant, a fallen hero. *But he is still Morgan,* she reminded herself, and he must never see the pity that wrenched her heart as she drew near to him.

"Nora," he said softly. "Ah, Nora, *ma girsha.* 'Tis really you. I am so glad, so very glad to see you at last."

He held out his hands to her. Nora tried to speak his name, but managed only a strangled sob. She hesitated only for an instant before leaning to press her cheek to his, accepting his embrace for what it was — a kind of homecoming, the welcome of a long-time friend and brother.

Daniel had all he could do not to crumble at the sight of Morgan in the wheelchair. It had been three years since he had last seen the hero of his boyhood, the one man he had respected and loved as much as his own departed father.

For years Morgan Fitzgerald had been a giant in his eyes. He was a powerfully set man, and most of the other youths in Killala had admired him, but Daniel's admiration and respect went far beyond an appreciation of Morgan's forbidding stature and breadth of shoulder. Daniel had esteemed Morgan for his intelligence, his wit, his daring, the reckless courage that had helped to keep at least a part of the village from total starvation.

An mhac tire rua, they called him. The Red Wolf of Mayo. Later, he had been given a title of even more respect and affection: the *Seanchai.* The Storyteller, a beloved figure, revered throughout all Ireland.

But more than all else, Morgan Fitzgerald had been a friend, the uncle Daniel had never had, a mentor and example, an ideal and an inspiration. Leaving him behind when they departed Ireland had been one of the most painful things he had ever had to do; at the time he thought he might just as well tear out a part of his heart and throw it into the sea.

But now Morgan was here, here in America, in New York. They were together again, at least for a time. They would play their harps together and Morgan would tell the old legends, and just like before, the two of them would spend time together, laugh together, walk together —

He caught himself and swallowed hard.

They could not walk together. . . .

As he watched the reunion of Morgan and his mother, Daniel forced the thought of the wheelchair out of his mind, along with the lost years and old sorrows of the past, and stood waiting, silently thanking God for this gift of a day. And when his mother finally moved aside to make room for him, he smiled into Morgan's eyes and stepped gratefully into the welcoming embrace of his former hero, his forever friend.

After Daniel John, the others converged on him, as if all at once.

Johanna was no longer a little girl. Morgan studied her, marveling at the graceful transition she had made from child to the threshold of young womanhood. The sharp little face with the pinched features he recalled from three years past had taken on a softness, a sweetness that could only be described as lovely. The dark red hair was brighter now, as copper-glazed as his own, its deep waves shot with gold and caught in a green silk ribbon at her neck.

She watched him as she signed his name on her hands, the way he had taught her so many years ago. And then she spoke it aloud, and Morgan thought he would surely weep at the sound of his name on those once silent lips.

"Un-cle Morgan." She said it twice, then smiled at him, obviously enjoying his delight in her accomplishment.

Even though Michael had written to him about Johanna's voice, the sound of it at this moment — the low pitch, the words articulated with such obvious effort — shook Morgan soundly.

Overcome, he could barely find his own voice. "By God's mercy, lass, your words are a song to my heart!" he told her, drawing her into his arms.

Whittaker stepped up next, passing the babe to Nora. Morgan had known about the man's losing his arm on board the *Green Flag*, but he had not seen the beard yet, so it took a second or two for recognition to dawn.

When it did, a slow grin broke over his face. Whittaker smiled back, and Morgan not only remembered how much he had liked the diffident Englishman, but realized how much he had been looking forward to seeing him again.

Whittaker extended his hand — which the English were not wont to do, Morgan knew. On impulse, he leaned forward and, instead of taking Whittaker's hand, pulled him into a quick, hard embrace.

He set him back then, just enough to study him. "Well, now, Whittaker, and aren't you the fine-looking gentleman these days? Being a family man would seem to agree with you, and that's the truth."

Nora produced their wee boy just then, and Morgan pronounced him a fine, sturdy lad, the image of his mother — adding a wry aside that in matters of heredity, Irish blood would win out over the British every time.

Morgan heard a quiet clearing of the throat at his right, and he turned to look. The dark-haired man with the badge had remained silent and removed from the welcoming party up until then. In all the commotion and excitement, Morgan had almost forgotten his presence entirely.

But now the fellow came to stand directly in front of him. Morgan studied the roguish handsomeness, the somewhat cynical long line of lip. Finally he met the dark eyes and held them for the first time. A powerful wave of remembrance engulfed him, and at that moment he saw past the random threads of silver in the hair, the added muscle about the chest and shoulders, the dark moustache. For a brief, overwhelming instant he was back in Killala, sitting on the rickety dock, looking out across the bay, with his best friend at his side: Michael Burke, a sturdy lad who even then had had the same quick, appraising eye, the restless energy so apparent in the man now standing in front of him.

"It cannot be," Morgan murmured.

"Ah, but it is, you red-headed roamer." The dark eyes danced, the wide mouth quirked, and the granite jaw gave way to a broad smile.

Twenty years of memory came flooding in on Morgan. Overpowered by an entire tide of feelings, he squeezed his eyes shut, just for an instant.

When he opened them, he saw that Michael's eyes were red-rimmed and glistening.

"Mo chara," Morgan said, "Michael, my friend. 'Tis really you, then."

"And didn't it take you long enough to recognize me, you rogue?" Though Michael's mouth still quirked with amusement, his voice sounded suspiciously unsteady.

He leaned toward him, roughly gripping Morgan's shoulders, pulling his head against his chest. They did not weep, of course. They were both strong men, after all; it would not do to make a display of their emotions in front of each other's families.

"Twenty years, man," Michael muttered in Morgan's ear. "You were but a long-legged *gorsoon* in those days."

"And you a hard-headed Mayo man set on making his mark in America." Morgan hesitated. "Twenty years. Can it be, Michael? Are we really middle-aged men by now?"

"Not at all," Michael shot back, still clinging to Morgan. "Do we not have beautiful young wives for ourselves? That being the case, man, we cannot possibly be middle-aged."

The mention of their wives brought both of them up short. It was long past time to present their families, which they both did with a great deal of pride.

In the midst of all the fuss and excitement, it occurred to Morgan that only the Irish could make a tribal ritual out of a reunion. But, then, only a people so often displaced, so frequently exiled, could know the rare wonder, the incomparable joy, of coming together with loved ones once counted as lost.

36

A Time for Sharing

I have a garden of my own,
shining with flowers of every hue;
I loved it dearly while alone,
But I shall love it more with you.
THOMAS MOORE (1779–1852)

Annie Fitzgerald awoke to a golden autumn morning, with sunshine flooding the bedroom. She blinked, waiting for her eyes to focus, then glanced about the room. For a moment she could not think where she was.

With a start she sat bolt upright in bed. Fergus! Where was the wolfhound? The great beast always slept nearby, at the foot of her bed. He would be eager to go outside. . . .

Then she remembered. *She was in America!*

The draperies were open. She had deliberately left them so the night before, intending to look out upon New York. Instead, exhausted from all the excitement of the day, she had dropped off the minute her head met the pillow.

But this was a new day. A day to spend in New York City, having the first real adventure of her life! Well, perhaps the second. Running off from Belfast to seek the *Seanchai* in Dublin City had been her *first* true adventure.

But surely this was an even greater event. She had crossed an entire ocean, after all!

Annie felt a brief pang of disappointment. She missed Fergus, longed for the nudging of his great wet nose in the palm of her hand. She wanted to show *him* the wonders of America. He was needed at Nelson Hall to protect Sister Louisa and Lucy, of course. But Annie wished desperately that they hadn't had to leave him behind. This morning was too important to savor in solitude. Such a morning should be shared.

She gazed wistfully at Gabriel, still sound asleep in the small trundle bed. Perhaps she could jostle him just a bit. On the other hand, he might be cross if she woke him before he was altogether rested. Bedtime had been late for them all the night before.

With a sigh, she decided to leave well enough alone. She swung her legs over her side of the bed and gave a huge stretch before stepping onto the floor. What luxury, feeling a soft, plushy rug under her toes first thing, rather than the cold, unfriendly planks in her bedchamber at Nelson Hall.

She reached to retrieve the soft rag doll she had slept with, then padded to the window in her bare feet. Yesterday had been filled with excited conversation, questions, and exchange of memories; this morning she would have a long, unhurried look at her surroundings.

Although the house did not appear so vast and rambling as Nelson Hall, the grounds seemed to have no end. Immense old trees towered near enough that she could have reached out and touched their branches. The grounds were precisely manicured, with even the shrubbery trimmed into interesting, ornate shapes. A stone lane ran the length of this side of the house, with an iron gate at both ends.

Annie went to the back window, from which she could see an enormous lawn with lush gardens and, at the far end, an odd-looking structure, roofed but open-sided, which resembled a small pavilion. She stood, hugging the doll to her as she looked out upon the gardens, still vibrant with late-blooming flowers, and allowed her thoughts to roam over the people she had met the day before.

Johanna she had liked almost instantly.

They had struck a quick rapport, communicating quite well despite Johanna's deafness. Johanna's brother, Daniel, seemed very nice — and wasn't he a handsome boy as well? It was a grand thing, to meet Tierney Burke's American friend and comrade, even though he somehow seemed much older and far more serious than Tierney.

She found the Whittakers to be splendid people. Annie would never have let on to the *Seanchai,* of course, that she knew he and Mrs. Whittaker had once been sweethearts, back in their home village of Killala. She had learned this fascinating bit of information from Tierney Burke, who had sworn her to secrecy. Of course, she would not divulge the secret, but she did think it wonderfully romantic that the *Seanchai* and the sweetheart of his youth had remained great friends, even with an ocean between them.

The Burkes were grand, and great fun. Almost immediately they had invited her to call them "Aunt Sara" and "Uncle Michael," which pleased her no end. Aunt Sara and her grandmother were true ladies, but clearly without airs. As for Uncle Michael, he had been a bit of a surprise. Having heard Tierney Burke grumble about his father every now and again, she had not quite known what to expect. But Uncle Michael had a hearty laugh, seemed quick to tease, and was actually rather handsome, for an old man. Annie had liked him immediately.

It was a wondrous thing entirely, to realize that he and the *Seanchai,* boyhood friends in Ireland, had remained close after twenty years or more. Annie wondered what it would be like to have a lifetime friend, and she suddenly found herself missing Tierney Burke and Jan Martova.

No doubt the two did not yet consider her a best friend, but they would come to, eventually. When she was older. Perhaps things would be the same for them as with the *Seanchai* and Uncle Michael and Nora. Perhaps the three of them would be friends forever: herself, Tierney Burke, and Jan Martova.

Both boys might even fall in love with her one day, and she would be forced to choose between them. She would choose Tierney Burke, of course. Jan Martova was darkly handsome and ever so gallant, but he was also years older — in truth a man, not a boy. No, she and Jan Martova would remain good friends, but nothing more. And he would understand. He would study her with his soft dark eyes, saddened that she did not love him as he did her, but he would be kindness itself and give his blessing to her and Tierney Burke.

Annie sighed, then put her thoughts of the future to rest as she came slowly, reluctantly, out of her reverie. Behind her, Gabriel stirred, and she turned to see him push himself up on his knees and give her a sleepy smile.

"An-ye?"

Crossing the room, she swept him off the bed and into her arms, spinning him and the rag doll all about the room.

He began to laugh, and Annie, unable to any longer contain her delight with this new adventure, laughed with him. "Wake up, wake up, little brother! Today we begin to discover America!"

In their bedroom, Sara came awake all at once to find her husband lying beside her, watching her with a studying smile.

"That is the most unnerving habit, Michael Burke — staring at me while I sleep."

He smoothed a strand of hair away from her face and went on smiling. "It pleases me to watch you when your defenses are down, Sara *a gra,* that not being a common occurrence."

"My defenses are *always* down with you." She yawned and stretched. "I still can't believe you're actually taking a week off. Other than when we were married, I can't remember you ever being around the house more than one day at a time."

She didn't say what she was thinking, that this was the way she had once imagined things would be between them. Before their marriage, she had dreamed of quiet evenings spent by the fire, golden mornings of waking up together, with plenty of time for talking and being close.

The reality was that her evenings were often spent alone with Grandy because Michael was either working or at a subcommission meeting. He frequently woke her when he came to bed long after midnight. As for the mornings, he was usually up and dressed before she awakened. The man seemed to run on almost no sleep at all, a trait that secretly irritated Sara, since she was little more than a slug with anything less than eight hours.

He drew her into his arms. "After this week, you will be ready to toss me out on my ear, no doubt."

"No doubt." She yawned again. "Seriously, Michael, I think it's wonderful that you're going to have some free time just to be with Morgan."

"And you," he added. He moved to kiss her, then stopped, rubbing a hand down the heavy stubble of his beard.

She noticed and pulled his head down to hers. "Gently," she reminded him.

After he kissed her, Sara lay smiling, her head on his shoulder, immeasurably content to have this rare, unhurried morning hour alone with him. But after a moment a less pleasant thought struck her, and she turned to look at him. "You're terribly disappointed that Tierney didn't come, aren't you?"

His answer held a note of sadness. "I had hoped, right up to the last, that he might be with them, that is true. But even if he'd known about Walsh before he and the Gypsy took off on their jaunt, I can't help but wonder if he would have come."

Sara remained silent, for she had wondered the same thing. "He'll come home soon, Michael. One day Tierney will come back, and when he does, things will be right between the two of you. I really believe that."

"I couldn't help but think of him yesterday, when we met the others at the harbor," he admitted. "What it would have been like to see him coming down that gangplank! And then later, watching Morgan with his teeny boy and Evan and Nora with theirs — ah, didn't that bring back the memories all in a rush?"

Sara ached for him. She knew that he not only missed Tierney, but also grieved because of the conflict that had clouded their relationship for years.

"I wish I could give you *another* son," she said impulsively, clinging to him. "Oh, how I would like a little boy exactly like you!"

He held her, stroking her hair. "I wouldn't mind a little girl, you know — a bright and saucy little miss like her mama."

Sara daydreamed for another minute about baby boys and girls, but said nothing more. Lately, she found that talking about babies only made her empty arms ache all the more.

"So," she said, trying for a cheerful tone, "what are your plans for the day?"

Michael propped one arm behind his head. "Well, at Morgan's request, I'm arranging for Jess Dalton to stop by so they can meet. Morgan's anxious to talk with him about his publisher. And your grandmother suggested a meeting with Mr. Greeley as well. Morgan is set on getting that famine journal into print as soon as possible."

"What about his appointment with Dr. Gunther?"

"It sounds to me as if he means to delay the examination until he ties up matters with the journal."

Sara raised herself up on one arm to look at him. "It must be very worrisome to Finola, if Morgan's really more concerned with a publishing agreement than with his own physical well-being."

He smiled wryly. " 'Tis a grace for us men, fools that we are, that our women are willing to suffer our headstrong ways. I for one will be forever grateful for the patience of my good wife."

"I should think so." Sara sank back into his arms. "I hope he doesn't wait too long, Michael. Perhaps you could talk to him, convince him not to delay?"

"I think I know what he's doing," Michael said quietly. "And I understand it, him being the man he is."

He lay studying the ceiling for a moment. "Joseph Mahon's journal is important to Morgan. Not only because the priest was his good friend and spiritual father, but because Morgan believes a wide reading of it could make a real difference for Ireland. He says the truth, once revealed, *always* makes a difference. I think he intends to see the journal well on its way to publication first thing — in the event that something should go wrong with the surgery." He stopped. "If indeed there is to *be* a surgery."

"Oh, Michael — this is such a critical time for him, isn't it? Surgery could change his entire life!"

"The way Nicholas Grafton explained things to me," Michael said, his voice strained, "this surgery will at the very least en-

danger Morgan's life."

"But he's willing to take the risk." Sara paused, thinking. "I believe you'd do the same."

"What man wouldn't?" Michael said softly. "If there's even half a chance of getting his legs back . . . aye, Morgan will risk it."

Unwilling to let him lapse into melancholy for what might be their only time alone today, Sara moved to change the subject. "Isn't Finola absolutely breathtaking?"

He smiled a little. "She's suited for Morgan, right enough. The lass looks like something right out of the storybooks. Like one of the enchanted princesses from the old legends."

"She's beautiful," Sara mused. "I don't believe I've ever seen a more beautiful woman than Finola Fitzgerald."

He looked at her, then moved to gather her closer. "As I said, she suits Morgan. For myself, though, I am a man who has always been partial to a dark-haired woman with great, soft eyes." He brought his face closer to hers. "A woman like yourself, Mrs. Burke, now that's the kind of woman that suits *me*."

Tenderly, he kissed her. When he drew back, he smoothed her hair away from her face and searched her eyes, smiling at the flush she could feel creeping over her skin.

Sara wanted to tell him she would be endlessly thankful that she suited him, but she could find no words to say what was in her heart.

Which was just as well, for Michael did not seem to want to talk.

Later that morning, as Finola put up her hair, she watched Morgan in the mirror. He sat propped up in bed, reading yet another of the American newspapers Michael had given him the night before.

He was totally engrossed. His eyeglasses had slipped a little down the bridge of his nose, and his brow was furrowed in concentration. Occasionally he would chuckle or give a sharp sound of surprise; once or twice he muttered in disagreement.

"I think I will like this man, Greeley," he said, exchanging one paper for another. "His editorials demonstrate great sympathy for the black slaves and Irish emigrants. I may be meeting him soon, did I tell you? Michael says Pastor Dalton thinks Greeley might consider serializing the journal in his newspaper —" He waved the paper in his hand. "The *Tribune*."

With a smile, Finola turned to face him. "I think much ground has already been broken for you, before we ever arrived."

Morgan laid the newspaper aside. His face was animated, and as he told her about his hopes for the coming days, he worked his hands as if he could not contain his energy.

Fascinated, Finola studied him. She had grown used to his intensity by now, the almost feverish way he pursued whatever he believed in. But she did not think she had ever seen him quite so spirited as at this moment.

Later, when he had finished relating his prospects for their American visit, she carefully broached the subject on *her* mind.

"Morgan . . . when will you see Dr. Gunther?"

His reply was immediate. "When I have all things in order for Joseph's journal." As if he sensed that she was less than satisfied with his answer, he hurried to reassure her. "It shouldn't take long, you know. As you said, Lewis Farmington and Pastor Dalton seem to have already set things in motion."

Suddenly it occurred to Finola that Morgan's eyes almost always caressed her face when he spoke to her. But now, she sensed that he was deliberately avoiding her gaze.

Troubled by his evasion, she rose and went to sit down beside him on the edge of the bed. When she reached to take both his hands in hers, he finally met her eyes.

"Morgan . . . I know Father Joseph's journal is very important to you. And I know one of your reasons for making the crossing was to see the work published."

He didn't answer, but his expression was wary, as if he suspected the direction her words might take.

"I must say this to you, Morgan; please have patience with me. As much as I believe, just as you do, that the journal should indeed be published and widely distributed, I will admit that is not the concern uppermost in my mind. Morgan, please . . . promise me you won't delay the examination with Dr. Gunther."

His glance darted to their clasped hands, and Finola realized only then how tightly she was clinging to him. Still, she made no move to let him go.

"You're not afraid I'll change my mind, *macushla?* I'd not do that, you know."

"Not that you might change your mind, but that in your determination to publish the journal, you will neglect yourself. I warn you, Morgan, I will not let you do so!"

His gaze went over her face, and he smiled. "If you are not careful, Finola *aroon,* you will become a terrible scold."

"A good Irish wife, you mean," she countered, trying to match his lightness of tone.

"You are already that," he said, lifting her

hands to brush his lips over them. "No man could hope for a finer wife."

"Then promise me," she demanded, unable to sustain the lighthearted tone of a moment before. "Promise me that you will see the surgeon soon, without delay, no matter what you accomplish — or do not accomplish — with the journal."

Still he teased. "Listen to the woman, with her ferocious demands."

"Morgan . . . promise me."

Again he brought her hands to his lips. "Ah, Finola, do you not realize by now I would promise you the world and the stars above it, if you but asked?"

"I am not asking for the world or the stars, but only for a promise."

He acquiesced with a nod and a kiss, then told her, "Have Sandemon come and help me out of bed, if you will. I must get dressed for the day."

"We can manage without Sandemon," Finola said, getting to her feet.

"I expect you're right," Morgan said dryly as she walked to the window and looked out. "But do not ever let him hear you say as much."

"Besides, Sandemon seems to be occupied. He is with your friend Michael, in the garden."

"Ah. Good. I had hoped those two would come to know each other better. Michael grieves so for his son. Perhaps Sandemon will ease his mind a bit.

"Well, woman," he said after a moment, "will I lie here all day like a great lump, or will you be helping me?"

She turned and smiled, aching with the sweetness of her love for him.

He met her smile with a rakish grin of his own. "Unless, that is, you would care to join me?" He patted the space beside him, then removed his eyeglasses. "I am not in such a great hurry, after all."

Michael had been on his way out back for his early morning walk in the garden when he spotted Morgan's man, Sandemon — the "West Indies Wonder" as Morgan was wont to call him — and went to join him.

Though the morning was cool, Sandemon was in his shirt-sleeves, walking among Grandy's tidy row of herb plants, his face lifted slightly as if to savor the fragrance. At Michael's approach, he smiled politely and gave a brief nod.

"I had hoped for a chance to thank you," Michael said without preamble. "Morgan told me my son owes you his life."

Sandemon shook his head, not looking directly at Michael. "Your son owes his life only to God," he said, still smiling. "I merely waited on the boy and his friend during the cholera, as best I could."

"Still, I am indebted to you for your kindness to Tierney. I do thank you." Michael paused, uncertain as to how to pose the question on his mind. "About this friend of his — Morgan says he's a Romany. A Gypsy."

"Jan Martova. Yes, he is from the Romany tribe."

"And the two of them have gone off together on a trip across the country. In a Gypsy wagon." Michael heard the edge in his voice, but he felt he had reason to be concerned. Of all the things he might have expected of his rebel son, taking up with a Gypsy would not have been one of them.

"Yes, young Tierney seems to have great passion for the land of his father. He wanted to see it for himself."

"A good deal more passion than his father ever had for it, I expect," Michael said dryly.

Sandemon started to walk, and Michael joined him. "What sort is he, this Gypsy?"

"Jan Martova is a fine young man with a tender heart. And he loves God. He is a believer."

Michael looked at him. "A Romany with the Christian faith? I would not have thought that possible."

"His faith came to him during the attack of cholera. I can assure you it is genuine."

The black man stopped and turned, looking Michael in the eye for the first time. "Perhaps you are aware that the Gypsy youth was banished from his tribe for choosing to help your son when he was ill?"

Michael nodded. Morgan had told him as much in one of his letters.

"Although Jan Martova is of the Romany tribe, he no longer practices their beliefs," Sandemon went on. "He has great affection for his family, and I'm sure he misses them very much, but he is not welcome at their campfire. Even if he were, I am convinced his Christian faith would prevent him from falling back into the old ways." He stopped, his dark eyes studying Michael. "You have a great burden for your son, Captain, do you not?"

Michael swallowed and looked away. He was not altogether comfortable with discussing his son with a total stranger. Still, Morgan did think the world of this man. And in spite of Sandemon's protests, Morgan had been adamant in his assertion that, had it not been for Sandemon's round-the-clock attentions, *both* boys — Tierney and the Gypsy — might not have survived the cholera.

"I want only what's best for my son," Michael said with a sigh. "Naturally, I would like him to be a decent man. A good man."

"Of course. And I believe young Tierney will eventually live up to your hopes for him, Captain."

Michael looked at him.

"Your son is brave, if a bit reckless at times — a common trait among the young, I have observed. He is also loyal and has a generous heart. Certainly traits of a good man, wouldn't you say?"

Michael looked into the man's face and felt himself drawn to the gentle kindness reflected there. "How is he? In his heart of hearts, how *is* he?"

Sandemon seemed to consider the question. "Your son is struggling to find the truth, Captain," he said, his voice quiet and thoughtful. "He is confused about many things, but courageous enough to explore. You may be surprised at my saying so, but I do believe this trip about the island with his friend will be good for him. Very good indeed. Jan Martova has a pure soul and a keen instinct for what is right and true. Your son could do worse in his choice of friends. I think the weeks or months they spend together will be time well spent."

Michael felt his heart unclench, just a little. "I'd like to believe that."

Sandemon regarded Michael with a look of gentle understanding. "Captain, I believe that most men, in their deepest souls, want to know the truth — and to be strong enough to live their lives by that truth. It seems to me that your son is fortunate, in that he has had people throughout his life — both family and friends — who love him enough to encourage him, to stand by him, to pray for him. I think Jan Martova will prove to be such a friend, and I believe our all-wise heavenly Father will be at work among the two of them as they make their journey." He ended with a faint smile. "And, one thing more, Captain. If you will permit me, I would like to say that, like the *Seanchai,* I have grown quite fond of your son over the past months. Indeed, Tierney is an easy young man to like."

Warmed by the man's simple, direct words, Michael suddenly felt better about Tierney than he had for a long time. Somehow, without really knowing Morgan's West Indies Wonder, he thought it must be a genuine compliment, a true honor, to gain the favor of such a man. For his son's sake, he was pleased; for his own, he was grateful.

Impulsively, he reached to shake Sandemon's hand. Afterward, as he walked back to the house, he felt encouraged and cheered, excessively pleased that God had allowed this reunion of friends. More than ever he was hopeful that much good would result from it, a good that would eventually bless them all.

37

Letters

Seek out reality, leave things that seem.
W. B. YEATS (1865–1939)

On Thursday afternoon of that same week, Quinn O'Shea was enjoying a rare hour to herself when she found another envelope slipped beneath the front door.

Instead of hurrying upstairs to her bedroom, as she usually did, she scooped up the letter and ducked inside the library. Mrs. Whittaker and wee Teddy were having a rest, and Mr. Whittaker was teaching his last class of the day before the boys' choir rehearsal. With Johanna at the academy and Daniel off to the Five Points with the visiting poet, Fitzgerald, Quinn felt reasonably sure she would not be interrupted.

Inside the library, she went to the tall window behind Mr. Whittaker's desk. The light filtering into the room was dim, all but blocked by the enormous old oak tree right outside the window. She held the envelope to the light, staring at the name for a moment, swallowing down a stream of emotions that ranged from anticipation to dread.

A part of her had hoped that no more letters would come. She knew she had to put a stop to Daniel's dreaming. There could never be anything between them, even if she had felt something more than friendship for the lad — which she did not. Besides, his sort deserved as good as himself: a pure girl, unsullied and unused — not one jaded and left hard by life's cruel twists and abuses.

Yet there was another part, a hidden part which she had tried to ignore, but could not quite silence — a part of her that cried out to the soul behind the pen from which the shy and gentle love poetry continued to flow. That timorous, yet somehow hopeful, shadow-part of Quinn was loathe to relinquish the sweet, if transitory, touch of healing the poetry had brought her.

Finally, with trembling hands, she opened the envelope. She ignored the painful tightness in her chest as she withdrew the single page and brought it close enough to her face that she could read the words.

As she had expected, it was another poem, this one slightly different. More intense, hint-ing of a growing impatience, it was neither demanding nor angry, but lacked the gentleness of those that had gone before.

She read the last few lines, then read them over again, her eyes straining in the pale light. . . .

"I have no fabric wove with golden
   threads,
No silk upon which starlight gleams,
No velvet trimmed with satin ribbons —
Woman, will you wear my dreams?"

A sob caught in Quinn's throat, and her eyes misted. For a moment she could not read the note's closing. When she did, the thin page shook in her hand:

If you have a heart at all, please meet me at half-past seven tonight at the band pavilion in Schedlen Park. We must talk. Or, at the least, I must speak what I can no longer hide.

A draft seeped through the window casing, and the paper in Quinn's hand fluttered slightly. Yet cool as it was in the shadowed room, perspiration traced her hairline and moved down the back of her neck. With a heavy sigh, she sank down onto the window seat and sat staring outside, to the park just a ways up the street, on the other side.

She sat there for a long time, the note dangling from her fingers, her heart aching, tears collecting in her eyes. Never before had she admitted to herself that, had she known the shame and guilt that would hound her every day since her last encounter with Millen Jupe, she would simply have allowed him to beat her to death without raising a hand to stop him.

Her life since that night had not been worth the price she had paid. And if she told Daniel Kavanagh the truth — and she would, if it took the truth in all its ugliness to discourage him — her life thereafter would be worth even less.

It would be her first time to attend a rehearsal since Patrick's death, and Alice Walsh felt a certain edge of nervousness as she walked up the steps to Whittaker House. She had talked with Evan Whittaker and his wife twice after the hearing, but she had seen none of the boys in the choir for several weeks. Still, if she were ever to reclaim any semblance of a normal life, she had to make a start — and very soon. Waiting would only make everything more difficult.

For her own sake and that of her children,

she had to face reality, a reality affirmed by the court hearing: Patrick's death had been ruled as an accidental shooting. Alice's part in the incident, according to the court's decision, had been a natural act of self-defense, as well as an attempt to save the life of Ruth Marriott — who in fact had died instantly from the fall down the stairway . . . although Alice could not have known this for certain at the time. She had been summarily pronounced innocent of any wrongdoing.

Innocent of any wrongdoing. What was she guilty of, then? Blind faith? Misplaced trust? An obsessive love for a man who had never deserved it, never returned it?

Perhaps she was guilty of all that, but she was also, she reminded herself firmly, *forgiven.* At least by her God.

Still, she struggled with remorse, with grief over the loss of her dreams and the loss of her husband. Even if he had pretended to be something he was not, Patrick had still been her husband, the one she had vowed to love and honor until death.

And now death had parted them — death by her own hand. The court had ruled her innocent. God had forgiven her. But it would take longer to forgive herself.

At the top of the steps she stopped to catch her breath. She tired easily these days, more than likely from the weeks of lost sleep and no appetite. For the first time since she could remember, she was losing weight, would actually have to have her wardrobe altered in the near future if she continued at this rate. There had been a time when that necessity would have brought her a great deal of pleasure; now it served only to remind her of the pain.

Her eyes stung from unshed tears as she entered the cool, dim hallway of Whittaker House. She knew the anguish of the past would be with her for a long, long time to come — perhaps forever. But she also knew it did not have to dominate her life, not unless she allowed it to control her.

Today was intended as her first step in putting the pain of yesterday behind her. Her mother had reminded her just yesterday, not for the first time, that Alice could either drown in her misery or gain healing in ministry.

Dear Mama! Alice had once resented her mother's stoicism, her insistence on good deeds as the cure for all malaise. She still didn't entirely agree with Ula Braun's regimented, Teutonic approach to life in general. But she *would* concede that, for the present at least, there was considerable wisdom in her mother's advice to keep busy, preferably by doing for others. After praying for the strength and the fortitude to do just that, Alice had made the decision to attend rehearsal today.

She hoped Mr. Whittaker would be glad to see her. No doubt he, like others, would be uncomfortable around her for a while. No one seemed to know quite what to say to Alice about her . . . *situation*. She thought she understood, but she also knew that she desperately needed at least a few people — besides her parents — to treat her with a modicum of normality. She rather thought she could depend on Evan and Nora Whittaker to do just that.

Inside, she found the spacious old house uncommonly quiet. She was early. Mr. Whittaker was probably still in the classroom with the children. Knowing Mrs. Whittaker's habit of resting after the noonday meal, she decided not to risk disturbing her.

The library door was ajar. Alice started to enter, then stopped at the sight of the girl on the window seat. Framed in the room's dim light, she appeared a slender, delicate silhouette, not quite real.

As she stood watching, Alice saw the girl's thin shoulders heave and shudder. The sobs ripping from her sounded as if they were being torn from the heart of a despairing child.

Alice realized that it was Quinn O'Shea, the

young Irish immigrant girl the Whittakers had employed as housekeeper. Nora Whittaker made no secret of the fact that they had come to depend heavily on the girl, and in the process had grown quite fond of her as well.

Alice hesitated, uncertain whether she should leave the girl alone or approach and try to help. She was hardly equipped to relieve another's distress, not with her own grief still so raw.

But the girl was so young, and in such obvious despair, that her mother's heart succumbed. She took a tentative step inside the room, then another, before clearing her throat to make her presence known.

As he waited in the Black Maria for Mike and Morgan Fitzgerald, Denny Price dug the letter he had been carrying for days now out of his pocket and unfolded it. He could not say how many times he had read the letter, but with each reading the same sick ache settled over him.

He read it again now, and once more felt his stomach knot. The letter from Ireland, a response to his own, had finally arrived nearly two weeks past. Since then his days and nights seemed to have grown longer and darker. Most nights he managed little more than two or three hours' sleep, sometimes not that much. Even during the day, as he carried out the routine of his job, he was continually mindful of the folded pages in his pocket.

His sleeplessness and restlessness were borne of common causes: a pall of sadness concerning the contents of the letter, and the sting of guilt for probing into matters that were none of his business. In truth, he had no right to the information he now possessed. More to the point, the act of obtaining that information could be construed as nothing short of meddling.

It made little difference that his actions had been motivated by a desire to help. Now that he finally had his answer, he could see how it might easily bring humiliation and distress to the very one he sought to help. He had overstepped his place, exploited his position as a police officer.

Yet despite the disturbing awareness that his actions might be questionable — or even worse, deceitful — he felt a certain grim sense of satisfaction that he had followed his instincts. At least now he knew the truth.

All that was left to him was to figure exactly how he should go about making proper use of that truth. Or if he should act upon it at all.

The girl looked up with startled eyes, jerking to her feet.

"Quinn? I'm sorry . . . I don't mean to intrude. But . . . can I help?"

The girl shook her head. Although she stood facing Alice, she did not look at her, instead, fixed her eyes on the doorway.

Alice felt an inexplicable urgency to detain the girl, to keep her from fleeing the room — as Quinn obviously wanted to do. On impulse, she turned to close the door behind her before walking the rest of the way into the library.

The youthful face was ravaged by the evidence of weeping, the sharp cheekbones tracked with tears, the unusual gold-flecked eyes red and swollen. The girl stood, a paper in one hand, her other hand clenched to a fist at her side, as if to steel herself from an invasion. But Alice did not miss the fact that she hadn't quite managed to check the tears.

Her first thought was that the girl had gotten herself "in trouble," a common predicament among many of the city's young immigrant girls. But somehow she didn't think that was the case with Quinn O'Shea. Indeed, Nora Whittaker had once remarked that the girl actually seemed to shun contact with young men.

Still, there was always a possibility. Alice had seen young Daniel's covert looks in the girl's direction, and once Mr. Whittaker had mentioned in a wry aside that Sergeant Price seemed to call frequently since Quinn O'Shea came to work for them.

Somehow, though, she could not give much credence to the idea that either Daniel or Sergeant Price might have taken advantage. Neither had the manner of a man who would play loosely with a young girl's affections. Alice was fairly certain that whatever distressed Quinn O'Shea had nothing to do with that kind of trouble.

"Are you sure I can't help?" Alice offered again. "I'm a very . . . safe . . . person to confide in these days."

Quinn O'Shea's eyes narrowed as she looked at her, and Alice thought the girl's defensive stance relaxed a little.

She couldn't define what prompted her to go on, to speak so candidly with one so young, a virtual stranger. But the words seemed to flow with surprising ease once she began. "I expect I've been miserable so long myself that I can recognize unhappiness in another."

She laid her music case on the desk, removing her gloves as if she meant to stay. "Of course, I was fortunate in having my mother to talk with. Mama has extraordinarily strong shoulders. I sometimes think she could carry the burdens of the entire universe, if need be."

Alice raised her eyes to search the girl's troubled face. "Most of us," she added quietly, "are not possessed of such resilience."

Something told her that this child — for Quinn O'Shea was surely little more than that — had never really known the comfort or the assurance of a mother with strong shoulders. Something in that furtive — or was it frightened — gaze hinted of rejection, if not outright abandonment.

At that instant, the pain in Alice reached out to the pain behind those wounded eyes, and she thought she felt the kindling of understanding. Suddenly, she ached to put her arms around the girl and simply . . . hold her.

Instead, she walked to the small sofa in front of the fireplace, motioning for Quinn to join her. "I'm much too early for rehearsal. Can't I convince you to come and talk with me while I wait, dear?" Her eyes went to the single sheet of paper that the girl continued to clutch in her hand. "Perhaps you might want to tell me what's in that letter that has upset you so."

38

Begin to Live

But tears, when turned inward,
are no longer cleansing.
And words, when not spoken,
get lost in the mind.
And feelings, when denied,
refuse to live.
Anonymous

Quinn hesitated as Alice Walsh sat down on the sofa. For a moment she stood watching the woman suspiciously. The unexpected invitation confused her. She could not understand this quick friendliness from someone so much older than herself, someone who lived in a completely different world. Nor did she entirely trust it.

And yet at that moment she desperately needed someone to tell her what to do. She could not speak with the Whittakers about such ugliness, could not expose the horror and shame of her past to those two fine, decent people — people who had in good faith brought her into their home when she had nowhere else to go, given her employment and a decent wage, and treated her as kindly as if they had known her forever. She simply could not reveal her disgrace to them.

But something about Alice Walsh made her think that, if she were ever to tell *anyone* her secret, she just might be able to tell this woman. Perhaps it was because Mrs. Walsh had shot and killed her own husband, in what could only be described as a terrible scandal. This was a woman who knew about disgrace.

There had been a great deal of gossip after her husband's death — not here at Whittaker House, of course, for the Whittakers did not gossip. But a number of shopkeepers along the street had wagged their tongues to anyone who would listen, and for days after the shooting Quinn had overheard all manner of exchange between the proprietors and their customers.

As rumor had it, Mrs. Walsh's husband had been a bad sort entirely, as bent as a snail's back. He murdered his mistress, and would have killed Mrs. Walsh as well — or so it was reported — had she not finished him first.

Quinn's mind locked on that fact. Her throat tightened, and she tried to study Alice

Walsh without actually staring. In spite of her wariness, she was drawn to the woman — drawn to her candor, her plain and unaffected mannerisms. She was especially intrigued by the fact that Mrs. Walsh had not only endured her husband's betrayal, but also the notoriety his death had brought upon her.

Quinn had always thought Alice Walsh a rather sad lady. Even when she smiled, her eyes still held a hint of sorrow. Perhaps that was why Quinn usually felt more comfortable with her than with others of a similar station. Today, however, she felt something else: an odd kind of *kinship,* a bond which for all she knew might prove offensive to the older woman, but one that seemed real enough to Quinn.

Slowly, with hesitant steps, she went to sit down beside Alice Walsh on the sofa. The woman smiled, as if pleased to have her company.

Quinn moistened her lips, unsure of herself. She looked at the older woman for another moment, then impulsively extended the note in her hand. "I keep getting these," she said bluntly. "I don't quite know what to do about them."

Alice Walsh took the paper, her eyes studying Quinn for a moment more before scanning the words on the page. When she was finished, she looked up. "You've had others?"

Quinn nodded, biting her lip. "A number of them," she said, knotting her hands in her lap.

"Have you any idea who's sending them?"

Quinn hesitated, then nodded again. "I'm sure it's Daniel Kavanagh."

Mrs. Walsh looked at her, lifting a hand to touch the broach at her throat. "I see. Well . . . obviously the boy is taken with you. His writing is quite lovely, really. But how do you feel about him — or perhaps I shouldn't ask?"

"No, it's all right," Quinn said, not meeting her eyes. "Daniel is a grand boy, and he has been very kind to me. He's helped me with my grammar and taught me a great deal about America." She clenched her hands even tighter. "But I don't have the sort of feelings for him that he seems to hold for me."

"Oh, dear," said Alice Walsh softly. "Then I suppose you must tell him so. Are you going to meet him this evening, as he asks?"

Quinn didn't answer right away. She stared into the fireplace, her heart as cold as the empty grate. She wondered if she was being foolish entirely, to spurn a fine lad like Daniel, who seemed destined to be an extraordinary man. Most girls of her station would be wild for such an opportunity. But the fact that he *was* such a good person was the very reason

518

she must not deceive him. He did not deserve shabby treatment. He merited a girl who would appreciate his worth . . . and one who deserved his affection.

"I expect I will meet him," she said at last. "I suppose I must. He's been sending the letters, the poems, for weeks now. I can't just let it go on, can I? I can't allow him to believe I share his feelings. It seems the only thing to do is face him with the truth."

"That will be very difficult for you," Mrs. Walsh said gently. "Especially with the two of you living under the same roof. Do you think you can make him understand?"

"I must!" Quinn insisted. "He cannot hold any false hopes about me. There can be nothing between us, and I must make him understand so."

Alice Walsh frowned slightly, regarding Quinn with a peculiar look. "Are you all that certain, dear? I'm sure Daniel would be patient, willing to wait —"

"*No!*" Quinn leaped to her feet, her breath coming rapidly in uneven shudders. "I'm not fit for him, don't you see? I'm not fit for him or any other man!"

Mrs. Walsh looked startled, then reached to take Quinn's hand. "Oh, my dear, whatever do you mean? You're a wonderful girl, Quinn. Why, the Whittakers can't say enough good things about you! I'm sure they'd be pleased to know you and Daniel cared for each other."

Quinn yanked her hand away. She saw the look of bewilderment on Mrs. Walsh's face, and knew she had made a mistake, thinking she could confide in a woman like this. What would a lady like Alice Walsh know of the sort of life she had lived? No decent woman knew of such things; no decent woman would even believe that men like Millen Jupe existed, much less fathom what his sort was capable of!

Yet the look on the older woman's face was not one of shock or repulsion, but simply that of compassion, of genuine kindness. It was the kindness that was Quinn's undoing.

When the girl yanked her hand away as if she'd been burned, Alice also flinched, appalled that she had somehow caused her distress.

Quinn stood, hunched, her arms wrapped tightly around herself as if to keep from flying apart. She was obviously distraught, her mouth trembling, her eyes frenzied.

"The Whittakers don't know me!" she suddenly burst out, her voice an angry hiss. "They would *despise* me if they knew the truth, would set me out at once! And sure,

they would let me nowhere near their precious son!"

Stunned by her outburst, dismayed at the girl's unmistakable despair, Alice could not think what to do. Again she tried to protest, but Quinn silenced her into utter amazement with what came next.

"I'm nothing but a *strumpet!*" she spat out. "A strumpet and a murderer!"

Alice watched with horror as the girl's normal reserve shattered in front of her eyes. It seemed that an enormous wave of anguish and self-hatred and rage had suddenly risen from some secret place deep within her, exploding in that one tortured, heartrending outburst.

She stood and moved to comfort the girl, but Quinn shook her off almost violently, shrinking from her.

"Oh, Quinn . . . child . . . I only want to help . . ."

As if her words had been the final blow of an entire onslaught, Quinn suddenly crumpled in front of Alice, staggering beneath the burden she had carried for who knew how long. With a shudder, she began to weep — the resigned, hopeless weeping of utter despair.

Alice went to her, and this time the girl allowed herself to be led back to the sofa. "Shh, dear. Whatever it is, you must not bear it alone any longer. Tell me, child. Just . . . tell me."

Her words seemed to open the floodgate to the girl's soul. Great sobs came ripping up from her throat, as if escaping from the deepest chambers of her being. For several moments she wept, while Alice held her, soothing her, consoling her as she would have her own daughter, her Isabel. Whatever had happened to this child, Alice thought it surely must have had its breeding place in hell.

The weeping finally subsided, but the girl still trembled as slowly, haltingly, she began to speak.

"I have never told a soul," she said, her voice little more than a rough-edged whisper. "None but my mother. But Mum, she didn't believe me . . . at least she claimed not to. She said I was selfish and wanton. And then she sent me away."

Alice swallowed, her own eyes filling with tears as she steeled herself for whatever might come next.

Quinn had gone to work for Millen Jupe for one reason, and one reason only: to save her mother, her younger sister Molly, and herself from the graveyard.

Situations in service were all too rare

throughout the county. But situations like the one into which Millen Jupe eventually drew Quinn were shamefully common, especially during the Hunger.

The landlord or his agent, whichever happened to be in residence, would send for one of the village girls, offering what seemed — at least to a starving family — like an extravagant wage for the position of housekeeper and cook.

More often than not, it was the young, comely girl who received such a summons. Refusal meant almost certain eviction of the entire family. With hundreds throughout the county falling over dead from the harsh winter winds and the famine, a bid from the Big House was often seen as salvation itself.

When the message first came for her, Quinn resisted, indeed refused to go. Later she begged her mother not to *make* her go. Although the agent, Millen Jupe, was neither old nor unattractive, he was known throughout the county for his vicious temper and debauchery. At the time, Quinn was but fifteen years of age, and the thought of living in the same house with the agent terrified her.

It was her mother who finally convinced Quinn there was nothing for it but to comply. And so finally, she had gone — for the sake of her little sister, whom she loved more than everything, and for her mother, whom she also loved, though her affection had never been returned.

For nearly two years she lived in the Big House, serving as housekeeper and cook — and, later, as the agent's mistress, and the object of his abuse.

"It wasn't all that bad, at first," she told Alice, her voice leaden. "In the beginning, he treated me decent enough. He paid me a fair wage, allowed me time off to visit my mother and Molly on Sundays, and later even taught me to read a bit — permitted me the use of his library as well."

The man had actually been kind to her at first, almost as if he valued Quinn as a companion. When he turned ugly, it seemed to happen all at once, without warning. He brought her to his bed and raped her repeatedly, then shamed her until she started to believe his accusations — that she had taunted him, enticed him to do the things he did to her.

"I tried to run away many a time, but when he brought me back the beatings were worse than ever. He grew uglier as I grew bolder. And he threatened to have the roof knocked down over my mother's head if I didn't cease the running. Between his threats and his savagery, I finally gave up and stayed with him."

524

"Didn't you tell your mother?"

Quinn stared down at her hands. "Aye, I told her. She said I must be doing something to displease the man, else he wouldn't be so bitter toward me. She told me I must try harder to win his favor, or we would all pay."

She looked up and saw the shock mirrored in the eyes of Alice Walsh. Shamed, Quinn quickly dropped her gaze and went on with her story.

She had not known a human being could perpetrate such cruelty on another. Although her mother had always been cold and indifferent, she had never raised a hand to Quinn or her sister. Quinn hardly remembered her da — he had died when she was seven — but her vague recollection was that of a bearded man with mournful eyes and a quiet voice. A gentle man.

There had been nothing in her life or limited experience to prepare her for a madman like Millen Jupe. Almost daily he inflicted an entire gamut of abuse on her, the depravity of which grew darker as his drinking increased. At the end, on those rare occasions when he was sober, he wounded her with his words instead of his hands.

It seemed to Quinn the man had been taken over by the devil himself, and in his madness he had resolved to exorcise his demons by destroying her. She spent her days in a prison of physical pain and emotional terror. She spent her nights in hell.

Perhaps, like Jupe, she went a bit mad after nearly two years of his abuse. Or perhaps her action was spurred by the latest in a particularly vicious series of beatings. More than likely, though, it was the sound of her sister's name on his leering mouth that finally drove her to that mindless deed of desperation which resulted in her fleeing her home . . . and her country.

"That last night, he beat me harder than ever before. Then he threatened me and my family, and beat me again. At the end, he said he was going to replace me with my little sister Molly.

"He taunted me, said Molly was nearly as old as I had been when he brought me up to the Big House. He said . . . he said he liked to raise up his little tarts to suit himself."

He had sat up in bed and, as was his habit, began to peel himself an apple with a kitchen knife. He continued to mock her and, seeing her fury, he flicked the knife at her face, as if to cut her.

Quinn snapped. She dived at him, wresting the knife from his grip and raking it down the side of his face.

Roaring like an enraged bull, he kicked her

from the bed, onto the floor, then stood over her and kicked her again. And again.

The knife went clattering out of her hand, across the floor. Somehow Quinn found the strength to lunge after it. As she rolled over onto her back, the knife in hand, Jupe fell on her with a demented scream, as if to murder her.

Instead, he fell onto the knife. With her last remaining shred of sanity, Quinn realized what had happened, and, hoping to save herself, twisted the knife into his heart even farther.

Dazed and in pain, she eased out from under his lifeless body and stumbled to her feet. He was dead, or looked to be. She did not wait to be sure. Her mind screaming, her body rebelling against the agony of the night's abuse, she bolted from the house and ran like a wild thing all the way home.

"Your mother . . . actually told you it was your fault?" Alice said incredulously. "She told you to leave?"

Dear God in heaven, what this child had endured! It was a miracle she had survived at all!

The girl nodded. She had not met Alice's eyes more than once throughout her narrative. Even now, although she lifted her face, she kept her gaze averted.

As carefully as if Quinn were made of fragile china, Alice touched her hand to the girl's chin, turning her face gently toward her. Tears spilled from those pain-filled eyes, tracking that splendid face. Alice felt her own eyes sting and knew that she, too, might weep at any moment.

"Listen to me, Quinn. What happened to you — that horrible time with the agent, that last night, the knife — none of it was your fault. *None* of it! Do you understand?"

The girl looked at her. "I should never have gone with him in the first place. I had a choice."

"Did you?" Alice probed. "Did you really? And what was your choice, Quinn? To let your family be thrown out of their home and die of starvation? Good heavens, girl, your own mother urged you on! You had no *choice!* You were only a child!"

"But if I could have gotten away from him before then . . . at least he wouldn't have died. . . ." The girl squeezed her eyes shut, as if she could not bear the memories.

"If you could have gotten away from him, you *would* have!" Alice said sharply. "You tried, child — you tried. It wasn't *your* fault you couldn't get away! Oh, Quinn, Quinn, you must understand — none of it was your fault!"

The girl opened her eyes. Alice could not bear the sight of such despair any longer. Gently she gathered the girl into her arms and pressed her head against her shoulder.

"Oh, my dear . . . my dear," she murmured, agonizing over the devastation, the evil, that had been inflicted on the girl. "You bear no guilt for what was done to you. You are not a murderer, child. You're a *victim!*"

They sat there for a long time, the shadows deepening in the room. Alice held her and let her cry away her shame and agony, the entire time repeating soft reassurances.

"God doesn't condemn you, Quinn, and you must not condemn yourself," she told her when the girl had quieted. "Why, there's a promise in His Word about this very thing," she said, trying to recapture from her memory the words she herself had learned to cling to in the days after the hearing.

" '*For if our heart condemns us, God is greater than our heart, and knows all things . . . if our heart does not condemn us, we have confidence before Him.*' "

"No court in the land . . . at least not in *this* land," Alice went on, "would hold you responsible for that man's death. Look at *me:* I shot my own husband! Yet the court declared me innocent of any wrongdoing. And I accept that decision. I can't take back what I did, can't change anything that happened. But I believe God has pronounced me innocent, just as the court did. And if I believe I am innocent in God's eyes — then I must not condemn myself in my own heart."

The girl eased back, lifting her face to look at Alice.

"That's what you must do, Quinn. You must accept your innocence. Give God all those years of torture and fear and hurt. Give Him your pain, your broken heart, your guilt. Give it all to Him . . . and begin to *live*."

As Alice watched, she saw a faint light of awareness, understanding . . . something . . . dawn in the glistening eyes. And in her own words of comfort to Quinn O'Shea, she seemed to hear the voice of her forgiving Father speaking to *her* with the same admonition. . . .

"Give Me your pain, your broken heart, your guilt. Give it all to Me, Alice . . . and begin to live."

39

The Abomination
of the City

This is the place: these narrow ways,
diverging to the right and left,
and reeking everywhere with dirt and filth.
Such lives as are led here,
bear the same fruits here as elsewhere.
CHARLES DICKENS (1812–1870)
(From *American Notes*)

The squalor and misery of the Five Points immeasurably exceeded everything Morgan had been led to expect.

Within minutes after entering the area ludicrously known as "Paradise Square" — a triangular space into which the five streets giving the slum its name converged — he began to wish he had not insisted on seeing the place for himself. Both Michael and Whittaker had done their utmost to dissuade him. Even Jess Dalton, who apparently spent much of his time here in ministry, warned that nothing in Morgan's past experience could possibly prepare him for the Five Points.

Morgan now saw for himself why they had been so adamant in their objections. The place was an abomination, a nightmare world which would surely defy any attempt to capture its ugliness and horror, its wretchedness.

He had seen the slums of London and Paris, knew the treacherous laneways of Dublin's Liberties all too well. But none of these had stunned him or sickened him quite like this American lair of filth and depravity.

He would have thought that by now he was past being shocked or horrified. He had seen enough suffering and rampant injustice in his own country to callous one's soul. But to find such a pit of human misery in the midst of a city often hailed as having "streets of gold" — and to know the place was chiefly populated with his own countrymen — was beyond belief.

As Sandemon wheeled him down one garbage-littered alleyway after another, flanked by Michael and Jess Dalton, with Daniel John out in front of them, Morgan felt as if he were journeying through the very streets of hell. Every building in view seemed to have a crumbling facade and broken windows, doors hanging ajar, torn free of their hinges. Broken whiskey bottles and animal offal literally paved the rutted lanes. The stench alone was enough to make a strong man retch. On almost every corner lounged inebriated beggars and slatternly women — these also drunk — while from each open doorway came the sound of shrieking or brawling or weeping.

The farther they ventured into the depths of the slum, the more unspeakable their surroundings became. But upon their return to the "Square," one building in particular caught Morgan's attention — a singularly hideous monstrosity that resembled a distorted, overgrown crab. He was certain he had never seen anything so extraordinarily ugly.

They came to a halt in front of the structure, and he glanced up at Michael. "What is that, pray?" he said, making no attempt to conceal his disgust.

"The Old Brewery," Michael said, his own voice laced with bitterness. "We will not go inside."

Morgan studied him for a moment, then turned his attention back to the building.

"The place looks almost alive," Sandemon commented. "Alive, and crawling with evil."

"It is that," Michael replied. "The sights inside that den would give you nightmares for months."

"But it is finally coming down," Jess Dalton said quietly.

"Coming down?" Michael's surprise at the pastor's announcement was evident.

Dalton nodded, the ghost of a smile touching his mouth. "I just learned for certain this week. The Ladies Home Missionary Society will finally see their prayers answered. Oh, it's a ways off yet; the actual demolition and rebuilding will have to wait until more money can be raised. But the Society has entered into an arrangement to purchase the building. They hope to see it leveled within two years."

Dalton crossed his arms over his massive chest and stood staring at the building with a look of satisfaction. "It seems fitting somehow, don't you think, that a new blow for the Kingdom will be struck in the very spot where darkness has held title for so many years? A hostel of vice and degradation is to be razed, and a new mission building erected in its place."

"Well, thanks be!" said Michael.

"Thanks be indeed," Jess Dalton echoed, still smiling. He turned to Morgan and Sandemon. "Without knowing the background of the place, you can't be expected to understand what a victory this represents. But as much as anything else that's been accomplished here in the Five Points over the past several years — possibly *more* than anything else — this news reaffirms my faith that God is at work in New York City."

Morgan gave a nod, but he could not still the anguish of his heart as he saw firsthand the conditions under which his people were existing. Thousands of them, fleeing their own country for the sole purpose of survival, had come to this "Promised Land" in hopes of finding a better life for themselves and their children. Instead, vast numbers of them had ended up here, in this pit of squalor and despair. Was Ireland's tragedy destined to continue unabated, even in the Land of Promise?

Worst of all, at least in Morgan's eyes, were the children. They broke his heart. Raggedy little beggars, obviously without provision of any kind for their very existence, scurried along the streets pleading for money, for food, or, in some cases, looking as if they had come in search of a touch that wasn't a blow. Morgan emptied his pockets in minutes, unable to resist their hollow eyes, their claw-like hands grasping at him.

Some, little more than babes themselves, carried infants on their backs. They had no doubt been tossed out, Jess Dalton explained, by abusive or indifferent parents. Many wore little more than tattered blankets to hide their nakedness; shoes were almost nonexistent.

And there were hundreds of them, scuttling through the streets like stray animals. For the first time Morgan caught a glimpse of just how sacred a work, how enormous a burden, Whittaker and Nora had taken upon themselves. And right there, in the midst of the gutters and garrets, he breathed a prayer for divine provision for their efforts.

"Now I understand what Whittaker meant," he mused softly. "Once, on the docks of Killala, the man stood and issued a caution to me, which I later came to suspect was more from the Lord than from Whittaker himself. We were little more than strangers at that juncture, Whittaker and I, but even then the Englishman did have a way about him. 'Fitzgerald,' he said to me, peering through those spectacles of his, 'Fitzgerald, you are a very big man, a strong, powerful man. But even *you* are not man enough to bear the pain of a nation, to carry the burden of an entire people, unless you in turn allow Jesus Christ to hold *your* heart and carry *you*.' "

Morgan looked about him, at the hopeless souls, the drunken wretches, the lost children of the Five Points. Then he turned back to the leprous old building which, according to Jess Dalton, sheltered evil beyond all imagining.

"Whittaker was right," he said quietly. "All this" — he made a sweeping motion with his hand — "this would surely crush even the mightiest of men, were they to undertake God's work on their own."

He looked up at Michael and Jess Dalton, then at Daniel John, who had dropped to one knee and was adjusting a filthy sling on the arm of a dirty-faced little boy. The child called Daniel John "Doc."

Morgan swallowed and raked a hand down his beard. "What I see here, in this place, makes me yearn even more to have the use of my legs again. It makes me want to walk through these alleys and pitiful dwellings and help somehow — as all of you are helping."

Michael put a hand to his shoulder. "Would you forget your writings, Morgan? The truth you have placed in the hands of so many? Heaven bless you, man, you have virtually assured that untold thousands will know the truth about the famine — and England's part in it!"

Jess Dalton also spoke up. "Michael's right. Because of your efforts, the history, the very heritage, of an entire people will be preserved for other generations."

Morgan lifted a hand to acknowledge their words, but they did not understand. He was not ungrateful for the agreements that had come to him this week: first from Greeley, who had promised to serialize Joseph's famine diary in his newspaper; and from S. W. Benedict, Dalton's own publisher, who was drawing up a contract for the book rights to the diary, with the promise to go to press just as quickly as possible.

But none of it seemed enough, somehow. He wanted . . . ached . . . for the mobility to go among his people, here, in the place of their exile, as well as back in Ireland, where thousands upon thousands still faced possible extinction.

He wanted . . . he needed . . . to *walk* again.

Ah, well . . . tomorrow, he reminded himself with no small amount of trepidation, he would take the "first step" to accomplishing just that.

40

An Encounter
in the Park

Forget not that no fellow-being yet
May fall so low but love may
lift his head. . . .
JAMES WHITCOMB RILEY (1849–1916)

That evening, as she started toward the park, Quinn O'Shea wondered why Daniel Kavanagh wasn't going to the concert with the rest of his family. The Whittakers and the Burkes were escorting their Irish visitors to Castle Garden tonight, joining vast numbers of others in New York City for an evening of music with Jenny Lind.

According to the papers, it was to be only one of many concerts performed by the famous soprano, and it promised to be a grand affair entirely. Quinn would have thought Daniel would want to be in attendance, to hear the one the newspapers called "the Swedish Nightingale." But she had seen nothing of him throughout the afternoon or early evening, and the family had left without him.

Earlier in the day, Quinn had thought she might be asked to stay with Teddy. She had hoped for an excuse to postpone this evening.

But Johanna and the Fitzgerald daughter had volunteered to keep the two babes, giving the grown-ups an evening to themselves. Under the watchful supervision of the big black man called Sandemon, they would keep an eye on the boys at Whittaker House.

Apparently, there was no way out. She had to do this — and she had to do it tonight.

As he sat in Castle Garden, surrounded by the largest crowd he had ever seen, Morgan marveled at the contrast between these surroundings and what he had encountered earlier in the day.

Apparently this island at the southern tip of the city, where the vast circular concert hall stood, had once been the site of a famous fort. Now it was the largest place of entertainment in New York.

They had been here since a little past five, even though the concert was not to begin until eight. The place was mobbed. Morgan estimated an audience of at least six or seven thousand inside, with hundreds of others bobbing about in small boats on the water surrounding the island.

Their own party was a large one; besides Morgan and Finola, it included Lewis Farmington and his wife, Winifred, a delight of an English lady who also happened to be Evan Whittaker's aunt; Nora and Whittaker, Sara Burke, and her grandmother. Daniel John should be joining them any time now. Michael would not be sitting with the rest of them, being one of the many police captains who, along with their men, were attempting to keep order within and outside the premises. As for Sandemon, he had opted to remain at home. Although he had not said as much, Morgan suspected the black man preferred the company of the children to the noisy throng of concert-goers.

He looked up, studying the tiers of seats that rose to a ceiling of remarkable height, then scanned the crowds throughout the building. As he sat there, waiting for the concert to begin, he contemplated the extremes of the day, from the squalor and misery of the Five Points slum, to the grandeur and gaiety of this packed, glittering concert hall. Yet from one place to the other, and all along the random sites he had seen in between, he thought he could detect the pulse of the city, indeed the very heart of the nation.

Someone had said that the key to America's strength lay in her diversity. Perhaps, he thought, but only if that diversity were respected.

It had been his experience that too often oppression was employed as the only workable approach to dealing with differences or divisions. In his own country, the English, in their attempts to conquer and colonize the land, had from the beginning adopted a policy of tyranny and virtual enslavement of the Irish people, rather than one of tolerance and respect. What might have been the consequences to both Ireland and Britain, he wondered, if the English had chosen to encourage Ireland's rich and ancient culture, rather than to pillage her lands and attempt to destroy her language, her history, and her economy?

If England had even guaranteed the most basic freedom to the Irish people, there might have been a chance for something more than conflict and hatred, and, eventually, war.

Morgan wondered whether America's future would turn out to be so very different. From what he had gleaned from the newspapers and his talks with Michael and others, the issue of racial and ethnic division was a gathering storm upon the country's horizon.

Jess Dalton, for one, firmly believed that a divided nation might emerge from the burgeoning controversy surrounding the slavery issue. The abolitionist preacher, with what might well be prophetic sight, feared a great battle looming in the near future, a war between North and South. Such a war — one which turned the nation against itself — would surely prove to be nothing less than cataclysmic.

Before he could descend deeper into his brooding, Morgan was jarred back to his surroundings by the orchestra striking up. After the overture, a baritone named Belletti came on stage and sang a brief solo. Afterward there was more stirring among the crowd, then a salvo of thunderous applause as the Swedish Nightingale — Jenny Lind — finally appeared on stage. The audience rose to its feet, quieting only when the conductor rapped his baton.

Morgan had heard the "Casta Diva" from Bellini's *Norma* sung before — but never like this. The famed soprano, while in truth a rather ordinary-looking young woman with strong but irregular features, possessed a voice that was anything but ordinary. As she stood there in her white dress, her pale hair coiled in a thick roll over each ear, she seemed to transcend the concert hall, the crowds, even the orchestra, with the purity and perfection of a voice that defied all description.

At Morgan's side, Finola drew in a shuddering breath of admiration, then turned to smile at him. Her eyes were misted with emotion, and Morgan could not deny the thrill that seized his own soul. He squeezed Finola's hand, gratified by her pleasure in the event, fortified by her presence beside him.

As the night deepened, and the Swedish songbird went on to captivate the thousands in Castle Garden, Morgan finally forgot his thoughts of divisions and conflicts, oppression and war. He even managed, at least for those few fleeting hours, to allay his apprehension about his next day's meeting with Jakob Gunther.

For a time, albeit all too brief, it did not matter that his legs would not support him. He was utterly caught up, transported beyond himself, by the wonder and the magic of the music.

The twilight had brought with it a cool, damp mist, lending its autumn melancholy to the gas-lighted streets and deserted park. Quinn's mood, earlier brightened by the encouragement from Alice Walsh, now grew somber as she steeled herself to confront Daniel Kavanagh.

She dreaded the encounter. Yet another part of her soul swelled with the newly acquired assurance that, whatever might lie ahead for her after this night, she would somehow learn to live again — without shame and self-abasement, without the terrifying, desolate feeling of being entirely on her own. For the first time in years, she had even made a halting attempt to learn to pray again, with at least a seed of faith that God would hear her.

For all that, she could thank Alice Walsh. She would, no doubt, thank that good woman every day of her life for years to come. But for now — she must get the immediate ordeal over with.

Quinn started up the gentle swell of land which eventually dropped off to the bandstand just below. As she walked, she filled her lungs with the autumn smells of woodsmoke and dying leaves and the faint, yeasty odor of the day's offerings from Gartner's bakery.

Something about the everyday, familiar scents brought a rush of sadness sweeping over her. Once Daniel knew the truth, she could lose it all — this place, her position in service, the people she had come to care for. Especially if he chose to tell his family.

Whittaker House was the first home Quinn had ever had — in reality the *only* home she had ever had. There she was accepted for what she was, appreciated for what she could do. She had enough to eat and a bit of peace for herself at sundown. She had grown fond of the people, especially the little boys, had even come to care about the neighborhood; its familiarity made her feel safe, gave her an odd sense of proprietorship.

In truth, she could scarcely bear the thought of losing all this after having it so brief a time. But she would do what she had to do, and take the consequences.

From the top of the rise Quinn looked down and saw a figure standing in the center of the darkened bandstand just below. She took a deep breath, pulled her shawl more tightly about her shoulders, then went on.

Her vision was even poorer than usual in the gloaming. She was almost at the steps of the bandstand before she realized her mistake.

She stopped, her eyes locking on the shadowed figure of the man who stood, obviously waiting for her. *A man too brawny by far, too solid-set, for Daniel Kavanagh.*

A chill of terror touched the back of her neck. Then he stepped out of the shadows, and Quinn saw his face.

Sergeant Price!

She should have felt nothing but relief, that the encounter she had been dreading was apparently to be postponed. Instead, she was overwhelmed by a wholly inappropriate feeling of pleasure at the sight of the smiling policeman.

Her pulse bounced like a hare as she stared at him. "What — what are *you* doing here?"

He took a step toward her, then another, holding out one large hand to help her up into the bandstand.

Quinn merely stared at the proffered hand, then looked back to the now solemn face. With his hair slicked back, he was all spit and polish, in a nicely cut jacket with snow-white linen.

Whatever was he about? What was he doing here?

Finally she allowed him to help her up the steps, where she stood staring at the man as if she had never laid eyes on him before this night.

"What are you doing here, Sergeant?" she asked him again.

"Ah, lass, I have a name, don't you know? Won't you please drop the 'Sergeant' at last and call me 'Denny'?"

He was acting very peculiar. Quinn's mind raced, and she said the first thing that came into her head. "Where is Daniel?"

The sergeant looked at her. "Daniel?"

Quinn nodded. "Daniel Kavanagh."

"Why . . . no doubt he is with his family and

their visitors from Ireland, at the Castle Garden."

Quinn shook her head. "No, I was to meet him here."

The sergeant frowned. "You . . . were to meet young Daniel here? Tonight?"

" 'Tis not what you think!" she hurried to tell him. She would not have the man suspecting what he looked as if he *might* be suspecting. "I came to . . . explain some matters to him."

He was studying her with his policeman's chicken-hawk eye. It was the look he might have turned on one of his criminal types, and it made Quinn squirm.

"You need not look at me so," she informed him. "This is none of your affair, after all."

"The lad asked you to meet him, here, at the bandstand, did he?" His voice was quiet, but Quinn did not like the tone he was taking. It was obvious he doubted her word.

"Isn't that what I told you?"

The sergeant dug his hands down deep in his pockets, eyeing Quinn as if her face were changing right in front of him. "And did the lad possibly request your attendance by way of a note?"

Quinn gaped at him. How could he possibly know about the note?

He drew a long breath, and a slow smile broke over his insolent features. " 'Twasn't Daniel who sent the note, lass," he said, his voice ever so soft. " 'Twas myself."

"You did not," she shot back. Caught off guard, Quinn almost laughed at his nerve. As if a thickheaded Irishman like himself would be caught dead writing love poems and sentimental letters!

" 'Twas myself, and that's the truth," he said, no longer smiling. "I wrote the note asking you to come here tonight. And I wrote all the poems that went before. They were for telling you my feelings, Quinn O'Shea, so don't be taking me lightly."

Quinn opened her mouth, but nothing came, only a choked sound, like a squawk.

"You thought it was young Daniel, did you?" He grinned and shook his head. "Aye. Surely a big oaf like myself wouldn't be writing such things." He paused, then began to recite the poems, line by line.

Quinn was astonished. But even more amazing was the natural and easy way the rhythmic words rolled off the man's tongue, like gentle water lapping the stones in a riverbed.

Her hand flew to her mouth. So it had not been Daniel at all who had gone sweet on her! Not Daniel, but this big square Irishman.

Was it possible? Could this rough-hewn, inarticulate policeman really be the poet who had wrenched her heart with his lyrical words, his lovely phrases?

She was stunned entirely, unable to think, shocked into immobility as her mind groped for reason. She could do nothing but stand and gawk at him.

He stopped quoting the poetry long enough to expel a long breath. "I couldn't think what else to do, lass. You wouldn't give me a chance to tell you how I felt. You were always so eager to run away from me. And even had you given me the opportunity, I've never been the man for flowery speech and fine words . . . except on paper, perhaps. I had to find a way to make you see what you have come to mean to me."

For a moment . . . one bright, poignant, achingly sweet moment . . . Quinn permitted herself to savor this discovery of his feelings, even as her heart silently acknowledged that she was not without some feelings of her own.

And then she caught herself, the full impact of his confession hitting her like a blow. This was worse, much worse, than she could have imagined, worse by far than if Daniel had been her poet! This Sergeant Price, who seemed to be taking up a great deal of space as he stepped closer to her, was a *man,* not a boy.

A man she could come to care for, Quinn admitted to herself for the first time. This was a man grown, and he apparently thought her a decent lass, a girl worth cherishing.

But he did not know what she was. And, oh, please God, she did not want him to know!

She shook her head, as if to shake off the shame and the disgrace of the past. That was then, this was now. Some things she could change, and some she could not. There was nothing for it but to tell him the truth. The fact that he was not Daniel had no bearing at all on what *she* had to do. She could not allow him or any other man to think she was something she was not.

She lifted her face to meet his eyes, shrinking inwardly at the unexpected tenderness reflected there. "You are saying, then . . . that you have feelings for me, that you care for me?"

He took a step toward her, but Quinn stopped him with a hand held up as if to ward off a blow.

"I am, lass. And my feelings are ones you need not be fearful of."

Quinn swallowed and found her throat dry and swollen. "You must not say anything more," she said dully. "There is much you need to know about me, and once you do, I will walk away, and you can do what you will with the knowledge."

She pulled in a shuddering breath, struggling to find the way to begin. "What I have to say is . . . ugly, and it shames me. But I have to say it, and you will understand why, once I tell you."

"No, lass," he said quietly, making Quinn flinch in surprise. "You do not have to tell me *anything*. I know it all."

Quinn went rigid. Even her heart seemed to stop its beating as she stared at him in disbelief.

He moved as if to close the distance between them, then seemed to think better of it. "I know your story, Quinn O'Shea."

His voice at that moment seemed the gentlest sound Quinn had ever heard. "I know your story, and other than my grief for your pain, it matters not in the least to me. Your past is of little concern to me, lass. 'Tis your future I would like to have a part in, you see."

"How?" Quinn finally managed to choke out. "How could you know?"

A look bordering on pain crossed his face, and for an instant he glanced away. When he turned back to her, his expression was one of regret. "I must ask your forgiveness, Quinn O'Shea. The guilt has hounded me like a plague for days now. I can only ask you to try and understand why I acted so. 'Twas only because I hoped to find a way to help you."

"What are you saying to me, Denny Price? What did you do?" Her words sounded as if they echoed from a great distance.

"I have a friend back home," he said, looking down at the planked floor on which they stood. "A policeman, like myself. I, ah . . . what I did, you see, was to write to Niall. He did a bit of asking about, you know, from some of the lads down to Roscommon. The story about what happened to you — to Millen Jupe — is still talked about in your town, in Athlone."

Still he did not look at her.

"You . . . know about Millen Jupe?" She stared at him in horror. "You know . . . that I killed him?"

"Aye, I do." His voice had hardened to flint. "And I know *why*."

Quinn was fast losing the battle against the tears burning her eyes. The humiliation flooding over her made her want to turn and run . . . run away from Denny Price . . . from New York . . . from herself. This man knew her shame. *He knew.*

He made the mistake of reaching for her hand. Quinn jumped back as if his touch would sear her skin, and he quickly raised both hands, palms outward, as if to assure her he would not press.

"How long have you known?"

His answer was slow in coming. "A few weeks. Not long."

A few weeks . . .

"The poems . . . you started sending me the poems . . . a few weeks ago. . . ."

His gaze was steady, gentle. "That's right, lass."

"You *knew* . . . and you wrote such poems to me anyway?"

He said nothing, merely nodded, his eyes still holding hers.

Quinn's chin began to tremble. "How?" she choked out. "How could you write such words . . . knowing what you knew?"

Again a look of pain swept over his features, then ebbed. "The only thing I knew that mattered at all was the fact that I love you, lass."

This could not be happening . . . such a thing could never be. Not for her. Never for the likes of Quinn O'Shea.

He paused, passing a hand over his eyes. "You might want to know, just for the knowing, that the talk about the town was all in your defense, that you acted only to save your life — and that the man had it coming long before. The thought is that it was a miraculous thing entirely that Jupe had not murdered *you* before that night." He stopped, then added, "There is no offense on the books for you, lass. No charges against you — none."

Quinn's legs shook beneath her. She was chilled and she was on fire, all at the same time. She wanted to laugh. She wanted to weep.

Once more the man held out a hand to her. Quinn stared at it, then searched his eyes.

"Give me your hand, Quinn O'Shea."

Quinn bit her lip till the pain made her stop. Then she stretched out her hand.

He clasped it gently, then just as tenderly drew her closer to him, close enough that she could see more clearly the entire tide of feelings that had risen in his eyes.

"Listen to me now, Quinn," he told her, still in that same soft voice. "Listen to me closely. I have loved you for a long, long time. I cannot keep it to myself any longer. I am asking you, Quinn O'Shea, to be my wife."

Quinn gasped. She tried to pull her hand away, but he would not let her go. "Wait, now," he said. "Wait. I am asking you to marry me . . . when you are *ready*. Until then — and forever after — I will be your friend. I am a patient man. I will give you all the time you need, however long it might take, for you to come to love me. And even if you never do — well, then, Quinn O'Shea, I expect I will still be your friend."

His eyes probed hers, and after a moment, as if he had seen what he was looking for there, he drew her closer, gathering her in his arms and holding her lightly, carefully, much as he might have held . . . a friend.

With her mind still reeling, her heart racing, Quinn stood very still, scarcely daring to breathe. For the first time, a man's touch felt almost safe, even welcome.

"I will never hurt you, Quinn O'Shea," he murmured, smoothing her hair away from her face. "And neither will anyone else. Upon my life, no one will ever hurt you again."

With only an instant's hesitation, Quinn pressed her face against the fortress of his sturdy shoulder. At last she allowed the tears to fall free and, as they flowed, to wash away her yesterdays.

41

The Surgeon
and the Seanchai

*What does he see, this peacock of a man,
when he looks at me through his proud,
condescending eye?
Am I flesh and bone, or merely a dot
on the map of his achievements?*
MORGAN FITZGERALD (1850)

Jakob Gunther was even more of a surprise
than his dimly lighted salt box of an office
near the East River.

With Sandemon, Morgan had been waiting
for the esteemed surgeon for nearly an hour.
For the last twenty minutes or so he had felt
his patience unraveling one thread at a time.
His self-composure throughout the morning
had been tenuous at best; at the moment he
wanted nothing more than to go charging out
the door and book the first available passage
back to Ireland.

They were the only ones in the pantry-sized

waiting room, which to Morgan's thinking made Gunther's self-endorsed skills highly suspect. Where were the patients of this great surgeon, if not clamoring for his attention?

The door finally flew open to admit a blast of cold air, followed by a lean, black-cloaked figure. As Morgan watched, the new arrival kicked the door shut behind him with a long, narrow foot, then flung off his cloak with a careless toss before turning to face Morgan.

"You are Fitzgerald, I presume? I am Dr. Gunther — Jakob Gunther."

At first Morgan could only stare at the man in surprise, biting back the urge to make a cutting remark. For some reason, he had concluded that Jakob Gunther would be well past his middle years, most likely balding and rotund. Perhaps because of the arrogant tone of the surgeon's letters, he had conceived the image of an aging eccentric, and a self-indulgent one at that.

But the man who now stood appraising him with undisguised boldness and a kind of clinical interest looked to be near Morgan's own age, certainly no older than his late thirties. He was fairly tall, angular, his face sharply molded — lightly scarred as well, probably from an attack of smallpox at some time in the past.

It took a minute for Morgan to recover. He

might have been wrong in his assumptions about the doctor's age and appearance, but he was certainly *not* mistaken about Gunther's arrogance. The iron-gray eyes flitted over him as if he were a questionable side of beef, of no particular value except as a suitable subject for research. The fleeting glance the surgeon afforded Sandemon registered nothing but utter indifference.

"I am quite late. It could not be helped." The surgeon was abrupt, even in his speech, the words shearing the air like hailstones. The accent of Vienna was still evident, but considerably Americanized. "So, then — let us begin. I will need your man's help in the examining room, large as you are. In here," he instructed over his shoulder as he whisked through a curtained doorway on the right.

And that was that. No word of apology. Not even the slightest sign of human warmth or interest.

Morgan ground his teeth as they followed Gunther through the doorway. His first impression of the man who might hold the power to change his life was anything but reassuring.

The examination itself required far less time than Morgan would have anticipated and seemed much too uncomplicated to be reliable. Neither was he prepared for Gunther's gentleness. Given the surgeon's earlier rudeness and brusque manner, it would have come as no surprise had the man taken to kneading him and punching him down like a stubborn loaf of bread dough. Instead, the hands that explored him were deft, but sure and gentle, the instruments carefully placed. Gunther even seemed to suspend his brusqueness, if only for the moment.

The surgeon hinted at nothing during the examination, other than to make an occasional soft utterance, the meaning of which defied interpretation. When he had finished, he left the room, allowing Morgan time to dress in private.

"What do you make of him?" Morgan muttered as Sandemon helped him back into the wheelchair. "Aside from his charm, that is, about which I cannot say enough."

Sandemon chuckled softly, waiting until Morgan was completely settled before replying. "Certainly, his manners could do with some improvement. But his hands are skillful, powerful. And his eyes hold the fire of genius."

"Or madness," Morgan said dryly. "Your sense of him is that he is capable, then?"

"More than capable." The black man's voice was quiet, his tone thoughtful. "Dr. Gunther would seem possessed of both confidence and competence."

"You failed to mention arrogance."

Morgan would have gone on, but Gunther swept back into the room at that moment. Seated across the desk — a Spartan, scarred piece which somehow fit Gunther to perfection — Morgan had a good opportunity to notice the man's hands. Splayed palms down on top of the desk, they did indeed convey the impression of strength and agility that Sandemon had observed. The fingers were unusually long and tapering, with large, rough knuckles and slightly reddened skin.

Morgan realized with a jolt that these were the hands of a man who was no stranger to physical labor. He remembered James Dunne remarking at some time in the past that the actual meaning of the word *surgery* had to do with "laboring by hand." He was struck by the seeming appropriateness of those words as they related to Jakob Gunther.

The surgeon lifted a hand and raked it through his straight, sand-colored hair, disheveling it even more than it had been. "So, then — if I might ask, how well do you endure pain, Mr. Fitzgerald?"

Unprepared for the surgeon's bluntness, despite his earlier behavior, Morgan tensed. "As well as the next man, I expect," he said guardedly.

"The procedure your condition seems to suggest would involve a great deal of discomfort and pain. Not so much in the surgical process itself, you understand, for I would employ ether as an anesthetic."

It was the period of recovery — which would be quite extensive, he went on to explain in his terse manner — that would be most difficult. "While you would seem to be in remarkable physical condition for a man with your injury, surgery has a way of breaking down the body's natural defenses, depleting you of your stamina, and weakening you in general. Recuperation would undoubtedly be long and difficult."

The entire time he spoke, Gunther's eyes probed Morgan's as if taking his measure. If he had arrived at any conclusions, he was keeping them carefully masked.

Morgan's mind fumbled to grasp the details of Gunther's explanation. Although he had heard the surgeon's warnings about pain and discomfort, at the moment he could not seem to move past the words, "a surgery such as the one I am proposing."

"Are you telling me then that surgery is possible?" Morgan abruptly broke in.

Gunther continued to hold his gaze. "Possible, perhaps. But highly risky and with no guarantees whatsoever."

Morgan slumped back in the chair. He felt Sandemon's strong hand on his shoulder and was infinitely grateful for his friend's presence in the room.

He let out a long breath. "Tell me all of it, if you will. Spare me no detail, please."

Gunther propped his elbows on the desk, his hands forming an arch in front of his face. "To be altogether honest, you would be an experiment. This sort of surgery has never been performed in the States. I know what I'm doing, of course, but there is no convincing the plodding old men who govern the medical profession in this country — or in Europe, for that matter — that we must take risks if we are to learn. In Europe they are not quite so timid, but neither do they understand the value of research and experimentation to our work."

Morgan sat up. "Do I understand that you have never *performed* such a surgery?"

Gunther actually smiled — a quick, thin slash that did not approach his eyes before it disappeared. "You would be the first. Let me explain that our knowledge of anatomy is still severely limited by poor educational methods. The entire surgical field suffers from a lack of subjects on which to experiment, not to mention a dearth of professors who know anything more than a first-year student.

That's why students are stealing cadavers from the famine hospitals on which to study, a practice which will no doubt be sharply curtailed once the authorities catch up with them."

He lowered his hands and began to tap his fingers on the desk. "A procedure such as I am suggesting to you will not be widely performed, at least in this country, for years to come. But I am not willing to wait until I am a palsied old man to attempt what I already know can be accomplished."

The uneasiness that had been circling about Morgan since Gunther had begun to speak now swooped down like a hungry vulture and began to peck at him in earnest. "Why — what makes you so certain you can perform such a surgery?"

Gunther seemed to bristle. "I have seen it done, on the Continent. By somewhat primitive methods to be sure, but I *have* seen it. I have observed, and I have learned. I can do the surgery, I assure you, Mr. Fitzgerald."

He paused, again turning that unsettling iron stare on Morgan. "What I cannot assure is its success. There are any number of possibilities, most of them unpleasant. You might awaken with the paralysis extended to your upper extremities. You might not awaken at all. If you do survive, you will surely suffer. In addition, there is no guarantee that you will walk. There has been considerable atrophy of your muscles by now — and there will be even more during recovery. As yet we cannot know the extent of nerve damage. Only your own strength of will and divine intervention — if you believe in that sort of thing — will ultimately determine whether or not you will walk."

Morgan moistened his lips and tried to swallow, but gave it up when he found his mouth as dry as batting. "Have you no hope at all for me?" he said, his voice hoarse. "I hear no reason — no *sane* reason — to submit to such a procedure. It seems you are predicting only my doom. I am no rat on which you may ply your tricks. I am a man."

Sandemon's hand tightened on his shoulder, but Morgan was fast losing his patience with the man across the desk from him. It did not help that any hope he might have felt before the examination was quickly being extinguished by the surgeon himself.

Jakob Gunther seemed to consider his words, then pushed back from the desk and stood, hands clasped behind his back. "How much is it worth to you, Mr. Fitzgerald? How much do you *want* to walk again?"

Morgan stared at him. The blunt question seemed in incredibly poor taste, and the words hovered between them for a long time, until they were no more than an echo in Morgan's mind.

How much indeed?

"Enough to risk what would appear to be a fairly decent quality of life at the present?" Gunther probed. "Enough to risk your very life?"

"I cannot answer such questions. Not until I have had time to consider the implications."

Gunther looked as if he were about to dismiss them from the room, but Morgan did not intend to be put off without more information. "Explain to me, if you will, why you responded to James Dunne's correspondence in the first place. I will admit that your letters to him and to me were anything but optimistic — and what I have heard from you thus far is even less encouraging. If the risks are so great, and the possibilities of success so slight, why would you presume I would agree? It seems to me that only a madman or a fool would involve himself in such a venture, and I like to think that I am neither."

Gunther lifted an eyebrow, the thin line of his mouth again curving in a slight smile. "Perhaps it is the surgeon who is mad. A mad surgeon on the hunt for another wild-eyed adventurer like myself. Except that what you call madness, I prefer to call boldness."

Morgan studied him, and without any basis for his judgment came to the conclusion that Gunther was anything but mad. Prideful, cynical, perhaps without human warmth — but not mad.

"Where would you perform the surgery?" he asked abruptly.

Gunther seemed surprised by the question. After a second or two, he came round the desk and stood, his hands still locked behind his back. "At Bellevue," he said, "for the practical reason that no other hospital in the city is willing to let me . . . 'ply my tricks' on their premises." He smiled a little. "Bellevue has grudgingly allowed me to practice on the indigent and a number of the poor wretches in the insane facility. As one of the administration so delicately put it, 'Who would care?' "

He went on then to explain something of the surgical process itself, which Morgan did not understand in the least. He did notice that Sandemon seemed to be taking it all in with some degree of comprehension.

"From what I know of your injury, Mr. Fitzgerald, and the nature of your present condition, I am inclined to believe the bullet caused a fracture in your spinal cord. There would have been severe bruising and swelling, as well as some nerve damage, which is irreversible. But the bullet itself could still be contributing to the paralysis — and, of course, could cause additional paralysis if it shifts." He continued, sounding more as if he were explaining the process to himself than to Morgan. "After the surgery, I would immobilize you in a type of plaster cast — much like a cocoon — from the neck to mid-thigh. For how long, I cannot say as yet. Certainly for several weeks."

Morgan flinched but said nothing. His mind rebelled against the grim details Gunther was disclosing with such clinical impassiveness. Only by sheer force of will did he make himself hear every word of the surgeon's explanation.

"Once the cast is removed —" Again the eloquent shrug, the lift of the eyebrows. "After that, we would see what we have accomplished. If anything."

For the first time since the surgeon had begun his explanation, Morgan took in a deep breath, albeit an unsteady one.

"I will ask you again," he said tightly. "Can you give me any hope at all?"

Gunther looked at him, his expression unreadable. "Hope? What can I tell you, Fitzgerald? Your Dublin surgeon mentioned that you are a man of great faith. So, then — perhaps the answer depends on you. *How* great *is* your faith? Men of faith often believe that hope can be found in places where others would not think to look."

Morgan found himself strangely irritated by the surgeon's words, as if Gunther were deliberately attempting to mock him. Yet his dizzying heartbeat was finally beginning to slow, his hammering pulse ebbing to a more normal rhythm. He was starting to move past the threats implied by the surgeon's recitation to the possibilities as yet unrevealed.

He answered Gunther's question with one of his own. "What of yourself, Doctor? Are *you* a man of faith?"

The smile turned to a cynic's sneer. "Doubtless you would like me to be, eh, Fitzgerald? Then we could pray together for a miracle. If the surgery is successful, you would give credit to your God, as if I had had no part in it. Well, I am sorry, Fitzgerald, but I fear that if you decide in favor of the surgery, you will be under the knife of a heathen. There's little I believe in besides the depravity of my fellowman."

Morgan studied the sardonic face, the mocking eyes. He did not miss the edge of bitterness in the surgeon's voice. He sensed that Jakob Gunther lived with some private pain of his own, a pain beyond the help of even the most skilled surgical hands.

"God can use the hands of a heathen just as easily as the hands of a saint," he told Gunther in all sincerity. "He has even been known to use madmen and jackasses for His purposes now and then."

The surgeon made no response other than to crook an eyebrow, but Morgan felt a certain satisfaction. He had at last breached the man's armor, if only slightly.

"Interestingly enough," he went on, "that depravity of man you referred to was the very thing on which my own faith was ultimately founded. Once I recognized it in myself, that is."

He gave the surgeon no opportunity to respond. "Thank you very much for your time, Doctor," he said, a bit surprised that he could actually be civil to Gunther with so little effort. "I am sure you will understand that I need to consider all this very carefully. If I send you my answer by tomorrow, will that be soon enough?"

The surgeon gave a curt nod and merely stood watching Morgan as he and Sandemon turned to leave.

Outside the office, Morgan drew in a deep breath. He barely noticed the vile stench of the river, so relieved was he to escape Gunther's cold cynicism. With his response to the surgeon weighing heavily upon him, again he questioned whether he might be foolish entirely, to consider placing his life in the hands of such a man.

But there was no one else. Jakob Gunther was his best hope, perhaps his only hope. A chilling thought, but one to keep in mind as he made his decision.

It was late afternoon before they got back to Michael's house.

Inside, Sandemon wheeled him to the parlor. They came to a sharp halt just inside the door. The room teemed with people. Finola was sitting by the fire. Annie and Johanna occupied the opposite corner of the room, playing with Gabriel and Teddy. Also present, watching Morgan with anxious eyes, were Michael and Sara, Nora and Whittaker — even Daniel John.

In a moment of alarm, Morgan wondered if some tragedy had occurred in his absence. Then it dawned on him that they all seemed to be waiting for *him*. Going the rest of the way into the room, he managed to force a note of lightness into his voice. "Well, now — we have had the reunion already, and I don't see a corpse, so it must not be a wake. What, pray, is the occasion?"

They all glanced among themselves — except for Finola, whose gaze clung to his.

Michael broke the awkward silence. "The truth is, you see, none of us seemed to be of much account, anxious as we've been for your news. We thought we might just as well wait together."

By this time, Gabriel had spotted his father and came running. Morgan lifted the boy onto his lap and gave him a squeeze, then turned his attention to the others in the room.

For an instant — and an instant only — he felt a slight edge of disappointment. All the way back from Gunther's office he had craved nothing so much as Finola's serenity, longing to talk things through with her and hear her response, knowing that no matter how she felt about the surgery, she would soothe him.

Then he realized how altogether foolish, if not selfish, he was being. Was he not a man blessed, to find a room filled with people who cared so about him? He would have his time alone with Finola later, but for now he would be with his loved ones.

Finola had risen and now came to kneel beside him, studying his face as if to read his thoughts. Morgan set Gabriel to his feet and sent him running back to Teddy and the girls, then took Finola's hand in his. He turned to the waiting faces, and with a smile that was not in the least forced, began to tell them what he had learned from Jakob Gunther.

42

In the Garden

In the dark night of my agony
Oh, Savior, let me turn to Thee,
Who leads me from Gethsemane
Beyond despair to victory.
Anonymous

It was late before the parlor doors finally closed on the last visitor, later still when those left behind went to their rooms.

In their bedchamber, after making certain Finola understood his need to be alone, Morgan prepared to seek out a place of solitude.

"You will tell me . . . when you have made your decision?" Propped up in bed, her flaxen braid tucked neatly over one shoulder, Finola searched his eyes, all the while clinging to his hand.

Morgan noted with some concern that she looked exceedingly weary. Her eyes were shadowed, her fair skin more pale than usual.

"Are you quite well, *macushla?*" he asked, his wheelchair pulled close to the bed. "You look exhausted." He reached to touch her cheek, and she covered his hand with her own.

"I am perfectly fine, Morgan. 'Tis not me you should be thinking of tonight, but yourself."

"You'd just as well tell me not to breathe as not to think of you," he said, smiling. "Now, will you promise to go to sleep?"

"I cannot promise you that I will sleep, but I will have a rest. Go, now, Morgan. I know you need to be alone for a time, but please — not too long. You, too, must sleep."

She brought her face to his for his kiss, and afterward he held her for a moment. "Finola? You have not told me what you think I should do."

"Oh, my love, you know I cannot!" Her eyes caressed his face. "Whatever you decide, you must do it for yourself, not for me. Only for yourself, and for our Lord, as He leads you. I can merely promise to be with you, to love you, no matter your choice."

He squeezed her hand. "No man could ask for more," he answered softly. "Rest, Finola *aroon.* I won't be long."

He did not reassure her lightly. But as he wheeled himself out of the room, he wondered how long it might take a man to make what might well be the most critical decision of his life.

From the first day of their arrival, Morgan had been drawn to the gardens behind the house. So tonight Sandemon took him across the wide lawn, to the sheltered pavilion at the very end of the gardens. Surrounded by a profusion of late-blooming flowers and shrubs, Morgan sat breathing in the rich scents of autumn with great relish, savoring the bracing effect of the night air.

Sandemon came round the chair to face him. "Shall I stay with you, *Seanchai*, or would you prefer to be alone?"

Morgan shook his head, lifting a hand. "You need not wait. It is late, and I know you must be weary. I can make my own way back. I'll use the side ramp."

He was keenly aware of Sandemon's hesitation, his searching dark eyes. The man's expression was uncommonly grave, with no hint of his thoughts or his feelings.

"Have you any word for me?" Morgan made no attempt at lightness; the time had long passed when either of them felt a need to dissemble with the other. "I would not be too proud to hear any advice you might care to offer."

"No advice, *Seanchai*," Sandemon replied quietly. "Only the conviction that, however you decide, our Lord will be with you."

Morgan nodded, and Sandemon squeezed his shoulders as he passed. Morgan had felt the need to be alone, yet the moment Sandemon left him, he shivered slightly — not from the chill night air, but from the rush of loneliness that suddenly came swooping down on him.

Weary beyond belief and chilled by the dampness of the autumn night, Sandemon thought wistfully of the warm fires inside the house. But instead of going back inside as he was tempted to do, he sought a private place of his own, beneath a large old oak whose branches still clung bravely to the last of their bronze leaves.

He pulled his cloak more tightly about him and prepared to wait. It was a clear, sharp night, the sky sprayed with stars and frosted with moonlight. With his eyes fixed on the hunched figure in the wheelchair, he was so keenly attuned to the young giant's torment that he could almost feel the weight of the burden upon his own back.

As he stood watching, he began to pray. He prayed first that the *Seanchai* would be given the faith and childlike trust to make a wise decision. Although he thought he knew what that decision would be, he would not presume, but would wait until he heard it for himself.

He went on to pray for a company of the faithful who would this very night begin to gather, united in the One God, to do battle during the coming days for one of their own. Too often it seemed that even God's own people were unmindful of what their united, intercessory prayers could accomplish. Although the Holy Word and the world's history were filled with examples of lives changed, battles won, and evil vanquished by a divine power working through the prayers of a believing people, too often every other effort *besides* prayer was employed in a time of crisis. It was a sad but undeniable fact that only when all else had failed did hearts kneel in desperation before the throne of heaven.

Sandemon prayed that God would call on all those who loved the brave young poet now struggling with his own life-changing decision — those who through the years had been touched or influenced by his words, his deeds, his very life — to muster their faith and join forces in storming the doors of heaven on his behalf.

Finally, he prayed for peace for the *Seanchai,* the peace that did indeed surpass all human understanding. . . .

*"Peace, Lord, for that troubled, searching spirit
. . . peace for that agonizing soul. A peace that
will abide, in the dark garden of his anguish,
through the haunted valley of the shadow. Prince
of Peace, bestow your peace upon your troubled
son this night."*

At first Morgan was tempted to think of this
night in the garden as his darkest hour, his
own Gethsemane. But such a thought seemed
almost profane, somehow. To cast himself in
the same light as his Savior was surely irrever-
ent to the extreme.

And yet he could not help but think of the
Son of Man, kneeling in a garden, agonizing,
even sweating drops of blood, over the terrifying ordeal that awaited Him. That Man,
too, had found himself alone in His garden of
torment, with no one who could drink His
cup of sorrow, share the suffering of His soul,
or lighten the burden of His heart.

At times like this, Morgan knew, in times of
momentous decision and great despair, when
everything in life — even life itself — seemed
to depend on the choice that is made, a man is
truly, utterly alone. And yet, after those first
tortured minutes of pleading for an answer,
for wisdom and enlightenment, he slowly began to realize that he was *not* alone. This fra-

grant autumn garden had been transformed into a hushed and holy place. The presence of the Lord was all about him.

He could not kneel, not with his dead legs. He had often thought that, if by God's mercy he should ever regain the use of his legs, the first thing he would do would be to kneel before his Lord, in humility and thanksgiving. But for now he could only kneel in his heart, his body hunched in the chair, his hands gripping the rungs of a garden trellis.

As he sat there, his spirit gradually quieted, growing more serene than he would have thought possible this night. The years of his life began to roll over him like an entire succession of tides. Scene after scene — his lonely boyhood, his youthful roamings, his foolish, thoughtless sins and errant ways — gradually unfurled, reminding him with startling clarity of the strange and unpredictable directions his life had taken.

Could anyone have foreseen the changes God had wrought, the surprising turns and twists . . . and falls . . . that had brought him to this place, to this night?

A mystery.

A miracle.

Suddenly, in one radiant, pristine moment of illumination, he knew that tonight he would not pray for a miracle, as he had earlier thought to do. The truth was that he had already been given his miracle. From a solitary vagabond, a wayfaring poet with little but the cloak on his back — a wanderer without a home, without family or means — he had been given a vast estate he had not earned, a loving wife he could never deserve, and two precious children he had not sired.

If that was not a miracle, then what was? Moreover, in the agony of his pain and humiliation, in the helplessness of his immobility, he had been bathed in infinite grace. In learning to live with his useless legs, to endure the pain that ever burned low in his spine and burned even hotter in his freedom-starved spirit, he had discovered the reality of a loving, forgiving, redeeming God.

In his weakness, he had caught a glimpse of divine power. In his anguish, he had been comforted by divine love. And in finally accepting the burden of his own cross, he had received divine peace.

For the sake of his soul, the decision he would make this night must be based not on the hope that he would walk again, but on the truth that whether he walked or not, God would still be God and would still be faithful. The promise for his life, the glory of all life, was not God's blessing . . . but God himself.

"My grace is sufficient for you. . . ."

If his healing, his deliverance, did not come in one sudden, brilliant flash of divine intervention, then it would come day by day, year by year, as he went on, walking with God in his spirit, if not on his legs.

By the gift of God's love and by the blessing of family and friends, he lived life, if not entirely as a whole man, at least as a fulfilled man.

He prayed that he might also live it as an unfailingly thankful man.

Morgan stayed a short while longer, then turned the chair to start back toward the house. He wheeled about, then stopped, startled by the dark figure who stepped into his path.

"May I help you, *Seanchai?*"

Morgan studied the serene features. "You need not have waited. You must be chilled to the bone, you with your love of tropical breezes."

Sandemon went behind the chair and began to wheel him down the garden path. "I wanted to wait with you," he said quietly.

"This day has been exceedingly long," Morgan said over his shoulder. "You must be weary."

"Not so much as you, I'm sure."

They continued in silence for a moment. At last Morgan said, "You were praying for me as you waited, I expect."

"For you . . . and with you."

The wheels bumped over a fallen branch, and Sandemon slowed the chair.

Morgan swallowed with some difficulty. "I am grateful to you for staying," he said, his voice roughened with emotion.

"It was my privilege, *Seanchai,* and my pleasure."

"The Savior should have had such faithful friends," Morgan said. "Instead, His followers slept while He agonized. How is it, I wonder, that a wretch like myself is more greatly blessed in his companions than our Lord was?"

"What I do for you," Sandemon said quietly, bringing the chair to a stop and laying his hands lightly on Morgan's shoulders, "is also done for our Lord."

Morgan nodded. "Aye, so it is. And He must be greatly blessed by your faithfulness, for surely I am."

They stayed that way for a moment. Finally Morgan cleared his throat and said, "I have made my decision. I will have the surgery."

The hands on his shoulders tightened almost imperceptibly. "Yes, I thought as much," came the quiet reply. "And do you have peace with your decision, *Seanchai?*"

"I do. Whatever comes, I have peace."

Morgan hesitated, then went on. "Two things I would ask of you, though in truth I have no right to ask."

"I give you the right, then, *Seanchai*. Ask what you will. You know that I will do all that lies within my power."

And so he would, Morgan knew, his heart swelling with gratitude for this friend who had enriched his life in more ways than he could number. "Should I not survive the surgery, I would hope that you might remain at Nelson Hall with my family — *our* family. Finola and the children would have great need of you. You would be taken care of financially, of course. It would mean more than I can say to have the assurance that you would remain with them."

"I would stay, *Seanchai*. Surely you knew without asking that I would stay."

Morgan *had* known. Still, he had needed to ask — for his own sake.

"And your second request, *Seanchai?* You said there were two."

Morgan drew a deep breath. "I would ask you to be with me in the surgery room, while Gunther does whatever he will. I cannot explain exactly. I only know it would give me some measure of peace, the knowledge that you are standing by me, praying for me, watching the entire time."

There was a long, bleak silence. Morgan was beginning to think he had asked too much. Even the most unselfish of men must surely have his limits.

When the reply came, it sounded strangely muffled, even somewhat choked. But the words were clear, and they warmed Morgan's heart like a soft blanket of down.

"If the surgeon has no objection, of course, I will stand by you throughout the entire procedure, *Seanchai*," Sandemon said. He paused, and in a slightly steadier voice added, "And throughout the days and months and years thereafter . . . may they be long and richly blessed . . . I will continue to stand by you."

Morgan could manage nothing more than a weak nod of gratitude. This, too, he had known without asking.

43

A Gathering at Bellevue

For where two or three are gathered
in my name,
there am I in the midst of them.
MATTHEW 18:20

Anxious not to get in the way of the doctors and aides rushing back and forth through the vestibule, Finola huddled against the corner in one of the chairs Michael Burke had secured for them. She could see nothing of the adjacent corridor or patients' rooms from where she sat, only the drab walls and cold floor of the small room where they had been told they could wait.

She had never been in a hospital before, at least not that she could remember. This Bellevue seemed enormous, its design haphazard at best. Grim as a prison and equally as intimidating, it reeked with the smell of sick rooms and acrid chemicals. As the morning hours went on, her stomach had grown increasingly unsettled from the noxious odors.

As Finola waited, she felt her senses heighten. Every sound drummed in her ears and played on her nerves: the abrupt exchanges between physicians, the groaning of patients, the heart-stopping screams that echoed down the corridor as if coming from a great distance.

Above the racket that drifted in to them from the hallway, she found herself keenly aware of even the faintest sounds made by herself or those waiting in the vestibule: Michael Burke's shoes buffeting the hard floor as he paced. The frequent sighs of his wife, Sara. Evan Whittaker's way of slipping off his eyeglasses and immediately putting them back on, the frames clacking lightly as he did so. Daniel Kavanagh's drumming fingertips on the small scarred table by the window. Pastor Dalton's walking in and out of the room, his low murmurs to one of the physicians passing by. Only Nora seemed to sit without making a sound, wringing her hands in her lap, occasionally glancing at Finola with a sympathizing smile.

They had been waiting since early morning — close on three hours by now. Even though the surgeon had cautioned that the procedure would be lengthy, with every hour that passed

Finola grew more and more fearful. Three hours seemed far too long to bode anything good for the surgery.

As if he had sensed her anxiety, Pastor Dalton crossed the room and stopped in front of her. "The morning must seem endless to you, I'm sure, Mrs. Fitzgerald. But no doubt we'll hear something soon. Is there anything I can get for you in the meantime? Anything I can do?"

Finola shook her head. She tried to smile, but instead suddenly found herself fighting back tears.

The big pastor dropped down in front of her. "Would you like us to pray again?" he asked softly, his eyes reflecting kindness and understanding.

Finola looked at him. "I would, please," she said gratefully.

There had been much prayer already throughout the morning, of course — the personal, silent prayer of individuals, as well as the combined prayer of the entire assemblage. But as the hours passed without word from the surgery room, the prayers seemed to increase, both in frequency and intensity.

After nearly three hours, Sandemon was keenly aware of the tension and anxiety swelling inside him. He felt somewhat light-headed, though more from the malodorous ether than from his close vantage point of the surgery.

A number of times he had had to remind himself that he must ask no questions, make no sound whatsoever, must not even breathe too heavily; such had been the surgeon's adamant orders before beginning the procedure.

So, as directed, Sandemon had spent the hours standing, unmoving, his insides growing tighter and tighter as he watched the surgeon and his slightly wild-eyed assistant operate on the *Seanchai*'s back.

But now, with his chest as tight as his nerves and his head beginning to swim, he quietly turned and went to stand at the narrow window that looked out across the river. He had anticipated the long hours, the tension, the discomfort of standing in the same position for such an extended time. He had even anticipated the unpleasant chemical odors. What he had not anticipated was the effect this unnatural invasion of the *Seanchai*'s large and powerful body was having on him.

As weak and ailing as Morgan Fitzgerald had been when Sandemon had first gone to stay at Nelson Hall, he had still been leagues beyond the perilous condition in which he now lay: utterly vulnerable, entirely at the mercy of a surgeon who appeared to possess little if any emotion or concern for the *person* beneath his knife.

As he stood there, drawing in deep, steadying breaths, Sandemon paused for only a moment in the prayer vigil begun during the hours before dawn. His concern was deepening as the morning wore on. Yet from the start of the surgery he had sensed a Power at work in the room that had nothing to do with the disdainful physician.

Clearly, Jakob Gunther's hands were those of a highly skilled surgeon, his mind nothing less than brilliant. All the same, he was only a man, subject to a man's inherent weaknesses and limitations. The great surgeon was still mortal. Thus it was both a comfort and a source of encouragement to Sandemon to sense that during these critical hours, that finite ability, albeit considerable, was being overseen and directed by a Divine Power.

The clattering sound of metal against metal caused Sandemon to jerk and whip around.

The physician glanced up from his work long enough to meet Sandemon's eyes. For the first time since they had entered the operating room, Gunther acknowledged his presence. "The bullet," he said brusquely.

Hope soared in Sandemon's chest, but it

faltered when the surgeon sharply warned him against any expectations. "The only thing we know at this moment is that his spine is free of the bullet. It is much too soon for optimism."

Sandemon knew the physician was right. Still, the bullet had been removed, and the *Seanchai* was alive. That was enough to bolster his hope, at least for now.

The surgeon and his assistant were working feverishly over the *Seanchai,* Gunther's hands quick and deft beyond imagining. The assistant seemed to have more than he could do just to keep up with his mentor.

Gunther's face and neck were drenched with perspiration. Sandemon saw that even the man's surgical coat was damp. Obviously the physician was struggling not to contaminate the incision with his own perspiration, for every few seconds he wiped an arm across his forehead to blot it.

Sandemon hesitated only a moment before picking up a clean cloth from the instrument table. Quietly he moved in next to the surgeon, who glanced up with an angry frown.

Gunther's gaze darted from Sandemon to the cloth, and understanding dawned. His expression cleared as he stilled his hands and turned his face, waiting for Sandemon to blot it with the cloth.

They worked that way, the three of them, for the duration of the surgery: Gunther plying his skills with a seemingly fevered concentration, his young assistant struggling to meet the doctor's sharp demands, and Sandemon wiping the surgeon's brow, all the while maintaining his own silent vigil of prayer.

When Finola heard the sound of footsteps approaching from the corridor, she caught her breath, waiting. She had been disappointed numerous times throughout the day, thinking word about Morgan was on the way, only to have the messenger walk past.

But this time the footsteps slowed just outside the door. Her heart racing, Finola stood, waiting.

When she saw Sandemon standing in the doorway, her first thought was that something had gone wrong and the surgeon had sent him with the sorry news. Then the black man's eyes found hers, and he entered the room, coming to stand directly in front of her.

With her pulse thundering almost painfully in her ears, she searched Sandemon's face. She could not speak, could not even voice the question that had been churning in her heart since the surgery began early that morning.

And then he smiled. A slight, wan smile,

but a smile all the same.

"The *Seanchai* has survived the surgery well, Mistress Finola," he said quietly. "The bullet has been removed, and he is resting now. Although the surgeon cautions that he will not speculate on anything beyond this hour, he is quite satisfied with the procedure and with the *Seanchai*'s condition."

The tears Finola had been fighting back for hours now escaped in a violent rush. "Thanks be to God!" she choked out.

Her words were echoed time and again as the others in the vestibule came to encircle her and the weary Sandemon.

44

For the Helpless and the Hopeless

He did not wring his hands, as do
Those witless men who dare
To try to rear the changeling Hope
In the cave of black Despair. . . .
OSCAR WILDE (1854–1900)

Through the rest of October and all of November, Morgan lay housed in the plaster cast designed by Jakob Gunther. As if the state of almost total helplessness, spasmodic cramps, lower back pain, and murderously itchy skin were not torture enough, the surgeon — whom Morgan by now had qualified as *demented* — had contrived with Sandemon a relentless daily schedule of therapy and traction.

Morgan was thoroughly miserable. He only managed to endure it at all because his thankfulness at being alive outweighed his discomfort. At least, that was the case on his better days.

Despite the excellent care he received from his wife and Sandemon, however — as well as the unflagging attentions from the rest of the household — his physical distress seemed to worsen as time went on. The cast — his *cocoon* — had been thoughtfully conceived for his comfort, was even lined with soft fleece. Even so, body sores were an ongoing problem, inactivity his personal demon.

He sometimes imagined that his body might be fossilizing inside the cast. More than once he dreamed of emerging from the cocoon only to have his brittle bones break apart and go scattering across the room. The restricted freedom of movement brought on aches in places previously undiscovered, and also made it difficult to sleep for more than a few minutes at a time.

But if he did indeed go mad, as he often believed he would, it would not be the pain or the boredom that drove him to the edge: it would be the infernal itching! Day and night, awake or asleep, it would not abate. After the first few days he had devised a number of ingenious mind games to get his thoughts off this particular plague, but none of them had been greatly effective. By now, they were all but useless.

But as bad as the physical torment was, the mental distress was even worse. He had always valued his independence. For years a solitary wanderer with virtually no ties, possessed of extraordinarily good health and energy, he had come to the wheelchair with great difficulty and an enormous burden of bitterness. Even after he had managed to accept the reality of the paralysis and learned to live with its imposed restrictions, he continued to suffer an ongoing battle with restlessness and melancholy. Yet through it all, Morgan had had the grim satisfaction of knowing he had faced and survived one of the worst calamities — so he had thought — that could occur to an ordinary mortal.

Only now did he realize how naive he had been in assuming things could not get much worse. His imprisonment in this plaster cocoon was worse than anything he had ever envisioned. Hope had become increasingly elusive. He did not know how much longer he could endure without succumbing to total despair.

He had never been a grumbler, at least so far as he knew. But these days he was finding it well-nigh impossible to brace up and not complain about his lot.

In truth, he had a horror of becoming so abrasive in his present discomfort that he would make everyone else as miserable as himself. With that fear ever in mind, he went to great lengths to paste on a cheerful face when anyone came into the room. Even when Sandemon set his legs in and out of the hated traction pulleys, he managed not to curse or roar, though he was sorely tempted.

Everyone was trying to help, that was the thing. Morgan almost wished they would *stop* trying, at least for a time. He had more visitors than the Queen, he was certain. No doubt they all feared he would give in to encroaching madness if they did not go out of their way to assuage his boredom.

And they were all so exasperatingly *pleasant*. So cheerful and sanguine. Even Michael, who Morgan suspected could still be every bit as annoying as he had been when they were lads back in Mayo, was never anything but lightness itself when he visited.

Daniel John came, and for the first few weeks the lad's company had been most welcome. But by now they had fairly well exhausted the subject of his plans for the university and medical college in the spring, in addition to exploring most of the chess strategy known to the modern world.

Annie, God bless her, continued to make a brave effort to amuse him. Upon demand, he had recited every legend and every tale of the faeries he had ever known, had continued to hear *her* recitations in Latin and the Irish so she wouldn't fall behind — all the while trying to figure some discreet way to break her of that grating Belfast accent for once and for all.

Ah, the lass! She was both angel and imp, with enough pepper to season them both.

Gabriel, of course, could not fathom why his da should be abed so long, much less encased from neck to knee. In this condition, Morgan was no amusement for the boy at all, and so it was only natural the tyke would grow restless after the first few minutes of his visit.

But Finola presented him with his greatest challenge when it came to concealing his distress. He fought an ongoing struggle with wanting her with him, while at the same time feeling more and more impatient with himself for being such a poor excuse of a husband.

Her very presence served to remind him of the great frozen lump he had become. His lovely young wife, in all her radiance and vitality, was chained to a man as useless as a tree stump.

He detested his present circumstances. He detested the loss of his already limited mobility — and his sense of virility. He detested in particular his total dependence on others — which was almost certainly beginning to wear on *them* as much as it did on *him*.

He worried that Michael and his family

were growing tired of their live-in guests by now. He worried that Finola was growing impatient with being tied to a worthless slab of plaster rather than a whole man.

Above all, he worried that he would go through this torment and, at the end of it, would still not be able to walk a step.

At least once a day he considered ordering Sandemon to take a sledgehammer to the hated cast and break him free. Not that Sandemon would respond to such a wild-eyed demand, of course. These days even the venerable West Indies Wonder seemed cautious to the extreme in Morgan's presence — a behavior that was anything but typical of the man.

What Morgan found himself hankering for, today at least, was the company of someone as crotchety as himself — someone who would not cater to his incapacity or his melancholy. Someone so mean-spirited and disagreeable there would be no need for forced cheerfulness or pretenses on his part.

Only then did it occur to him, with an accompanying degree of perverse pleasure, that today was Friday: routinely the day when Jakob Gunther, esteemed surgeon, made his call.

"When exactly will I be released from this

torture chamber?" Morgan demanded as the surgeon performed his usual examination.

It did not seem to him that Gunther could possibly detect any change in his condition, given the perfunctory nature of his assessment.

"You have asked me the same question twice since I arrived," replied the surgeon with maddening calm.

"And you have not answered as yet," Morgan snapped.

Gunther arched an indulgent eyebrow, then made a clicking sound with his teeth. "Testy today, are we?"

Morgan glared at him but made no reply. The truth was, he had come to rather enjoy the distant, enigmatic surgeon, actually looked forward to his Friday calls. For all his acerbity and brusqueness, Gunther intrigued Morgan. Not only was he a formidable chess opponent, but he had an incisive wit and a brilliant grasp of literature and philosophy.

It was true that Gunther was entirely without religion; he would unfailingly level a stony eye on Morgan at even the slightest mention of matters of faith. Morgan had tried all manner of ploys to circumvent the man's resistance, but had as yet found no way to breach the wall.

In any event, he was immensely grateful for

a visitor who would not patronize him or attempt to cheer his spirits. The surgeon's personality simply did not lend itself to superficial niceties. Morgan could be himself, could even vent a measure of his churlishness without risking Gunther's taking offense. The man seemed altogether unaware of rudeness, in himself as well as in others.

In light of Morgan's expectations, it was small wonder that Gunther's next remark set him back. "This is all very difficult for you, I'm sure."

The surgeon was still bent over Morgan, tapping the cast as if expecting it to reply, his intelligent brow furrowed in what would appear to be genuine understanding.

Morgan eyed him with suspicion. "Since when do you take note of a patient's difficulty?"

Gunther cracked the quick, tight-lipped smile that Morgan always found oddly arresting, perhaps because the man seemed so ill at ease with even the smallest hint of human emotion. And then he did a most incredible thing: he laughed. A tight croak of a laugh, to be sure, but an audible sound of amusement nevertheless. "You are much too large to ignore, Fitzgerald," he said, straightening. "Besides, having encountered the Irish temperament on numerous occasions, I know how you must prize your independence."

"I see. And what, pray, makes up this 'Irish temperament' on which you are apparently so knowledgeable?"

Gunther crossed his arms over his chest, regarding Morgan with the clinical detachment that was his common expression. "Melancholic, given to too much introspection. Fiercely independent. Argumentative. And highly explosive."

"You are to be commended for not mentioning our more unsavory traits," Morgan said through clenched teeth. "Now, then, if you are quite finished insulting me, Gunther, I would like an answer to my question. When, I repeat, do I shed my cocoon?"

The surgeon seemed determined to sidestep the subject. "Let me ask you a question first, if you will, simply to satisfy my curiosity. How is it that a man who has been paralyzed all this time is so fit, in body and — in spite of your present testiness — seemingly in mind? You are in remarkable condition, you know."

"Sandemon," Morgan said without hesitation. "The man is a martinet. He started on me his first day in my employ and has never let up. I was actually a very poor specimen when he came to me," Morgan went on, smiling at the memory of his friend's arrival. "I had grown despondent, was steeped in self-pity as well as pain, and had lost a great deal of weight. He devised an exercise regimen specifically for me, and it wasn't long after adhering to it that I began to see improvement."

The surgeon, his arms still crossed over his chest, regarded Morgan with a studying look. "You are quite fortunate. Anything less than total fitness would have worked against you more than you might imagine." He paused. "Even so, as I've told you, time is your enemy. Are you prepared to deal with the disappointment if you never walk again?"

Morgan frowned at him. Gunther seemed to have not the slightest warmth about him to diminish the chill of his character. Yet he could not actively dislike the man, could only puzzle over what sort of factors might account for such a disposition.

He feigned surprise. "Have you so little faith in your own ability, Doctor? I cannot believe that magnificent ego of yours would allow for even the possibility of failure."

Gunther shrugged, a mannerism he seemed to have refined to a gesture of elegant indifference. "You knew the odds before you went into this. I was quite direct with you, was I not?"

"Brutally so," Morgan said dryly. "Nevertheless, I thought the risk worthwhile."

Gunther's eyes glinted with something Morgan could not read. "And do you still?" the surgeon said quietly. "Think the risk worthwhile, that is?"

Morgan hesitated, his own choleric thoughts of the morning stabbing at him like needles. He found himself suddenly ashamed of his earlier descent into self-pity. Gunther's question, which no doubt was meant as a challenge, had instead reminded him just how much was at stake in all this. And it had also renewed his awareness that he had made a commitment before God to accept the outcome — to make the best of it, and live with whatever transpired.

He attempted to explain as much to Gunther, but when he reached the part about going on as best he could and remaining faithful, no matter the aftermath of the surgery, he could see the drawbridge begin to raise.

"I know you do not understand," Morgan finished lamely. "How does one explain one's faith?"

"One does not try. Not to a heathen like myself," Gunther said caustically. "But I do not begrudge you your illusions, Fitzgerald. If they are of any help to you in all this, then guard them well."

With one brisk movement, he picked up his medical case and took a step toward the door.

"Ah —" He turned to look at Morgan. "About the cast —"

Morgan clenched his hands.

"Monday," said the surgeon in his off-handed way. "We will remove the cast on Monday."

Morgan watched Gunther leave the room, banging the door behind him as was his way. A torrent of relief washed over him.

Monday. On Monday he would be liberated from this plaster prison. Although he knew that days, even weeks, of the most rigorous physical training still awaited him, for the moment he refused to think of anything but the fact that on Monday, he would have a proper wash. Turn over in bed as often as he liked. Enjoy the blessed absence of the itching and burning. On Monday, he would hold his wife in his arms. Hug his children. Scratch wherever it itched. Repeatedly.

Then the fear set in. A certain dread of the therapy to come was natural, Morgan supposed; Gunther had already warned it would be painful and relentless, enough to try even the most stalwart will.

And then there was the ongoing fear about what might come after the therapy — or, more to the point, what might *not* come.

Although, at this moment, Monday and the weeks thereafter seemed almost a lifetime away, Morgan was realist enough to know that the time was fast approaching when the question that had nagged at him for months would be answered: would he walk? When all the pain and struggle had finally come to an end — would he walk?

He dared not allow himself even to speculate on what might lie ahead. But there was one thing he could not ignore. He had not spoken of it to Gunther — had not told anyone, even Sandemon — for he was not yet prepared to give any credence to what might be merely a trick of his imagination.

During the past two weeks, mostly in the late night hours, he had thought he felt a stinging sensation in his legs. The first time it happened, he allowed it might have been a dream. But it had occurred since then, more than once.

With the cast, it was nearly impossible to identify the location of such vague feelings, if indeed the feelings existed at all. There was also the fact that he had imagined sensation in his legs on numerous occasions after the shooting, long before there had even been a thought of surgery.

God alone knew what it meant, just as He alone knew what the coming weeks would bring. And at this point in time, Morgan thought he should be grateful for that. He was facing a rigorous struggle, the culmination of which could not be predicted. What man would be strong enough to persevere if he already knew that at the close of his efforts nothing waited but the end of a dream?

A few minutes later, Sandemon entered the room.

"So then — is there any news from Dr. Gunther today?" he asked, smoothing the bed linens and straightening the table beside the bed.

Morgan looked at him. "Our esteemed surgeon actually laughed," he said, holding his larger announcement for the moment. "Aloud, can you believe it?"

Sandemon's eyebrows lifted in surprise. "An amazing thing, surely."

Morgan saw his thoughtful expression. "What? I know that look. You have had an idea."

Sandemon smiled. "I am wondering if we may not eventually learn that this surgery was not entirely for you."

Puzzled, Morgan frowned. "What do you mean?"

Sandemon shrugged lightly. "I think Dr. Gunther may also benefit from this acquaintanceship. He is growing to like and respect you, that much is obvious. Perhaps you can have a gentling influence on him. Our Lord might even use you to soften the surgeon's heart."

Morgan gave a slight wave of the hand in dismissal of such a notion. "The man is hopeless."

"No man is hopeless," Sandemon said easily.

"That one is, I assure you. Besides, we will be gone, on our way back to Ireland, long before even the smallest seed of influence could penetrate that stubborn head."

"Nevertheless, a seed planted . . ." Sandemon let his words drift off, but his meaning was clear.

Morgan merely uttered a short sound of disbelief, then said, "He will remove the cast on Monday."

The other's dark eyes searched his. "At last," he said softly.

"Aye, at last. But we still have a long road to travel."

Sandemon nodded. "Remember that you do not walk the way alone."

Morgan looked at him and managed a tight smile. "Pray that I walk it at all, *mo chara*. Pray that, if you will."

45

These Bright and Shining Gifts

He'll meet the soul which comes in love
and deal it joy on joy —
as once He dealt out star and star
to garrison the sky,
to stand there over rains and snows
and deck the dark of night —
so, God will deal the soul, like stars,
delight upon delight.
ROBERT FARREN (1909–   )

Christmas Eve, 1850

"Quinn? Could I have a moment, please?"

Quinn O'Shea stopped, eyeing Daniel Kavanagh with caution as he descended the stairway. She still felt awkward with him, almost as if she had failed him somehow. He was just as ill at ease with her, she knew. Ever since he'd learned about her and Denny, he had avoided her. Yet he was never anything but polite, if remote.

Occasionally, Quinn still caught him watching her with wounded eyes. It seemed that he had not completely given over his infatuation. She wondered if the Whittakers had made Daniel aware of her past. There was no reason to expect them *not* to tell him, of course, but it was difficult all the same to think of him knowing.

His family had been kindness itself when she finally told them the truth. Denny had gone with her, and although that hadn't made it any easier, his presence had at least supported her through the ordeal.

Quinn had detected no change in their demeanor with her since then, but there was no reason to assume it would be the same with Daniel. Still, he was smiling just now as he came toward her.

He stopped a comfortable distance away and stood, one hand at his side, the other behind his back. He looked uncertain, as if now that he'd approached her he might change his mind and walk away.

Finally he spoke. "I just wanted to tell you — to thank you, that is — both you and Sergeant Price — for offering to stay with the boys tonight, so my family could spend Christmas Eve at the Burkes. It was very kind of you — and the sergeant."

He seemed to stumble over Denny's name, as if it stuck slightly in his throat.

"Why . . . it's no trouble at all," Quinn replied, still somewhat guarded as to his intentions. "It's our pleasure, to be sure."

When he said nothing more, but simply stood there, looking altogether uncomfortable, Quinn moved to ease the stiffness between them. "Your friend, Mr. Fitzgerald — how is he? Has there been any change?"

Daniel shook his head. "None, I'm afraid. Oh, he seems to be feeling a bit stronger, but he can't — he still has to use the wheelchair."

Again there was an uneasy silence between them. After a moment he brought his hand from behind his back, holding out to Quinn a small, finely wrapped gift.

"This is for you," he said, watching her.

Quinn looked at him, then at the package in his hand.

He inclined his head toward the gift. "You can open it now if you like. But there's something I'd like to say first."

Quinn lowered her eyes before his steady gaze, troubled at the thought that he might still have feelings for her. She valued Daniel's friendship, had hoped for an end to the stilted formality between them. After another instant's hesitation, she took the gift, at the same time bracing herself for whatever it was he had to say.

A thin line of perspiration banded his forehead as he clenched and unclenched his hands at his sides. "I just want to tell you —" He cleared his throat before going on. "I'm awfully glad, for you and Sergeant Price, that is. He's a fine man. My folks think the world and everything of him, and I like him a lot, too. You're — you're a wonderful girl, Quinn, and you deserve the best." He paused. "That's all I wanted to say. You can open your gift now, if you want."

Dumbstruck, Quinn stared at him. *He knew.* He knew the truth, she was sure of it. And this was his way of telling her he thought no less of her for it. Like his family, he was accepting her just as she was.

To her dismay, she thought she might burst into tears. She bit her lip, then attempted a smile. "Why, what a nice thing for you to say, Daniel Kavanagh."

A light flush crept over his features, and he glanced away for a second or two. "Aren't you going to open your gift, then?"

"My gift . . . oh yes, of course!" Her eyes widened with amazement as she withdrew a small, narrow box. With one finger, she tipped open the lid. Inside was a pair of delicately fashioned reading glasses.

Quinn gaped at the glasses with disbelief. "Oh . . . oh, Daniel!" She let out a long breath, staring at the spectacles. "Oh, my! These — these are for me?"

"Put them on, why don't you? Let's see if they're right for your eyes."

No longer could Quinn hold her tears in check. Indeed, she could scarcely see at all for a moment as she carefully picked up the eyeglasses and slid them on.

"Here," Daniel said, reaching into his vest pocket and handing her a small card. "Read this."

Quinn drew in a sharp breath as her eyes scanned the small, precise printing on the card. "Oh, isn't it clear entirely?" she burst out. " 'Nicholas A. Grafton, M.D.,' it says!"

She looked up. "Daniel Kavanagh," she choked out, "never have I had such a fine gift! But how — how did you know I needed eyeglasses?"

"How —" Daniel blinked. "Well, I expect I assumed as much when I saw how you pressed your nose into the spine of the book at our grammar lessons." He paused. "Good Christmas, Quinn O'Shea. And — tell Sergeant Price the same for me, if you will."

Quinn thought he might have looked a bit wistful as he turned and went back upstairs. Perhaps not, though. Perhaps it was only that she could see his expression so much more clearly now, with her new spectacles.

In their bedroom, Nora pinned up the sleeve of Evan's jacket while he sat beside her on the bed. "Isn't it lovely of Sara and her family to have all of us for Christmas Eve? And planning a late supper, so we could have our worship and treats with the boys before we go."

"Sara could give almost anyone we know lessons in thoughtfulness," Evan said, smiling. "Certainly, this should b-be a special Christmas for all of us."

Nora stood, waiting to help him with the jacket. "Aye," she said as he rose from the bed and slipped it on, "and let us pray that it will be special indeed."

She moved behind him to check the back of his collar. "Next year," she said after a long sigh, "Daniel John will be away at university, thanks to Aunt Winnie and Mr. Farmington." She gripped his shoulders. "Wasn't it grand of them to offer their support for his tuition?"

Evan nodded. "Aunt Winifred can be very persuasive, in case you hadn't noticed. And the money from the music will help, too."

"Daniel John will realize his dream at last," Nora sighed. "A great gift from God — and the Farmingtons. A great gift." She paused, and her voice turned wistful. "But he will be gone, Evan. And Morgan and his family will go back to Ireland. Who knows how we may be scattered before another Christmas?"

She lifted a hand to smooth his lapels, but Evan caught it. "I am quite certain that Daniel will come home for Christmas, darling. And perhaps one day soon, we m-might even make a trip to Ireland, to visit the Fitzgeralds. Who can say?"

Nora raised a skeptical eyebrow. "And shall we be taking all our little boys with us, then, when we make this journey back to Ireland?"

Evan chuckled. "Only if we c-can afford to hire an entire staff of help for the duration." He studied her for a moment. "Wouldn't you like to go b-back at some time, Nora? To see your home again?"

She had thought about it, of course. "I expect I would, just to visit. Ireland is, after all, my home." She paused, considering. "But my life here is so full — I am content, Evan."

Nora smiled at him. "There now. And don't you look positively grand in your new coat, Mr. Whittaker?" she teased, kissing him on the cheek.

"Do I?" He stole a glance at himself in the vanity mirror, then turned toward her. "Well, if I m-may say so, you look extraordinarily lovely yourself tonight, Mrs. Whittaker."

"It must be my new brooch." Nora touched the small garnet stone, set in the shape of a heart, at her throat. "Though I still think it's much too extravagant, Evan."

"Nonsense. Why, I c-can scarcely see it unless I'm nose-to-nose with you," he said, pulling her close and smiling into her eyes. After a moment he eased her away from him, just enough to study her face. "Tell m-me something, darling. Do you feel even half as well as you look tonight? I declare, you're actually glowing!"

"I *do* feel well, Evan, and that's the truth. Which reminds me, I have some news from the tests Dr. Mandel ran earlier in the week. He stopped by for a moment while you were with the boys this afternoon."

A stricken look crossed Evan's face, and Nora hurried to reassure him. "*Good* news, Evan, not bad! My, how you do fret! Dr. Mandel seems quite pleased with my progress. He thinks I'm doing very nicely. He said I can be up and about for longer periods of time now. He's even decreasing the medication a bit."

"Oh, Nora, that's splendid! Why — that's the b-best Christmas g-gift I could possibly imagine."

Nora laughed at his obvious relief. The

man did take on over her.

And wasn't she blessed that he did?

Nora raised her face to his, locking her hands behind his neck. "And you, Evan Whittaker," she said softly, "you are my own treasure, my special gift from God." She paused, an unexpected heaviness stealing over her.

Ever sensitive to her feelings, Evan searched her eyes. "What is it? What's wrong?"

Nora shook her head. "There's nothing wrong. I was just . . . wishing that God would share some of the healing He's given me with Morgan as well. The last time we saw him — he was trying to be so cheerful, but underneath the pretense, he seemed worried."

Evan nodded. "Who *wouldn't* be anxious, after going through so m-much with not even the slightest hint of change? But we mustn't give up, Nora. Morgan hasn't. He is alive and getting stronger. Perhaps that is God's answer to our prayers."

"Yes," Nora said softly. She knew Evan was right. But she could not help but wish that God had answered in a more tangible way.

At the last minute before going downstairs, Sara stood, her back to Michael, as he fastened the clasp of her mother's emerald necklace.

His hands settled lightly on her shoulders for a moment, and Sara smiled to herself, imagining his response to the Christmas gift she was about to give him. She shivered when he pressed his lips to the back of her neck, then turned her around to look at her.

He drew in a long breath, his dark eyes glinting. "Lovely," he said softly. "I declare, Sara *a gra,* you are positively radiant tonight. You make even your mother's emeralds look dull."

Sara smiled at him, thinking, as she always did, that the man was simply too handsome.

"You said you had something to tell me," she reminded him. She was increasingly anxious to give him his gift, but she didn't want to take away from whatever news he had been keeping.

"Did I?" He looked at her blankly.

"Michael — don't tease! We have to go down in a minute. Tell me *now!*"

His hands circled her waist. "Actually, I want to ask you something, rather than tell you."

"Don't play coy with me, Michael Burke. Tell me at once!"

His expression gradually sobered. "Very well, then," he said, searching her eyes. "I've been wondering how you would feel if I were to leave the force."

Whatever Sara had expected to hear, it wasn't this. "Leave the force? Michael, are you serious?"

He nodded. "I believe I am, yes. Simon Dabney has approached me again, about the alderman slot. I'm tempted to make a try for it, Sara."

She studied him. "You would actually leave the police department? Leave your men, your work? It's been a part of your life for so long."

"Perhaps too long," he said, letting out a long breath. "I'm growing tired of the violence, the corruption — and the long hours. I know how you worry about me — and you *do* worry, don't think I haven't noticed. In truth, I sometimes worry about myself. Being a cop can make you — hard," he said. "Eventually, it can even callous your soul. I don't want that to happen to me."

Sara studied him frankly, with some concern. "Michael, I won't deny that I'd be relieved. Even though I know you're quite wonderful at what you do, you're right: I do worry about you. But — are you sure? Are you sure you *can* leave, and still be happy?"

His hands tightened on her waist. "I won't know that until I try, now will I? Besides," he said, his face drawing into a somewhat peevish expression, "there is the fact that I'm not getting any younger. I'll soon be too old to go chasing after hooligans, you know. I'd like to get out before I'm too old and used up to be good for anything else."

Sara's eyes went over his handsome face — still decidedly youthful for a man who groused about his age as much as Michael did — and she couldn't stop a faint smile.

"Well? What do you think?"

"I think," she said deliberately, "that a man who is soon to become a new father is anything but old and used up."

Michael's entire face went slack. He looked positively ashen as he gaped at her. "I'm not!" he blurted out.

"Oh, but you are, darling," Sara said, laughing at his astonishment. "Really, you are."

His eyes glistened, and his voice went soft. "You are quite certain?"

"Beyond any doubt." She paused. "That's my Christmas gift to you, Michael."

He made a strangling sound, and then he began to laugh. He swept Sara off her feet and swung her around and around, until she warned him she would surely faint.

As if suddenly remembering her condition, Michael set her gently to her feet and clasped both her hands in his. "Sara . . . ah, Sara . . . what a gift you are to me! And what a gift you have given me this night! I cannot wait to tell everyone!"

"Michael!" Sara felt a wave of color creep up her face. "You can't tell *anyone*. Not in public. It simply isn't done."

He reared back. "You can't mean you expect me to keep silent about such a thing? I will not! I *cannot!* I will tell everyone in the house, and I will tell them tonight!" He beamed at Sara. "And then I will go out into the street and tell the neighborhood. And the city — perhaps I will tell the entire city. What do you think of that, Sara *a gra?*"

"I think you are mad," Sara answered, laughing in spite of herself at his boyish excitement.

He kissed her soundly on the forehead, then each cheek, then the tip of her nose. "Indeed I am," he agreed, his eyes glinting. "I am mad entirely. Mad about my wife, the mother of my child."

His expression sobered as he set her slightly away from him so he could look at her. "Sara, promise you will help me to be a better father to our child than I ever was to Tierney."

Sara stared at him. "Oh, Michael! You were a *good* father to Tierney! And one day he'll realize just how much you mean to him. He'll come home, Michael, you'll see. Tierney will come home again."

Even as Sara spoke the words, she somehow knew that she was right, that Tierney *would* come home again. She believed in the unbroken circle of a family's love. She believed in the power of God to heal the wounds that even in the closest of families could cause division. And she believed in Tierney, for she had seen the love in his eyes for his father the day they parted.

Tierney would come home. And when he did, he would find his family waiting.

46

Morgan's Star

You are God's smile upon my life,
My soul's bright star, my joy . . . my wife.
MORGAN FITZGERALD (1850)

The late Christmas Eve supper had proved to be a splendid idea, everyone in attendance agreed.

Seated at the long dining table in the vast hall, each family member and friend seemed relaxed and aglow with the season's cheer. A profusion of evergreens, berries, and dried flowers sprayed seasonal colors about the room. Daniel Kavanagh's Christmas harp, which by now had become an annual tradition, rested proudly at the front of the hall, its frame decorated with colored ribbons, Christmas greens, and tinsel.

The food was lavish — baked hams and roasted turkeys, scalloped corn and candied sweet potatoes, oysters and dressing and an endless assortment of baked goods. A feast!

Gifts were abundant. Smiles were bright. Hearts were warm.

It was Christmas.

Morgan felt as if he might have been seated at his own table, back home at Nelson Hall, so good and natural was it to be in the midst of these loved ones this night, after so long a time. Beside him, Finola was radiant, her skin aglow, her eyes reflecting the light of the candles that blazed throughout the spacious room. Each time their eyes chanced to meet, she would smile and discreetly slip her hand into his beneath the table.

The last dessert had been cleared away, and gifts were now being exchanged in earnest. Both table and floor were strewn with bright wrappings and ribbons. There was much reminiscing between the opening of packages, much laughter as well.

All of them were here tonight: the Fitzgeralds, the Burkes, the Whittakers, the Farmingtons. Sara's grandmother. Sandemon, who, to Morgan's relief and satisfaction, had been invited to join the circle of friends and family. Only wee Gabriel and his new friend, Teddy, after having an early meal and the Nativity Story read from the Scriptures, had been put to bed in anticipation of Christmas morning.

With so many gathered in one room, noise and confusion naturally reigned, but nobody seemed to mind. As Morgan sat, allowing his gaze to travel round the table, taking in each smile, each bright expression, he knew an almost overwhelming sense of well-being. His only disappointment had been the absence of one invited guest: Jakob Gunther.

Strange, how keenly he felt the absence of the physician. With Sara and Michael's permission, he had issued an invitation to Gunther, knowing full well the man might laugh in his face. The holy significance of Christmas Eve would mean nothing to the unbelieving surgeon, of course. Yet he genuinely wished Gunther had come.

He had prepared himself for the surgeon's rejection; he would not have blinked if the man had openly mocked him. What he had not been prepared for was Gunther's awkwardness in the face of the invitation.

The man had appeared ill at ease entirely, even embarrassed, his eyes darting every which way, his reply mumbled. "Most kind of you, I'm sure, but I doubt that I can manage it."

Morgan had not pressed, but had simply reminded Gunther that he would be more than welcome, and that Morgan personally would be gratified by his presence.

The fact that Gunther had not come was certainly no surprise, but it was a disappointment. Yet the night was far too merry, too special, to allow himself to dwell on the surgeon's absence.

He glanced at Finola, beside him. She was dressed in an ice-blue gown, and she wore the ivory swan pendant that had been his wedding gift to her. On her right hand was the sapphire and diamond ring which he had presented her earlier in the evening. The ring had belonged to his great-grandmother and had been passed down through the family over the years. Morgan had brought it all the way from Ireland in anticipation of giving it to Finola at Christmas, in the event they remained in the States throughout the season.

He leaned close to her, squeezing her hand. "You are the only woman I have ever known," he murmured for her ear alone, "whose beauty makes even a sapphire go begging. You are a star, the brightest star of my world."

She smiled into his eyes. "The gift is too much, Morgan. It takes my breath away."

"As you do mine, *macushla*. But I have one more gift for you, one I saved for last."

Giving her no time to question him, Morgan glanced across the table to catch Sandemon's eye. The black man gave a brief nod, then rose and left the room.

Morgan watched him all the way out the door. When a figure appeared in the doorway a moment later, he was surprised to see, not Sandemon, but Robert, the elderly butler, ushering Jakob Gunther into the dining hall.

The lean-faced surgeon stood, visibly uncomfortable, his gaze scanning the room. Under one arm he held a parcel, while with the other hand he nervously stroked his chin.

A rush of pleasure swept over Morgan, and he lifted a hand to hail the surgeon. "Gunther! A grand surprise, this! Come in, come in!"

At the same time, Lewis Farmington and Michael rose to receive Gunther and escort him to the table, where a maid hurried to add a place across from Morgan and Finola.

"You have missed the meal," Morgan said when the surgeon reached him. "But no matter. You will have a dessert, at least."

"No, please, don't trouble yourself for me," Gunther protested. "I intended to arrive earlier, but was delayed by an emergency at Bellevue. I apologize for the lateness of the hour."

Morgan somehow believed the surgeon was sincere, that he had in fact intended to come earlier. He quickly moved to reassure him. " 'Tis not late at all. And I am delighted you've come. This is an informal gathering, to say the least, Gunther. You will feel like family in no time."

The surgeon looked at Morgan steadily. "I'm afraid I wouldn't know much about that sort of thing," he said, "having never *had* a family." He cleared his throat, obviously uncomfortable with the exposure of this human facet of experience.

Oh, the questions Morgan could have asked, had the time and place been right! As it was, he only managed to restrain himself with effort. "Well, then," he said heartily, "our family is as good as any to take up with, I expect."

Gunther turned to Finola then, giving a stiff little bow. Morgan would not have been surprised had the man clicked his heels. "With your permission, Mrs. Fitzgerald," the surgeon said formally, handing her the parcel he had brought with him into the room.

Finola made a great fuss upon unwrapping the delicate French figurine. The surgeon seemed pleased by her delight, although at no time did he actually meet her eyes.

Suddenly a thought struck Morgan. Perhaps Gunther was socially inept not because he was mean-spirited, but simply because he was unaccustomed to being with people. Perhaps the man was lonely. Morgan had no time to pursue that surprising thought, because at that moment he turned to see Sandemon coming back into the room, a sturdy pair of crutches in hand.

The room seemed to hush all at once as others became aware of Sandemon's entrance. Morgan felt Finola's questioning eyes on him and gave her hand a quick squeeze. "The gift I promised you, Finola *aroon*. A gift especially for you."

He left her then, pushing away from the table and wheeling himself down the length of the dining hall to where Sandemon stood waiting.

He brought the chair to a stop, and Sandemon bent to lock the wheels in place. The black man straightened and, as if he sensed Morgan's sudden uncertainty, met his eyes and held them.

"Remember, *Seanchai,* that you have already accomplished this many times before tonight. All the other times were for you. Tonight — tonight is for those who love you."

Morgan swallowed, then took a deep, steadying breath and gave a nod. "I am ready."

Sandemon's strong hands grasped his, supporting him as Morgan slowly struggled to his feet.

He was aware of the stirring in the room,

the collective intake of breath, as he hauled himself upright and waited while Sandemon helped to adjust the crutches under each arm.

The braces concealed by his trouser legs felt heavier than they had during the practice sessions. His head was light, almost giddy, from the anxiety that had been driving him most of the evening.

After one more long breath, Morgan slowly lifted his head to take in the crowded room. He saw the expressions on the faces turned in his direction, the mixture of shock and incredulity.

He reminded himself that, as Sandemon said, he had done this many times, in the privacy of Sandemon's bedchamber. Ever since the day some weeks before when he had known for certain that he had some control of his legs, he had strained and struggled and pushed himself beyond all limits. He had refused to tell anyone — other than Sandemon, of course. Not Finola, not Michael. No one. He was determined to be absolutely certain before revealing his secret.

But now it was time. Finally, he took a step. Then another. He heard a soft cry, saw Finola come to her feet at the far end of the room. He stepped out again, now almost mindless of the weight of the braces on his legs, intent only upon setting one foot in front of the other as he began his slow walk to Finola.

Finola stood, weeping as she watched him make his arduous way down the room.

He wore a suit of soft fawn hue, much like his wedding suit. The coat strained at the seams with the effort of his massive shoulders as he applied the crutches. His steps were heavy, labored . . . but firm.

He had thought she didn't suspect. And at first she hadn't. All those early mornings when Sandemon came to help him from the bed, then wheeled him quietly from the room, he had explained as "therapy." And she had believed him, in the beginning.

Only later, when in the night he would grow restless beside her . . . and move his legs . . . or when she heard the thumping noises in the next room . . . only then had she known.

But she had also known it must be desperately important to him that he surprise her, and so she had kept her silence. She wanted this surprise for *him* as much as he apparently wanted it for *her*. And tonight, watching him strain toward her, seeing the blaze of determination and exultation in his eyes, she was infinitely grateful that she had protected his secret.

Only in the vaguest sense was Morgan

aware that, as he walked on, those seated at the table had risen to their feet. At the back of his mind, he recognized the sounds of soft weeping, the whispered cries of surprise, but so intent was he upon his journey that everything else in the room seemed to recede.

He caught a glimpse of Annie, tears flowing from her dark eyes, both hands clenched to fists in front of her mouth.

Aine, my daughter . . . this is for you. . . .

Michael stood, legs apart, both hands extended palms out, as if to catch Morgan if he chanced to fall. Morgan smiled, remembering the ever-watchful eye of the young Michael, who even as a lad back in Killala had looked to the safety of the younger children in the village.

Michael . . . ah, Michael, friend of my boyhood, friend for a lifetime . . . this is for you. . . .

He passed by Nora and Evan, who looked as if they were locked together, weeping unabashedly, their smiles shining through their tears. With them, Johanna, her bright green eyes — so much like his own — shining, even as she sobbed.

God bless you, my dear ones . . . friends, family, each precious one of you . . . this is for you. . . .

Everyone seemed to have moved back from the table, and he passed among them unhindered, heading for Finola. Unbelievably, they hailed him, cheering him on with their applause as he dragged one leg after another. Perspiration wreathed his forehead, and his heart thundered with the exertion, but he went on, setting each foot down with great care and determination.

He looked at Jakob Gunther, and what he saw almost made him stumble. Gunther was on his feet, bringing his hands together slowly and deliberately in applause. Morgan was close enough now to see that the surgeon's eyes, usually devoid of all emotion, were ablaze with what might have been a combination of pride and elation — and something else. Something indefinable, but which looked suspiciously like a kind of fierce admiration.

As Morgan passed by him, the surgeon caught his eye and spoke one quiet word: *"Bravo."*

To Morgan, that one word of acclamation was a gift.

He had almost reached Finola now. He saw her hands clasped tightly together over her heart, the flush upon her lovely face, the tears streaming from her eyes.

She stepped out to meet him, and Morgan began to smile. He smiled, indeed could not stop smiling, as he finally reached the end of his long trek and came to a stop directly in front of her.

Only once had he stood with her. On their wedding day, Sandemon had trussed him in iron to allow him to stand for the exchange of vows. But on that occasion, he had known that the moment was but a temporary grace, that he would return to the wheelchair as soon as the ceremony came to an end.

Not so today.

He spoke to her in the Irish, softly, for her alone. "This is for you, Finola *aroon*. Especially for you. Without you, it would never have been. You are my soul's bright star, my joy."

"Oh, Morgan . . ." Her face as she lifted it to him was as radiant as if she had been painted by the sun. *"My love, my life . . ."*

The applause had ended. The room was quiet again, except for a muffled sob here and there. Finola moved to embrace him, dampening his suit coat with her tears.

Next came Annie, laughing and crying as she threw her arms about his waist.

And then Morgan found himself surrounded, as they all came . . . Michael and Sara, Nora and Whittaker, Daniel John and Johanna . . . all of them, one after another, to embrace him in love, to share his joy, to wish him long life and good health and God's grace.

Through it all, Morgan stood beside his wife, stood as tall as he could manage, which felt very tall indeed.

One Faithful Harp

One sword, at least, thy rights shall guard,
One faithful harp shall praise thee!
THOMAS MOORE (1779–1852)

March 1851

To those passengers arriving in New York Harbor, as well as the countless numbers waiting to depart, the large party massed on the dock seemed to be individuals of some quality and influence — perhaps even royalty.

Only upon closer appraisal could an alert bystander detect that the assembly responsible for the ceremonial fuss and flourish was made up, at least in part, of *Irish* persons. The ancient flag of Ireland, the gold harp on green silk, as well as the newer tricolor of green, white, and orange, waved in the morning breeze, along with America's Stars and

Stripes. A kilted piper stood off to himself, playing a number of the strange, droning tunes associated with the Hibernians.

Odder still was the sight of two rows of young boys — a number of whom were black — mixed in with the respectably attired members of the assembly. Each boy held a banner of white silk, on which had been embroidered green shamrocks. Beside them stood a meek-looking, bearded man wearing spectacles — and with one empty sleeve where his left arm should have been.

The unusual group had drawn close around a platform decorated with green bunting, while just outside their circle massed what looked to be a crowd of hundreds. Unsavory looking characters — immigrants, no doubt — pressed in among those of more reputable appearance.

The focus of every eye was obviously the man on the platform — a rather rough-hewn sort, despite an adequately tailored brown suit and watered silk neckcloth. Even on crutches, the fellow looked to be a colossus of a man. With his wild copper hair blowing free in the morning wind, he was the embodiment of the bronze-bearded, craggy faced chieftain sometimes portrayed in the history books.

Behind the tall man on the platform stood a statuesque young woman, whose cloud of flaxen hair highlighted a face of breathtaking beauty. She held a child in her arms, obviously her own: a lovely, golden-haired boy who was the image of his mother. Beside them towered an impressive-looking black man in a seaman's cap, and a young girl of saucy appearance, whose dark eyes fairly crackled with energy.

The piper concluded his selection, and the copper-haired giant on the platform commenced to speak to the crowds milling about. He possessed a strong, robust voice of obvious Irish cadence, but — at least to the discerning ear — a voice which held a distinct note of educated refinement.

Onlookers agreed that this was a very strange gathering for such an early hour, even in New York Harbor.

Those in the crowd teeming about the platform had heard it said that Morgan Fitzgerald was not a man for speeches, although he had been known to hold forth in his younger years. But when word got out that Ireland's most illustrious poet and *Seanchai* was about to leave New York for home, a number of representatives from the Irish and Irish-American communities had prevailed upon him to at least offer a word of encouragement to his people before departing.

He spoke for a few moments about his impressions of New York. He went on to remark on what was coming to be called the "Irish contribution" to America. He talked about peace — and the lack thereof — in Ireland, his tone surprisingly free of anger or bitterness as he bluntly indicted the English Crown for the "policy of oppression and colonization which had victimized Ireland for centuries." Even when he laid the blame for the Great Famine squarely at the feet of the British empire, no resentment could be detected in that magnificent voice.

At the end, as the *Seanchai* stood looking out over the vast ocean of faces lifted toward him, his final words rang out across the harbor like an anthem:

"You ask me how your children and your children's children can hope to avoid the same brutality, the same deprivation, the same bitter loss that you yourselves have endured . . . and survived. And I tell you that the hatred and division among all peoples — not only between Ireland and England, but in nations throughout the world — will *never* end until we finally come to understand that we are all children of One God — one Creator — whose heart breaks every time one of us wounds another."

The *Seanchai* straightened, drawing himself up as tall as possible on the crutches that supported him. His eyes seemed to hold a sea of ancient sorrows as he looked out upon the people pressing closer to hear:

" 'Tell your children,' our God said. 'Let your children tell their children, and their children another generation. Tell them a nation has come up against my land, powerful and without number. Its teeth are lions' teeth, and it has the fangs of a lioness. Tell them my fields are laid waste, the ground mourns, the grain is destroyed.' *Tell* them."

The great voice quieted, and his listeners strained not to miss a word:

"Tell your children who they are, where they came from, what they mean to you — and to their God. Don't let them forget that they are Irish, yes, or Irish-American — but neither let them forget that they are God's." He paused. "Peace will never dawn in Ireland until the love of God finally dawns in our hearts."

There was much flag-waving and cheering, much weeping as well. The *Seanchai* stood quietly, his eyes going over the crowd as if to take in each individual face, while the boys with the shamrock banners sang "My Country 'Tis of Thee," followed by "Let Erin Remember."

Tears tracked the faces of those standing

closest to the platform as Morgan Fitzgerald braced himself on his crutches and began to strum the ancient-looking harp placed in his arms by the black man. It was an old song he gave them — "The Minstrel Boy" — a song by Tommy Moore that was said to wring tears from the thorn bushes. And as Fitzgerald sang it through, the few dry eyes left in the crowd began to cloud with tears.

After the *Seanchai* and his family had embraced their friends in tearful farewells and walked away to board their ship, some claimed they could still hear the old song echo across the harbor, sounding among the big packets arriving from foreign lands and the ships sailing out, bound for distant countries. . . .

"Land of song!" said the warrior bard,
"Though all the world betrays thee,
One sword, at least, thy rights shall
   guard,
One faithful harp shall praise thee!"

Principal Characters

IRELAND

Morgan Fitzgerald: Poet, patriot, and
(the *Seanchai*) schoolmaster.
Grandson of British
nobleman Richard
Nelson. Formerly of
County Mayo.

Finola Fitzgerald: Wife of Morgan
Fitzgerald.

Annie (Aine) Fitzgerald: Belfast runaway
adopted by Morgan
Fitzgerald.

Gabriel Thomas Son of Morgan and
Fitzgerald: Finola.

Sandemon: Freed slave from
(the *"West Indies* Barbados. Hired
Wonder") companion and
friend of Morgan
Fitzgerald.

Sister Louisa: Nun employed as
teacher by Morgan

Fitzgerald for his
new Academy.

Tierney Burke: Rebellious son of
Michael Burke.
Formerly of New
York City.

Jan Martova: Romany Gypsy who
befriends Tierney
Burke.

Lucy Hoy: Friend and nurse to
Finola.

AMERICA

THE KAVANAGHS AND THE WHITTAKERS

Daniel Kavanagh: Irish immigrant,
formerly of Killala,
County Mayo. Son
of Owen (deceased)
and Nora.

*Nora Kavanagh
Whittaker:* Irish immigrant,
formerly of Killala,
County Mayo. Wife
of Evan Whittaker.
Mother of Daniel
Kavanagh.

Evan Whittaker: British immigrant,
formerly of London.
Superintendent of
Whittaker House, a
home for orphaned

and abandoned boys in New York City.

Theodore Charles Lewis Whittaker ("Teddy"): Son of Evan and Nora.

Johanna Fitzgerald: Irish immigrant adopted by Evan Whittaker and Nora. Niece of Morgan Fitzgerald.

THE BURKES AND THE FARMINGTONS

Michael Burke: Irish immigrant, New York City police captain, formerly of Killala, County Mayo.

Sara Farmington Burke: Daughter of shipbuilding magnate, Lewis Farmington. Wife of Michael Burke.

Lewis Farmington: Shipbuilder, Christian philanthropist.

Winifred Farmington ("Aunt Winnie") Wife of Lewis Farmington. Evan Whittaker's aunt, formerly of England.

THE DALTONS
Jess Dalton: Mission pastor, author and abolitionist, former West Point Chaplain.

Kerry Dalton: Irish immigrant, formerly of County Kerry. Wife of Jess.

Casey-Fitz Dalton: Irish immigrant orphan, adopted by the Daltons.

Amanda Ward: Orphan living with Jess and Kerry Dalton.

OTHERS
Patrick Walsh: Irish immigrant, formerly of County Cork. Crime boss.

Alice Walsh: Wife of Patrick. Mother of Isabel and Henry.

Billy Hogan: Fatherless Irish immigrant, formerly of County Sligo. Resident of Whittaker House.

Quinn O'Shea: Newly arrived Irish immigrant with

troubled past. Formerly of County Roscommon. Employed by the Whittakers.

Denny Price: Irish immigrant, New York City police sergeant, formerly of County Donegal.

Nicholas Grafton: New York City physician.

Jakob Gunther: Viennese surgeon now practicing in New York City.

Acknowledgments

I would like to express my appreciation to Dr. Eoin McKiernan of St. Paul, Minnesota, founder of the Irish American Cultural Institute, for his assistance and encouragement throughout the writing of the *Emerald Ballad* series.

A special note of thanks to the people at Bethany House Publishers — each special one of you — for your hard work, your commitment to excellence, and your encouragement to this author throughout the ongoing development of the *Emerald Ballads*. Too often your efforts are unrecognized, even unknown, by those of us who write the books, but that is not to say they're unappreciated. You are a unique team, and I am deeply grateful to all of you.

As always, my heartfelt thanks to these very special editors — and friends:

Carol A. Johnson, Editorial Director, Bethany House Publishers, is the true trailblazer in spiritual fiction, and with God's help has moved more than her share of mountains to give the genre — and of late, the Irish — a respectable place in literature.

Sharon A. Madison, Editor, Bethany House Publishers, holds a special place in the hearts of many authors who have come to count on her cheerfulness, her thoughtfulness, and her unfailing sense of humor. She is an inspiration to us all — and great fun on the telephone.

Penelope J. Stokes and Cindy L. Maddox of SilverFire Editorial Services are two very tough editors with uncompromising standards and an endless supply of patience — and fax paper. They have gone beyond the extra mile on my behalf many times, for which I am immeasurably grateful.

A Note from the Author

When I first began to research the idea for the first book in this series, *Song of the Silent Harp*, I discovered a strong religious thread throughout the history of Ireland. I hope I have communicated to my readers a clearer understanding of how Christianity influenced the lives of some of America's Irish ancestors.

During those years of study and writing, I became aware that it is virtually impossible to separate the past from the present. The struggles and successes, the trials and triumphs of our forebears, make up not only a rich heritage but also contribute in immeasurable ways to what we — and our world — are today. Like young Daniel Kavanagh, I believe that, from God's perspective, yesterday, today, and tomorrow are one vast *panorama*, a continuing epic which our Creator views in its entirety, from the dawn of time through the present to eternity.

Further, history *does,* indeed, repeat itself. Most experiences of the past continue to happen. The horrors of famine and hopelessness that surround many characters in *An Emerald Ballad* still exist. Month after month, year after year, the innocent victims of war, disaster, political indifference, and oppression go on suffering and dying, just as they did in Ireland during the Great Famine.

Government programs and private charities cannot begin to meet the escalating demand for worldwide assistance. I believe the Christian church should be at the very front of international rescue operations, for it is the *church* that bears the responsibility — and the privilege — of giving love to a world that needs it.

I invite you to join me in finding practical ways to help. I have selected World Relief Corporation, but there are many organizations that provide an opportunity to put faith and love into action. One person *does* make a difference.

B. J. Hof